I0831175

SHADOWFIRE

D.S. QUINTON

ISBN: 979-8-9900455-2-1

Copy Editor: Tee Tate

Cover design: Jeff Brown Graphics

Interior formatting: Mark Thomas / Coverness.com

PROLOGUE

The city of New Orleans has never been kind.

She seduces with brass and blood and takes more than she gives.

Her siren's song echoes down cobbled streets and shadowed alleys, loud and laughing, drawing the curious, the desperate, and the damned. They come chasing riches. Solace. Escape.
And the spirits moan that the dead will be many.

She rewards those who linger with a heady intoxication—an elixir distilled from dark desires and whispered secrets. They drink of her freely. And in return, they give her everything. Their stories. Their sorrows. Their bones. The names of the people are lost to history, but their souls remain.

And the city remembers.

And in time, a girl named Del was born into her keeping. At eight years old, she nearly died in a fire no one could explain. The flames stole her family. The city gave her back, orphaned and marked.

Ten years later, she stepped out of the orphanage gates with a worn satchel, a bruised heart, and the foolish hope for something ordinary.

But fate is not a thing you choose. It chooses you.

And hers was written long ago,

In a time nearly forgotten.

A time when some things refused to die.

CHAPTER 1

Somewhere in a bayou, Louisiana 1866

The conjurer raised his arms and the fire flared. An orb of light, the color of an escaping flame, appeared between his hands and took shape.

A circle of worshippers, naked and kneeling, ringed the man and the fire. Their rhythmic chanting was low and steady. With undulating bodies and outstretched arms, the worshippers sent whatever power they had to the man, praying that he—or the thing that he summoned—would show them favor. This evening, each one prayed that they would be the recipient, that their bodies would be the vessel, for whatever spirit he raised.

The worshippers totaled twelve in all, alternating around the ring, one man, one woman. In a way, they were more than mere worshippers, they were disciples, for the conjurer, a voodoo man, truly was their savior. And he was the all-important thirteenth.

The swaying devotion cast snaking shadows backwards onto

the canopy of Cypress trees—a nest of ghostly serpents dancing for attention. Outside the sphere of firelight was an impenetrable wall of darkness. They could have been the only humans in existence.

The disciples were all the same color, the color of swamp mud. Each one had stripped off their clothing during the long walk to the isolated swell of land where they now worshipped. To begin the ceremony, each one had baptized themselves in the dark waters, then slithered, in reverence to Le Grande Zombi, the serpent god, through the mud, up out of the swamp, to the edge of firelight. The whites of their eyes showed like tiny twin moons, swaying from side to side as an invitation to the spirit in the fire.

The man spread his arms wide, giving the orb freedom to roam. The spirit had not shown itself yet for it had not selected a vessel, but that time was near.

As the orb moved within the circle of light inspecting the vessels, the disciples' undulations grew bolder. Tongues waggled up and down, pink and wet. Outstretched hands mimicked technique. Breasts were squeezed into fullness. Hips were thrust forward to show prowess. Moans of expectation rose and fell as their bodies shook.

With increasing speed, the orb circled the fire, stretching its ghostly filament ever closer to the vessels, testing and tasting. Hands groped at the filament, trying to catch it. Open mouths snapped at the air where a wisp had just been, snatching for power they couldn't comprehend.

Then it happened.

The spirit orb chose its vessel— a woman with a long snaking tongue. It flew into her mouth, snapping her head back. It was already slithering down her glowing throat before the gasp escaped her mouth. Her stomach began to glow, then her groin, as she fell backward into the mud. Then the devotion was upon her.

The two men to either side of her had the best chance, but the closest women would fight hard as well. The first person to mate with the spirit, now in its chosen earthly vessel, would be granted great favor from it. For that is what the spirits missed the most from the living world, the electric touch of flesh on flesh. And it would get its fill tonight before granting any requests.

The original vessel was quickly lost under a mass of writhing bodies. Arms and legs intertwined. Pleading promises were whispered into ears. Groping hands reached to help. The devotion, although formed from individual and selfish wants, collectively knew that pleasing the spirit was their main goal. For if the spirit was satiated—and that could take many hours—it may show favor on them all. So, all pleasures were given.

Over the course of the night, the spirit, sensing the exhaustion in its current host, would jump to a new vessel. The glowing part of the body signaling its new desire or prowess. It tended to shift from female to male, alternately, it had many vessels to use after all. But sometimes stayed with one body type for multiple sessions.

After many hours, as the disciples lay in utter ruin, and the last carnal act was completed, the spirit orb floated free of its vessel. It had swollen to great size over the course of the evening, half the height of the conjurer now, who had stood watching the entire time. The spirit, now rippling with all the colors of the fire, took on the rough shape of a human head and torso. Sometimes it was an animal, sometimes the shape was so indescribable it could not be looked upon. But tonight, it was nearly a human shape. Its ethereal form twisted slowly in and out of existence, flames sparking to life from nothing, only to fade to nowhere. Its glowing head turned slowly as if inspecting the carnage.

"I am pleased," the spirit said, its voice coming through the flames. "What do you ask of me?"

"Tell me what I have become," the conjurer said.

The spirit vibrated as a faint tinkling sound filled the air. The sound was that of giggling children and broken glass. It nearly cut the ears to hear it. The spirit was amused.

The disciples, covering their ears from the harsh sound, slithered back from the heat of the demon. For they now recognized it for what it was. Each one tried to disappear into the mud as they turned their faces from the hellish light. They would not seek its favor tonight.

The demon swelled, seeming to have grown legs from the very fire itself. It stood equal height with the man now. Its eyes had formed as two black holes in its burning head. Its mouth was lightning. Its voice crackled with electricity.

"You have become what your heart desired," the demon said.

The man shook his head but was silent. *No.* This had not been his wish.

The demon titled its head as if not understanding the man's denial. Its flame body appeared to jump back and forth as if it were a swaying snake.

"Did you not, John Montanet," and here the demon chittered its child-like broken-glass laugh again, "*Doctor* John..."

The words, '*Doctor* John' echoed mockingly from a thousand child voices.

(…Doctor John…   hee hee   …Doctor John…)

"…raise a spirit and make a bargain with it?"

"Yes, but—"

"And did you not gain great power from this bargain?"

The man said nothing.

"And have you not bound so many souls into your own playthings?" The flaming demon head turned slightly to gaze into the distance. "Mr. Sandgrove for instance." At the sound of its name, a ragged beast, hanging upside down from a tree branch, opened its eyes and fixed its head toward the fire voice. Its split tail twitched in the air, sensing the situation. A tiny, man-shaped body no bigger than a doll, suspended from the beast's shoulder by a long hat pin, twitched slightly, but made no sound. Too little energy had passed between the beast and itself to generate its voice. After a mournful gaze, it closed its eyes, and both went back to sleep.

"That is not what I ask," the man whispered.

The demon turned its black gaze back to him. "But it is. You wished for me to tell you what you have become. Is it not evident?"

Before the man could speak, the demon addressed the supplicating disciples. "Children, do not fear me." Long tendrils of flame stretched out from the demon's body, motioning for them to come closer. "Raise your faces and look upon your savior."

Reluctantly, casting glances back and forth, the congregation raised their faces from the mud and looked.

With a flourish, the demon swung its arms and flames grew long and wild, swirling high in the air. The disciples gasped as a column of fire rose above them. For a moment, the swamp glowed red. Then an instant later, the column of fire descended, exploding outwards in a fiery blast. The voodoo man, having been wrapped in long flowing black robes caught fire. Just a single touch from the demon fire and a brilliant flash of light burnt his robes to ashes. The man only gasped in surprise. The clothes had burnt so fast he hadn't felt the heat.

He now stood before the congregation as naked as they were, and was the color of mud also, but for a different reason. A brown lumpy skin covered him from chest to foot.

It had been rumored over the last year that the great feud between John Montanet and Marie Laveau had ended when she'd finally cursed him and his eldest daughter with horse pox. This, only after he had cursed her oldest boy with consumption; the boy having died in her arms. John's daughter, having been teased to no end about being afflicted with horse *herpes* and what she must have done to contract them, had already gone mad and ran into the swamp to hide her shame. But John, who was consumed with gaining knowledge and power, had pressed on, ignoring the lesions that had begun to grow over his body. Besides, his face was so scarred with country marks and tattoos they were less visible on him. But the bumpy brown skin was not what made the disciples gasp.

Highlighted by the flaming body of the demon, the outline of John's body shocked the senses, for it was a true deformity. The brown, pus-filled bumps that covered his torso and back seemed to have flattened and hardened along the lower portions of his body. One leg was that of a man. The other was badly deformed and articulated backwards at the knee. Below the knee, the leg jutted forward ending with a clawed foot. At the base of his tailbone, previously hidden by the long cloak, a split tail protruded from his skin. One part of the tail, as thick and scaly as an alligator's, nearly reached the ground. The other part, a deformed and impotent twin half its size, hung there feebly, wobbling for attention. The reptilian portions of John's body were covered with hard patches of skin that more resembled scales than anything.

The disciples murmured and moaned in confusion.

"This is what you have become," the demon said. "This is what your heart desired. You prayed on it, after all."

The demon, now preaching to the wide-eyed congregation, spread its fire-arms wide, beckoning them to hear.

"You, John Montanet, in your ultimate wisdom," the demon said.

The child voices giggled. *(…ultimate wisdom… hee hee … ultimate wisdom…)*

"…called forth a very special spirit."

The demon's voice dripped with sarcasm.

"Oh, the power you must control,"

(…the power… hee hee hee …oh, the power…)

"to call forth Legba the Trickster God and strike a bargain with him!" Now the demon bellowed its own laugh, deep and thunderous.

"And he saw into your heart and gave you what it desired."

John raised his scarred face to the demon.

"To be an abomination," it said. "Behold children, behold your savior, the Gris-gris man!"

John, the Gris-gris man, growled through clenched teeth. "Aarghh, help me control it! Help me fix it. Help me and I'll bring you all the pleasure you desire." He spread his own arms now, motioning to the disciples.

The flaming demon settled a bit, its black non-eyes staring into the shadows. "There aren't enough souls in the world," it said.

Nothing moved within the sphere of the firelight. No one breathed. The demon seemed to be lost in an ancient thought.

Then, as if struck by sudden insight, the demon tilted its head and turns its attention back to John, the Gris-gris man. John had the uneasy sense that a smirk had formed on the demon's lightning mouth.

"But I foresee one who perhaps—"

"Who?" John nearly grabbed the demon in haste. "Tell me who."

Now the black demon eyes squinted as if looking far into the future. Flames that may have been hands or fingers danced on the air, scrying for a glimpse of a future that may still come to pass. "There *will* be one," the demon corrected, "who can… *unmake* what you have become."

Now the disciples began to giggle, uncontrollably, with the demon-child voices. Hundreds of voices, giggling and glass-like, echoed out of each horrified, gaping mouth. The insane chittering rose to a thunderous noise and the swamp creatures fell silent in fear.

The demon's head tilted back as if remembering something, or, as John now thought, watching his future unfold. It laughed as it began to fade. But before it vanished completely, it left John Montanet, an abomination that had become the Gris-gris man, with these final words:

In ages forth through moonless mist,
you seek the one that shadows kissed.
A fleeting form in dreaming state,
with ancient power to life abate.
Footsteps echo, never near,
a haunting hum that none can hear.
She wears the night like ink on skin,
a black streak hides the truth within.

CHAPTER 2

New Orleans, September 1964

As night fell over the Crescent City, the dead waited to speak. Their forgotten voices, having not been heard in years or sometimes decades, were as a whisper in a storm. And each night, as their feeble pleas slipped away unheard, this never-ending tapestry of dead jostled for position near the only light their dead eyes could see, a young woman lying alone in her bed.

Delphine Larouche, feeling crushed beneath the weight of their silent cries, tried not to hear.

Del's journey, her unwanted promotion to *circus freak for the dead*, had happened rapidly. In less than a year, from the time she'd left the orphanage and learned of her 'gift', she'd seen more death than many people did in a lifetime. It seemed to be drawn to her.

Death itself was not drawn to her—although sometimes she wondered—but the *dead*, certainly. Like moths to that final flame, the infinite tapestry of dead that marched ever-forward, had become aware of her. They felt her presence the way the tide feels the pull of the moon, ebbing to and fro, dancing and bobbing for her attention, but rarely reaching her protective shore.

But they all sought her council.

Since that fateful day when her mentor, Mama Dedé, had guided her in her first trancing session, the dead had felt a presence unlike anything they'd known before—except for Life. On their journey to the Desert of Dust where they would eventually decay into oblivion, there was no light, there was no hope, but then suddenly and inexplicably, there was Del. At least, there was the essence of her. And that was enough.

For months, starting with the manifestation of the Gris-gris man and his unholy beast, to the strange encounter with Madame Broussard and Scarmish, finally ending with Arlo and Billy Bash, Del had encountered a world of unbelievable possibilities, a world of unfathomable layers, a world that prior to leaving the orphanage, she didn't even believe in. But when one had seen the things she had, there was no denying them. And there was no longer any way *not* to hear them.

So, Del lay in the dark, and holding the voices at bay, waited for sleep to take her.

Her mind drifted over many things. Sensing the old creaks of Armand's grand house was a lullaby. Listening to her extended family go through their nightly routines was a comfort. Hearing shadows whisper at the window was… not as disturbing as it had once been, although it was getting harder to distinguish those voices from the real ones.

As far as the living voices went, Mama D's was muffled but strong as she fussed in the downstairs kitchen, quietly lamenting about how things had been left at the end of the day. Armand's was soft and thoughtful as he talked to the objects in his library, just down the hall from her room, trying to work out where a forgotten thought had gone. Jimmy's, a voice she had known since the orphanage, would be saying goodnight to things in his room: toys, shadows, the mirror.

The only extended family member she didn't hear on a nightly basis was Frank, but only because he *usually* went home at night. Unless he'd fallen asleep in the big chair in the library, with an empty brandy glass on the table and cold cigar ashes in the ashtray.

These were the voices—as strange as they were—of her adopted family. All of them, the living voices as well as the dead.

And perhaps because of their strangeness, or the fact that she was exhausted from previous sleepless nights, she didn't hear the new voice that floated on the wind, just outside her window.

Not even when it screamed.

*

Armand walked quietly back and forth across the library floor. His hands were folded behind his back and his pipe hung smoldering from a corner of his mouth. Now that his family was back together, meaning that Del was home and Mama D was on the mend, of course Jimmy would live wherever Del was, he felt whole again. And his wardrobe reflected this.

Armand had always been one for more formal attire. He never thought of it as being pretentious, but wool or corduroy trousers, a white dress shirt and ornate vest—of which he had many—just naturally fit his slim physic. He rarely wore a jacket in the house, except for holidays and special occasions. But, during the *Dark Time*, as he had come to think of the period when Del was gone and Mama D had fallen ill, he'd grown so lethargic and… out of sorts, that he'd fallen to wearing the same crumpled shirts for days on end. Sometimes even walking around in his stocking feet, dragging his pant cuffs along the carpet. Heavy bags had formed under his eyes during that time and although they hadn't disappeared completely now, he was feeling his old self again.

Having been a lifelong bachelor and academic, he'd grown used to his solitude. But when Del, Jimmy and Mama Dedé came to live with him just over a year ago, something had awoken inside him. He was surprised to learn that he enjoyed—no, loved—having this adopted family under his roof. Then, when the *Dark Time* occurred, and he'd almost lost them, he'd nearly been lost himself. Now that everything was set right—at least for the time being—he fretted over the thought that it could all happen again. After all, many unanswered questions still lingered around this family.

Del was still at the beginning of her ten-thousand-hour journey. That journey that everyone must take when they're searching for, and mastering, their true talent. Armand suspected he knew where her journey would lead her—whether she wanted to go there or not. They'd all witnessed the strange things that happened around her, and he didn't expect them to stop. But he could be ready to help her—and the family—when they did, so he'd vowed to do just that.

Strolling through the library, taking a mental inventory of the occult knowledge sitting on his shelves, he believed he had the means to keep his vow. However, considering how the spirit board situation had gone with Jimmy, he knew he had to be careful in his approach. Mama D was still mending after all and Del was… well, Del was a teenager. A very powerful one, he admitted, but still a teenager, for just a while longer. And although Jimmy showed to have some unexplainable abilities himself, the poor boy was afflicted with more scientific problems. Things that could not be fixed by a charm or spell. So, he could not be relied upon for any type of practical defense.

This left Armand with his library and his thoughts, and he felt the weight of it throughout his body. And somewhere deep in his shoulders, a pinprick of tension had just emerged, as if predicting a coming storm.

*

Jimmy sat in front of his chest of drawers saying good night to his treasures. The bottom drawer was filled with them: marbles, interesting rocks, old bottle caps, miscellaneous playing cards, broken crayons, and a host of other items which just showed up.

He'd had other items in here a few months ago, but they had been taken away after Del found the note from that other strange boy.

Jimmy couldn't remember how the whole thing had happened, but at some point, when Mama D was sick, and after Armand asked him to play the *Talking Board* game with him, strange things began happening around the house. There were the black crickets that hopped everywhere. He didn't mind those because it gave him something to stomp on. Then there was the voice in his mirror. That was scary at first, but when it spoke, and the words glowed with light in the mirror, it was like having a funny nightlight, so he didn't mind it. It wasn't like the time when his train lamp went crazy and tried to burn him up in the engine. And besides, he was pretty sure the voice in the mirror had taught him how to fly on the giant bird, and that made him happy.

But then the pointy scissors had gotten into his room and hid beneath the bottom drawer. Sometimes he heard a *snip, snip, snip* at night when they sharpened themselves. He was pretty sure they were bad, but Armand had taken care of them. Just like he took the book of matches, the little paring knife and the box of rat poison that someone had left in a closet. He didn't remember where these things had come from, but they talked a lot when he lay in bed, always telling him to do things. So, in a way, he was glad they were gone. But sometimes he missed them.

That just left him with the stuff he was looking at now. But he knew that he'd find some new treasures soon. Slinky the shadow brought all kinds of stuff back to his closet.

And just as the thought of Slinky crossed his mind, Jimmy heard a tiny scratching sound come from his closet.

He looked over just as the door began to swing open.

*

Mama Dedé finished puttering in the kitchen, made a cup of tea, and carried it to the parlor. She sat in a comfy chair and held her teacup and saucer on her lap. She looked around for something to do. She was stalling.

She thought about going back into the kitchen and check on the dishes. But the kitchen didn't really need straightening the first time, so, it certainly didn't need it now. After all, Armand hadn't regressed completely to bachelorhood during her… sickness.

She always hesitated to categorize *That Time*—which ended a few months ago—with anything more concrete than a *sickness*. Her strange condition, her unexplained gaps in memory, her general feeling of having been utterly violated in a mental sort of way, none of these things had a good explanation. And having no good way to categorize them, she simply thought of it as *That Time.*

But, during that time, when Armand tried to manage the house, he'd done a decent job. So, there wasn't much for her to do, now that she was on the mend. Not to mention, it wasn't her house anyway, so she didn't change much, but she did tinker.

In fact, she was beginning to wonder if she hadn't adopted some strange compulsion during her time away. Since recovering—although she was certain it wasn't complete—she'd become obsessed with removing and replacing the silverware in the drawers. It was harmless reorganization she told herself. And it was a large house filled with all sorts of things that needed organizing. Still, she'd never been like this in her old home. Granted, the Transitional Home for Girls, where she initially met Del, had not been a New Orleans mansion like this house, but it had a lot of forks. And they worked just fine even if they got stored in the spoon or knife slot in the drawer.

Looking around the parlor, she sipped the pungent black tea then sat the cup on a side table. It had been a long time since she'd had to resort to the tea trick. In fact, she suddenly realized, the last time was when she had led Del on her first session. That was back in the old house after Del left the orphanage. She'd loved that house—as ramshackle as it was. There she had her own parlor, and in fact, it was in that parlor where she and Del had sat, drinking this very same brew.

That seemed like a lifetime ago, now. And in a way—a way in which she tried not to think about—it *was* another lifetime ago. Hadn't she met the end of her original life just a few months back? The night she and Armand had fallen ill from the possessed brandy. Del said that she'd been cold, and that she'd taken her to Del's well of life. This still hurt Mama D to think about, but it was too late now. And at Del's well of life, something had happened. Some restorative power had been gifted to her, which allowed her to survive long enough for Del to discover what was wrong with her and ultimately save her. So, in a very real way, this was now her second life. And she intended not to waste one moment of it. Forks be damned! She had stalled long enough. There was something going on in this house and she meant to find out what it was.

She crossed her hands in her lap, closed her eyes, and began to trance.

She thought back to when she'd had to use the tea for her own trancing sessions and felt a tinge of pain strike her heart. As a young practitioner, she had reached a point where she could slip in and out of trances as easily as changing her blouse. True, Del had reached that point much sooner than she had, but Mama Dedé had come to terms with her abilities compared to Del's—at least, the way they *used* to be.

Now, as she sat still with her eyes clenched tight, the trance was slow to come. And this frustrated her beyond anything. She could feel it building inside her head, she could … *hear* it in a way. Like static on a radio, but as she felt her mind moving towards it, *dialing it in*, she would suddenly *pass* it somehow. As if the trancing vision were a radio station with a single beam that had to be pointed directly at her ear. If you moved your head, or took a step, you were no longer in line with the signal and the message disappeared. It had never been like this before, and she couldn't understand why it was like this now.

She even caught herself tilting her head from one side to the other as if she were a set of rabbit ears sitting atop a television set.

She opened her eyes and sat in quiet frustration. Her lips were puckered into a determined line. The night she'd come out of her sickness, the night Del fought Billy Bash, Mama D had jumped into her trance. Perhaps even *awoken* into it. She couldn't be sure. One minute she was in the worm nightmare, a hundred feet below the ground, the next minute—as far as she could remember—she was in a trance. But how?

Had Del pulled her into the trance without knowing it? Was that even possible? Mama D looked around the room at nothing particular. Like Armand, she imagined that the answer was somewhere on one of the many artifacts in the room, and that she simply needed to touch or look at enough things to eventually find it.

But it wasn't working.

Could Del pull me into her own trance? Or pull Jimmy, or Armand?

Frank would be too spooked, so Del would be better not to do that. He'd die of a—

Damn! She clenched a fist at the poor choice of words.

She grabbed up the teacup and drank the remainder in a quick gulp. She was determined to break through this...*psychic dry spell* if it took her all night.

And it wasn't just selfish pride driving her. A deep uneasiness had settled over her of late. She felt that Del would need help soon but feared she may not be ready when the time came.

CHAPTER 3

Somewhere on the Mississippi River, September 1964

At 11:59 pm, a paddle wheeler slipped silently into existence on the dark Mississippi. It made no sound at all; it was formless as a shadow. At this transitional moment the river was utterly quiet, and the ship did not disturb the silence. In fact, it *was* the silence. The still water with its black inkiness and fetid smell could have been a tarn festering before a crumbling manor house, had it not been for the slowly snaking current running beneath its surface.

The shanties that sat along this part of the river—stilted, leaning hovels that bent crookedly towards the water—housed weathered and superstitious people who loved and feared the great river. The abundance of fish aside, it was their lifeline in many ways.

Before the age of the steam-driven paddlewheel, a great raft of logs may have come floating by, led by nimble men who danced across their rolling surfaces, guiding them to a sawmill downstream. These crews were filled with hard and hungry men who would bargain with the shanty people; food, clothing, and pleasure could be purchased for a few coins. And the crews always needed extra hands, assuming one could stay on top of the logs. For the men who could not, amputations or burial services could be had for just a few coins more.

In the golden age of the paddle steamer, a man could chop a cord of wood and sit by the shore waiting for a steamer to dock, the captain ready to bargain for the fuel. If one lived back a tributary that fed the great river, other occupations were available. Small excursion boats were sometimes launched from the steamships in the dead of night. Quiet men would row up the tributaries to rendezvous points where secret trades were made. Then the goods were hidden in the bowels of the ship until some point further along the river.

All manner of people traveled the great river, fortunes were made or lost during a journey, lives as well. And of course, there was gambling: dice, poker, and roulette for the gentile class, boxing and brawling for the rustic, and for all classes, there was the oldest trade in history. Man or woman could make a living somehow on the river.

But over time, as the old steamers fell out of fashion, first from the expansion of railroads, then by diesel-powered barges that could carry a hundred times more cargo, life on the river changed. The shanty people, most of them, moved closer to towns where work could be found. Many of the questionable methods of making a living along the river—bootlegging and smuggling—were reduced to a minimum. And as the old ways died out, so did the superstitions.

Most of them.

For the river folk who remained, they held onto their superstitions. In a way, they kept the tales alive, just as the river kept them alive. It was a dark and symbiotic relationship, not unlike a bird which feeds from inside the mouth of a crocodile, cleaning its teeth of harmful parasites. The old tales of river sirens and spirits were still whispered from old to young at night in front of fireplaces. Children were warned to not follow shimmering lights—*will-o'-the-wisps* along the upper riverbanks, *fifolets* along the lower—into the forests, or they would never return. And the myths of dead men—or their spirits—being reborn from the mud of the Mississippi river banks, always set old heads to nodding. "I seen it," an old voice would croak. "Sure as I'm sittin' here." Other voices would murmur quiet confirmation, remembering the tales of voodoo and the Gris-gris man that had been told them in their youth. "Right outta 'da mud it crawled. I seen 'da tracks."

And then… the details would come.

"…sometimes handprints, sometimes bare feet…"

But the worst details were always murmured so low children nearly had to guess at the words. But they always sounded the same, "… sometimes tails." And with these details the old people would wonder in silent fear who would be cursed next. Who, through some terrible old magic would be turned into something unholy.

Which is why the remaining shanty people, in the year 1964, would not have been surprised to see the black paddle wheel materialize from the unnatural fog.

It was nearly midnight, afterall.

The sign on the lead paddlewheel read: Morrow and Nightshade's Circus of the Arcane. It was an archaic statement for the year 1964, with talk of moon landings and British pop music invasions. It was a statement that harkened back to an older time and place; a time when superstition ruled over science, a place where dark things ruled the night. But the river had seen so many things in its long life it cared not if signs seemed misplaced. Neither did it care for what people called it, having had many names over the eons.

Most Native American names referred to its general size—whether from the Algonquin words *Misi-ziibi*, meaning "Great River," or the Illiniwek people's words *Mecha Sepé*, meaning "Big River." Other tribes such as the Choctaw honored its *time* calling it *Misi sipokni* meaning "Beyond Age." For having formed thousands of years ago it was truly beyond the time of anyone who had walked the lands, and the waters held no memory. So, it had no opinion if something that floated on its surface was from this time or another.

The river was simply there.

And sometimes things came out of the river which had no earthly explanation.

Two other paddlewheel boats followed, as silent and foreboding as the first. The third boat emanated a fearful sense of dread, as a whipped dog might do as it followed a cruel master because anything was better than starvation. The third boat seemed to *hunker*, its bow hanging dejectedly towards the water.

On the lead boat, a silhouette was barely visible in the wheelhouse.

The silhouette was of a tall gaunt man, eerily lit by a flickering lantern. The sickly yellow light seemed to struggle forth as if it had traveled a great distance to frame him. In a strange way, unknown to the lantern that had produced the light—or anyone who may have seen it—it had. The yellow light had come from a time and place that was long gone, but oddly, from an instance of burning oil, that had just occurred. Just now. The next instance, the light from the lantern left its earthly body—the wick and shot off into the night. It had just escaped a strange happenstance. The light didn't know this, as it had no memory, just as the river had none, but it was finally free, nonetheless. And anyone who lived in the leaning hovels, who may have seen this extraordinary scene, would have inadvertently witnessed a great mystery.

One that had just begun to unfold.

*

At precisely midnight, when the third and most dreadful paddlewheel exited the black fog, Ernest Crowley looked up. His gnarled black fingers were working a fishing hook through the eyes of a minnow. He always ran his limb lines at night knowing better than to leave a good catch on the line for more than twelve hours. There were plenty of bigger things in the river that would gladly take the easy meal of a fish caught on a line that couldn't escape. He'd learned this as a little boy, and now, sixty odd years later, it was part of who he was.

He only flinched slightly when the hook went into his thumb instead.

His eyes scanned the black night but were of little use. Between his cataracts and the river fog, he was never sure what was really in front of him. He couldn't be sure that he'd seen anything. But he *had* felt movement in the air.

Bobbing silently in his aluminum boat, he was mostly hidden in the shadows of the brush that grew close to the river. This wasn't a strategic plan other than the fact that he didn't like to run jug lines or trout lines which typically floated in the middle of the river. He liked running limb lines which kept him close to the banks. And running, or servicing, these types of fishing lines meant you spent a lot of time jamming the nose of your boat into thickets that grew along the edges.

And even though he was deep in the shadows of the brush, something told him he wanted to stay hidden, so he quietly turned down the flame of the kerosene lantern that sat between his feet, then off. The minnow was left to flop in the shallow pool of water at the bottom of the boat.

He'd felt the heavy clouds settling over the water for the last hour but had largely ignored them. Having spent many years here, that hadn't surprised him until the gooseflesh crept down his back; it was only then that he sensed the unnatural fog that had already surrounded him, and he remembered the tales he'd been told as a child. Those tales of spirits being born out of the mud, *"sometimes bare feet, sometimes tails..."* Or of fishermen getting sucked into fog, never to be seen again. Until they came back, mad and screaming.

A faint voice spoke in his mind,

Heed yo' mama! Go back. Go back now!

but he was already halfway up his run of lines and so, found himself in this backwater channel. This place of still waters and shadows. A place that had suddenly become *Misi sipokni:* Beyond Age.

Ernest listened for the wind. He could always gauge a storm by the sound of the wind through the trees, but there was none tonight. He turned his head as if he were listening to the floor of the boat and the night sky at the same time. His eyes were closed. His fingers intertwined. He heard nothing but the smallest ripples lapping against the boat.

As if understanding his struggle to see, the lead paddlewheel suddenly came into view through an opening in the trees. Ernest hunkered, instinctively. Looking for the source of light that illuminated the monstrosity he found none. The moon was hidden. There was no lantern swinging from the sides of the big boat. But it was illuminated somehow, as if the first breath of air—outside the dark fog—had sparked it to life. The planks glowed faintly, just enough to reflect in the water.

The paddle wheeler was a floating nightmare. Old and decrepit, it sat on the water. Black as night, it moved in and out of the shadows, as if debating to materialize. Ernest didn't know why but imagined a thick carpet of black moss covering its surface. All three boats were infected thus, and he imagined their poison leaching into the water as snaking sheens of oil.

His eyes were too bad to have read the sign: Morrow and Nightshade's Circus of the Arcane, but as if hearing its name called from an old nightmare, and needing a ring master to present its case, the boat presented its emissary: the silhouette of the gaunt man came into view.

The slightest intake of breath gave Ernest away. Surely, he hadn't made a sound above that of a whisper. He hadn't knocked his boot against the metal side or dropped a pair of plyers onto the metal bottom. It was only a small gasp…

But the gaunt man had heard him. From a hundred yards away, across the water, through gnarled and wooly branches, the gaunt man heard Ernest and turned his head.

A decrepit face, an ancient face, fixed his position.

His boat began to move.

Yellow eyes, first like tiny fireflies, caught his attention. They danced hypnotic. He felt the gaze of those yellow eyes burrow into his own, slide around his eyeballs, past his lids and hook his mind. He was now the minnow.

Steadily, of its own accord, his little boat pulled itself through the brambles of the backwater where he was hidden, and out into the main channel. It turned its bow and steered itself towards the lead paddle wheeler and the gaunt man.

Larger now, the firefly eyes became sickly yellow moons protruding like insane tentacles from a deformed head. They were antennae, he thought. Strange, reaching antennae from a monstrosity birthed from a river myth—or more likely, from a river curse.

The cold goose flesh running down his arms told the tale. Something that had been cursed long ago or made to be hidden in the river, ancient and decrepit, had just awoken. It had lain waiting, hidden in the timeless mists, listening for the words that would call it forth into the time of the words.

The gaunt man's face, twisting into shape, appeared in the fog that hung around the boat. The yellow antennae eyes had just come through the fog face when a giant mouth opened. The mouth on the face, still fifty yards away, yawned open like a great cavern and a black tongue snaked forth into the water.

The little boat flew across the water as if heading for a final plunge over the edge of a great waterfall. Ernest gripped the sides tightly, a scream locked in his throat.

The face of the gaunt man, the face of the boat, for Ernest had just come to understand that they were one in the same, breathed in the air. It drank in the water. It bulged at him, pulling him forward. Pulling him down. And in a final act, pulled his boat beneath the water. For a brief second Ernest was in the water, tumbling and disoriented, then the underside of the boat absorbed him and let him slip through the porous moss-riddled planks.

And he was in the belly of the beast.

*

Ernest woke up in hell.

Although, it wasn't the hell he'd been warned about as a child, for there were no flames. But surely, he was dead, he thought. And this was some type of watery hell.

Something had happened to him the last time he'd gone fishing. He'd fallen into the river somehow, maybe having had a stroke, slipped beneath the water and drowned.

He distinctly remembered going under the water. The other images... well, old folks say that your life flashes before your eyes right before you die, and you see everything that has ever happened to you. But he'd never heard of people seeing glimpses of hell *before* you landed there.

And wasn't that what he'd seen?

Hadn't a demon or specter raised itself from the river and cast images of hell into his mind as he died?

—yellow bulging eyes—

Those eyes.

Yella' demon eyes, for sho'.

(Not just eyes. Antennae-eyes)

Yes, bulging yellow antennae-eyes that reached out from the fog.

Yellow and glistening...

Wavery and reaching...

Glistening and... sticky... his mind told him, like the tongue of a lizard that shoots from its mouth at lightning speed. A sticky substance on the end that snares its prey, then... it gets sucked into a giant, yawning mouth. Into the belly of the beast.

Only these antennae-eyes had reached into his mind, slipped around his eyeballs and glued themselves to his soul, snaring him like a minnow, and reeling him in.

He tried to scream but only managed to cough out a large splash of water. Air rushed into his lungs triggering a longer coughing fit. He rolled to his side as the river water gushed from his lungs.

Voices murmured in the dark.

Struggling to his hands and knees, he felt the voices—then imagined they were hands—reach for him. Voices and hands, tangled together, hovering around him, coaxing him back to life. They were one thing, he thought, the voices and hands. It was as if the desire to speak and the desire to feel were the last two vestiges of a wretched crew of souls, and all they could do was plead for attention in the dark. Although, he felt no warmth from either.

Ernest suddenly felt dizzy, as if he were rolling down a hill, although he didn't think he was actually moving. His mind told him the room—or whatever this place was—was moving around him. A sense of spinning darkness pervaded his body, threatening to flip his stomach over. A deep shiver wracked his old body, and a flush of heat ran up his spine. Beads of sweat formed on his balding head. It was the type of sweat the body used to excrete a deep poison from itself. He wanted to lay down and sleep. Lay down and let the spinning room take him off to whatever hell awaited him.

The sighing, moving shadows continued to taunt him. Around, they snaked, twisting the darkness at the periphery of his vision.

He suddenly thought of his family and wondered if he'd ever see them again. They'd be ringing the telephones of neighbors, asking if they'd seen his boat on the river. He should have been home by now, was the message they would share. His wife, Mattie, would be sending a smoky blessing of sage and other herbs up the chimney of their little home, hoping the protective aroma would find him, showing him the way home. He doubted any blessings or prayers would find him in this place.

Footsteps creaked old wooden boards above him and the voice-things drew back. Like gossamer threads from some shy, fragile underwater creature, he felt them retreat into the shadows, their voices mute.

The footsteps stopped as if listening to the wayward shadows, naughty children caught out after bedtime, then continued. They walked slowly, almost casually for several more feet, then began to descend. A wooden staircase creaked to his right.

Ernest felt something like fear radiate through the darkness from his right. The staircase shivered a nervous warning, and the darkness transmitted the message. Oh! something was near. Each groaning board, each squeaky nail, whispered of the horror to come and pleaded with him to flee, to throw himself back into the river and die a proper death, for there were already too many abominations here. Too many souls tied to this *Misi sipokni*, this *Thing Beyond Age.*

But their lamentations were muted by the suffocating dread of the specters, so were masked simply as the grumblings of old boards.

With head hung low, Ernest opened his eyes and saw a sheen of river water forming beneath him, most of which was still dripping from his hair and clothes. He saw the outline of a face in that dark, reflective surface. It was not complete but was more of a place where a face ought to be. The insinuation of face that somehow rippled in the darkness.

Although there were no lanterns here, he now understood that he was in the bowels of a large boat—feeling the sodden planks beneath his hands. The floating face—which now shimmered on the floor beneath him—carried its own illumination.

The gaunt man, he thought.

The face from the riverboat.

Leaving the final step, a deformed and scaled foot touched the floor upon which Ernest knelt. Four clawed toes, the middle two larger than the outside stabilizers, dug into the sodden wood.

Yellow bulging antennae-eyes.

(Yes. And hooked like a minnow.)

A similarly deformed second foot soon came into his periphery view. The shimmering face reflected large and grotesque across the wet planks. Perhaps because of the dripping water and uneven boards, or more likely because the face wasn't fully formed, the reflection seemed to move in and out of existence. The features of the face were broken and misplaced, as if it couldn't remember how it was to be structured. Or, as if it was deciding what it would become.

Ernest slumped back onto his haunches, pulling his hands into his lap. His eyes were fixed on the floor. The distorted, shimmering face said nothing, only waited.

Ernest said a silent prayer and sighed. The face distorted again as if somehow being able to read his mind, was amused by this action.

He felt sorry for Mattie in that instant. At least if he'd drowned, there would be a chance that his body would have been recovered. A body can be buried. It can be mourned over, wept over, even cursed at for its stupidity, but it can be seen, then buried. But whatever this *was*, wherever he was *at*, whatever he would *become*, he feared could not be described to anyone. Mattie would never know what had happened to him.

He nodded his head as if accepting his fate, then raised his eyes.

And with that, he looked into the face of the Gris-gris man.

CHAPTER 4

New Orleans, September 1964

Del popped out of bed, despite having only a few hours of good sleep, like a child on Christmas morning. She finally had a real job.

Taking a quick shower and wriggling into her best jeans—there were very few choices—she wiped the mirror of the bathroom and looked at her wild hair in the reflection. She twisted her mouth from side to side as she tried to imagine a better hair style.

Maybe I'll get it straightened, she thought. But the cost of that was probably—no, certainly—beyond her budget. And even though she was back sleeping in her own room—at least, the one she used while staying at Armand's house—she was still conscious of her finances. How could she afford a house for herself and Jimmy if she blew her money on things like that? So, with a sigh, she slipped on a t-shirt and tied her hair back with a bandeau. Wiping the mirror again and noticing that this t-shirt seemed far too thin in the damp air, she crossed her arms over her chest and walked down the hall to her room.

Her meager belongings were either folded in a single chest of drawers, or scattered across the floor, waiting for the wash. They were all pretty much the same consistency of the shirt she had on, which wouldn't do for work. She spied the closet and knowing it to be stuffed with clothes from whomever owned the house before Armand had purchased it, threw open the door and began to rummage. The previous owner had either been the owner of a costume shop, an actor, or simply a hoarder of vintage clothes, because every closet was bursting at the seams like this one. Her trademark leather motorcycle boots and jean jacket had come out of this very closet when she first moved in, but she didn't think those were appropriate for work either. So, after scattering items to the floor, she came across a white button up shirt, that could have been for a man or a woman. It was of good quality, but had an old design that could have fit either gender. She put it on and rolled up the sleeves. Next to it hung an old vest, which surprisingly was her size, in a baggy, Charlie Chaplin sort of way. Donning them both she stuck her hands in her jean pockets and looked in the mirror.

Tilting her head and hips one way, then the other, she decided this would do fine. She thought the androgenous mix of clothing fit her and looked cute.

Then her gaze fell to the ratty sneakers.

She didn't mind the Charlie Chaplin look, because her curves filled out the shirt and vest just fine, but the sneakers had *The Tramp* written all over them, and that wouldn't do. She kicked them off, pulled on her leather boots and reinspected herself. The masculine cut of the boots hugging her shapely legs also worked well. A quick adjustment of the headband and she couldn't help but smile at herself.

It had been a long time since she'd felt this good.

*

Del arrived at the main office of the Times-Picayune newspaper fifteen minutes before her starting time. She locked her bike to a lamppost, looked at her watch, then peeked her head around the big plate glass window in the front of the building. She didn't want to go in just yet—seeming too anxious—but she didn't want to seem like a creeper either, so after a quick glance inside, she slowly walked in front of the window, minding her own business. She'd go to the end of the block then turn back.

Passing the plate glass windows of the office, an oversized print of a front-page news article screamed out.

Beatlemania Sweeps New Orleans — Beatles Day Declared!

City officials declare September 16, 1964, to be Beatles Day.

Del knew the article by heart. It went on to describe how the "Fab Four" would come to New Orleans and play the City Park Stadium for 12,000 screaming teenagers. Staring at the headline she imagined what it would be like to be there in person, right next to the stage, watching Paul play his guitar and sing.

She sighed. What was she thinking? She didn't know anyone who was going. And five dollars per ticket was out of her price range. Besides, she wasn't sure how many people who looked like her would be there anyway. So, she shoved her hands into her jean pockets, kicked at a spot of gum on the sidewalk, and continued walking. Better to spend her time thinking about her job instead of stupid concerts.

Her pace had quickened. She knew that she didn't have an official starting time with this job. In fact, in the South, most meeting times were more of a suggestion anyway. But she'd been waiting for this opportunity for a long time and didn't want to take a chance of being late, so she turned around.

She had made her third or fourth pass in front of the plate glass window when a man stuck his head out the front door. He had a long, thin face, prematurely aged by too much sun or too many late nights. A lightweight tan fedora, complete with a black band and feather on the side, was pushed back on his head. A lit cigarette curled smoke into one squinted eye.

"Are you…?" He looked at a piece of paper in his hand.

"Del!" Del said too loudly. The man, startled, looked up.

Her hands shot back into the front pockets of her jeans as if the volume control to her mouth was there.

"Ugh," her voice dropped, "I mean, Delphine."

Her hands came out. "Delphine Larouche."

She wiped them on her jeans, imagining them covered with sweat.

The man squinted at her, with smoke curling up under the brim of his hat.

"Uh, but you can call me Del." And with an embarrassed but hopeful smile, she extended her hand to shake. In the back of her mind, she wondered if she'd remembered to pee before she left the house this morning.

The man, with his head still sticking halfway out the open door, looked down at the paper, then back to Del. Slowly, a smile crept across his face, then he joined her on the street and took her hand.

"Del, nice to meet you. I'm Bobby Dupre." A southern drawl

dripped from his words like molasses; Dupre came out slow and sweet like "doo-praay."

"I know who you are, Mr. Dupre," Del said. "I read your column in the Times-Pic—"

He released her hand and waved her off. The spent cigarette dropped to the sidewalk and disappeared under a black polished shoe.

"Bobby's fine. Truth be told, if people 'round here hear you callin' me Mr. Dupre, they liable to start askin' me for somethin' and I already gave at the office."

Del's hands looked for somewhere to go. "Uh, yes sir, Mr. Bobby."

Bobby Dupre was a tallish, thin man, with a languid stance. That is, he appeared to not use all his height. Del realized there was a bit of a stoop about him. Not the stoop of an old bent man, more like that of someone who felt no need to use the energy to stand up completely straight, and who was perfectly happy leaning. His long hands and fingers could have belonged to a pianist, she thought, but one who played in a smoky speakeasy, as opposed to Carnegie Hall. She suddenly imagined that beneath his lightweight slacks and white shirt, he was simply made of cigarettes bound tightly together by cellophane and the lean in his stance was due to some unseen slippage in his construction. A loosely knotted tie and missing jacket—certainly thrown carelessly over the back of his desk chair—completed the package. He was the quintessential newspaper man.

He walked to the edge of the sidewalk and stretched his back, absently stuffing the folds of shirt into the back of his pants. "Frank and I have a bit 'ah history, ya' know. Hell, I was a junior reporter when he cracked that Glapion case. Damndest thing I ever saw." He turned and looked at Del. "When he called me—" One eyebrow raised in a question. "Uh, you know he called me, right?"

Del nodded. "Yes, sir. I'm grateful for any opportunity to—"

His hand waved her off. "That's fine. I was happy to help. Frank was good to me when I was startin' out. Threw me a few scraps about the Glapion case. Interestin' side stories, ya' know. Helped me to eventually get my column started."

"The NOLA Pulse!" Del said. Her eyes were afire. Then she recited the tag line. "Exploring the heart and soul of the Crescent City."

Bobby chuckled, nodded his appreciation, and fished a pack of smokes from his shirt pocket. Snagging a cigarette with his lips, and as if in anticipation of a curl of smoke, his left eye squinted, he said, "Ready to explore the heart and soul of the city Del?"

"You bet!" Del beamed.

Bobby struck a match and held it in the air above the waiting cigarette. He studied it as if it were a mystical talisman. He lit the cigarette, watching the first wisp of smoke float away.

He blew out the match with a puff of smoke and said, "Looks like our story is that way." He pointed in the direction the smoke had gone.

During the morning, Bobby explained to Del that his job was actually pretty simple. It's not like they were brain surgeons, or astronauts. No one's life hung in the balance of their actions. But their job *was* closely related to this idea. Their jobs, as reporters—at least for the type of column Bobby Dupre wrote—were to observe the actions of people's lives, and the external factors that put pressure on them.

Del was a bit disappointed that she wouldn't be investigating a major crime scandal, but knew she had to start somewhere. And secretly she suspected that she'd do just fine at this job, because although she was new at the newspaper business, she was already fairly seasoned at understanding the hidden things that put pressure on people's lives.

In a strange way, Del was the perfect person to begin a career exploring the hearts and souls of the people of the Crescent City.

*

After a long exposition on some of the best columns he'd written, and a brief example of what he found interesting about the people they passed on the street, Bobby and Del decided to split up.

"We'll cover more ground this way," Bobby said. "Let the wind blow you, then let's meet up at say… one-thirty, Café du Monde."

Del nodded. "Sure. Sounds good."

"Aw'right then. We'll meet for lunch, compare notes and gawk at some tourists. My treat."

"Great," said Del. "Thank you Mr. Du— uh, Mr. Bobby."

Bobby Dupre had already turned to cross the street and gave Del a brief wave over his shoulder. Across the street, in the direction he was walking, a woman stood in the doorway of a tavern and called out to him.

Del was on her own, and happy to be so. She liked Mr. Bobby and was grateful for any help he could give her, but she was anxious to start *looking in* on some of the folks around her. Actually, she'd been trancing lightly—*flashing*, was how she thought of it—during most of their walk. But, given the need to follow the conversation and not seem rude, she hadn't really collected anything of interest. In fact, she didn't recall one interesting person from the last thirty minutes.

Del continued, letting her mind drift. The excitement she felt thinking about writing her first newspaper article had her mind jumping from person to person: a businessman planning for an upcoming meeting, several men from the Department of

Transportation working on a stoplight, a police officer thinking about their kid's ball game.

A middle-aged woman coming towards her was worried about her aging parents. Del didn't spend enough time on her to understand what the concern was, as she didn't think that would make a very interesting story. She did however, trance enough to visualize a few seconds of the path the woman had walked just before she came into Del's sight. It was an interesting phenomenon that Del had only recently discovered.

In the past, when she needed to trance deeply and really follow the path someone had previously walked, she had to be seated. It was simply too hard to trance and walk at the same time. And it wasn't like the time she'd followed the man to the murder house, as she thought of it. With him, his thoughts were so angry, and she was already walking behind him, it was easy enough to follow where he was going. It wasn't like she was trying to follow, in her mind, where he'd *come from*.

And it wasn't like trying to pat your head with one hand while you rubbed your stomach with the other, which she could sort of do. It was harder than that. Trancing backwards onto someone's path, while walking, was more like trying to solve a puzzle maze, if you had to draw the line backwards in a mirror.

She used to work those maze puzzles out of old crossword magazines she found in the orphanage. And having heard of one of those old Greek guys, Copernicus or Da Vinci, who used to write their discoveries backwards so no one could steal them, she'd tried doing the puzzle backwards, once.

Drawing a line from a reflection in the mirror was harder than it looked. Your brain wanted the line to go one direction, but your hand had to draw it the opposite way. It was like this when she'd first tried this trancing trick.

The first several times she'd tried following someone's path, particularly someone who had gone *past* her, while walking, she looked like a drunk going down the sidewalk.

If she was walking straight, but the person had turned a corner *before* they'd come into her view and passed her, when she got to that part in her trance, she would suddenly turn left or right for no apparent reason—at least, not apparent to the people around her. Multiple times she had turned right into someone who was next to her on the sidewalk, and once she almost stepped in front of a car. It had something to do with trying to reconcile someone else's path in her mind while she was moving. They tended to get mixed up.

The way she overcame it was to incorporate short little pauses in her walk, which allowed her a second or two to trance, then she'd resume walking. The sudden stops, while annoying to people behind her, was better than plowing straight into someone. Eventually, she learned to not trance so deeply—but something more than a flash—and keep her legs moving forward. It was slow and choppy for a while, but one day it all clicked, and her mind understood what to do. That was the day the *false sight* had come to her.

As if Del didn't already see enough strange things, she was a little disheartened when this new phenomenon started. *Trancing* vision, while seated, was second nature to her by now, and was the closest thing to watching a movie—albeit a grainy, two-dimensional one. The *pulling-back-the-veil* vision that Arlo had shown her was disturbing—and she still couldn't do it—but it was more like pulling aside a curtain and looking through a window. And she usually wasn't moving during those times anyway. The spirit-cord thing had only happened twice, and that was more of a *state-of-being*, she thought, than an actual vision. Plus, again, no movement. But the *false sight* was really weird.

The combined effect of her walking forward, while trancing *backwards* on someone's path that had walked towards her, made her feel like she could see where the person had been for a few brief seconds.

It was like she could see their imprint from where they had been ten feet ago, then five feet closer, then two feet closer, etc.

She thought it had to be a trick of her mind, like when heat from a blacktop road made it look like something was hovering above the ground. She supposed a mirage worked like that in the desert but had never seen one.

But in this scenario, when the phenomenon didn't cause her to stop dead in her tracks, it was like seeing a trail of ghost imprints of where the person had been. One time, she saw four or five images, like a skipping movie reel, of the person for the last few seconds they had been walking. Combined with the fact that her eyes were open, she was moving, and people were walking through the ghost trail images, gave the images a weird 3D effect. The other odd thing about it was that the newest imprint, the one generated from where the person had just been, was the most visible. All the others, the few that she could see, would quickly dissolve, leaving the oldest imprint, the one furthest away from where the person had been at that moment, nearly invisible.

When the *false sight* phenomenon started, she went back to looking like a drunk on the sidewalk for a while. It was very disorientating, and she quickly learned to only try it in small doses. Seeing multiple copies of someone moving past you, simultaneously while the 'copies' were dissolving, would have convinced her she was losing her marbles if it hadn't been for the many strange things she'd witnessed over the last year and a half.

But, on this happy day, where her job was simply to observe people and wonder what was important to them, she let the false sight slip into her mind.

The middle-aged woman who'd been thinking about her aging parents was already too far past her to try this new trick.

Up ahead, an old man was seated, waiting for a bus, and Del tried him. Unfortunately, he'd been sitting there for a while and having moved very little, she didn't get the same effect as if he'd been walking. In fact, all she caught was a slight shiver of his arms as he had straightened his pants legs.

Approaching a park, Del heard the faint clip-clop of horses as they pulled carriages through the city. Somewhere beyond that a trumpet sounded, a busker warming up for a sidewalk show. This was the soundtrack of the city, and it resonated deeply within her. She saw a young girl skipping rope near where her mother sat talking with someone. The false sight projected from the girl looked like an out of focus bubble. Del presumed this was made by the jump rope as she swung it over her head while jumping in place.

Walking through the park—and now having a better understanding of a 'good' target—she focused on a single individual who was passing from left to right about twenty feet in front of her.

She watched them, wide-eyed, for several seconds. The false sight was in full effect, doppelganger images and all. So much so, that she felt the slight tinge of dizziness that had nearly undone her the first time she'd tried. But now she grinned like a Cheshire cat. Seeing the world like this—if you didn't fall over—was fascinating. And, it had nothing to do with spirits.

She picked someone else. They were walking at a different angle, but still, it produced a perfect false sighting. She giggled.

Looking behind her, she saw that the jump-rope girl was now running across the park, yelling for her mother to time her. With a slight wave of her hand, the mother motioned to her and resumed her conversation with the person next to her on the park bench. The girl, now at the far side of the park, came racing back toward her mother, which would bring her directly in front of Del's path.

Del sped up enough that she would cross behind the girl just a few seconds after she passed. Right in her *cosmic wake*, so to speak. Del tranced and walked. The false sight came forward—the *doppelganger vision* as she now thought of it—and was amazed at what she saw. Whether because her mind was getting better at this, or because of the speed of the girl, Del saw eight to ten, no, perhaps as many as twelve ghostly doppelganger imprints streaming off behind the girl. There were so many that Del had no trouble seeing the imprints as she walked straight through them.

And she gasped as she did.

Not only did a static tingle run up Del's arms as she passed into the cloud of images, but a feeling of warmth enveloped her. It was so unexpected that Del stopped in her tracks with her hand clamped to her mouth. Tears sprang to her eyes.

Somehow, she'd just passed *into* something from the running girl.

(Happy aura thoughts?)

Frozen in place, trying not to draw attention to herself, she let the girl's aura wash over her. Amid the cloud—she was literally standing in the middle of the girl's cosmic imprint—she could see the ghostly images of the girl as they collided with her own skin. Several of the doppelganger images—now swirling together like smoke in a breeze—

began to disappear with tiny flashes of sparkling light as they landed on Del's arms, face and hands.

And she couldn't help but laugh.

The happy aura of the girl was like a nose full of laughing gas from the dentist's office. It invaded her, suddenly and completely, overwhelming her senses.

With both hands clamped to her mouth now, she was able to stifle the joyous laughter that threatened to bubble out of her. But she couldn't contain the tears. Some warm feeling of youth, gifted to her by the little running girl, had swelled inside her, and overflowed through the happiest tears she had ever cried.

Then she began to twirl.

Like a schoolgirl, without a care in the world, Del stuck out her arms, threw back her head, and spun in a circle as the remnants of the girl's presence lit her body with tiny flashes of sparkling light.

And as she sparkled, the Crescent City saw her in a new light—as did other things.

*

Standing in a third story window of the Hotel Monteleone on Royal Street, a dark-haired man gazed out the window. He was both young and old in a way few could understand. Dark brown hair fell in waves to his white collared shirt. A timeless suit jacket hung casually over a chair somewhere behind him. Manicured fingers of an elegant left hand pushed back the sheer curtains of the window. His gaze floated across streets and buildings he had seen more times than he could remember; and his memory was long. On his right pointer finger was a ring of unknown metal. Set upon it was a gem of equally unknown origin. Sometimes the gem was clouded with a deep smoky grey. On rare occasions it was fiery red. Today, as his thumb absently rolled it around his finger, it was a calm, pale blue. For his thoughts were of a calm blue nature.

The man did not live permanently at the Monteleone, for his travels took him far and abroad. But he was a special guest of the iconic hotel. So much so, that he had a standing reservation for several months of the year. His bill had been paid in advance a long time ago.

He had business to attend to on this day, but it was the standard mundane decisions that he'd grown bored of long ago, which is why his mind was adrift.

He sighed lightly and nearly let the curtain fall back into place when a movement to his right caught his attention. He let the curtain fall and walked out onto the balcony.

There, he peered up Royal Street. It was a one-way street running towards him. His sharp eyes focused, first past the hanging flowers that adorned his balcony, then over the low row of buildings at the corner of the block, then through the narrow sliver of alley that was aligned with his vision, and finally, to the park on the next street beyond that.

He couldn't pinpoint the movement that had drawn his attention—it was more of a feeling than anything—so stood and watched. His skin prickled with a telltale sign, and he leaned over the railing.

The normal players were moving in and out of the park, one that he'd frequented many times. But something new and interesting had just happened there. His nostrils flared slightly, as if to help him home in on what the disturbance was. Then he saw it.

A young woman was standing in the middle of the park, spinning, and laughing.

The man on the balcony, Étienne Cristophe Montclair, decided to take a walk.

*

Del had hardly touched her lunched. Not because she wasn't hungry—ever since her run-in with Billy Bash she'd had a nearly insatiable appetite—but mostly because she hadn't stopped asking Mr. Bobby questions, and knew it wasn't polite to talk with food in her mouth.

The ideas rolled out of Del's mouth in one long breath. "...so then I saw a woman that looked deep in thought and I wondered what her concerns could be and thought they might be financially related and wondered if the city had programs for people in need and maybe I would look into that—" She stopped for a long breath. "...and—"

Bobby held up his hands in surrender.

"Take a bite before the flies run off with it," he said. "We got plenty of time."

Del, not disappointed, only perhaps, slightly deflated that Mr. Bobby hadn't praised her keen sense of observation, grabbed her hamburger and took a large bite. Now that she had food in her mouth, she realized how hungry she was and added two French fries with it.

Bobby chuckled, grabbed his pack of smokes off the table and nearly speared one into his mouth six inches from his face. The cigarette practically flew from the pack only to be caught in his lips like a bear catching trout from a stream.

The smoke was lit as he spoke, left eye squinting defensively. "They're all good ideas, Del. Don't think I'm dismissin' 'em off hand." The spent match flew to its place in the ashtray with a flick of his wrist. "And you're probably right—" He tilted his head back and shot a column of smoke in the air before relocking her gaze. "Hell, I know you're right. This city needs all kinds of programs for the homeless and the unwed mothers and whatnot. But that's just not the *pulse* that people are lookin' to read in the newspaper."

He reached over and snagged one of Del's French fries as if he were a familiar uncle, before tilting his head back to its thinking position.

Del stared in wonder as he managed to eat the fry and smoke the cigarette at that same time. She almost imagined each side of his mouth working separately at their own task as if nothing was odd about it. It was only due to his eyes being closed in a contemplative manner that gave her the courage to stare a little at the trick.

Another column of smoke shot up from his throat, then he said, "No, the newspapers are already crammed with bad stories, stories of real life and how things *happened*. What people are looking for are feel-good stories—but not fairytales—of real life and how someone overcame their circumstances."

Still with his eyes closed, and maybe a bit to show off his own powers of observation, he said, "Take for instance the mother and daughter that got seated," and nodded his head to his left, "about ten minutes ago. What do you think is drivin' their quiet conversation?"

Without thinking, Del flashed to the two women, confirmed that he had the relationship correct, replayed the last few minutes of conversation in her head, and before Mr. Bobby could offer his own opinion said, "Oh, they're concerned about paying for her junior college now that the father ran off with the—"

Del stopped suddenly, wondering if she had in fact, just blurted the whole thing out loud.

Bobby's eyes sprung open. A look of surprise, which slowly narrowed to suspicion, covered his face. The specifics of her comment surprised him. The cherry on his cigarette glowed orange, as smoke curled before his face. It nearly formed a question mark before he blew it away with a snort.

"What, you a psychic or somethin'?" he asked.

Del shoved three French fries into her mouth as if to plug a leaky hole. Maybe this way she wouldn't blurt something else out.

"No," she mumbled, wide-eyed, past the food.

Bobby chuckled and shook his head. "I believe you're a bit of an odd bird, Del." He stubbed out the cigarette and reached for the pack. "But you are genuine." He shook his head again, as if in laughter, but magically came up with another unlit cigarette. "I didn't really think you were psychic." He winked at her. "But you do have an opinion, don't you?"

He looked directly at the mother and daughter, then watched with surprise as the elder woman pulled a folder from a cloth bag. He caught only a glimpse of the logo on the folder but immediately recognized it as that of the Mid-City Baptist Junior College. Both women leaned forward, with hands on their foreheads, as several papers were pulled from the folder.

Bobby's gaze slid back to Del, who was pretending not to notice the folder by looking in the other direction.

She flashed to the scene of her and Bobby sitting at the table. Doing this made her feel surreal and a bit creepy—watching herself and a guest from above, like it was an out-of-body experience—but she had to confirm if Mr. Bobby was still staring at her. He was.

"What about that person?" Del said, more as a distraction than anything. "What do you think is important to them?"

Bobby lingered for a moment longer, then looked, trying to spot the target. She hadn't pointed directly at anyone, but he began to pontificate on what he thought the people during that day were concerned about.

Her thoughts began to drift as Bobby talked, and she slipped into something like the doppelganger trance she'd managed earlier. Although she wasn't moving, she could still see the stuttering imprints of people as they walked by. She wondered what these people would be interested in reading if she wrote a newspaper article, then realized she could just search around in their reading habits and find out. She wasn't sure whether this was considered cheating or not, but thought it might be OK to do, if it helped her get—

She tensed in her chair. Mr. Bobby was still talking and hadn't seemed to notice.

Flitting her eyes left and right, she searched for the image that had just passed through her vision. She didn't want to be so obvious as to put her head on a swivel.

Had she dozed off just now? Had she imagined the whole thing?

Scanning through the doppelganger images of the people she'd been staring at, she replayed the tangled paths they had walked—their old selves crisscrossing where others had just been. It was a giant tapestry that hung before her. Not one of death per se, but of life-that-had-just-been.

She vaguely remembered their images and colors. But she was looking for something else.

A man.

The faintest imprint of a man had entered her trancing vision but was now gone.

But how could that be? She wondered. There was no long, ghostly trail of him having walked towards her. There were no fading imprints of where he'd dissolved into the other doppelganger images that crowded the air. There wasn't even any evidence of him having left the scene. It was as if he'd only existed for a mere second, then—

Then she found it.

Like a lost photograph, or an errant frame in a movie upon which the film projector had gotten stuck, she saw the image of the man.

Dark wavy hair hung to his white collared shirt. Elegant and timeless features composed his face and hands. The glint of a ring sparkled like sun off the water, cool and blue.

And in this single, snapshot of an image, Del saw his entire beautiful face. For although his body was positioned to walk past her, outside the seating area of the café, he had turned his head and had stared straight at her.

CHAPTER 5

"A movie?" Jimmy said. His eyes sparkled with wonder. "Whah kinda' movie?"

Armand snapped the newspaper open to the entertainment section. Although he had several research topics on his mind, including Jimmy, he'd been thinking about his adopted family all summer. Their lives had been so inextricably thrown together, and in that forced proximity they'd overcome great dangers. But now, in mid-September, as his mind moved towards that October country that he so loved, that time of year when things began to die, he wondered about his family's future. Where would their lives take them? Did he have the means to support them after he was gone? How long would he be around?

Armand didn't know why these thoughts had suddenly flooded his mind, but it was as if an invisible clock had suddenly struck a late hour. Which hour it was, how close to his *final midnight*, he could not tell. And this bothered him. For perhaps the first time in his life, he felt the winds of mortality at his back, and they blew hard. Where they were blowing him, was something he chose not to explore. Not yet anyway.

And for these reasons he'd begun to think about all the things he'd never had a reason to do before.

"Whah movie?" Jimmy asked again.

Armand came back to the conversation and snapped the paper again. "Well, Master Jimmy, let's see what our options are."

He laid the paper on the kitchen table and smoothed it out. He scanned the titles one by one, reading them aloud.

"*Dr. Strangelove*. Hmm, strange indeed."

"*The Pink Panther*. Mmm, perhaps."

"*A Hard Day's Night*." Then under his breath he said, "Oh my, one hundred screaming Del's. Perhaps we'll avoid that one for now."

"Whah wong wit Deh?" Jimmy asked.

Armand shook his head. "Nothing. Let's see. *Seven Days in May*. A political thriller I believe."

"Mama D," Jimmy said as she entered the kitchen. "We goan' to ah movie. You wanna go?"

Mama Dedé looked at Armand with a bit of surprise. This was the first time he'd ever suggested something like this.

"What?" He supplicated his hands. "One needs a bit of sophistication, do they not? Besides, it would be a nice surprise for Del after her first day at her new job."

"Yeah!" Jimmy stated. "But whah kinda' movie?"

"Egh!" Armand sounded disgusted. "Most of these are sappy romances or—" His finger stopped, and he peered closer to the paper. "Wait a minute. I think we have a winner."

"Whah?"

Armand looked up triumphantly. "Mary Poppins!"

"Who?" Jimmy wrinkled his face.

"Mary Poppins?" Mama D tilted her head at Armand as if to look over the top of invisible glasses.

Armand, now convinced that this was the best idea in the history of movie choices, fell into his professorial defense mode. "Why yes, of course. You see, it's about these two sad children who are visited by a mysterious nanny with a flying umbrella, and go on wonderful, magical adventures together. It's Walt Disney after all.

"In fact, now that I think about it, it's not unlike our little family here."

Mama D tilted her head. "Whatever you say, Frenchy."

He continued. "And it's playing at the Saenger tonight at 7:00. I'll call Frank."

Mama D turned to go upstairs. "Heh! You do dat. The day you get Frank Morgan to go to a Disney movie is the day I become Mary Poppins and fly up the chimney!"

Armand spent the day doing errands around the house, finishing with an early dinner of shrimp étouffée. He wanted everyone to save room for popcorn.

When Del finally came home, Jimmy ambushed her at the kitchen door with the exciting news.

"A movie?" she said. "Tonight?"

Jimmy nodded.

Del looked at Armand and Mama D, who were already eating. "Oh, I was going to do some research for work, and…" Her voice was low as she thought about the mysterious man she'd seen at the café.

Armand shoved a bowl of food at her and said, "In celebration of your new job and all." He nodded towards Jimmy. "He's been waiting all day to tell you."

"He has?" Del spooned food into her mouth. "All day?"

Jimmy piped up. "Aww day!" And began to spin around in a helicopter motion as if that clearly showed the extent of his waiting.

Armand watched Del with a twinkle in his eye. Having Jimmy as an ally was as good as any secret weapon.

Her mouth twisted with indecision. She felt like the freedom of adulthood, of having a real job, maybe even a boyfriend, was nearly within reach, but clearly outside the doors of this house or some movie theatre. How would she ever get back out on her own if she kept doing kid stuff? But as she watched Jimmy spin with excitement, her indecision was replaced with a strange feeling of emptiness, knowing that someday she wouldn't be here for him. "OK. Is it the new Beatles movie?"

Armand cringed. "Well, we thought perhaps something a little… quieter."

"Oh, alright." Del's eyes sparked. "The James Bond one?"

"Uh, less violent."

Now Del was at a loss.

"Let's just call it a surprise," Armand said. "Eat up. Quickly now! We want good seats.

*

Returning home after the show they tumbled into the house feeling closer than they ever had before.

Jimmy had a stomach-ache from eating too much popcorn, but every time Armand would start up another chorus of the iconic song, *Super-cali-fragilistic*, to which Del would groan, he'd do his best to sing the words. The sound of the syllables was generally in the right place, but sounded something closer to: "Suppah-fadjuh-madjuh-biscuit...," then the words would stick together like peanut-butter syllables, as his head rocked from side to side. But he was always waiting on the turnaround to start up with, "Suppah-fadjuh-madjuh-biscuit…" as loudly as possible.

Armand glowed from the success of the evening. "Ah, if only Frank could have attended, our little adventure would be most complete."

"When was the last time anyone spoke with him?" Del asked, pulling a crumpled box of Jujyfruits from her pocket.

"Hmm," Armand said, "let's see, it's only been… well, how long has it been?" He looked at Mama Dedé.

"It's been a spell," she said, nodding. "Might want to swing by tomorra' and see."

"Yes, yes," said Armand. "I'm sure everything's fine. I'll drive over tomorrow and find him tinkering in his garage."

The night ended in the usual manner, each one going their own way. Each one with secret thoughts.

*

Del sat on her bed with her notebook, pencil poised to write. Bobby Dupre had told her to jot down interesting things she'd seen throughout the day, and they'd talk about them as potential topics for an article. But nothing was coming to her.

She considered flashing back to the movie house and filching an idea from someone in the audience, but she'd actually liked the movie, so hadn't noticed anyone in particular. There were several families there, however. Lots of kids. So, the parents surely had concerns that would make a good story.

Abandoning the pad and pencil, she leaned back against her

pillows and stared at the ceiling and the slowly moving shadows. Nothing ominous tonight—yet. Her eyes grew heavy.

Her thoughts drifted over the topic of family. She was on her third version now. The first, with her real mother and father, was quite faint in her memory. At times she'd tried to remember them—she *should* have been able to, she thought—but it was always difficult. She'd been eight when the fire had occurred, and that was old enough to have many memories stored away. But they just weren't there. The few scenes she had were obscured and hazy, as if shrouded by… well, as if shrouded by smoke.

She fingered the scar that ran up the right side of her neck. The one thing about her first family that she could never forget. She closed her eyes and dropped her hands back to the bed.

Outside her bedroom window a mist began to swirl.

Her second family, she thought, if one could consider her time at the orphanage familial, had left her with many memories, most of which she'd like to forget. If only there was some type of mental fire she could conjure to burn up the bad memories. That would be a great power to have, she thought. But she'd met Jimmy at the orphanage, so that counted as a good memory. Sister Eulalie certainly did *not*. Jo… that was complicated on many levels.

The mist gathered weight and pressing itself against the panes, spread over the surface. It was looking for a way in.

But now her third family—another adopted one, but in a good way—was around her now. And although she was happy here, and loved each one of them dearly, it had more than its share of bad memories. In fact, considering how new this family was to her, having formed about a year and a half ago, it had far more bad memories than it should have. Not because of the people around her

(The live ones you mean.)

Yes, the live ones, she thought, just as a face formed in the window. Its hollow eyes began searching randomly around the room.

But because of the things that had occurred here. How long could a family stay together under those conditions? Would she ever have her own family? A real one, like with a husband and kids? How could you have a family with dead things always—

The face in the window screamed, just as it had a few nights before.

*

Del's eyes shot open as her hand flinched, sending the pad and pencil flying off the bed. She was immediately in a trance.

The spirit face, as if not aware of the commotion it had just caused, continued staring blankly into the room. The holes that were its eye sockets moved slowly around, searching, but not always in the same direction. And although one of them had just passed over Del, it did not see her.

They're the blank eyes of Jimmy, Del thought. That distant, searching stare reminded her of how Jimmy sometimes looked, especially the day she'd brought his birthday cake to the orphanage. She'd seen the same vacant, tongue-lolling gaze staring out the window as he'd waited for her.

In her trance she saw the spirit and the strange mist that supported it. She'd never seen this before. For a moment she wasn't sure if she was awake and physically pinched her leg.

She was.

In her room she saw the spirit-face peering aimlessly through the window. In her trance, she saw the same thing, only with more detail. There was clearly a spirit floating outside her window, but it was as if it couldn't see her. And worse than that, it was like the spirit had needed help finding her window. The mist *around* the face was made up of other spirits, as if they had guided the first, and were now supporting it. And just as she realized this, they pulled back from the window as if to leave.

With an overpowering curiosity and empathy, Del's trancing mind floated out the window and followed them.

CHAPTER 6

Ernest cowered in the dark as he felt shreds of sanity pulled from his mind. At first, he imagined it had been in slow drips, like a leaky faucet, although now he knew they had been *nibbles*. Something had been nibbling at the edges of his mind, tentative and unsure. But over the last twelve hours or so—he couldn't really tell time in this dark, watery hell—it was as if his mind had finally been opened, an oyster succumbing to the prying knife, and whatever there had been of Ernest Crowley was quickly being consumed.

He saw only flashes of memory now, pieces of a life that may, or may not, have belonged to him. Glimpses of a yellow-eyed face, there, but not there, deformed and clawed toes, fleeting warnings. Then the spirit-things came.

At first, they came as shadows, as soft and fleeting as thoughts. They couldn't believe their good fortune, the shadows, and had to reinspect him several times to confirm his presence. They were curious things, child-like, brushing against him in the dark, then fleeing away to safety. He swatted at them franticly like a drunk with the DT's—imaginary bugs crawling over his skin. This may have gone on for minutes or hours, he couldn't tell. Each one's touch sent a brief cold sting through him, restarting his horror all over again.

Then one, being past its initial curiosity, began to nibble at his mind, and Ernest screamed. The screams confirmed to the shadow-spirits what Ernest really was, a living person, and their shyness disappeared. And like when they were living disciples and fell upon each other, they now fell upon him in a swarm.

As the disciple-swarm pried at his mind, he heard words, fragments of thoughts, frightened and confused.

(...what? ...how? ...dead? ...mother? ...where? ...how?)

The voices, now many of them, tumbled over each other in a cacophony of fear. Ernest tried to shrink away from them, tried to close his mind to their pleas, but could not. There were too many of them. And more were coming from the dark recesses of the boat. Those, the late-comers, had watched longingly from the edges as the bolder ones had inspected Ernest first. But now, realizing what was happening, and that the person lying there on the floor feeding them, may not survive long, they came forward, adding to the madness.

Ernest heard his voice screaming, but from a faraway place. The swarming spirits, while snatching morsels of his soul, had also caught a bit of a scream. Yes, even his screaming voice was being carried off to feed some unimaginable horror.

He had the sensation of blacking out, but it could have been his mind protecting him. He perceived that the feeding frenzy went on for a while, then subsided. The spirits had not been satiated, he felt, but wanted him alive for a while. Then the questions came.

(How did this happen? Where are we? Who are we? Are we dead?

Where is he? Has he forsaken us? Yes, where is he? Where is he?)

Then the yellow-eyed face came into his mind and the spirits pulled back. They waited anxiously at the periphery.

The yellow-eyed face

(...Gris-gris man...)

calmed the disciple-swarm by its presence. It had been in the background, Ernest suddenly realized, the entire time. It had been there when the feeding frenzy began. It had stopped the swarm—even those *eater of screams*—from killing him. But now it would do its own feeding. But first, it had a question.

(What year is this?) The Gris-gris man asked.

Before Ernest could open his mouth, the thought of what a strange question this was came to his mind.

What year?

(Yes. It's a simple question. What year is this?)

In a way, Ernest was happy to entertain the psychic conversation. Perhaps he was imagining the whole thing anyway, but it kept the hungry mouths at bay for a while longer. He could go on like this for a while, he thought, talking to himself. But in the end, would it matter? He was so tired. He was so... thin. His mind was failing; he could feel it. Just a few more questions, then a few nibbles, and he would be undone completely, and his hell would end.

1964, he thought in response.

The spirits were startled at this and crowded in at him.

(...what? ...lie! ...false ...demon! ...he lies! He lies!)

The essence of the Gris-gris man—for Ernest could not tell whether he was physically there or not—lashed out at the spirits and they fell back again, shirking from their reprimand.

He turned his attention back to Ernest.

(The year is nineteen-hundred and sixty-four?)

Yes.

(What place is this?)

Place?

(What town?)

Bayou Sara. The image of the small back-water town jumped into Ernest's mind. That was the town he had lived in. It was also the name of the river he'd been fishing on when he'd seen the paddle-wheelers come out of the mist. But if he wasn't dead and imagining this, and if he was really inside the paddle-wheeler which was moving, then he couldn't be exactly sure where he was now.

(...Bayou Sara?..)

Ernest felt the confusion in the voice as easily as his mind heard the question. An image of a river map came into his mind. On the map, the Mississippi River snaked through Louisiana on a winding, southeasterly path. The area of Bayou Sara was a small pinprick on the map, which sat on the north side of a bend in the Mississippi. The smaller river flowed south feeding into the Mississippi northwest of Baton Rouge which was a larger dot. And finally, as the big river flowed Southeast, the city of New Orleans appeared before the southernmost swamps began.

The spirits—very much like anxious children now—jostled with excitement but held silent.

The Gris-gris man, cloaked in shadows, became a shape in the darkness—Ernest could see part of his face. The man closed his yellow eyes and breathed deeply. The scent of the river had changed little over the years, but the paddle wheeler had been gone for so long it had been stripped of actual odor. It was as if the ship and crew had dry rotted and were now saturated with the dusty-gray smell of nonexistence.

But the river, which pushed water in and out of its weed-choked and fish-strewn tributaries, smelled full of life. And even the oldest of memories can be brought back by smell.

"I remember now," said the Gris-gris man. His physical voice was still faint and shaky but seemed to reverberate around the room. It was as if the boat wanted it to be strong.

"We are near New Orleans," he said.

Ernest watched his face fade back into the shadows, a smoldering ember not yet strong enough to burn.

(We will find her in New Orleans.)

And with that, the spirits fell upon Ernest again.

*

Later that evening, the paddle wheeler slipped into a dark backwater near a place called River Ridge. Built by French colonists in the late 18th century for sugar plantations, the marshy land was subdivided into traditional French long-lot style farms that extended far back from the river, deep into the land.

John Montanet would have known that many slaves were housed in the area during this period. One of the largest plantations, the Providence, owned by the Sauve family, was reported to have housed nearly one-hundred and fifty slaves at the height of its production. John had plied his trade many times to the plantation owners and knew the land well. It was barely a four-mile walk straight north from the river, and one would come to Lake Pontchartrain and its swampy surrounds. If a runaway slave could make it that far, there was a fair chance they wouldn't be seen again. But not being seen again did not always equate to escape.

But for now, the Gris-gris man, with the shadow memories of John and others, needed to rest. And regenerate. The process of *reemergence*, or whatever he had experienced over the last twenty-four hours, had left him incomplete.

And the spirits

(…disciples…)

were hungry. The feeding they'd done from Ernest had provided very little considering the number of them. Many had not even made it to the feeding. Certainly not the wretched thing housed in the last boat.

A vague recollection of what lay in the third boat came to the Gris-gris man's mind. Had it survived? Would he even recognize it if it had? He let the thought slip away. His immediate attention was on finding another food source. Preferably one younger than their current guest.

As if feeling his master's will, a faint blue light shimmered forth. The shape of a beast, something like a large mangy wolf, began to materialize. But it would not fully form.

The Gris-gris man stroked the air where its back formed a weak outline. A faint blue mist floated from his unformed hand and into the beast. This action, the meager energy he could spare, was enough to bring the beast forward. It was opaque with mass now, but still not complete.

(Why, Mr. Sandgrove, what is the matter?)

The forming body of the Gris-gris man slipped back into the gloom, only a partial face and one hand materialized. More energy was sent to Mr. Sandgrove, the Gris-gris man's beloved creation.

The body of the beast filled out. Its split tail swished the air. Its giant claws flexed against the wooden floor.

The Gris-gris man's hand, no longer petting, groped the back of the beast, searching. Something was missing.

(But… where is he? Where is Toth?)

The beast, Mr. Sandgrove, could not speak. It only looked at the Gris-gris man, its master, its creator, with a look of longing and despair. A part of it was missing. The voodoo doll Toth, which had been stuck to the beast's back with a long hat pin, was gone.

Then the man's hand slipped under the beast's neck. Another surprise. Attached to the crude collar hung the tiny doll of a woman. It had dirty yellow hair and one eye stuck open like a broken toy. This child's doll had not started the journey with them. It had been added later.

The ghost hand of the Gris-gris man dropped away, and the beast laid down, resting its ragged head on a quickly fading paw. Something was wrong, the man thought. Their reemergence from the *Misi sipokni mist*, that mist from the great river which was Beyond Age, had not gone as expected. That, or there wasn't even enough energy to form the correct impression of the beast. Why wasn't there at least a hint of Toth? A shadow of its outline? Had it somehow been turned into the tiny woman?

No. The Gris-gris man felt in his thin shadow-core that something was wrong. Toth was somewhere else. Or, perhaps, some*when* else.

(Preserve your energy.) The Gris-gris man thought to the beast.

(Rest and preserve. We'll be safe this way. I'll send the three.)

*

Sometime later, three spirits emerged from the shadows. These three had been the first to awaken and feed, so they were the most complete. In life, these three disciples had been the strongest and most loyal. And John Montanet, Dr. John, who became the Gris-gris man, had granted them many favors.

But now, as he looked upon their wretched state, and because they were so unrecognizable, he couldn't even recall their names.

Weeks before his undoing, during the period of his original life, the Gris-gris man had worked at a feverish pace preparing his escape. He had felt his time growing short, not just because he was being hunted as an abomination, there was that. But he'd felt a narrowing of his mind, as if it were fading to nothing. As if the candle flame of that life was sputtering out. And during those weeks, he, and the three disciples had transformed, binding themselves, over and over, to become as strong as possible for the journey. They were to become his personal protectors. They were to become wraiths.

The disciples, feeling blessed to be of use and elevated to such status, fed from John's magic during these transformation sessions, but at a terrible price. Each time they let their souls be bound—to reach wraith status—he pulled the strongest pieces of them to himself and kept it. Now, hovering before him were the tattered remains of the three disciples, and they were a horrid sight. Time within the mist had been hard on them all, but these wretched things would barely complete a soul if bound together.

Misshapen and thin, the wraiths trembled in the air, awaiting their master's command.

The Gris-gris man searched his memory. He had to remember *something* of these creatures, he had to name them at least, if he were to use them properly. Slowly, from the mist, the dream fragments came.

The first wraith reminded him of his most loyal disciple, a woman. She had been the first to convert, and he was comprised more of her soul than any other he'd bound. Whatever her name had been in the past did not matter now, for that soul no longer existed. But the essence of her devotion was still there. He could feel it. And when he thought of it, the wraith trembled in response. A phrase came to his mind. *Umbra Fidelis*: Shade of Devotion.

(Umbra,) he said, naming the first wraith.

The second wraith emitted a low, despairing little sound, something of a warble. Whether it was a sound of displeasure or warning he could not tell. But he suddenly remembered a disciple, another woman he thought, who had been loyal, but cautious as a field mouse. Having some bit of foresight, she'd always warned him to be careful. She felt that one day someone stronger would come along and steal the power he'd gained, and then she'd have to serve a new master. She'd always been fearful of a new master. A smile crept onto his ghost face as another phrase came to mind. *Susurrus Ruinae*: Whisper of Ruin.

(Susurrus,) he said. Thus, naming the second wraith.

The third wraith, the most incomplete, was a forsaken revenant. Its utter decay, either by the mist or some unknown malevolency, was horrible to behold. The few shapes it could form, three limbs of gossamer shadow and something resembling an eye, hovered in the air, barely attached. Despite its state of unbeing, a sharp pulse of energy radiated from it. There was a feeling of power in the thing. And because of this, the Gris-gris man felt this spirit must have been one of his male disciples.

There had been one nearly as ambitious as John who had fancied himself a potential rival. Perhaps Susurrus had warned him of this one at some point. But in the end, John had won out. He remembered a particularly brutal binding that had nearly ended in disaster. The disciple had reacted so violently to the binding that it threw him backwards into the fire, where he was badly burned before the others could pull him out. John buried him up to his neck in swamp mud for three days trying to heal him. The disciple was nearly insane after the ordeal. Another phrase came to mind. *Praeco Cineris*: Harbinger of Ash.

(Praeco,) he said. The third and final wraith was named.

The wraiths seemed to vibrate, in a way, as if gaining a filament of energy from being named. They were connected mentally to their master, as all his creations were, and needed no instructions. As part of the collective, which was the Gris-gris man, they felt his hunger, theirs, and that of their siblings, the other disciples who had yet to reform. The three wraiths now had to hunt. They had to feed their family.

As the face of the Gris-gris man faded into shadow, he remembered River Ridge when it was cane fields and blood, when he could ply his trade to the plantation owners unbothered.

Now, the city crept toward it with roads and wires. But the swamp still whispered his name. And like them, it was still hungry.

The wraiths spread out through the land like a living plague: deadly, hungry, and hunting.

CHAPTER 7

On the corner of Dauphine and Mandeville streets, in the old Faubourg Marigny section of the city, sat a row of abandoned buildings. Half-way down the block a dark opening led to a small alley that crept behind the abandoned buildings. The unnamed alley dead-ended in the center of the block at a singularly odd building.

It was a building that, either through some trick of its geometry, or a spell no one understood, could not be seen. And because it could not be seen, at least by any normal definition of the word, it had been forgotten to have existed at all, except by a few.

Its main occupant, Madame Broussard, had resided, hidden, in the building for a long time. She had paced its inner rooms, watching the living fresco, for a span of memories, looking for a way out.

Another presence, which had been in the building as long as she, lay still as death. Even Madame Broussard didn't know whether it lived or merely lingered. As far as she knew, no other thing had ever been put into such a state. But she knew that it was the state of this spirit that kept her hidden and safe. But how long it would keep her safe she did not know. And this thought weighed heavily on her mind as the years passed.

Outside the invisible building, also hidden from view, was a dark ring of shadows. They had formed quickly after she'd gone into hiding. Over the years, more shadows had collected and the color of the ring, as seen on the fresco on her wall, had grown darker. It was nearly black now.

And very recently, appearing occasionally as a small dot on the fresco wall, someone new was seen to stand outside the invisible building. Madame Broussard wasn't sure if the person could sense the black ring of spirits around the building, but suspected it was possible. But she was certain of one thing, the person standing outside her building was Arlo, the eldest of the witch sisters, and a sworn enemy to her.

The thought of the three witch sisters took Madame Broussard far back into her memory. She had first encountered the sisters shortly after her arrival in the Crescent City. It pained her heart to think of those days when she'd been so free, so powerful. Had it not been for them, she'd still be free, and even more powerful. But a series of small events changed everything. And her life, that which it was, had changed forever.

Thus, Madame Broussard spent her days and nights watching the outside world on the fresco that covered her walls. And through this portal she had watched the return of Scarmish, the black spirit ring around her, the newly formed white ring around the spirit hunters house—Del was her name—as well as Arlo now standing outside her own home.

She took these events in stride, as so far, Del had been the only one who had found a way into her inner sanctum. Through some strange ability, Del had followed the path of the Alvie-bones as it had moved through the shadow-roads back to her. But during their brief encounter, Madame Broussard had not detected a threat from Del. In fact, Del had pulled a rather clever trick on her to free a young girl from her. And although this had been an inconvenience, Madame Broussard had not sought retribution. After all, she hadn't come to the New World to abduct children. In fact, hadn't she herself been abducted when she was… that other name? That other girl she'd been before she had been cursed with the Black Gift?

She sighed. Yet another story for another time.

So, when Del had tricked her and freed the girl, Madame Broussard began to think seriously about her own escape. If Del could find a way in, someone else could too. And there was always the threat of someone turning Del against her. After all, Madame Broussard had watched on this very fresco as Arlo had taught Del about the silver cord. And she had been impressed, rightfully so, when Del had used that ability against a man who had attacked her.

The thing about the fresco was that she couldn't see great detail on it. Certainly not that of humans going about their everyday lives. And she couldn't even see the details of the attack that night, when Del had unleashed her terrible power. But large flashes of supernatural power were easy to see; they showed like lightning flashes in a dark sky. Large gatherings of spirits were also easy to see, like the rings. And specialty items, like that of the Alvie-bones—her own creation—or Scarmish, a most unfortunate creation of the cosmic order, could also be easily detected. It was as if the fresco was tuned to seek out these things.

So, she noticed the wraiths the moment they slipped into the city—black stains spreading across her fresco.

Madame Broussard had been reading from an old book. She thought it had once belonged to her Uncle Lucian, but could no longer remember. For months she'd been working with the Toth-skeleton trying to communicate with it. Her first version of the Alvie-bones had been nearly destroyed by the stone maiden which protected the spirit hunter's courtyard. She still didn't know how it had been enchanted, but it had made short work of the Alvie-bones after they'd first been animated. Somehow feeling the pull of Del, the Alvie-bones had followed her home and wreaked havoc in the house. Somehow, being merged with an intruder, the man and the bones had run from the house, only to get caught up by the stone maiden and nearly destroyed. Luckily, the boney hand had the sense to reach for the shadow-road and was whisked home, mostly intact. The body of the man the bones had inhabited, had been pulled into the depths of the fountain and never seen again.

Madame Broussard thought the bones had been a complete loss, not having any real thought processes of their own, until she discovered the magic hidden in the Toth doll. Positioning the doll behind the skull by way of the hat pin that held it upright, Toth appeared to ride the Alvie-bones. Embedding the hat pin into the spine of the skeleton, Toth's stubby arms and legs stuck out on either side of the skull. Its head stuck up just above the crown of the skull where its red bead eyes could see over the top. The combination of the two of them, which she now thought of as the Toth-skeleton, was the second incarnation. And although she knew not how, she felt that the Toth-skeleton would be her key to escape.

And her ability to communicate with the thing was nearly complete.

Feeling a faint electric buzz in the air, Madame Broussard looked up at the fresco. The Toth-skeleton followed her gaze, somehow knowing where she was looking. When the skeleton head moved, imbued with the magical blood from her use of the Thirteen Passage—that ancient rite of transference—Toth's red bead eyes glowed, and its red bead mouth emitted a low murmur. If by a trick of the light, or some magic she didn't understand, the arms and legs seemed to move slightly as if turning the skull head like a rider on a horse.

On the fresco, three black shadows were moving quickly, but randomly, through the outskirts of the city. They'd just come from the West; some place off the edge of the fresco map. That most likely meant the river, she thought. During her many years of watching the fresco, she'd seen many things come from that direction. And in a strange way, thought that was part of her salvation. There was something about the river that she could use to escape. But she didn't have it worked out yet.

The shadows, wraiths she thought, were moving haphazardly through the streets. They reminded her of stray dogs, who'd recently escaped the dogcatcher. They skittered—or floated, she presumed—helter-skelter from one place to the next, sniffing, pissing, and moving on. Their movements were jerky, urgent, and unpredictable. Her own hackles were suddenly up. This was something new that had just come to the city, and she felt an unease in the pit of her stomach.

She didn't care for the wraiths. Watching them closely, her nostrils began to flair, as if preparing for a hunt. She and the Toth-skeleton stood up almost simultaneously. She hadn't commanded it to stand. It simply felt her intention.

Now, Madame Broussard and the Toth-skeleton stood at the fresco wall, watching the three wraiths invade their city.

CHAPTER 8

When Del's trancing mind left her bedroom window to follow the spirit, she thought her journey would be short. Not that distance was a factor when dealing with the dead, but the spirit-requests she'd entertained over that last year had been quite specific and relatively quick to fulfill.

Soon after she came into her power, Mama D had quietly advertised her abilities to a discrete circle, from which she'd begun to get requests. They'd spanned the gamut of typical appeals: fortune telling, a blessing, the occasional love potion, even curses. But Mama D, who understood that Del's power was far different than most, had declined these on her behalf. The few she passed onto Del, advising her as to the reason she should consider them, were those that dealt with calming spirits back to some state of rest.

That skill, Mama D had assured her, was the mark of the truly gifted, and she should leave the fortune telling and potion making to others. So, at her mentor's advice, Del had done just that. She'd dealt with a handful of truly lost souls that for one reason or another could not find their paths forward.

Now, as she followed the spirit-mist—for the face still had its supporting cast—she wondered what she would encounter tonight. Free of the house, and watching the cloud drift out before her, she paused to appreciate the view of the neighborhood. Who else had this perspective? Floating high above Armand's house, she saw the network of shadow-roads that knitted the city together. Like a dark and floating yarn, the shadow-roads were everywhere, crisscrossing the sky like an ancient and forgotten weave. And in that instance, she wondered if the city could survive without them, for surely, they were the threads of the tapestry that the city was painted upon.

Absently following the spirit-path, wondering about the layers yet to be discovered, she suddenly jerked her eyes up and stared in surprise.

They'd just arrived at the St. Louis Cemetery #1.

*

This cemetery was famous for many reasons. Marie Laveau was reportedly buried there. And, although not confirmed, John Montanet aka Dr. John was also. Although, which crypt was his was up for debate. Regardless, the people that revered—and thought they followed—either one, would regularly visit the respective tombs to leave offerings and prayers to their chosen leader.

Del knew this place for another reason. Through a strange series of events, Del and her adopted family, along with Josephine, her friend from the orphanage, had ended up here the night they'd fought the Gris-gris man and the beast.

She'd tried to forget that night but having watched her friend Jo—

who had saved her life—get sucked into the void and snap out of existence made it impossible. If this was what the spirit had wanted to show her, she had no interest.

But to her surprise, the spirit—which she now thought of as the ghost of a child afflicted with something worse than Jimmy's handicap, perhaps blind, deaf, and dumb—led her past the crypt of Marie Laveau, past the open area in the center where the void had consumed the Gris-gris man, to the back of the cemetery. There a vine-covered, over-sized crypt sat. And she remembered it well. Over a year ago, she'd knocked three times on it to call forth the Gris-gris man.

Atop the crypt, and unlike any other in the cemetery, crouched the strangest gargoyle she'd ever seen. It was made of stone, although the discoloration was off—it looked relatively new. Clawed toes grew over the edge of the crypt, anchoring it to its perch. Gangly arms, and a beak-like nose, gave it an unsettling, human feel. The first upgrade of a neanderthal cousin, which perhaps wasn't far from the truth. But the truly odd thing about this sculpture was the extra digit on the right hand. Six claws total.

Del stared at the grotesque as a vague uneasiness grew in the pit of her stomach. This place already had bad vibes for her, but the fact that the spirit seemed to be focused on the crouching gargoyle made it even worse. To her dismay, the spirit turned in her direction, warbled a low cry, then turned and floated toward the crypt, stopping off to one side of it.

The grotesque waited patiently.

*

Del floated toward the crypt and felt a strange energy radiating from it. Something like a radio signal crackled in her mind. But this wasn't a signal that would play the Big Boppers Top Twenty, she thought. This was a low-grade thing. Psychic static. And somehow the spirit had detected it, for it was circling the crypt now—with no help from the others—in a slow clockwise manner. Every time around it would stop, turn, and scream its bleating warning at Del.

She scanned the area but saw nothing outside of the normal ghostly apparitions. They were beginning to congregate now, feeling her presence. She'd have to work quickly, the last thing she needed was more spirits clambering for her attention.

What are you trying to show me? Whatever it is, I don't see it.

Are you simply lost? How can I help you?

But whatever she did, the spirit simply couldn't hear or understand her. But it knew her, somehow. And for that reason, she was sure it was trying to tell her something.

Finally, after several more attempts at communication, Del retreated from the cemetery. Outside the walls, she watched the little spirit continue its vigil around the mystery crypt. It stopped and bleated its warning in the direction of where she had been. But it seemed as if it hadn't detected her departure yet.

There's something about the gargoyle, she thought. She vaguely remembered it from that night so long ago but didn't think it had anything to do with the Gris-gris man—besides sitting atop the rumored crypt of John Montanet, that was.

What am I missing? She called once more to the circling spirit. *What do you want to show me?*

But the spirit went on circling and bleating its warning.

(So, you're just going to leave it wandering around aimlessly?) a part of her mind said.

What else can I do?

(Guess you're not so powerful after all.)

Who asked you anyway?

And with that, she turned her back on the cemetery and was back in her room. Sliding down into the pillows, she pulled the covers up to her chin and closed her eyes.

In the St. Louis Cemetery #1, the gargoyle—which had once been called *Six-finger Eddie* before he'd met the Gris-gris man—opened his.

CHAPTER 9

Earl "Buddy" Tibbets looked at his watch. It was 3:45 a.m. and he had only begun to unload the ship. When the heavy fog had rolled in earlier that evening, the ships waiting to dock at the old Todd Shipyard had begun to back up on the river. Because several ships had docked at the same time, and with the loading dock crew being shorthanded, the workers had been split up. He was left alone with a motorized hand pallet truck and over thirty crates of seafood to move. Middle-aged and overweight, Buddy gave off a pungent smell of fish rot and eggs. His eyes were red-rimmed and leaky, and sweat ran down his ruddy face in great runnels.

The Todd Shipyard crouched on the south side of the river in Algiers, just across from the Ninth Ward. Built in the 1920s, it had boomed into a fifty-building sprawl by the Second World War. Now, half-rotted and forgotten, it served as a ghost of its former self—and the perfect place to offload cargo no one wanted documented.

Five crates into his load and the hand truck began to stall. Either a short in the wiring from the hand control, or a bad belt was causing the truck to move intermittently. Buddy grumbled under his breath at the delay, lamenting his ongoing bad luck. "Shitty equipment," he muttered. If he'd kept a better dock job, he wouldn't be here at all. But that's how Buddy's life had gone for the last several years.

Fired from his jobs and estranged from his family due to his increasingly drunken outbursts, he'd taken to sleeping in his truck as he'd tried to right his capsizing life. But after his ex-wife died and his in-laws were granted custody of his daughter, it had capsized completely. Now he spent his time sleeping in his truck and sometimes on an old cot he'd hidden in one of the abandoned buildings in the shipyards.

As he wrestled the heavy cargo deep into the holding area, his mind slipped back to a better time. His wife and newborn daughter had been a high point in his life. A time when he honestly thought he would break the bad habits that had plagued him most of his life. If he could only go back and do things differently, he thought. If one of these crates would bust open and spill out a magic lamp, he wouldn't even ask to use all his wishes. He just wanted one wish, to go back and do things differently. Just one little wish.

Half pushing and half cursing, he coaxed the dying hand truck to move the crate close to its designated area. Close enough, he thought. The trucks from the fish processing plant would be here in a few hours anyway and they had their own forklifts.

Leaving the cargo, he moved back into the depths of the warehouse. There he could have a smoke and a drink, and have them in peace.

The back of the warehouse was a maze of hallways and small rooms, mostly made from thin, single-plank walls that had been nailed to large support posts. He thought the rooms had been used for management activities such as counting inventory or general coordination during the shipyard's heyday. He'd even heard rumors that the military ran contraband through here during the war, but didn't know if it was true.

He found an abandoned room which had a long wooden counter built into the wall opposite the entrance. Several desk chairs were scattered about as if the counter had served as a long desk area for several people. He didn't try the overhead hanging lights, not wanting to draw attention to himself. But enough light from the loading area leaked back here so that he could move about.

Sitting in an old chair, he positioned himself so that he could see up to his loading bay, if he leaned over and looked out of the opening. If someone came looking for him, he'd just sneak up to where he'd left the handcart and begin cursing at it, as if it had just died. He lit a hand-rolled cigarette, then took a long pull from the bottle hidden in his lunchbox. The whiskey burned, but it kept the ghosts quiet. Most nights. Other times, it was a bottle full of memories, not escape. He closed his eyes and listened to the sounds of the river, smoking and drinking.

Images of his deceased ex-wife and daughter eventually crept into his mind.

*

The wraith, Umbra, Shade of Devotion, having followed the river for several miles, found itself drawn to the docks and the forlorn men who worked it. Their silent lamentations pulled it like a siren's call.

It knew not of the others, or their locations, but felt a deep devotion to its master, and heeded the need of the collective. They were starving. Now that the Gris-gris man had awakened, and the first of his disciples released, a ripple of anticipation had moved through the collective disciples. The wraiths could feel it. They could feel their unformed siblings calling to them, pleading with them, to hurry. It wasn't fair that the three were released first. It wasn't fair that the food hadn't been shared equally. And now, the food was nearly gone. So used up that the food-thing could only twitch as it slobbered onto the floor of the boat. And besides, the master was using it.

With that thought, Umbra crossed the great river, following silent pleas of a lonely man. And entered the Todd Shipyards.

*

Buddy sat in his chair and dozed. His red face slumped against his chest. The bottle of whiskey sat half-empty and tilting in his lap, loosely held by his hand. He twitched the dance of half-sleep as his body tried to fall forward.

Then a sound brought him to the surface, and he snorted awake.

Opening his heavy eyes, he saw a faint light. It was coming from a makeshift hall that was connected to the room he was in. He hadn't noticed the hall when he'd sat down, but it had been very dark. His head was heavy, and he tried to blink his eyes open.

What was that sound?

Weakly scanning the room, he mumbled to a thought that was fleeing his mind. He thought he recognized the sound—something familiar, maybe from a dream—but it slipped away before he could name it.

His eyelids drooped again.

(Buddy,) someone whispered.

His arms and legs jerked out in surprise, and the whiskey bottle went skidding across the floor.

"Who'zat?" he mumbled. He stood up with a screech of the chair legs, wobbling in the dark.

The light in the hallway seemed further away to him. It was a tiny light now, far away. His dilating eyes tried to follow it, tried to focus on it, but they weren't working well in his current condition. Leaning forward, his legs took slow, clumsy steps towards the hall and the light. He never saw the shadows creeping up the walls.

(Buddy, I'm lost,) the voice said. *(You left me, and now I'm lost.)*

Fear jumped up into his chest. "Sally?" He steadied himself against the wall at the opening of the hallway. An innate sense of caution kept him from moving forward into the narrow hall. "Sally, is that you?"

He hadn't heard his wife's voice since she'd left him. It didn't sound exactly right, but maybe she was sick.

The light at the end of the hallway pulsed, growing slightly. It was a friendly, inviting pulse of light.

"Sally, I'm here," Buddy said, one hand still clutching the wall.

As the light grew, he held up his other hand, squinting, trying to see.

A form appeared in the middle of the light.

(You left me Buddy. You left me and your daughter, and now we're lost.)

He shook his head violently. "No! I didn't leave. I didn't want to leave." His legs carried him into the hallway towards the light. Shadows moved in the darkness behind him.

How long had it been since he'd heard his wife's voice? It had been years since she'd left him. Is that what she had sounded like? He couldn't remember.

The apparition grew brighter.

(You left me for the bottle.)

"No!" He shook his head.

(You left US for the bottle. We're in the bottle now Buddy. You left us in the bottle and we'll never get out.)

He stumbled forward, faster now, pawing his way through the light. He had to get to Sally. He had to get to his wife and daughter, and get them out of the bottle.

Shadows moved in the darkness, swelling up behind him.

"No, I swear. I tried to stop. You know I did. I just… couldn't."

A thought came to him so abruptly that his eyes flew open as if he'd been shot. "You're dead!"

He began to back away from the light.

"That's not you. You're not in the bottle! THAT'S NOT YOU!"

He turned to run, but the room was gone. He was in a long, dark hallway that had no end. A round hallway, like the neck of a bottle. And it went on forever. The round hallway was a long, swirling tunnel of shadows. A tunnel of wraiths.

At some point in the night the other wraiths had heard their sister and joined in her hunt. Umbra, Shade of Devotion had sought the man out, hearing his woeful tale and setting the trap. Susurrus, Whisper of Ruin, pulled his dead wife's voice from his memory and fed it back to him as best it could. It had been a clumsy imitation, but the man had wanted the sounds to be the voice of his wife, so the ruse worked. Praeco, Harbinger of Ash, struck the first blow.

As Buddy Tibbet fell into the tunnel of wraiths, his mind went blank. Accepting the swirling phenomenon as another drunken stupor, his mind simply shut down all but the most essential functions—heart and lungs—and closed his eyes. This was a fortunate blessing for Buddy, for the wraiths feeding, especially Praeco's, was so violent that

Buddy ignited in black-green Shadowfire and collapsed in a heap of smoking flesh.

The wraiths, unrestrained by the presence of their master, consumed the food source of his soul—his Aether—in a heated frenzy terrible to behold. Nightbirds nesting in the rafters of the old warehouse cried a warning and flew from the building, alerting no one to the presence of the evil that had just grown stronger.

As the wraiths raced back to their master with their newfound energy, the remnants of Buddy Tibbets lay smoldering on the floor. He would be discovered in the morning and after a brief inspection by the coroner, labeled as accidental death by self-immolation. It was the opinion of the coroner that he'd simply gotten drunk, spilled whiskey on himself while sleeping, and ignited himself on fire with a smoldering cigarette. After all, when he was found, the only parts of his body that were recognizable were one hand that lay near an empty whiskey bottle, with the wrist still smoldering. The other hand had the remnants of a charred cigarette caught between its fingers.

One thing the coroner couldn't explain was why his feet were so far away from his body, as if they'd tried to flee his own burning body. But there was nowhere to go in the little room. It wasn't connected to a hallway or any other room except the open storage area where his hand truck had been found.

Two other interesting notes—and these the coroner only wrote down as afterthoughts—regarded both the color and distribution of Buddy's ashes, for he had burned completely through the middle.

The ashes didn't look like anything he'd seen before. They had a faint oily green iridescence to them which shimmered slightly in the light.

And regarding the distribution of the ashes, they appeared to have settled into a strange shape during the process of burning. Perhaps a burning body created its own small vortex, the coroner had thought.

His note read: *Ashes formed three loose circles.*

His unrecorded thought was: *Almost like a signature.*

CHAPTER 10

Armand sat in his library thinking. He'd tried to ring Frank on the telephone, but there had been no answer. He told himself that he would drive over later and visit his old friend. It had been quite a while since they'd spoken, and he missed the friendly banter.

He thought about all that had happened to them over the last eighteen months and shook his head. How quickly one's life can change, he thought, with just the addition of one person. Granted, that one person, Frank, whom he'd known before, had introduced another, Del, then two more, Mama D and Jimmy. But it had all started with an inquiring visit about a strange book.

The number of supernatural events that had occurred since that time was utterly amazing, he thought. Most people went their whole lives without even one such encounter, but here they were, this strange, adopted family, in the center of something that no one understood. And he suspected that they were far from done with the hoodoo. The supernatural events seemed to be seeping from the pores of the city.

Armand puffed gently on his pipe and looked at his bookshelves. He was sitting in Frank's usual seat which faced the shelves. Armand, being in a thoughtful mood today, had decided to roam around his library sitting in each chair, letting his mind open to the different viewpoints. He suspected that he'd sat in each chair in this room before but couldn't be sure. Most times he stood behind his long worktable, except during conversations with the group. And during those times, each person sat in their usual spot. But today the house was quiet, and not feeling like working on the outline of his manuscript, he thought he'd try a little experiment. He imagined it was like when he had to touch random objects in a room piecing his thoughts together, only today, he wasn't after a particular thought, but was more interested in the random ones.

He moved from chair to chair, puffing and thinking. Then he walked over and sat on the love seat that sat along the balcony railing. This caused him to think about Del and he wondered how her job was going. He then moved to the chess table where Jimmy often sat, and began to randomly move the chess pieces. He recalled the strange game he'd seen Jimmy play on occasion, the one with the black queen in the middle of the board, with concentric circles of pieces surrounding it. He'd played this version on several occasions, but could never describe to Armand what he was doing, or how the rules worked. But over time, by watching him secretly, Armand had determined that it was only the black queen that ever stood in the center. No other piece could occupy that space. And the object seemed to be to kill her. Although, Armand wasn't sure how often that happened. In most cases, he thought, the black queen persevered. At times, Jimmy would play the game for hours, before dinner, after dinner, even early in the mornings. Armand rarely saw a game from beginning to end, but could always tell when Jimmy was playing it. The boy would whisper commands, or encouragement, to the pieces that surrounded the queen, but they rarely overcame her.

In fact, Armand could only remember one time, out of all the games, that the pieces had beaten her. And when it happened, Jimmy seemed so surprised, and… upset, that he'd jumped up from the chair and ran into his room crying. That night, Armand could not console the boy and Mama D had to make a special tea to get to him to calm down and finally go to sleep. He suspected that the magic ingredient in the tea may have been nothing more than a bit of whiskey and honey but did not ask. Mama D was sensitive to Armand's prying about supernatural goings-on.

This train of thought—like a rich vein of gold—stuck in Armand's mind. He absently puffed at his pipe as he looked around the room, tracing with his mind, events of Jimmy. Besides the chess table, there was the incident with the strange papers they'd found. They all suspected that Jimmy had written them, considering the childish, crayon letters. But the boy didn't remember.

Armand walked to the bookshelves trailing his fingers over the objects there. He thought back to that night.

Del and Mama D had been discussing whether Mama D had been dead or not, when Del had interceded. Then, poor Del had tried to discreetly describe what the worms were, hiding the details from the men, but at Armand's insistence at being included, showed them the true horror of the situation.

"Regrettable behavior," Armand said, chiding himself quietly. "Truly, regrettable."

Then of course, Armand had to explain the whole Talking Board game situation to them.

He brought a hand to his face. "Oh, my," he said, shaking his head. It was as if he'd forgotten the whole incident. Shamed by his reckless actions, he now feared that he'd suppressed substantial portions of that night.

Pacing around and puffing his pipe to a chimney-state, he began to carry on a conversation with himself. He often did this in his head, but on occasion, when he was deep in thought, would unknowingly speak aloud.

"What else have we not dealt with?" he said.

(We all agreed to give it time.)

"I know, but it's been months now. And we still don't understand—"

He stopped and spun to walk back the way he'd come.

(Understand what?)

"The letters, of course." His hand waved impatiently. "Do they mean what we think?"

The question hung in the air.

(Could we do anything if they did?)

"Could we—?" Incredulous, Armand scoffed at the defeatist tone. "What, are we to do nothing? And what about the strange game? Hmm? What about that?"

The room was silent.

"Bah!," he continued. "That's ridiculous. Of course we can. There's always something that can be—"

He stopped, head cocked at an odd angle.

"No, of course not. I would never try that ag—"

Now on the other side of the worktable, Armand grabbed the brandy decanter.

"No, no, not like that."

He poured two glasses.

"No. It's something though..." Setting down the decanter, he took one glass in his left hand, sipped it, and began pacing again.

"Yes, yes, I know, quite a fragile state. And he's such a sweet—"

Armand stopped in the middle of the room, as if listening to an interesting idea.

He sipped at his brandy, rolling the idea over in his mind. The brandy glass went down as his right hand brought his pipe to his mouth. He tapped two fingers over the bowl, as he lightly puffed.

"Fascinating. Regressed memory?" he said. "Why yes, it's possible." He resumed his slow walk around the room.

"In fact, it is more than possible. It is *probable* that his mind remembers more than he can recall himself. Are there not cases of savants after all, who cannot function in society?"

Armand's head nodded to the silent room, as a smile crept onto his face. His eyes began to twinkle as the mouth-end of his pipe became a pointer in his hand.

He stabbed it in the air with finality. "That, is an excellent point!"

He walked to the stairs to go down and get something from his room, not noticing the second glass of brandy still sitting on the worktable.

CHAPTER 11

Del came downstairs to the smell of tea and entering an empty kitchen started to pour herself a cup.

She was surprised that someone was up already considering it was barely six in the morning. She'd planned to make coffee and getting an early start. She figured she'd be gone before anyone else awoke.

Mr. Bobby had explained to her that he worked when the muse hit him, so they only needed to meet every few days. She'd hoped to have a full article written by now but had gotten distracted. There were so many things to think about as potential newspaper articles, she couldn't settle on just one and spent the last few nights running over a dozen stories in her head. Having never written anything before, she wasn't sure whether this was considered writers block or not but felt guilty at being unprepared just the same. She was to meet Mr. Bobby later today.

She was surprised when Mama Dedé came into the kitchen from Armand's den, carrying a cup of tea.

"You're up early," Mama D said.

"Oh, morning," Del said, surprised. "So are you."

Mama D took the teapot from Del. "You don't want dat." Then added, "It soured. I'll make some coffee."

"Oh, ok," Del said, rubbing her eyes. "I'll get the paper."

As Del walked to the front door, Mama D poured the rest of the bitter tea into her cup and drank it down. It was cold by now, considering she'd made it hours ago, but it was all she could think to do. Then she started on the coffee.

Del returned with the paper, already reading an article.

"How's work?" Mama D asked.

"Hmm? Oh, ok I guess," Del said, sitting at the table. "You know, just waiting for my muse to hit."

With her back turned to Del, Mama D chuckled silently at the comment. "Dat so?"

"Mmm," Del muttered.

Closing her eyes, Mama D concentrated on the kitchen. She'd made some progress this morning but was surprised by Del's early appearance. She'd hoped for more time. With a bit of effort, she worked up a mediocre trance. A faint image of the kitchen formed in her mind where she saw herself and Del. She tried to focus on the article Del was reading but it was grainy. With a bit of effort, she got it to clear slightly, but Del turned the page and the image was lost.

"Damn," she muttered.

"What?" Del said. The newspaper rustled loudly.

"Hmm?" Mama D responded, seeming to ignore her.

Del folded the paper briefly and looked up as if just noticing her mentor. "What are you doing up so early?"

Mama D turned and set some leftover cake on the table. Armand had taken to making desserts lately and after the third night, Mama D had asked him if he was pregnant. "You sure are nestin' a lot, Frenchy," she'd said. "You sure you ain't pregnant?" To which he'd replied with an exasperated look saying, "Please, can I not spoil my favorite girls?" To which Jimmy had wrinkled his nose and replied, "Hey, I'm noht a giwl!"

"Oh, just lookin' for my muse," Mama D said.

Del mumbled thanks and grabbed a piece.

Mama D returned to the counter and took down two coffee cups. "You know," she said, "while you're lookin' for your muse, you might want to muse on over and check on Frank. He ain't—"

"Oh my," Del said quietly. The newspaper rustled again. "Oh."

"What?" Mama D said, turning.

"I gotta go," Del said with a mouth full of cake. She grabbed another piece for the road, and headed out the back door.

"Wait. Did you hear what I said about Frank? Someone needs to—"

"Just did," said Del. "He's sleeping. See you tonight."

And with that Del was gone.

Mama Dedé went to the back door and watched Del mount her bike, then ride it out through the big metal gate. "Damn," she said under her breath. "Dat girl."

She turned and looked at the empty tea pot. With a short heavy sigh, she set her shoulders, went to the teapot, and began filling it with water again.

*

Twenty minutes later Del crossed Tchoupitoulas Street and stopped on the high levee overlooking the Mississippi River. It wasn't a very pretty view where she'd stopped, but she wasn't sightseeing.

The Mississippi was a working river, and New Orleans was a trade city. Besides the river being a constant muddy brown color from all the silt it carried, the area was rough and dirty due to the work done here. Ships, barges, and boats of all sizes came and went along the river which snaked around the city. From wherever the river started, somewhere up North she knew, it ran on a fairly straight course to the South, until it got into Louisiana. Once it hit Baton Rouge, and as if to start its slow turn around Lake Pontchartrain, it snaked up and down running East until it got past the city, then turned South again, heading through the swamps down to the Gulf of Mexico. This meandering of the waterway caused daily congestion, which meant the boats and barges sat longer in one place puffing out exhaust from their diesel engines. It was a hard life for the people who worked here. She wondered briefly if any of them cared about Mr. Bobby's NOLA Pulse articles, for she couldn't remember him ever having written about the life of a dock worker.

And that's why she had come here. A newspaper article had caught her attention this morning. A dock worker was found dead yesterday. The poor man had accidentally caught himself on fire somehow. The article didn't have many details about his life, but Del wondered about his family. She felt sorry for them, even though she didn't know them.

The accident hadn't happened on this side of the river, otherwise she would have gone to the location. The article said the accident happened at the Todd Shipyards which was somewhere on the South side of the river. There were a lot of docks along the south side which was pretty rough, besides, she didn't want to ride her bike all the way over the Greater New Orleans Bridge just to get there.

She looked across the river not expecting to see it. The riverbanks looked pretty much the same where docks were concerned. But still, she wondered about the man and his family.

She rode her bike Northeast, switching from streets to alleys, and then back onto the levee paths, following the curve of the river. She knew if she rode this way far enough, she'd eventually hit the French Quarter and Jackson Square where the riverbank viewing had been built up for tourists. But she didn't need to go that far. Soon enough she found a small viewing area that overlooked the river. She stopped and sat on an empty bench. She would try and trance on the man she read about in the paper.

Del had yet to fully understand her gift. When first shown how by Mama Dedé, they'd focused on something familiar to her. She remembered that day in the halfway house when Mama D asked her to think of something familiar, and of all things, Del had thought of the orphanage.

She supposed now it had been because she'd just left it. Or possibly because Jimmy had still been stuck there. And, the terrible Sister Eulalie was planning to have Jimmy committed, although she didn't know it at the time. So, it wasn't a surprise that it had been top of mind for her.

Later sessions had focused on things she could see or that were nearby, but perhaps she wasn't as familiar with. Over the last year and a half, her abilities had expanded. The doppelganger vision being the latest variation, but she wasn't sure if there was any use to that. It was more of an amusing trick, she thought. Sort of like when children discover that crossing their eyes gives them double vision.

Of course, there was the combination of abilities to consider. The whole Billy Bash situation had only ended in her favor because Arlo had told her about the silver cord. Not to mention, helping her see it, then telling her to bite it. She supposed that there was no great skill in biting something, but considering it was invisible until the trance kicked in, there was.

This is where things got muddy for Del, suddenly remembering the pact she'd made with Arlo. Mama D was a voodoo practitioner and used her skills to help people. At least, she thought she did, although had never dug into her past. Arlo on the other hand was… well, she didn't know what Arlo was, but suspected she was something else. Maybe even a witch.

Del supposed this was a possibility, although just eighteen months ago, hadn't believed in any of this. But she'd seen too much—done too much—to not believe. But now, sitting here wondering about it, she wasn't sure how far her belief went. If Arlo were a witch, and she'd made a pact with her to find her path, did that mean that she was now a witch?

Del didn't think so.

However, the little girl at the ice cream shop had thought so. She'd even asked Del, point blank, if she was a witch.

Maybe it was the scratch on my neck.

Del remembered the nasty scratch she'd received during one of her first paid sessions trying to settle a spirit. That seemed so long ago.

Tired now from all the thinking, and having left the house without any coffee, Del thought that the morning may be a loss. She'd come here to trance on the man from the newspaper article, but had never tried to visualize someone she didn't know, who was in a location she'd never visited. The closest she'd come to that was when she'd followed the Alvie-bones as they'd traveled back a spirit road to some hidden location. But she'd only found the hidden place by accident, considering the animated bones had somehow gotten into Armand's house.

But if she *could* trance on some person and place she'd never known, that would be a pretty good trick. And if she could, why couldn't she trance on someone—anyone—that lived anywhere in the world?

What if she just made up a name, or an imaginary place? Could she trance on that?

That's silly. That's no different than daydreaming. Start that and you'll end up in the loony bin.

"Err," she grumbled, rubbing her head. She was suddenly angry with herself for letting her mind go off on another tangent. This is what it was like most nights when she tried to sleep. There was simply too much going on in her head, too many questions, to get to sleep easily.

It's also why she had begun to doubt that she could be a good newspaper reporter. She'd come here to concentrate on an idea for an article and had been daydreaming the entire time.

Out of sheer frustration, she closed her mouth tight and growled. She mentally willed her thoughts to fly across the river and do something, anything other than mill around here distracting her.

For a moment, all she managed to do was make her vision red. It was probably the increased blood pressure in her head. Then, as if her eyesight had suddenly sharpened, she saw the other side of the river. It was a zooming effect that was so startling, she fell out of the trance immediately.

Looking around as if someone may have seen the far shoreline suddenly jump closer, she confirmed that no one was watching her and tried again.

Another mental squeeze of her mind and she felt her vision slide forward. Slowly this time, but it was moving. The far shoreline was moving closer.

It was a strange sensation, seeing the trance from this perspective. Maybe this is how it had always worked, she thought, but hadn't noticed because her eyes were always closed.

Her mind floated with the vision, first hovering over the water, then pausing above a random building. She was aware of the people and boats moving about, but didn't know where to go next. Letting the trance drift, she simply took in the vision as it came to her. The doppelganger vision was not in effect here. But she didn't expect it to be. In fact, she didn't expect anything really, still surprised that it worked at all.

The trancing vision moved along the shoreline, faster now. The sensation became familiar, felt more natural, and she settled into it.

She closed her eyes to let her mind roam, and immediately slipped into the past.

*

One minute she was seeing the day as it was unfolding, the next, it was dark. And it was a different day.

Del stood on the southern riverbank, with her feet in the water. Small waves lapped over her sneakers and the bottom of her jeans were wet. A steep bank of cobblestones lined the river here. The bank sloped up, leveling out about ten feet above her head. There, the cobblestones became a rudimentary road that was used to service the docks on either side of her. Huge metal chains were anchored into the cobblestone and ran back down into the river, connecting to something she couldn't see. A decaying, fishy smell hung in the air here. Beyond the cobblestone road, forlorn looking buildings spread out to her left and right. They ran as far as she could see and faded into the mist. Their shapes were outlined by the feeble nightlights that dotted the river. She walked up the embankment leaving wet footprints on the stones.

At the top of the embankment, she was met with a wall of fog. She knew the buildings to be here, she'd just seen them. But now they were obscured by a thick mist. The night was oddly quiet. Too quiet. She suddenly felt that she had intruded on something, and like a skittish animal, the events that were about to happen had paused, curious about their visitor. She simply stood and waited.

The mist swirled for several seconds, then, as if now accustomed to her presence, began to fade. Old warehouses appeared.

Not knowing this part of town, she didn't know where to go. Briefly, she wondered why she'd come here at all and why she'd been standing in the river. Then a name came to her: Todd Shipyards. The words came from an old memory, and when they did, the mist obeyed.

Instead of turning left or right, to walk to the building she wanted, the buildings—or her perception of them—moved for her. Somehow, behind the thin veil of fog—for it was clearing now—the long row of buildings slid before her, then stopped.

She saw an empty room and knew that she was inside the building now. She hadn't walked into it, she was just suddenly there, like in a dream. The walls of the room were comprised of old wooden planks that had been nailed to the larger posts of the building. It had no door, just an opening to the larger part of the warehouse. An old work bench ran down one side of the room, and a few wooden chairs were scattered about. Dust and debris littered the place: scraps of paper, empty bottles, and an old calendar that hung on the wall.

A single light bulb hung above the center of the room. Although the light was off, Del could see the objects there as if they were a black and white sketch. The room felt real to her—three-dimensional—but formed in a way that could have been a drawing or photo. If she had somehow fallen into a black and white newspaper photo and come to life there, she thought that it would feel like this room. Real, but not real.

A scratchy record began to play somewhere in the dark. It was faint, but it was there. Del thought she recognized the music.

Occasionally, Armand would play records on his old Capehart phonograph. It was an ornate piece of furniture the size of a side table, that he kept in his bedroom. It was made of polished wood and was carved with delicate curves. He loved the old thing, and Del sometimes heard him dialing up staticky old radio stations on it. As if he were trying to tune in to a time that no longer existed.

Only once or twice had she heard him play a record, but he always turned it off if he thought someone was listening. Those were the only times she ever thought he'd been sad afterword. It was something in his demeaner. But she'd never asked.

Now, from somewhere far away, she heard the old music. Images of grand homes and lavish parties slipped into her mind. Images from another time, as if ghosts, carrying the remnants of their former lives, and wanting to share the feeling, had found their way to her.

As she listened, the music faded into the background and her focus settled on the light bulb hanging from a high rafter. She watched as the black and white outline of her hand reached toward the bulb. Her fingers grasped the small chain that hung beside it, then pulled it. Nothing happened.

A long finger—hers, as her hand seemed exceedingly long—tapped the bulb. Faint color flickered on and off in the room as if it—the room—had a bad connection with the socket. And, if the connection were just made complete, the room could light itself.

She grasped the bulb and gave it a turn. A faint, gritty squeak settled the bulb deeper into the socket. She pulled the chain again.

An odd radiance suddenly coated the sketch of the room. The bulb hadn't turned on necessarily, but the color of the room had changed. The objects within it pulsed with a weak light, helping them to stand out as something more than a flat image.

The scene now resembled a type of trance she recognized. Faint traces of red and blue drifted off the objects indicating that parts of them were moving towards, or away, from her. This would have been odd any other time, considering she'd only seen whole scenes moving in the past, but this was a different type of trance. The faintly colored scene seemed to not know which direction it was going, or more likely, it didn't know if it was a scene from the past or the future. Therefore, it simply vibrated in an odd state of stasis.

The music had stopped. She only realized this because she heard a man grumbling outside the room she was in. She thought he must be a dock worker.

Suddenly, the man walked through the opening in the wall, and came right at Del. His red-rimmed eyes staring right at her. Frightened, she jerked the chain on the light bulb.

The man disappeared.

Del stood in the dark for several seconds, not sure what had happened. She realized that the room wasn't completely dark; she was back in the black and white version again. But the man was gone, and the record was playing again.

Her mind raced, trying to understand what had just happened. As far as she could tell, she hadn't gone anywhere. She hadn't changed her trance. All she'd done was pull the chain—an imaginary chain at that—and the vision had gone away.

Looking at the tips of her fingers, still hovering near the chain, she saw a slight tremble and tightened them into a fist. Now wasn't the time to get distracted by nerves, she thought. The old record played its melancholy song—scratchy and faint—as if lamenting the end of some tragic movie. She swallowed, took a deep breath, and stretched her fingers towards the chain. She grabbed it and pulled.

The colored image of the room came back, just as the music went off.

Now, the dock worker was sitting in a chair, smoking, and drinking from a whiskey bottle. Oddly, seeing the man as if he'd jumped forward in time didn't bother her. The part that *did* bother her, the part that almost *unnerved* her, was the fact that part of the man protruded from her body.

Looking down, she saw that the man sat right where she was standing. His head appeared to grow from her abdomen and his right arm was a terribly misplaced appendage growing from her side. A bottle of whiskey tilted precariously in one of his hands while a lit cigarette smoldered in the other.

Del didn't move in fear of alerting the man to her presence but was soon calmed by the sound of his snoring. After all, she realized, even if he could have detected her, he'd have thought she was some type of apparition or delusion.

After several seconds, Del pulled the chain again. And again, the colored version of the room, and the man, disappeared as if their presence was linked to the chain. She saw only an empty warehouse.

Del wanted to leave. She wanted to end this crazy dream, ride her bike back home and crawl into bed. But she couldn't. Something wouldn't let her. Some part of her wanted to pull the chain again. Some part of her wanted to see what happened to the dock worker.

Although, if this were the same man she'd read about, she already knew what that was.

She pulled the chain again and the colored room returned. Only this time, a hallway jutted out through the wall across from her. A chilly wind flowed out of it.

She hadn't remembered seeing the hallway before, but it was there now. And if she'd had her senses about her, she would have realized that she'd never felt cold before in a trance. But she was cold now.

Then the hallway began to twist.

Del immediately thought of the void that had been conjured up that night in the cemetery. Conjured by the strange song that had gotten stuck in Jimmy's head, the swirling void had opened right out of thin air. And it had nearly sucked her in if not for her friend Jo. But it had sucked in the Gris-gris man as well, him and his awful beast, before snapping shut.

The man in her vision began to move. A light at the end of the hallway had woken him. He stood up, his head occupying the same space as Del's. She looked down with surprise as her stomach seemed to expand to three times its size, as his shape stretched out beyond hers. Then the man was talking.

She couldn't hear his words. They were garbled and staticky in the vision. But she knew he was speaking; his words sent tiny ripples through the vision of the room.

The man—struggling to keep his balance—walked down the hallway. He was gesturing and speaking. He didn't notice the shadows growing darker behind him.

The light at the end of the tunnel seemed to pulse in response to the man. Del thought they were having a conversation—the man and the light—but it sounded like static to her. Then the man yelled. He stopped and yelled, then turned to run. He tried to escape the light, but it was the tunnel that would take him. Del saw that now. The slowly twisting tunnel had constricted in the last few moments, thick with shadows, and began to close in around him. Barbed shadow-fingers shot out, hooking the man, and he screamed.

The wraiths fell upon him in a frenzy.

Del watched in horror, frozen, as the wraiths slowly tore him apart. They swarmed over him, circling, pulling at his very being. The finger-barbs hooked threads of his essence, his soul, and pulled. Long strings of light were pulled from the man like threads from a garment. Each one came free of his body with a spark and a faint *pop*. They were tasting him. Nibbling. Then, as if satisfied to the quality of his being, the wraiths pulled him apart in larger pieces. Whole sections of his being came loose with electric, ripping sounds. As they pulled, the filaments of his soul broke apart in green sparks. The Shadowfire was near.

His skin began to smolder. He screamed in terror and agony as his mind unraveled. The sparks ignited his skin, then his clothes. He thrashed for only a few seconds before falling to the ground, completely consumed in the greenish-black fire.

The wraiths fed for a few moments longer, then disappeared as quickly as they had come.

Buddy Tibbets lay motionless as he burned.

A scream finally escaped Del's mouth, pulling her from her trance. She'd been shocked into silence as the horror played out but was now sitting on the bench screaming. Her right hand clenched over her mouth as she stood up and stumbled forward. She ran unsteadily, as the horror scene played in her mind. Faint images of buildings and staring people slid past her blurry vision as she fled. She didn't know where she was running to, only away from the bench.

After several blocks, and realizing the danger was over—if there ever had been any danger—she began to walk. Her heartbeat slowed and her legs steadied. She pulled her hand away from her mouth. It was aching.

At some point during the trance, she'd begun squeezing her hand tightly. Only now did she realize the pain she felt there wasn't just from squeezing it. It felt like her palm was burning.

Opening it, she saw that her right palm was red and covered with lines. She nearly panicked again until she recognized what it was.

Her palm was covered with runes.

They were the same rune lines that had formed after she'd made her pact with Arlo. And with sudden dread remembered what the pact had been. It had been a pact to help Del find her path. And she feared that the wraiths and burning man were a part of that.

Gaining composure, her strides took on a look of determined purpose. She still didn't know if she could trust Arlo, and in fact, hadn't seen her for a long time. But something different had occurred today. She felt that she was meant to see the horrible death of the man in the warehouse. She didn't know why, or how she could have stopped it, but felt certain of this fact.

And if this were to be her path, if she'd been given this gift of sight to prevent the same terrible fate from happening to someone else, she would accept it.

She walked on with purpose. Now determined to understand where her path really lay.

*

An hour later she was sitting at Café du Monde with her knees drawn up on her chair. The covered, outside dining area was quickly becoming one of her favorite places. Here she could watch people from all walks of life meet and interact on common ground. The café wasn't overly expensive. It wasn't exclusive. And the regulars enjoyed it as much as the tourists, which was rare for a lot of establishments.

Hugging her knees tight to her chest, she gazed off to a random point in the air. She wasn't replaying the scene from the warehouse, as she didn't care to relive the poor man's torment. But the new sense of purpose that swirled around her was centered, somehow, on what she'd witnessed. It was the combination of the natural—the man who had been alive—and the supernatural—whatever the shadow-things had been.

She thought about Mr. Bobby and his newspaper column. She understood that people wanted to read about pleasant things happening to good people. And she understood that people needed to read about serious matters as well. No one she could think of wanted to read about terrible things caused by supernatural forces. But wasn't there a place where these things overlapped? Could it be possible that good and bad things might happen to someone based on supernatural events? Was it that much different than religion? If doctors gave bad news to someone about their health, stating that science had done all it could, wasn't that person more likely to pray for a miracle? In that instance, they'd be inviting the supernatural to intervene over their natural lives. In fact, people had been doing this for thousands of years; the major world religions were based off the idea.

Hadn't Armand said something like this the first time they'd met? Something about the religion of voodoo being *almost* as bad as the Catholic religion.

She'd been surprised at his statement until he used the act of communion as an example. *The eating of the body of Christ and the drinking of his blood.* Some people called that cannibalism, others called it worship. His point was well made.

It wasn't that she was suddenly defending the religion or practice of voodoo—she wasn't even sure if her gift still fit into the category—but there had been a number of historical people that had claimed divine insights or abilities, and history had labeled them as prophets and saints. Except of course for the women burned as witches…

But, over the centuries, accepted dogma had normalized—no, in some cases sanctified—the person's supernatural abilities. So why should she shun hers?

Considered another way, was she sinning—in the eyes of whomever—by trying to *not* use her gift? Would Moses have been considered a sinner if he'd run away from the burning bush?

Unknowingly, Del rocked in her chair as her mind spun. For too long she had carried this weight on her shoulders; this weight of abnormality. And she was tired of it. After all, people were born the way they were born. Some were pretty and some weren't. Some people had cancer, and others didn't. And where would the world be if Galileo or Einstein had ignored their own minds?

A clank of dishes pulled Del from her revery. Her eyes shone with the light of purpose, and a tight line of determination set her mouth.

An odd feeling settled over her. It was more than a sense of purpose—that had been percolating in her for some time now. It was more than purpose, more than drive and determination. It bordered on righteousness, directive, fate. She'd been gifted with a power that few others had. She'd been chosen in some strange way. Then it dawned on her what she was feeling, a sense of permission.

Coming back to her surroundings, she looked around the café and saw all things at once. Her mind was open and absorbing and drunk in her surroundings like a sponge. This was her gift. She had a right to use it. And like any other person with an abnormally acute power of observation, she *would* use it.

Only then did she notice that her bike, which she'd forgotten at the bench where she had tranced, was leaning against the lamppost just outside the café's seating area. With a quick doppelganger trance, she scanned the area for whoever brought it here, for it meant that someone had followed her.

Just like before, after several attempts, she finally found the image. It was a single image of the handsome man with the dark hair. And in that single frame, his face was turned to her with a look of curiosity upon it.

CHAPTER 12

After meeting with Mr. Bobby and discussing Del's ideas for his next article, she was on her own again. He'd agreed to consider a piece about dock workers—considering the recent focus on them from the newspaper article—but wanted it to be lighter in nature. He asked her to think about a positive angle they could take, and said they should meet in a few days.

She appreciated the guidance but was starting to wonder if she'd be given an actual writing assignment. As accommodating as Mr. Bobby had been to her ideas, she figured he would have given her an assignment by now. Perhaps he was just being polite and didn't want to tell her that her ideas were no good. But she wasn't sure if that even mattered now. The overwhelming sense of relief she now felt, after simply accepting her gift for what it was, was liberating. And she decided to enjoy the day.

Café du Monde sat on the corner of Decatur and St. Ann Streets, across from Jackson Square. Artists and musicians of all types occupied the streets that lined the square—except for the Decatur side which bordered heavy traffic. But the two side streets and the back street—which ran in front of the St. Louis Cathedral—would begin to fill up around ten o'clock each morning and stay busy well into the evening. Visitors were mostly tourists and vendors were always locals, and over the last eighteen months the square had become a favorite place for Del to people-watch. So, after leaving Mr. Bobby, she crossed the street and meandered.

A person could buy almost anything along the square from paintings, to old records, to t-shirts, to hand-carved fetishes, to food. And if there was one fortune-teller sitting behind a table, there was a dozen.

Any number of musicians could be found in singles or groups, playing a variety of music, but which typically landed in the realm of Zydeco or Jazz.

It was here that Del straddled her bike seat, and with toes stretching to the cobblestones, walked it through the throng of people, daydreaming. Being late afternoon, and pleasant weather, the place was packed, including the grassy park in the center.

She was looking for an angle on her dockworker story and having no idea how to go about traditional research, decided to use her God-given talent, and simply snoop. And in reality, she no longer thought of it as snooping, although she did once. Now, she thought of it more like *mental listening*. After all, she couldn't help it if people spoke loudly around her, and she caught parts of their conversations. So, she couldn't help it if her mind *listened* and caught parts of their thoughts.

Images of people's lives flashed through her mind but soon faded into the background behind the music she heard. She'd just passed a group of four young men who were playing an upbeat tune with a trumpet, a trombone, a washboard, and someone drumming on an overturned plastic bucket.

After them, and past a long row of bright yellow paintings, were three younger boys, tapdancing with bare feet. Not having tap shoes, the boys had taken off their regular shoes—assuming they had any—and stuck bottle caps to the bottoms of their feet. Whether through pressure, glue or gum, they got the caps to stay, and proceeded to dance at a fiery pace, and quite in unison. Del suddenly wondered how far these boys could go—or others in their situation—if they'd had the proper gear. Another great human-interest story, she thought, but not necessarily uplifting.

She avoided a hotdog vendor just as two men began to cat-call her from a nearby bench. They were permanent residents of that bench, she thought, and ignoring them, turned her bike left, onto the wide walk of Chartres Street.

Although the two side streets that lined the square, Peter and St. Ann, were through streets, the sections that bordered the square were narrowed and blocked to vehicle traffic. The section of Chartres Street that ran in front of the cathedral was the same way, so when she turned onto it, she was still in the middle of a crowd, most of whom were standing around in front of the steps of the cathedral.

Halfway down this block, which put her near the center of the cathedral, she heard a strange sound. Someone was playing the guitar, but in a way she'd never heard before.

A crowd had gathered near the steps at the far end of the cathedral. A man sat on the steps with a guitar. The music was coming from him.

Creeping her bike forward, she heard a haunting, lonely tune that she didn't recognize. She couldn't see him well due to the crowd but felt that he was oddly misplaced. His head was down, looking at his guitar, causing his dark hair to hang around his face. She glimpsed dark pants and a jacket. She'd never seen someone wear a suit and sit on the dirty cathedral steps before, least of all a musician.

His left hand slid smoothly up and down the neck of the guitar as the song changed. Something glinted from his pinky finger. Del realized why she hadn't recognized the style of guitar playing before, he was playing a slide guitar. During her time waitressing at the *Jazz Note*, there had only been a few times when someone had attempted to play slide guitar—probably because they booked more cover bands than anything—but the few who did, usually played it to ear-cringing effect.

She hadn't known that those sounds could be made from a guitar. Hypnotic and beautiful, in a dark way, the haunting melody resonated with her. There was something primordial, yet elegant about it, and she was completely drawn to it.

The song faded to its conclusion, then with almost no pause—or a well-played transition—another took its place. The slide had disappeared from the man's finger, and he was now playing an intricate finger-style piece of dark jazz.

Some of the crowd moved on, giving Del room to inch closer. She could now see him clearly—except for his face—and thought again that he was not only oddly, but clearly, misplaced. The pants and suit jacket shone with an expensive sheen. His shirt was crisp. His shoes looked new. And the hint of silver flashed from his right hand but was hard to discern due to the movement of his fingers.

Del straddled her bike in rapt attention, not noticing that the crowd had dispersed. Oddly, no one else came up to listen.

The man finished the song, and before Del had a chance to clap, he looked up.

Del's mouth fell open in shock.

She was looking at the same face she'd caught a glimpse of in her trance. The single doppelganger image of the handsome man who had walked past her when she was speaking with Mr. Bobby, then who had returned her bike to the lamppost.

Étienne Montclair looked at Del. As he did, one corner of his mouth turned up in a mischievous grin.

*

"I see you got your bike," Étienne said. A friendly baritone voice, warm but firm, resonated in her ears. His arms hung languidly over the guitar as he sat, relaxed, upon the stone steps. His fingers absently traced the curve of the guitar cradled in his lap. His head had tilted slightly when he'd addressed her and was now staring at her with hazel-colored eyes, awaiting her response. When one did not come forthwith, a look of amusement crept onto his face, but he held his tongue.

Del, suddenly remembering that she was standing astride her bike with her mouth hanging open, clamped it shut with a loud snap and crossed her arms over her chest.

"I see you've been following me," she said. She watched him, trying to reconcile the face she'd seen in her trance with the one before her now. It was a handsome face, but out of place. It reminded her of a picture she'd seen once. Whether it was of a painting or a sculpture she couldn't remember, but it was of a man from another time. The features of his face, clean-lined and elegant, did not look like the faces she saw around here. Perhaps he was a tourist from another country, but if so, why the guitar? When he gave no response, her eyes narrowed. "Care to explain why?"

He spread his hands with a casual air. When he did, a silver ring glinted from his right hand. “I wanted to return it,” he said. “You… left in a haste. And I thought you might want it back.”

Del suddenly realized that he had not only been following her but must have seen her get scared out of her own trance, and stumble away. She felt a flush creep up her neck, threatening to redden her cheeks. She was embarrassed that someone may have seen her acting like a crazy person, running from her own shadow. But it hadn’t been the first time she’d looked like that, and certainly wouldn’t be the last. Still imbued with her newfound resolve to embrace her gift, she dismounted her bike, holding it by the seat and lifted her chin slightly. She no longer cared if her cheeks were red.

“I did,” she said. “Thanks.”

Del and the man were a dichotomy: he with his elegant face and expensive clothes, she with her worn jeans, thin t-shirt and sneakers. His shoulder-length hair fell in soft dark curls. Her wild hair partially escaped her bandeau. As if to accent the differences even further, a slight wind roamed through the square. On that wind, drifting toward Del was a musky scent, primordial, as if from a mystic animal. Then the breeze changed, floating up around her and away. She smelled her own body lotion and sweat—the later a daily gift from her mode of transportation—and watched as the breeze brushed a bit of hair hanging in the man’s face.

His head tilted back as if deep in thought—or smelling a faint scent. His face, upturned, and with closed eyes, stayed that way for several seconds.

“Well then!” he said, clapping his hands loudly. Del jumped, startled. “Now that we’ve established the ownership of the bike, perhaps introductions are in order.”

Del's heart thumped in her chest. The sound of the clap had taken her by surprise, and she feared he could hear it pounding from where he sat. Before she realized it, her hand went to her hip and a snarky comment came to her rescue. "Ah. So you know who to send the bill to?" Her eyebrow raised, playfully, of its own accord.

The man chuckled so quickly, if he'd been drinking a glass of water, he would have spit it out.

"No charge, my dear," he said, and spread his hands toward a white silk handkerchief laying on the ground. Upon it, several coins and a few dollars had been collected as tips. "I have all I need. Purely a community service I perform."

"What's that?" Del asked.

"Orphans, of course. I—"

"What?" Del asked quickly.

He stopped briefly, hands suspended, then continued. "I… find orphaned bikes and return them to their most forgetful owners." His smile was playful.

"Oh." Del smiled, embarrassed.

His relaxed nature never changed as he leaned forward and whispered. "It's an epidemic."

Del chuckled. "Guilty, as charged."

And suddenly, the man was standing in front of her. Del immediately thought of the single doppelganger vision she'd seen before, that brief image in time with no trace of what had occurred before or after. She hadn't been trancing just now, she'd been too engaged with judging the man's intentions, so wasn't distracted from his movements. But somehow, as if she'd closed her eyes for a full second or two, she hadn't seen the man stand up from the steps. One minute he was seated, and the next he was standing before her.

"Étienne Montclair," he said, extending his hand. "At your service."

Del stifled a snicker at the archaic greeting. Extending her own hand she said, "Del Larouche, um… bad bike owner."

They shook hands, Étienne's long fingers wrapping gently around Del's, before she pulled away suddenly. For a brief second Del thought she'd seen something in his eyes—a change of color, perhaps—when their hands had touched, but it was gone in an instant.

"I liked your music," she said. "Have you been playing long?"

With the guitar hanging from his neck and shoulder, Étienne looked around the square as if seeing it from a memory. "A while," he said, nodding. "But I'm a quick study."

He turned and went to the handkerchief.

"I haven't seen you out here before," Del said. "I recognize a few of the regulars, you know, like the trombone guy. But… I don't really come here much, so..." She looked at the ground and nudged some rocks with the toe of her sneaker. When she looked up, the handkerchief and money were gone, and he was standing in front of her again.

"I don't get a chance to do this often myself," he said. The slide was back on the pinky of his left hand, and he began strumming the guitar softly. They turned and walked towards the street corner leading away from the square. "But who wouldn't recognize the trombone guy?"

Although there were many musicians in New Orleans who played the trombone, there was only one trombone guy. He was a favorite of local musicians and tourists alike. He wore a pair of black and white pinstriped suit pants, a white dress shirt with no sleeves, an old silk paisley vest, and a beat-up fedora with a peacock feather jutting from the hatband. It was rumored that if he showed up in the second-line of someone's funeral, playing his horn, then the deceased had called to him, and good luck would befall the immediate family.

Étienne produced the silk handkerchief from his pocket. It hung like a white purse with the four corners tied in a knot. He dropped the silk purse of money into the hands of a beggar woman sitting at the corner. "Good health to you, mother," he said.

Feeling the silk blessing, the woman cracked a toothless grin and looked in his direction. "Bless you, Éti," the blind woman said.

As they walked past, Del looked back at the woman then over at Étienne. Even though she was taller than average, standing at around five and a half feet, she still had to look up at him when they talked. She guessed he was closer to six foot one.

"Éti?"

He smiled faintly and shrugged.

"I've known her for a long time," he said.

"But you called her mother. Surely, she's not…"

"No," he chuckled. "Not mine." He looked at Del. "But hopefully someone's. It would be a shame to think that she was no one's."

Del thought this a strange sentiment.

"Well, have you asked her?"

"No."

"Why not?"

"Because then I'd know," he said.

Del stopped her bike. Étienne took a few more steps before noticing she wasn't there. He turned and looked back at her.

"That doesn't make any sense," she said, then resumed walking her bike.

"Why not?"

The reporter was coming out in her. "If you wanted to know, you should have just asked her."

"But I don't want to know," he said.

"And why's that?"

This time Étienne stopped and looked at Del for several seconds. She again had the sense that his eyes had changed colors for a moment, but then it was gone. It's his hazel eyes, she thought. It's just a trick of the light.

"Because if I knew," he said, pulling a black silk handkerchief from within his jacket, "it would no longer be a mystery." He tossed the handkerchief in the air and let it fall over his left hand. With one quick movement, he snatched it away. In its place, a black dove fluttered up from his cupped hands. The handkerchief was gone.

"And isn't a mystery beauty in its rawest form?"

Del stood silent. She'd always liked magicians but until recently, had admired their slight of hand over anything mystical. She hadn't believed in mystical things then. But now—considering her own abilities—she couldn't be so sure.

"Nice trick," she said, ending the debate in her head. She nearly performed a trick of her own, casting an image of a white dove into his mind, as a bit of tit-for-tat competition, but didn't. She wasn't sure why she held back, but something inside her told her to be cautious. Besides, the sudden emergence of the dove had drawn the attention of several people.

Étienne simply shrugged, then pointed across the street at a hotel. "That's me," he said. Then walked into the middle of the road.

Del went to warn him of cars but was suddenly struck by a doppelganger vision. Like a bad movie reel, the scene of Étienne crossing the street skipped forward in jerky, frozen frames. Cars changed positions in large jumps. People came into and out of her side vision. And Étienne stepped between them all as if strolling in an empty park. The last scene of the vision, before her mind began processing at normal speed again, was of Étienne standing on the steps of a hotel, looking at her, with a crooked grin. Then he was gone.

Del stood still for several minutes letting her head clear. People streamed around her, mumbling their displeasure. Slowly, she began to walk her bike forward, then to peddle. She knew where she was. The whole time they'd been walking away from Jackson Square and towards Armand's house. But somewhere along the way they'd turned to come to this place, his place, the Hotel Monteleone.

As she picked up speed, the noise of the city resumed. Her mind drifted as she rode, but occasionally she couldn't help thinking that she'd just heard a fragment of a song coming from some open window. It was an old tune, one that she'd heard only once before. It was a slide song that an old swamp man had played for her. In fact, he'd put her own name into it.

Delphine, Delphine, don't liiie to me, tell me where did you sleep last night?

CHAPTER 13

All day Mama Dedé had worked on her craft. She was only interrupted a few times when she heard noise in the kitchen and had to go in to see that it was being kept in order. Armand had gotten better over the last few months, but Jimmy still needed some fetchin' up. The sweet boy was all too happy to help scrape the plates or wash the dishes. But, she'd soon realized that more times than not, there was more clean up needed after Jimmy *helped*, than if she'd just tidied herself.

Aside from the few distractions, she'd had the entire day to herself. And, to a bit of relief, had made some progress on her visions. But it was still far from perfect.

It had been years since Mama Dedé had had to ask for help with this. She'd been doing it for so long, she'd forgotten about the struggles that people had when first learning. She didn't understand why she was now back at this stage but could empathize with anyone just starting out. Her mentor was long dead and considering that Mama D hadn't been a regular practitioner—one who advertised her abilities as a full-time service to hire—she had lost touch with the more active women in the community.

She knew there were some men who were white practitioners, but there were very few, and it wasn't the same anyway. It was the women who always took on the difficult cases.

As she sat in the parlor, and having lost track of the amount of tea she'd consumed, she thought she'd look around the house. It had been a long time since she'd inspected the perimeter and doubted that Del had done it over the last few months.

With effort, she got into her trance, watching herself sitting in the room. The clarity of the vision was poor, but it was there. She was surprised how old she looked. The dramatic weight loss that had occurred during her illness did not sit well on her. She certainly wasn't thin, and never would be, but now looked partially deflated, as she had lost weight unevenly. Although she was gaining some weight back, her once plump and beaming face sagged considerably now. Her eyes were closed in the trance, but she knew they looked old as well, for all the times she'd peered into them in the mirror. A weariness had settled in them, somehow; they weren't as bright as before.

She sighed and let her vision drift to the kitchen, where she tried to pull up an image of Del from this morning. This trick was still difficult for her to do, and it frustrated her to no end. Seeing future scenes was completely out of the question, but since she'd never been great at them, she didn't miss them as much.

A faint image of Del sitting at the table came into her mind. Mama D tried to focus on the newspaper article she'd been reading but it was too fuzzy to read. She remembered asking Del about Frank and she had said—almost as an afterthought—that she had just checked on him, while she was getting ready to leave. If that was true—and Mama

D didn't think Del had any reason to lie about it—then her trancing power had grown considerably.

What other things had Del learned while she was gone, she wondered. She'd meant to check into the whole cord business, but getting her mind back right had taken longer than expected.

Concerned about Del working in the newspaper industry, which was nearly all men, Mama D intended to check up on her from time to time. Del might consider it snooping, but that was only because she was young and foolhardy, Mama D thought. The young girl still had a lot to learn about the world, had a lot to learn from Mama D if she'd just slow down a bit. But Del wasn't slowing down. And Mama D was worried about that as well. Since she'd been back, Mama D watched, day after day, as Del seemed to speed up. It wasn't a frantic pace, at least not yet. But something propelled Del forward, each day, just a little faster. And it was that force, whatever inner fire that had ignited within the girl, that Mama D meant to discover.

*

Armand sat in his library, happily surrounded by large stacks of books. He'd recently returned from the public library where he'd checked out several volumes of birth records, miscellaneous shipping logs, and an old version of Clark Hull's groundbreaking work from 1933, *Hypnosis and Suggestibility – An Experimental Approach.*

Although he knew he should be working on the outline of his book about legends and their origins, he justified the distraction by telling himself that this research was important because it helped the entire family. He was just surprised he hadn't thought of it before.

Ever since Del, Mama Dedé, and Jimmy had come to stay here, he'd wondered about their families. His innate curiosity would bother him to no end throughout the day, forming questions, positing theories, making connections, to the point that by the evening, he'd collapse in his chair, utterly spent. It was always his intention to untangle the theories the next day, but his mind would drift to something else, starting the entire process over again.

He suspected that Del suffered from a similar affliction, but one caused by a different source, and manifesting to a different level of severity.

And what of the boy? He obviously suffered some *variation of fate*, with his diminished capacities, but to what end? And what other capacities had grown, or abilities awoken, to compensate for the deficit?

Was it all simply chance? Was it a cosmic accident that simply floated around, landing on people at random, as Frank had once suggested?

Armand didn't think so. He liked to think there was something more to it. In his bones, he felt there *must* be more. It may be hidden. It may need to be ferreted out. But wasn't he a man of research? Did he not have keen powers of observation? And if whatever he discovered could help his family somehow, even in the smallest way, would he not do it? Of course he would. And he intended to.

The time had finally come to look into Del and Jimmy's family lines.

And he'd start with Jimmy.

CHAPTER 14

Somewhere on the Mississippi, 1964

The Gris-gris man stood in the wheelhouse of the boat, clutching the wheel for support. He peered into the mist cloaking their hiding place, wondering how long he could hold them together.

It had been days since his reemergence and he'd yet to fully regain his strength. The night the wraiths had returned from their first hunting trip, he'd nearly been made whole. Fat with Aether—the soulstuff they craved—the wraiths greeted him like a mother to her babe. Lying prone in his bed, only partially there, with a ghostly image of the beast streaming from a limp hand, Umbra, his most devoted wraith, hovered over him and let him suckle her.

The extraction of Aether from Buddy Tibbets had been a violent affair. Insane with hunger, the wraiths had gorged themselves, ripping at his essence, which had caused the Shadowfire to start—the greenish-black fire that can only be caused by the soul's decimation. Had they shown more restraint, the wraiths may have been able to milk the fat man for many days, for despite his earthly weaknesses, he was full of life. But their frenzy reduced him, like overcooked steak fat, to a shadow of his potential. In essence, the Shadowfire had cooked away the best part of him.

The Gris-gris man had fed, then dispersed the three wraiths to feed the others. But the meal was thin, as there was a terrible number of suckling mouths. And the Aether was gone before all could feed.

The thing in the third boat emitted a low, rumbling sound at this affront, and the wraiths trembled. The sound conjured the image of a groaning ship, which instead of carrying cargo, was filled with a giant stomach and fathoms of intestines, contracting, rippling, to the promise of food. The sound so disturbed the living that fish near the boat died instantly, floating to the surface of the river and washed downstream.

After the feeding the Gris-gris man thought he was whole but the power it took to keep the three boats in place and hidden, was more than he'd expected.

He thought back, trying to remember why he'd gone into the mist. His memory was that of an old film reel, rotted and dry. Images flickered in his partial mind, but large gaps hid the whole story. It was as if the scenes had been burned away, or simply not yet reformed. He didn't know why he'd come to this time. He couldn't remember how he'd set the spell to be regenerated. But he knew he was looking for someone.

He was looking…

*

Somewhere in a bayou, 1866

The old woman knew when the spirit approached. She'd been waiting for it after all.

In a way, she'd heard it, although that's not how regular folks would have described the sensation. Her hearing *was* sharp—compensating for her cataracted eyes—but it worked differently for her. What she'd actually heard were the shadows moving to make *way* for the spirit—the fifolet to be exact.

Her shadows had been with her for a long time and like the old woman, they were set in their ways and preferred not to be disturbed. There was no need for a shadow to make room for another shadow—say, one that was made by a passing bird—for both shadows could exist in the same space and time. But fifolets were different. Fifolets *moved* like shadows, but had a substance of their own, being actual spirits. And somehow, perhaps because the old woman was expecting a visitor, the shadows she kept in her company knew it as well; that part of the relationship she'd never been able to explain. And knowing that this visitor had recently adopted the habit of moving in fifolet form, but would need more space for the actual meeting, the shadows shuffled away, looking for a quiet place. This is what the woman heard.

So, when the blue fifolet appeared, shimmering at the edge of the clearing, the woman knew her subject had arrived.

The 'clearing' was nothing more than a small island of swamp mass that had somehow kept itself above the water line despite the ever-changing landmass. Locals—the few that had need of, and could pay for, the talents of the old woman—had to visit by boat, for there was no road to this spit of land. Old maps from the time of Spanish explorers showed a connected landmass here, even a road, but that had been long ago. Now, the clearing was demarked by a circle of five covered wagons, each pulled into a wide circle as if camping for a night or two. No one knew where the wagons had once been headed. And, if the old woman were somehow a descendent of the original group who had led the wagons here, she'd never told, or perhaps could no longer remember. But the wagons were now part of the island, part of the swamp, and appeared to have been accepted by the indigenous plants and trees as having earned their right to exist here, for nothing encroached upon the circle.

The general color of the area around the circle, including the shadows, whether by accident or not, was a constant shade of dark green. It was as if this part of the swamp was in perpetual twilight and the fire which burned in the center was always able to hold darkest midnight at bay. Perhaps, because the circle of wagons had been here so long, they'd grown a type of shadow moss which discolored everything within eyesight, but the color was pervasive.

The other odd thing about the clearing, among many, was that an endless supply of firewood was always available. If the old woman ever considered this odd, she made no mention of it to the shadows. But swamp locals, the few who knew where to look, told stories of the never-ending fire that burned on that small island. In fact, the bravest of them used that fire to navigate into the deeper parts of the swamp, when they had the blackest of business to attend.

The blue fifolet shimmered outside the circle of wagons for a few moments longer, then, as if taking on weight like a heavy fog, descended to the ground. A man took shape within the mist and stepped forward. The Gris-gris man had arrived.

Trailing after the man and forming from the remains of the blue spirit mist, the beast walked forward. Its shaggy head turned from side to side sniffing the old air. A miniature voodoo doll, suspended above the beast's shoulder blades on a hat pin, rocked slowly back and forth with the motion of its footsteps. Its red bead eyes sucked at the firelight that fell upon it and gave nothing back. Although it was a dead thing, it still remembered life and was want of it.

The Gris-gris man approached the wagon on the opposite side of the never-ending fire. Its crooked stovepipe chimney being the only one exuding smoke. In its day, the wagon—all of them he thought, but especially this one—had been quite handsome, being decorated with vibrant colors. Blues, yellows and reds had colored every inch of its surface. Ornately carved wood decorated the eves of the roof. But now the wagons had taken on the dark green hue of the entire area as if to eventually fade into the background. A small Dutch door with the top half open, marked the entrance and was also decorated with strange carved scrolls. Dim candlelight flickered within the dark opening of the door.

He stopped at the foot of the wooden steps.

A leathery voice croaked from within the wagon. "What do you seek?" Although the voice was feeble and sounded as if it came from ancient lungs, he heard it as clearly as if she had whispered it into his ear. He flinched slightly, imagining that she had.

"I seek your foresight," the Gris-gris man said.

"Come up," the voice said, but not before emitting a sound of amusement.

He ascended four steps and peered into the wagon of the fortune teller.

An ancient woman sat barefoot and cross-legged on an elevated bench cushioned with Mediterranean pillows. Heavy drapes and tapestries covered the walls. Candelabras and lamps hung precariously from the walls and ceiling.

The woman was clothed in wraps of silk fabric that had faded over the years. Gossamer strands of gray hair floated from her head. Her skin was the color of aged leather, a light brown, that hid her nationality. Her wrists and ankles glittered with silver and gold bracelets. Her blind, cataracted eyes showed milky white. A small pipe of dark wood, from which floated a pungent smoke, jutted from the corner of her mouth. She removed the pipe with a gnarled hand.

"Devil John comes seeking foresight?" the woman said. "Have the voices abandoned you?"

Her voice was surprisingly devoid of the Creole patois, and although John couldn't place it, he thought she still carried a hint of an old Eastern European accent.

John, still standing outside the wagon door, started to speak, but was interrupted by a wave of her pipe hand.

"Come, sit," she said. "And show me your offer."

John opened the bottom door, entered the wagon and sat cross-legged in its center. This put him slightly below the old fortune teller.

"And the other," she said with a wave of her hand.

The beast walked up the steps and into the wagon. Its standing height was taller than John seated. Silver strands of slobber hung from its jowls and a rank smell of wet dog filled the small space.

The woman seemed to perk up when the beast entered. Although her face and dead eyes were turned to a point above John's head, her hand closest to the beast motioned it forward, then reached out for it. The beast moved past John, allowing her to touch its ragged head.

The Gris-gris man spoke, after all, this *was* his creation; the old John Montanet could not have managed such a thing without his transformation. "Please meet my newest companion. That is… Mr. Sandgrove."

Her crooked fingers skimmed over the dirty and mottled fur. In several places her fingers drew back as if she felt a wound, or great pain living beneath the fur. As if just arriving home after being lost, the beast closed its eyes and slumped against the bench that elevated the woman. Her head shook slightly, hardly believing what she felt. The binding of a human soul into such a creature was almost more than she could believe. But the evidence loomed before her. Then her hands felt the hat pin.

"Ahh..." she whispered. "What do we—?"

Her hands felt the doll and drew back.

"Oh," said the Gris-gris man, "and that... that is Toth."

As if at the sound of its name, but more likely the caressing touch of the old woman, Toth's read bead eyes began to glow, and a faint sound slipped from it bead mouth. "Ngyihng..."

A smile crept onto the woman's face as if she were seeing a newborn babe for the first time.

Such a curious thing, the woman thought, a tiny, tiny person. And although she suspected the voodoo doll was formed of wrap and stuffing, she felt in a way that it was a person, for she felt life, or the desire for it, pulsing beneath its bumpy skin.

John cleared his throat for attention. Since receiving the cryptic message from the demon, he'd expended as much energy as he could muster to unravel it, but to no avail. There was no way he would go to Marie Laveau with this request, as they were now mortal enemies. But, he had vowed to get his revenge on her after she'd cursed him and his daughter with the horse pox that drove her insane. This was just another step closer to gaining the power he needed to do that.

"Yes?" said the woman. Her hands, now in her lap, attended to her small pipe. She brought it to her mouth and puffed. A thick cloud of smoke snaked up past her eyes, mingling with her flying hair.

"I seek your foresight," John said. "I seek a person that is unknown to me. Their face is hidden from my sight. For that knowledge, I've brought this offering." From beneath his robe, he took a human skull and held it up to her.

"Bah. What need do I have of that?" She spread her hands wide, motioning to the walls. "When I have so many."

As if by a trick of light, John suddenly noticed the skulls that adorned the wagon walls. Jutting out from between the hanging folds of material, some skulls were used as candle holders, some were painted or carved with strange symbols, and still others had shiny objects stuck in their eye sockets. These were positioned to look in all directions as if for protection.

John sat the skull aside and reached into a leather bag that hung over his shoulder. He brought forth a full bottle of whiskey and held it up.

The old woman, still gazing above him, but in a different direction, cocked her head to the side and sniffed. She snatched the bottle with surprising speed and weighed it in her hands. John did not miss the flick of her tongue as it passed over her thin lips, imagining the taste.

She stowed the bottle next to her on a pillow.

"What else?" she said.

John looked around the room. He had little else with him. Finally, he said, "What would you have?"

A smile crept onto the leathery face. Without a word, the woman reached out and even though the beast had settled below her, her hand found Toth as if she'd placed it there. She nodded slowly as if imagining casting life into the wretched thing.

"No," the Gris-gris man said. "I could never."

The woman drew back her hand. A slight frown on her face.

John continued. "You must understand, Toth is… well… Toth is family, you see."

The woman nodded appreciatively. "Yes, family." The end of the word snaked out in a long eee sound, not unlike a rusted hinge.

A long silence played out, then the woman continued.

"I too desire a family. Mine," and here she motioned to the skulls again, "have been asleep for so long. This is what I require."

She reached out her hand motioning for the skull John had set aside. When he placed it in her hands, it went with the bottle of whiskey.

"These…" meaning the objects by her side, "and… one of your females."

John's head cocked slightly at this.

"One of your… disciples?" Her head tilted, asking if that was the right term. "I require her monthly bleed. I'll return her in time."

"Done," John said.

With the negotiations out of the way, it was time to get down to business.

"John Montanet, you come seeking foresight, a person you say. But what do you ask?"

He told her of his affliction and that a demon had stated that someone could fix him. Although, he hadn't used the exact terms. Then he repeated the strange poem.

In ages forth through moonless mist,
you seek the one that shadows kissed.
A fleeting form in dreaming state,
with learned power to life abate.
Footsteps echo, never near,

a haunting hum that none can hear.
She wears the night like ink on skin,
a black streak hides the truth within.

The woman nodded her head. Her unseeing eyes stared off to a forgotten place. Smoke curled from her pipe as she puffed and considered the verse.

"Give me your hand," she said.

John extended both hands and she grabbed his right. Surprising strength pulled it close to her face. She flattened it and let her fingers run over the lines there: the lifeline, the heart, fate.

Then her eyes began to change.

Holding his hand now by the slightest touch, she rested her stubbly chin on his inner fingertips. Transfixed, he could not pull his hand away. Slowly, parting lips glued together with ancient saliva, sliding past gums decaying into bone marrow butter, an old tongue peeked out of her decrepit mouth. The tongue, mottled with spots resembling those in a petri dish, quivered slightly in the air.

The tongue was sensing the air, sniffing, tasting, quivering. Bending and twisting, the tongue finally found the inside of his fingers. Snaking down between the fold of his pinky and ring finger, he could feel tiny bumps, like a cat's tongue, scraping his skin. Slowly moving between fingers, John imagined a slight stinging sensation, minute shocks from an ancient electric eel.

Finished with the folds, the tongue snaked out even longer and traced the lines of his palm: head line, heart line…fate. The lifeline, easily seen when the thumb is swiveled in toward the palm, runs from the middle of the hand, around the fat of the palm toward the inner wrist. Having found it, the tongue quivered as if in ecstasy. Like

Pavlov's dogs, the lifeline triggered an effect in the ancient mouth; saliva filled the insides of her cheeks. John thought he saw a shiver run through the old woman's body but couldn't tear his eyes away from her. As if following tiny pathways, he saw rivulets of saliva emerge, running up, out of the mouth, over bumps, and slowly down the snaking tongue, glistening in the dark. He watched the acid saliva run along the tongue. Slowly, after clinging to the tip for several seconds, the first drop fell onto his palm, settling into the crease of his life line, greasing the way for the mottled tip, and running toward his wrist.

Her face stretched into a grimace of ecstasy; the old woman shuddered each time the tongue snaked forward. Her hands trembled. Her eyes, now grossly engorged and bulging, did not see. Her mouth gaped open, making no sound. Her tongue, unnaturally forced out ever farther, stretched into a rope of sinew. Threatening to tear the ligaments away from the back of her throat, the old woman tortured her tongue out of her throat as if seeking the last morsel of food that would save her life. Suddenly, as if she had just touched the end of a battery, her tongue snapped back like a breaking rubber band. Her head shot back, lolling to one side. She dropped his hands and looked at him. Her trancing eyes were now blue and as clear as the night sky.

She spoke.

"You have set your path, John Montanet. I see a long and tortured life for you, although your time here is nearly at an end."

"At an end? How can that—?"

"You have been bound, John. Bound by a black magic that was shown to you in a false bargain. Are you not an abomination like these poor creatures?" Without looking, she motioned to the beast and Toth. "Do you not suffer transformations that you cannot control?"

John's face flushed with a seething anger at the cruel trick played upon him. It was true that his transformations had gone awry, and in fact were more frequently out of his control. He could feel his very being changing in some fundamental way. He feared that one day soon he would wake up and not know himself at all. It was true, he felt his time *was* short.

She continued. "That is the nature of your deal with Legba. Your binding transformation will continue. What you will become… I cannot say. But the child the demon spoke of has yet to be born. Nay, not for a long time will she come. But, one day, through an intricate weave of bloodlines, she will come forth. And only then can you be… undone."

"Undone?" John said. "I wish to control this magic! I *will* control it! One day. And when I unlock its secret, I will curse Legba and watch *him* grovel!"

The woman shook her head. "John, this magic is not for the likes of us. It cannot be—"

"I did not ask for mothering!" John said. "We have a bargain. Tell me how to find the girl."

Her hands settled into her lap as she closed her eyes. A moment of silence whispered away. When she opened her eyes, the milky cataracts had returned. The trancing session was over.

"You must go into the mist, the *Misi sipokni*. You must go beyond this time, outside of it, and there you must wait. How you will return, I cannot say, for that is not my ability. But only then, only in *that time* will you find the one you seek. Only then will you find… Delphine."

The woman slumped slightly as if ashamed of her own abilities. Speaking the girl's name felt like a terrible betrayal, but a bargain had been made. And her part was now fulfilled.

John suddenly knew what to do. This curse that had been laid upon him would be used to his advantage. After all, Legba, the trickster god, the guardian of the gates between the living and dead, had imbued him with some new power when he'd been locked into this transformative state. What was supposed to be a joke played upon John, had created something unintended. He knew of the mist beyond time and now understood how he could use it to wait. To wait for the one named Delphine.

His mind spun with the revelation. He'd have to think of a way to survive the wait. He needed a place of safety to come back to. Who knew how long he'd have to wait? And his disciples, he'd take them as well. But how could he protect them all through the ages? How could he come back and move freely in a time that he wouldn't understand? How could he stay hidden until his strength returned, until he found this girl?

A slow smile spread across his face. The old woman drew back, feeling a change in John. The beast picked up its ragged head, feeling the call of its master.

John needed a boat. And on that boat…

*

Somewhere on the Mississippi, 1964

And on that boat the Gris-gris man tightened his grip on the wheel. He felt strength—or it was resolve—flow into his hands. His sinewy arms flexed against the wooden pegs of it. The wheel, old and worn, was a symbol of his journey. He'd gone into, and come out of, the mist by way of this wheel. It had brought him to the time and place he needed to be. He just needed more time. They needed more energy. And when they had it, they would be whole again, the savior and the disciples would be made whole. Then he'd find the girl. He'd learn the secret to his curse. And his reign would begin. Then, and only then, would he awaken the thing in the third boat.

He reached his hand out and let it fall upon the shoulders of Mr. Sandgrove. The Gris-gris man, in his sudden surge of will power had attracted much attention within the boat. The beast, his favorite abomination, stood by his side in anticipation. But there was still something missing.

The Gris-gris man stroked his back longingly.

"I know," he sighed. "I too, feel his loss."

Slobber dripped from the beast's jowls. He began to pant.

"I miss Toth as you do," said the Gris-gris man. "But I feel we will see him again. In fact, I mean to find him. And when I do, we'll make you whole again."

The beast's split tail twitched in anticipation, as a low growl vibrated the floor.

"Patience, Mr. Sandgrove. Just a while longer. You'll see."

And with that, the three wraiths filled the cabin. They'd heard their master's call.

"My family is hungry," said the Gris-gris man. "Feed us."

And the wraiths flew away on the night air.

CHAPTER 15

Arlo stood in the shadows near the Lafayette cemetery #1, looking up at a lighted window. Her flowing robes matched the rhythm of the wind and with little energy or thought, she melted into the background. Only her mind and a keen sense of observation existed to betray her presence.

The shadow of a cat had just disappeared around the corner, hugging the old stone wall of the cemetery.

"You know yer path, don'tcha?" Arlo whispered. The shadow cat did not respond. It merely ascended the wall, looking once up at the window, then disappeared over the top. It knew it would not be needed this night so would spend its time exploring. All manner of things tended to collect in cemeteries, and it hadn't been to this one in a long time.

But she don't know hers, Arlo thought, staring up. *Not yet. And now wit' dis new problem.*

The moon slipped up from behind the roofline of the house, just as the last thought entered Arlo's mind. It hung in the sky just above the window she watched. It had an opinion on the current situation but like always, remained silent.

Bah! Arlo waved it off. *No one coulda predicted dat. Why he's even back, I don't know.*

A faint tidal sound resonated in the old woman's mind, as the partial moon watched her. One eye, sleepy and nearly closed, had recorded the events that unfolded over the last few days. Soon, it would sleep on the matters it cared about, and when it awoke, it would give its opinion. It had much to consider.

Arlo twisted her hands, then looked at her palm. Years of runes—learned spells and pacts with others—were layered there in a tangled weave. To the human eye, the lines would appear muddled like old scars. But to her eyes, it was a universe of knowledge.

She stared at the runes like an old librarian. She knew that upon her hand lay the knowledge of a thousand years. She knew the answer was wrought somewhere in her flesh. It was just a matter of finding it. As her eyes searched for the answer, her palm seemed to gain depth, growing long, longer, infinitely deep. The lines became three-dimensional as her mind probed them, searching for the knowledge she sought.

Upon finding Del, she thought her task would have become easier, that the spell would present itself, or a series of steps. But that had not happened. After Arlo had taught Del how to sever the silver cord—and she'd unexpectedly had to use it on the intruder—she thought her plan would fall into place and she'd be done with the business.

But Del had barely survived the ordeal, and had it not been for the shadow cat, cleaning away the poison of the silver cord, she would not have.

Arlo had watched from the shadows, just as she was doing now, during the time of Del's recovery. And the months after. She'd been surprised that Del had elected to move back into the house of her benefactor. Perhaps she'd overestimated the girl's independence in the beginning. Or she simply didn't understand young girls any longer. In her formative days, girls became women quickly, just as boys had to become men. After all, newly wed couples barely of twenty years ran homesteads and plantations in her days. They controlled large households and commercial dealings. But now, the youth could barely survive without needing someone to come along and pick them up every time they stumbled.

"Bah!" She shook the notion away. Lamenting about the stock she had to choose from did no good. She had to fight with the army she had. And she knew that Del was the center of it. But… there was still the lingering question in the back of Arlo's mind, had Del swallowed any of the cord juice? Even just a drop? And if she had, what would that mean? As far as Arlo knew, this exact situation had never occurred before.

And to complicate matters further, Étienne had to show up. And not just show up, but to randomly meet Del on the street.

Just then, a movement in another window caught Arlo's attention. A curtain had been shuffled, letting some light escape the room. Within the window, a silhouette appeared. Arlo watched as the figure fused with the curtains, finally getting them apart. A short, plump outline stood in the window, looking out at the dark night. Then Arlo remembered something.

The first night she'd met Del, the night the men had chased her down a street, bringing mischief to her door, Del had mentioned her konseye. When Arlo had learned that Del had not been set on her path yet, she'd asked the girl why her konseye—her mentor—hadn't taught her.

Had she angered her mentor? No, Del had said that the woman was sick.

Then Arlo asked if her mentor was dying. The girl seemed to have taken offense at the question, at first, but was uncertain with her answer.

Arlo smiled and looked up, just as a cloud passed over the fading moon. The moon nodded its approval. Arlo was on the right track.

Del's mentor had been sick but apparently was on the mend. The silhouette in the window, who stood so still, looking for something in the dark night, was the person who taught Del. It was the person who unleashed her ability. And this would be a good person to know, Arlo thought. She still didn't know what to do about Étienne, but she had an idea of what to do about Del.

In the fading moonlight, outside the Lafayette cemetery #1, Arlo's path became very clear.

*

By the evening, Mama D was exhausted. She'd spent the day in and out trancing sessions, slowly gaining ground. Having focused on the objects closest to her: the parlor, the couch she sat on, the old paintings that hung from the walls, she'd been able to keep her sessions going longer and with better clarity. Her mental vision still wasn't great, but anything was better than it had been. And there had been enough progress over the weeks, and especially the last few days, to give her hope.

And she needed hope more than anything right now. The thought of never being able to trance again had kept her up at night. To a practitioner, losing their mental sight was like losing a part of their actual vision. And having experienced that loss over the last few months—even temporarily—had terrified her.

Mama D had come to think of this ability no differently than a muscle that had been neglected. Her own body cried out for relief after an easy day around the kitchen, when it had never done that in the past. Having lain in bed for months on end had weakened her muscles and she ached daily as she used her body more. Why would her trancing be any different? She'd heard some folks describe the brain as a type of muscle, and although she wasn't sure about that, she now believed that with work, she'd gain her ability back.

The question was how long it would take.

Mama D sensed something of late and needed to find out what it was. So, her vision had to return soon.

Maybe the uneasiness had been there for a while, and she'd just been too weak to feel it. But she felt it now. There had been plenty of odd things happen in the house, and she knew from experience that a house could attract its own negative energy. But this was different. And she thought the difference was Del.

It had dawned on her recently that whenever Del was in the room, or right after, her own trancing ability was better or worse than the norm. At times, she felt stronger when Del was near, as if some of the girl's power had radiated out to her. During those times her own sight felt strong. And perhaps this is what happened during the Billy Bash incident—Del, in an effort to save her own life, pulled Mama D to her—but the concept was beyond her ability to work out.

Other times though it was the opposite. Sometimes, if Del was tired or cranky, it would sap Mama D's strength, as if Del were absorbing more power, more *mental oxygen*, than her fair share, leaving little for anyone around her. Could someone mentally suffocate if Del absorbed too much for too long? Was that even possible?

Mama D shook the thought from her mind. Too many of these wild scenarios had plagued her of late. They were becoming a distraction. Besides, she doubted the girl did this on purpose. Most likely, she didn't know she was doing it at all. But she was. It was as if Del's body, like an animal sensing a storm, was storing up energy.

She'd never known anyone to do this and had admitted to herself that it could just be her tired mind inventing stories. But just when her mind would start to settle, she'd be reminded of it again the next time Del was in the room with her. And after a while, it was too much to ignore.

This was why Mama D was so happy when her trances had moved beyond the closest objects. Her reach was returning.

And when it had, she'd explored even further. Just tonight, with the others occupied, she'd let her vision slip beyond the confines of the house and explore the grounds. And what she'd found there had shocked her senses.

A ring.

A ring of spirits had formed around the house and were simply waiting. She couldn't see them individually, and even just viewing them briefly drained her considerably. But they were there. A ring of spirits had surrounded Armand's house.

Had they always been there? she wondered. Had she known about them before falling ill and simply forgotten? She shook her head in dismay. Too many things were happening, and far too quickly for her liking.

Now, standing at the window, peering out into the dark, she saw only shifting shadows. The Lafayette cemetery #1 was right across the street from her, and in her trance she thought there was more there than just the spirit ring. But the vision had faded too quickly to discern any details.

Looking through the window did not help. She only saw the night and shifting shadows. But she knew something was there. She could feel it.

*

Armand packed his pipe and listened to the old house. Although he was not alone, the evening was settling in nicely. Del was noisily attending her wash downstairs. Mama Dedé had also taken to spending many hours downstairs, either rearranging the kitchen drawers, or simply sitting in the parlor. He sensed that she was still out of sorts a bit, but saw signs of improvement—however small—each day. So, he thought it best not to interfere. Each in their own time, he thought. And he knew that to be true from a few of his own experiences.

He checked his pocket watch. He'd been standing here for several minutes, waiting, and knew the time was close. He'd wait to light his pipe after it happened—if, it happened.

And it did.

Just as the time hit 8:19, he heard Jimmy's door open.

Armand couldn't remember when he'd first noticed Jimmy's strange behavior but had observed it for several weeks now. And the boy never failed.

Whether through some strange ultradian rhythm, a trigger that Armand could not detect, or the most fascinating coincidence he'd ever witnessed, each night after dinner, once everyone had settled to their own pursuits, Jimmy appeared at precisely the same time.

When Armand had first noticed it, he dismissed it as what he called the *alarm clock effect*. That was where one woke up in the middle of the night, and looking at the time, noticed an eerie symmetry in the time. Perhaps it was one minute after one in the morning, or thirty-three minutes after three.

He'd never noticed the phenomenon as a young man, but then again, with the old style clocks, one could imagine that the minute hand was simply near a number, and not on it. But with the invention of the Copal flip clock, which had thin metal plates with numbers on them that would flip over every minute, it had become easier to see the odd symmetries. More times than he cared to remember, he had awoken to the time of 12:34, 1:11, or 3:45.

His mind, as with all things, latched onto the phenomenon, trying to ferret out its meaning. He understood that the scientific term for it was numerical pareidolia, referring to the human mind's tendency to perceive patterns where there were none.

Yet others, those of a more sensitive mental nature, may refer to them as Angel Numbers, assigning a higher significance—such as in Numerology—to their occurrence.

Regardless of its origin, it was this very phenomenon that he'd noticed with Jimmy.

The boy had taken to the chess table like a prodigy, yet Armand thought it was fleeting. His fascination with the table itself—a handmade piece with an inlaid chess board cut from small squares of wood—may have been due to its own symmetry. The rows and columns of alternating colored wood was pleasing to the eye, afterall. But his grasp of the *game* of chess still eluded him. Night after night, Jimmy played the game of the Black Queen, despite Armand's attempts at explaining how the pieces really moved.

Now, at precisely 8:19, Jimmy opened his door, walked down the short hall, and sat at the chess table.

He was ready for another game.

"Hi, Ahman," Jimmy said as he passed by.

"Good evening, Master Jimmy. And what will be tonight's entertainment?"

"I gonna pway ah game."

"Indeed." Armand walked behind his worktable and sat on a high stool. Striking a match for his pipe, he said, "I'm just going to do a bit of work myself. Don't let me disturb you."

"OK," Jimmy said. "You dohn 'sturb me." He was already positioning his pieces.

Armand sat silently smoking his pipe and watching the boy. His eyes sparkled with curiosity and the joy of discovery. In one of his many journals, he wrote quickly but softly, recording all the pieces on the board, and every move they made. He'd nearly filled this journal with notes of the many games he'd watched.

*

About forty-five minutes later, just as Armand's pipe was dying, so was the last piece on the chess board. The black queen had survived, as Armand knew she would.

Armand's vigil had served multiple purposes, just as it had for the last several weeks. He had collected more data for his study of the *black queen endgame*, as he'd come to think of it. Believing that there was more to the game than just nonsensical play, he was determined to unravel its secrets. Secondly, he'd given time for Del and Mama Dedé to settle into bed after their nightly routines. He needed privacy and quiet for what he was about to attempt.

Walking to the chess table, he sat in the open seat, across from Jimmy, and discretely sat a battery-operated tape recorded on the table. The boy was organizing the pieces for another game.

"Master Jimmy," Armand said, then paused. He hadn't thought to rehearse this part, but now wished he had. "May I ask you a question?"

"OK," Jimmy said, looking up.

Armand leaned forward with his forearms on the table. His fingers interlocked into a tight ball. He cleared his throat.

"I uh… well—"

Jimmy watched him quietly.

"You see, I want to ask you a question and—"

"You fohgot you q'esion?" Jimmy offered.

"Heh-heh. Well, no, not exactly. You see, I didn't forget my question, I don't know *how* to ask my question and—"

Jimmy's eyes narrowed at this. It seemed silly to him that someone who didn't know how to ask a question, would have one to ask in the first place. Then he thought that someone should tell Armand this, but the concept seemed too complicated to think about, so, he forgot it.

Then an idea came to Jimmy and his face brightened. "Ohh, you ax 'ike dis." And he began to mouth words with his mouth, in an apparent silent inquiry.

In that moment, Armand felt an overwhelming love for the boy swell up inside him. The utter trust on Jimmy's face nearly set him off his course. But in his mind, he knew this was important. In fact, he felt it may be the path to discovering what threatened his family the most. And for that, it was worth it.

Jimmy stopped mouthing his silent words and sat waiting.

Armand unclenched his fingers and with his eyes locked on

Jimmy's he quietly pushed the RECORD button of the tape recorder.

He sighed visibly as if the act of pushing the button was the official start of the whole business.

Jimmy seemed not to notice the action, and this felt odd to Armand. Jimmy was a curious boy and asked about all sorts of little habits that others ignored. Why would he not care about something this… obvious?

Armand watched the boy watching him. An eerie silence grew in the space between them. Armand swallowed once, thinking that he'd postpone the experiment. Then a thought came to him. It was as if Jimmy knew what Armand was about to do and was waiting for him to do it.

Armand's head tilted back slightly, as if to view the boy from a different perspective. Jimmy seemed not to notice Armand's discomfort, or, if he did, was simply waiting for him to overcome it.

Armand imagined a slight nod of Jimmy's head, as if to say, "You've gotten this far, don't turn back now."

And with the smoothness of a magician, Armand pulled a gold pocket watch and chain from his vest pocket. He looked at it for only a moment, then, setting his elbow on the table, let the chain slip through his fingers until the watch hung, suspended in the air. Jimmy's eyes went to the shiny gold object. Slowly, Armand began to twist the chain in his fingers, first one way, then the other, causing the watch to spin back and forth.

Jimmy's eyes never left it.

Back and forth it twisted.

Back and forth.

Armand whispered. "My question is here in this watch."

"In you watch?" Jimmy asked.

Back and forth.

"Yes. Its name is Sparkle and it's hiding," Armand whispered. "It's shy, but it wants to come out."

"It does?"

Back and forth.

Armand took long, slow breaths timed with the twisting of the watch.

In and out went his breath.

Back and forth spun the watch.

"Yes. Sparkle wants to come out," he said softly, "but it's afraid."

"It is?"

"Yes, it is. Will you protect Sparkle if it comes out?"

Jimmy nodded slowly. His head bobbing to the rhythm of the twisting watch.

In and out went his breath.

Back and forth spun the watch.

"When Sparkle comes out," Armand whispered, "it will try to get away, because it's scared."

Jimmy's eyelids began to flutter, and Armand knew the time was near.

"But you can protect Sparkle with your eyes."

Back and forth.

"When I snap my fingers, Sparkle will jump to your eyes and hide. But you must shut them, or Sparkle will fly away."

A concerned look fell over Jimmy's face. He didn't want Sparkle to be scared or fly away.

"Do you understand?"

Jimmy nodded.

"OK, here comes Sparkle. One,

"Two,

"Three." Armand snapped his fingers.

Jimmy started slightly as if surprised by the sound, but snapped his eyes shut. Armand held his breath, watching the boy intently, waiting to see if the suggestion took.

"Keep your eyes closed so Sparkle will be safe. Sparkle was in the spinning watch, it caused the watch to sparkle, but now it's in you. My question is hiding behind your eyes, which made your eyelids heavy. Can you feel it?"

Jimmy, with eyes closed, nodded.

"Do you see Sparkle?" Armand asked. "Is Sparkle in your eyes?"

Jimmy's closed eyes narrowed as if he was looking for something, then his mouth curved into a faint smile. He nodded.

"That's good, Master Jimmy. Very good. Now keep your eyes closed," Armand said. "Is Sparkle beautiful?

The boy nodded again.

"Are you keeping Sparkle safe?"

He nodded harder.

"That's good. Now, Sparkle wants to look for its answer. Can you let it do that?"

The nod slowed, as if Jimmy didn't understand.

"Sparkle is my question," Armand said. "And you're keeping it safe. Now it wants to go look for its answer."

Jimmy nodded.

"And the answer is deep in your mind. Very deep. But Sparkle will find it if you let it."

Armand watched closely. Jimmy seemed to have accepted this suggestion as well.

"Will you let Sparkle look for the answer?"

A quick nod.

"Good. Very good. Now, just relax and let Sparkle look around in your head. You won't feel a thing." Then he added. "It might even tickle."

Jimmy smiled at the thought of Sparkle tickling his mind.

Armand prepared his first question.

CHAPTER 16

Lying in bed, Del tried to corral her racing thoughts. So many things had happened over the last few days it felt like it had been a week.

She was worried that she needed to produce something, anything, to discuss with Mr. Bobby. But it was easy to see that he had a very laissez-faire attitude about reporting, so thought she still had some time. Besides, there were more pressing concerns before her now.

The strange visit from the spirit, which had led her to the cemetery sat in the back of her mind. She considered flashing back, just to see if the spirit was still there. She hated the thought that it could spend its eternity floating around in a circle, but she didn't know how to communicate with it. Besides, it didn't appear to be doing any harm. She'd ask Mama Dedé about it later. Or even Armand. He'd love to research something like that, if he didn't already have a theory for it.

The wraiths and the poor dock worker, on the other hand, *that* had been disturbing. She'd never seen anything like it before and needed to think about what to do. She'd promised the others that she'd be more open with these topics but didn't want a repeat of the worm event. Mama D may not survive something like that again. So, she'd do her own research first—she was a reporter after all—and bring them the scoop when she had it.

Only, she didn't know exactly how to describe *how* she'd seen what she had. Her mind was inventing new ways to blend her real sight with her mental sight, faster than she could understand them. The doppelganger sight for instance. It was interesting but didn't seem overly useful. And the teleportation bit—where she'd suddenly appeared in the warehouse—was just weird.

But had she really *been* in the warehouse? Hadn't her shoes been wet when she got back? Something else to check on.

Maybe her brain was just shorting out from too much thinking. Could she over trance and wear it out?

She groaned, rolled over and looked at the clock. It was almost 11:30 and she could still hear Armand talking to himself in the library. She thought about popping in to see what he was studying but told herself not to. She wasn't a snoop—just curious.

Then her mind went to Étienne. What was he about anyway? There were plenty of eccentric people in New Orleans but something about him didn't fit. She couldn't put her finger on it, but she felt he was… misplaced, somehow. That was the only way to describe it. But she assumed he'd be gone soon. How long does someone stay in a hotel anyway? So, as she pulled the covers tight around her—the old AC rattled and groaned, freezing her room—her mind slipped into its nightly ritual.

*

Her thoughts drifted—in some form of a trance—around her room in a slow circle. Ever since the Billy Bash incident, she had become intensely aware of doors and windows that weren't locked. She'd never worried about them before, but now, among many things, it was a recurring bell that rung in her head. Fighting it was useless—also like many things—so she just let it happen.

In her mind, her vision floated around the room in a tight radius. It looped her body three times looking for something she couldn't name, then drifted to the room's edge. After inspecting the windows and doors, it floated off in an ever-larger circle, looking for ways into the house. During these sessions, she was aware if people were in particular rooms, but they were always fuzzy and muted. She never stopped to listen in on their conversations, and wasn't sure if she could, as the inspection routine had its own purpose.

After inspecting the house, her vision would move to the garden, and she always felt a sense of security when she caught a glimpse of the stone maiden. She felt it was somehow a lone warrior that was put here to stand guard, and at times had meant to ask Armand about its history.

The high stone wall would come into view next, and she'd check the heavy iron gate that closed off the drive. By this time, her vantage point was from high above the house, as if she were a cloud.

That's when she would see the white ring of spirts that surrounded the house.

Goosebumps crawled across the back of her neck. *There could be anything hiding in there,* she thought. An uncontrolled shiver ran through her body.

She couldn't recall when she had first learned of the ring. But as long as she'd been having these *inspection trances* it had been there. In this fuzzy, muted vision it could have been a ring of fog surrounding the house, but she knew better. Fog rings didn't cut through the middle of houses.

Around Armand's grand estate, was a menagerie of buildings. On one side was the cemetery with its high wall. On the other three sides sat a variety of homes and one small park. Most of the buildings were masked behind the large trees that surrounded the house, so there was a sense of privacy here despite the proximity of the neighbors. But from Del's elevated view, she had a clear line of sight of the ring and everything it passed through.

The white spirit ring didn't follow the square confines of the house and block upon which it sat. It spread out in a rough circle around the house, which is what caused it to pass right through the center of nearby buildings, kitchens and living rooms.

Del wondered if the neighbors experienced odd happenings in their homes, especially the rooms that seemed to be infested with spirits, but didn't have the nerve to ask. And what would she say anyway? "Excuse me, but has anyone seen my ghost circle lately?"

Perhaps they didn't experience much, but as thick as the ring had become, she thought *something* weird had to be happening.

The white ring, which looked like fog, had a few layers to it. The innermost layer—closest to the house—was thick and solid white. It appeared to be a border or boundary line. She imagined a sentry of spirits holding back an army, or perhaps an angry mob. She couldn't be sure which one it was.

Outside of that, a middle layer of spirits congregated. And beyond that, a sparse layer of spirits—as if it were formed by those who had just come to watch—had begun to amass.

Why they were amassing, she didn't know. At times she thought it was simply her gift that was drawing them close. But when she had finally noticed the dense inner line, what she thought was a boundary line began to look differently to her.

It looked like an army.

And it made her think of an impending battle.

CHAPTER 17

The fourth floor of the Touro Infirmary was quiet. A few of the night nurses were on their lunch break, which left few people on the floor. Head nurse Maggie DuBois sat behind the nurse's station reading a paperback novel. The smell of old coffee and antiseptics clouded the promise of coconut rum and palm trees, the kind of healing only her books ever offered.

She'd often thought of a tropical island getaway. Gary, her sometimes husband was occasionally in these daydreams, but over time had faded out of the picture.

She wished she'd be daring enough to book the trip for herself. Gary would scoff at the idea outright. It was always his position to assume the cost of traveling anywhere was a waste of money. Although investments in dubious land deals and profit shares were doled out with regularity, none of which ever produced a profit.

The idea of divorce had been a frequent thought of late. But who wanted to be divorced when forty was staring you in the face? She was still in decent shape but not as thin as she'd once been. She envied the young girls these days. She sensed a type of feminine freedom springing up around them. Something that her generation would not have done. But it was too late for her to join that movement. Besides, she'd look silly if she tried. She felt trapped, too old to be young, too young to vanish.

When her backup returned, Maggie dropped her paperback on the counter and went downstairs. A few people were in the cafeteria and the smell of frying bacon made her stomach rumble. Scanning the pastry station, the donuts called to her, but with sunned bodies dancing in her daydream, she passed them by and just grabbed a coffee.

Outside, in the alley behind the hospital, she fished her smokes from the pocket of her scrubs and lit up. Although everyone else smoked in the hospital, Maggie felt that recovering patients should be breathing the cleanest air possible, so only smoked outside. She knew it was a silly idea, but it had become a habit somewhere along the way.

The night was warm and closing her eyes, she imagined herself walking along a beach. In her fantasy, her coffee became a rum drink, and her cigarette became a joint. After all, she was on a tropical island, and, when in Jamaica, she would do as the Jamaicans did. The fantasy moon floated high overhead illuminating liquid diamonds that washed ashore on gentle waves. The night breeze brushed her skin, and the smell of salt air tickled her nose.

Ahead of her on the fantasy beach, a handsome man stood up from tending a fire and motioned to the blanket he'd laid out for them. This was their secret rendezvous place. His silhouette stood before the fire. A bright line of firelight clung to his black skin hiding his nakedness. But his white teeth and eyes hinted at an eager smile. She thought about dropping her own bathing suit in the sand, but preferred to let him remove it at his leisure.

Another few steps and she would be in his arms. They'd fall to the blanket, they'd roll in front of the fire,

the fire would warm them…

the fire…

The man looked down at himself. Green fire flickered—then pierced his chest.

At first, just a wisp of smoke, barely visible, Maggie thought it was smoke from the fire curling around him.

But it had just come *through* him.

The man watched in surprise as a pinpoint of fire opened his chest, and like a flame burning through paper, his skin curled away in a black, ragged opening. The burning hole widened, slowly at first, then with increasing speed. When it reached his stomach, she could see through him and to the fire behind him. The fire on the beach had become a long, swirling tunnel of flames. It stretched backwards into the darkness, its mouth emerging from the surface of her lover's body. He looked up in surprise, but before he could cry out, the flames consumed him in a blinding flash. And the wraiths fell upon Maggie.

Knocked to the ground by a stunning blow, Maggie realized she was in the alley behind the hospital. A cascade of stars shot before her eyes when her head struck the cobblestone sidewalk. Her arms went protectively over her face, expecting more blows from her attacker but she saw no one. Her lungs reacted to having the breath knocked out of them by drawing in a large breath. She screamed, but it had no sooner left her throat, and she heard it die with a strange warble. The warble was her throat collapsing under great pressure. The wraiths, swarming her like a thick, black cloud, were smothering her in their frenzied feeding.

Fortunately for her, she lost consciousness before she caught fire. The wraiths, despite their directive for restraint, consumed her Aether in large, gluttonous slumps. Her essence tore free in wet, ragged streaks. Her subconscious mind was only briefly aware of this violation, and having no reference to the experience, simply shut itself down.

The chaotic feeding of Maggie DuBois went on for several more minutes. By then, she was fully engulfed in Shadowfire, but this did not hinder the wraiths. And due to the seclusion of the alley, their feeding would have gone unwitnessed, but for a strange occurrence.

Del's subconscious was pulled to the violence, as if it had been seeking this very thing.

CHAPTER 18

The restless mind of Del, having made its nightly rounds of inspection around Armand's house, and having inspected the white ring of spirits, had continued its journey long after her conscious mind retired.

During her waking hours, Del had come to suspect that something like this had been happening. She suspected her mind slipped off without her. But it was hard enough to separate the visions of her waking trances, much less track what her brain did at night. If she tried to figure that out, she feared she'd never go to sleep. So, she'd become used to waking in the morning with any number of strange images fleeing her mind. And trying to capture the dream behind those images before they fled completely was a game of frustration, and she'd given up on it long ago.

But tonight, as if sensing something was amiss, she slept restlessly. She was pulled near the surface of consciousness by her mind. Something of importance was happening that it felt she should bear witness to. But then by some opposing force, she'd be plunged back into sleep, as if the event had to be hidden from her.

Her subconscious pitched and reeled like a boat in rough water.

As her thoughts wandered of their own accord, and through some cosmic happenstance, they'd come to witness a violent scene in an alley.

Del stirred, her body coiling in response. From her dreaming, elevated vantage point, she could see far and wide. And as if by the force of a magnet, her vision had been pulled to this scene, but was now sinking closer to view it entirely.

A woman had just collapsed in an alley, surrounded by a swirling black cloud. Sleeping Del felt a revulsion when she saw the cloud, but like most people, couldn't look away.

Before the woman hit the cobblestones, tiny sparks of light had begun to jump from her body.

Sleeping Del groaned and mumbled at the pain she felt radiate from the woman. Her sheets began to twist around her, unconsciously mimicking the swarm of black shadows around the woman.

Although a part of her mind wanted to come fully awake and end this nightmare—end it for her own sanity or come awake to save the woman—it would not. Something held it back. Something was preventing her mind from jolting herself awake. Something wanted to watch the scene play out.

A force had awoken in Del's mind the day she tranced on the dock worker. Perhaps witnessing the wraith attack—although after the fact—had connected her to their presence somehow, tuned her to their energy. Whatever it was, her thoughts were now drawn to the wraiths and their terrible power.

The woman burned—ragged orange licking through her bones.

The ripping strings of her essence showered sparks onto her clothing. Oddly, the glow of the flames looked muted as the light filtered through the blackness of the shadow-wraiths.

Intrigued by what was happening, Del's mind floated closer. It was only then that she noticed the woman's silver cord. Or what was left of it.

Two of the wraiths, after having consumed... whatever they were eating of her, had fled. Not in fear of detection, she'd felt, but more under a sense of urgency. The third wraith, a larger, darker specimen, had stayed behind and was now consuming what was left of the cord. In a matter of seconds, having been completely severed by the force of the feeding, the cord had been torn apart. When that happened, it vanished in a shower of disintegrating ashes.

Something about this scene stirred old fears in Del's mind. She swallowed reflexively. Lying in her bed, her body twisted in revolt. She felt herself look inward, look for whatever part of her mind that kept her locked in this vision. And that's where her mistake was made.

This mental disturbance caught the attention of the third wraith, and it turned its gaze to her. Somehow, through some terrible negligence, the third wraith, the most fearsome, looked and saw Del's trancing mind. It looked into her and saw a reflection of itself. Scene after scene of Del's recorded visions unfolded before the wraith and suddenly it was seeing itself consume the dock worker, then the woman in the alley. In that moment, it realized that this person had been looking for it. Maybe not for the wraith itself, but for the power that the wraith represented. In that moment, the wraith both feared and desired her, for it felt her mind had the power to unmake it—or, to make it whole.

This realization was enough to sever the vision. In a violent flash, Del and the wraith were expelled from the vision. She started awake in her bed with a stifled scream, scanning her room for an unseen attacker.

The wraith, confused by the encounter, but exhilarated, and full from the feeding, fled into the night.

It did not return to its master.

As Del lay in bed with her heart pounding, she listened for the intruder she thought was outside her door. A quick flash showed her that no one was there. She sat up in bed, pulling the covers up to her chin, waiting for her heart to settle. She knew that she would not be going back to sleep tonight.

But the damage had been done.

As Del sat there waiting for her mind to clear and wondering what was to be done with the rest of the night, something else was settling back to sleep.

The Dark Dreamer, Del's buried other self, the black streak of Del that had lain silent in her thoughts, was there. The thing that had nearly convinced Del to swallow the cord juice of Billy Bash had been awakened by the discovery of the wraiths. And during Del's exhaustion, when her racing mind felt the need to search the house and surrounding area for intruders, it had guided her thoughts on a hunt for the wraiths. And now that contact had been made, finding them again would be easier.

In fact, the wraiths, and whatever master they served, may be looking for Del right now.

The Dark Dreamer felt this to be a very real possibility, for the sheer power that it had just witnessed was beyond imagining. Like great tidal forces, these two beings, Del, and the wraiths-collective, had the power to move the world.

Whether individually or by the combination of both, ultimate power had just been witnessed.

And the Dark Dreamer meant to have it.

CHAPTER 19

Madame Broussard watched the wraiths as they fled the burning woman. Their second attack in less than a week, unless she'd missed one, had been just as vicious as the first. Concerned about their sudden arrival, she'd held a nightly vigil over her fresco ever since first detecting them. How long it had been since this type of devilry had freely roamed the streets, she couldn't remember. Several decades at least. Maybe longer. But she'd never seen the green fire before. She thought she had an idea what it was but had no idea what it meant.

The fresco had shown her many things over the years, mostly mundane human movements. But it had shown her many surprises as well. The last year and a half had been quite exciting, making her yearn even more for her freedom. But when she caught the sense of Étienne, she was almost taken aback. Where had he been for so long? Had he gone back to the old country? What caused him to reappear now? But the biggest question, the one that should have surprised her the most, was how on earth had he come to meet with Del, the Spirit Hunter?

When she'd first detected their meeting, while keeping her vigil for any sign of the wraiths, she *was* surprised. But it was such an unlikely and fortuitous meeting, she'd tried to dismiss it as mere coincidence. But the odds...

The mechanics of the universe were unknown but moved in a great synchronicity. Their meeting was simply another cog, in the infinite wheel of time, that had turned a fraction of a degree. It was a lever that moved imperceptibly towards an unfathomable position. In other words, the two most unlikely people to meet, actually meeting, at this time in her life, was nothing short of a planned intervention. She was sure of it. Madame Broussard didn't believe in fate, per se, as she liked to think that her own free will made a difference in her life. But at odd times throughout her life, she'd had the feeling that someone knew the end of her story.

But that story would have to wait for another time. And she turned her attention back to the wraiths.

The fresco did not provide great clarity of the attack, and she lost them when they fled, but it showed enough to concern her. The last time things of this nature were set upon the city, she had been free of her confines and was able to defend herself. But that *was* a long time ago.

During that time, she and her kind—the few that existed then *(Étienne)*—roamed freely and without fear, mostly. There *were* older and more powerful things to fear, primordial things that had lived for eons in the swamps, but her kind knew not to bother them.

And the ancient things hadn't concerned themselves with humans either, that is, until humans had made them a concern. Foolish people who had tried to harness the old knowledge and use it to their advantage. That's when the abominations—the intentional cross-binding of different species—had become a plague. The magic—the best she could tell—had come out of Africa with the slave ships. She'd heard there were paths of ancient knowledge that crisscrossed that continent all the way back to the Egyptians. And where they had acquired the knowledge, no one knew. But once it came to the new world, filtered through the superstitions and beliefs of so many African people, it had been changed into something new. The New World was truly a melting pot. New religions were formed. New powers were attained. Old powers were reimagined. And they became like Gods.

And it was during her own god-like reign that she had been crossed. Crossed and tricked by creatures that through a strange turn of events, both trapped her and hid her in this very building. The turn of events that caused this was one of the most fortuitous of her lifetime, second, perhaps, only to how she'd been given the Black Gift. Although, she hadn't thought of it as a gift when it happened. And her poor uncle… What had become of her Uncle Lucian? That was a long, sorted affair; again, a story for another time.

Because now, right in front of her was a danger that could be her undoing. Now that she knew Arlo was close—for she had seen her standing outside the building—and she'd detected interactions between Arlo and the spirit hunter, she wondered if the wraiths were not her doing as well. After all, the black ring of spirits that surrounded her hiding place had stood watch at Arlo's command. Now, if she controlled the wraiths, that must mean only one thing, Arlo was preparing for an attack.

Madame Broussard nodded, and the Toth-skeleton mimicked her. Both mother and child—for it was of her blood—looked at the spot on the fresco where the wraiths had just been and nodded. They understood, mother and child, that if they were to survive, they had to do it together. After all, misery acquaints a man with strange bedfellows. And was she not in a tempest, or very nearly?

She looked at the Toth-skeleton and the head looked back. It was a strange creature that stood before her—an abomination unto itself, yes, but in some ways, even more representative of the idea of strange bedfellows. Toth, the little voodoo doll imbued with cunning but with no means of locomotion, and the Alvie-bones, with means of moving, but no mental capacity, could only exist as one creature. And that creature, needing her own blood for a semblance of life, stood before her now. But the individuality of the parts were still discernible from the whole. For when the mother looked upon the child, it was the head of Toth that looked back first, then, by the slightest movement of its little arms, moved the Alvie-skull to look in the same direction. The delay was almost imperceptible, but it was there.

The stubby arms of the doll, which usually stuck straight out from its body, were thrust forward, touching the back sides of the Alvie-skull. When she turned her head, she could see the arms of Toth push on the skull to orient its direction. She smiled at her creation.

But the Toth-skeleton had not been made for her amusement. It had been made for her salvation. And now, with the hour growing late, it would have to leave the safety of her home, traverse the shadow-roads, and help her to form an alliance.

An alliance between creatures that perhaps had never existed before.

An alliance with Étienne, herself, and the Spirit Hunter.

And if an alliance could not be reached, then perhaps the Spirit Hunter had more enemies to contend with.

But, if nothing else, she always had Scarmish.

CHAPTER 20

Del, after seeing the wraiths in her dreaming trance, and tossing fitfully in bed, had finally gotten up. It was hopeless to think she'd get back to sleep, so, decided to start her day early. Afterall, 5:10 in the morning wasn't crazy early. She knew lots of people had to get to work before the sun was up. But not journalists, she thought. She doubted Mr. Bobby would be up, typing away on his next story. In fact, it was possible that he had gone to bed not too long ago. New Orleans brought out the night owl in a lot of people.

In the kitchen, she grabbed a day-old biscuit, thought about making coffee, then decided to skip it. She didn't want to risk making noise and waking anyone up. Besides, now that she was up and moving, she was anxious to get going. She had no work deadlines, as of yet, so *starting her day early* felt better to her, than say, *bumming around.*

Armand had made it clear, multiple times, that the room she slept in was *her* room. There was no rent. There weren't any assigned chores, although each person had fallen into their own routine which benefited the whole house. But Del still felt restless about her situation.

Her path was far from clear to her. And in a strange way, she realized, that may be the only thing that *was* actually clear to her, not knowing her path.

Slipping out the backdoor, she grabbed her bike from the porch and wheeled it towards the big iron gate. She knew the disturbing images of the wraiths would plague her throughout the day, so she tried to fill her mind with other thoughts, anything other than the death that seemed to be drawn to her.

She looked around at the grand courtyard. She and Jimmy had done a pretty good job getting the garden back in shape since they'd been here. The flowers were just beginning to release their morning smells and would fill the air with exotic scents by late morning. It was a magical place, the courtyard. There were many times that Del had sat on the back porch in one of the old rockers, and let the afternoon lull her to sleep. It could cast a spell over any who lingered on it. And Jimmy seemed to be the lord of the garden, under the protective eye of the Stone Maiden, of course.

Del looked at the maiden as she wheeled her bike past. The stone guardian stood silently above her reflective pool of water, seemingly lost in deep, contemplative thoughts.

Outside the gate, and peddling slowly down the dim street, her mind stayed on Jimmy and the strange things that occurred in his orbit.

Jimmy spent a lot of time talking to the stone maiden. Many times a day he could be seen sitting on the rock ledge around the little pool, murmuring to himself. Sometimes he'd look straight into the maiden's silent face, other times, deep into the pool of water.

When asked who he was talking to, he'd say something silly about his friends in the water.

"Friends in the water?" she'd asked him once.

"Yeah, da'y my fwends," Jimmy said.

"In the water?" Del said. "Are they fish?"

"No, Deh! Dey not fish. Dey people!"

Jimmy looked hurt and angry at the implication that his friends were fish.

"Oh," Del said sheepishly. "Sorry." Then, deciding to probe a bit further she'd asked, "How do they breathe in the water?"

Jimmy had looked at Del trying to decide if she was playing a trick on him, or really didn't understand how people breathed.

"Ike 'dis." And he breathed angrily, three times, through his nose, his nostrils flaring above a curled upper lip.

"You makin' me cazy," Jimmy said, shaking his head.

Del had laughed at the reprimand, and wanting to end the conversation on a good note, probed a bit further.

"I see, so your friends aren't swimming in the water, their sort of… under the water?"

Jimmy's head tilted, considering this.

"Like in a secret room, or something?" Del said.

Jimmy's face lit up. "Yeah! Inna sec'et woom. I showed 'em how to get out."

Del was surprised here. "You showed them how to get out? So, they were lost?"

He nodded.

"How many were there?"

Jimmy screwed his face up, one eye closing in concentration, and thought. "Deh was, Miyo, and da' boy, and da' giwl, and… da utter giwl, and…"

"Wait, you know their names? One's name was Milo?"

He nodded.

"And what were the other names?"

"Uh… I fohgot," Jimmy said. "But dere was bad fings too."

"Bad things? Like what?"

Jimmy thought a minute, then made his arms into waving, rubbery appendages. He was surprisingly good at this. Then he added a throaty growl, clearly imitating some type of monster.

"Wow, that's pretty scary. Are there other things like that, you know, around the house? Scary things that live in weird places?"

A spark of light flashed behind Jimmy's eyes, as if the question had just passed from one side of his brain to the other. He opened his mouth to respond, but she could see that he was deep in thought. It was as if she could see his eyes looking inward for guidance on what to say. After several seconds, his vision changed, looking outward again. But the spark of inspiration was gone or had been muted by something inside.

"No," was all he said.

Del remembered that she had wanted to follow up on that line of questioning but hadn't. She needed to spend more time with Jimmy, but for some reason never accomplished it. There were a lot of things she wasn't accomplishing. Her thoughts were going in too many directions. And hadn't Arlo warned her of this when they'd first met? She'd said something about you can't halfway follow a path because you won't get anywhere. And if you follow no path at all, you'll end up where you don't want to be. And that was exactly how Del felt now.

Adrift.

And like her body, her mind drifted as she peddled. Street after street passed by in an early morning daydream. In an odd way, she felt free and confined all at the same time. The forward movement of her bike was a poor replacement for the lack of movement in her life, but at least it was movement.

Movement of her bike.

Movement of her bike from her spot on the bench, to outside the café.

The doppelganger vision.

The movement of Étienne… or the lack of it.

The *strange* movement of Étienne, and the fact that she regularly could only catch a single-frame glimpse of him in the doppelganger trance…

What was that about?

What was *he* about?

What *was* he?

Her mind snapped back to the present. A crowd was gathered in front of her. She had just stopped in front of a crime scene.

Letting her instincts guide her, Del had ridden her bike through familiar city streets, turning automatically as her mind had wandered. Now, she was stopped in front of an alley that was blocked with police tape.

She'd unknowingly ridden to the crime scene of Maggie DuBois, the woman she had seen attacked in her trance last night.

*

Del was suddenly and completely overwhelmed with the scene of the feeding wraiths. If her dreaming-trance had been a vague vision that had nearly disappeared from her early morning ride, it had reemerged in full color the moment she stopped, as if it had been stalking her.

She did not hear the murmuring voices of the onlookers, nor the indifferent descriptions between the coroner and detective. She only heard the last excruciating moments of Maggie DuBois.

Like an invisible whirlpool, Del's mind was pulled to the spot in the alley where the remains of the dead woman lay. The scene of the feeding wraiths materialized before her. Black writhing shapes swirled in a mad frenzy around the woman, pulling at her very being. The woman had already fallen to the ground but was still alive in this scene. And in Del's mind, she was standing right next to her watching it happen.

Like the time she'd sat on the bench overlooking the river, and had tranced into the Buddy Tibbets scene, she saw herself standing in a place different from her physical body. The woman lay on the ground screaming. She was lost in a black mist that was the feeding wraiths. She flailed her arms to no avail, thinking for a second that she'd had a seizure, or a stroke. Something that her medical mind could hold on to. But when the tearing of her soul began, that violent ripping of her being, and when the tiny green sparks began to leap out of her body, she could think no more. Her mind could not comprehend what her eyes saw. Which, in the end, was a blessing. And all Maggie DuBois had left to do was to scream and to die. But she would not do it alone this time.

Del felt her pain. And sometime in the last few seconds she had dropped her bike and fallen to the sidewalk.

Del screamed the agony of the dying woman. The onlookers, first startled, then terrified, pushed back.

Del saw the tiny sparks of Shadowfire leap from her own body. Then, in a confused mix of reality and dream-trance, she saw her own clothes catch fire. She flailed her arms, beating at the green flames that were spreading across her body.

Help me! Why doesn't someone help me?

The crowd only stared in terrified disbelief.

She felt her skin bubble, burn, and crack open. Her body contorted from the pain. She was burning alive, and the pain was unbearable. How long could someone survive this?

Her mind flashed to the next moment and the next, where no one helped her, just as no one had been there to help Maggie. In another fraction of a second she'd be fully ablaze, but unlike the woman, who's mind had graciously gone to sleep, Del's mind would not. In fact, her mind was wide awake, perhaps the most awake it had ever been. It was like watching an accident occur in real time, when everything runs in slow motion. Her mind ran so fast that she could see the individual movements of the flames as they consumed her clothes. She saw the invisible fractures begin in her torso, then open, as if pulled by unseen hands. She saw light, her lifeforce, as it began to stream out of her, or more correctly, as it was sucked out of her.

She had to act.

In an instant, she was falling—no, rushing—through a blackness of space and time. One moment she was watching the wraith-fire consume her body, the next moment she was in a deep cavern. In a panicked trance, she'd fled to her Well of Life.

But it was not a peaceful arrival. The faint backwards dripping of her life force—the *evaporation* as Mama Dedé called it—could not be heard. Nor did she hear the more urgent backwards rain, like when she'd used her well to heal her mentor. What she heard here, what she felt running through the core of her body, was something elemental. Before she'd even arrived at this place, triggered by the trauma she was experiencing in her trance, a pressure had begun to grow. Like a shock wave caused by an underwater earthquake, a pressure within her well had begun to swell and it was rising rapidly up to meet her.

What she heard here was thunder. It was the roar of a life force rushing forward to save itself. It was a well of power, that having spent millennia under great pressure, finally cracked the surface of the vessel it served. And with all the violence of the oceans, a tidal wave of water rushed up from her well, exploding up, up and out.

And a downpour of rain drenched the shocked onlookers who stood outside the police tape.

They'd come to see about the dead woman in the alley.

They'd been terrified by the young girl who had just had some type of seizure on the sidewalk.

But they were truly mystified by the brief downpour of rain that fell from a clear, early morning sky.

Del looked up, also surprised, as the sudden drenching shocked her from her hallucination. Laying prone on the hard sidewalk, she frantically checked herself for the life-threatening injuries she was sure were there.

She found none.

There was no burning or crackling skin.

There were no swirling wraiths.

There was not even the hint of singed clothes.

But the experience had been real. Or, as close to real as Del's beautiful mind could make it. A beautiful but deadly mind that controlled a power beyond imagining, perhaps beyond control. And as that realization washed over her, as her hands trembled uncontrollably before her face, she could only cry in despair at what she was becoming.

Not surprised, however—for it was his job to be open to all possibilities—was Detective Marcel Valcour. He'd seen many strange things in his profession. And when his inspection of Maggie DuBois had been interrupted by the shouts of the onlooking crowd, he'd walked over to the police tape thinking it was a frantic relative of the victim. But upon looking down at a familiar face—a face that was connected to more than one strange death—he'd simply crossed his arms, waited, and watched. After all, it wasn't the first time this girl had had an apparent seizure outside of a crime scene.

When Del came out of her terror, when her trembling hands slowed and her watery eyes cleared, she looked up to see the detective watching her with keen interest.

CHAPTER 21

Armand sat at the long research table in his library, running his hands through his wild hair. He'd been up for hours already but had missed Del at breakfast.

"Beating the streets early, my dear?" He'd mumbled the accolades of her perceived work ethic to the empty kitchen as he made coffee. "Good for you!" As he waited, he scanned a few headlines, but the newspapers were filled with political pieces due to the upcoming election.

Johnson Airs "Daisy" Nuclear Warning Ad

Goldwater "Mentally Unfit," Says 1,000 Psychiatrists

Even the local news wasn't much better.

Governor McKeithen Urges Calm Amid Civil Rights Tensions

"Ugh," he muttered. "Nasty business."

So, he'd left the paper unread and retired to the library.

Within minutes he'd forgotten politics, Del, and hadn't even made it to Frank, when his thoughts were drawn down a rabbit hole of research that would have far-reaching consequences: Jimmy and the hypnosis session.

Armand's initial goal had been simply to learn more about the boy. He'd started with basic research before going into the actual session. The sparse records he'd found from the orphanage had listed Evelyn Lareaux as Jimmy's mother, with a birth date for the boy of March 15th, 1947. There had been no mention of the father.

He'd made a cursory search for Evelyn but had discovered nothing. The Lareaux surname, despite its similarity to many Creole names, was not assigned to anyone of note. Oddly, it was the same for Del's name. A search on Larouche didn't produce much, despite—according to Mama Dedé—Del being related to the infamous Marie Laveau through a long and winding lineage. It was possible, Armand thought, that the family names had been confused or misspelled over the years and noted it as something to follow up on later.

Armand knew that a March 15th birthday put Jimmy squarely in the zodiac sign of Pisces. This fact alone supported the idea of the boy having some psychic or mystical abilities, if one assigned any weight to the practice of Astrology. Practically every culture Armand had studied assigned some supernatural significance to people born under this sign. But he was cautious in his studies not to lean too heavily into one pseudoscience over another.

However, it was hard to ignore the many theories about personality proclivities. Many prophets and mystics were said to be born under the sign of the fish. The idea that these people were touched by a type of *divine madness* had been well documented through the ages.

And, depending on the cycle of the moon when these March births occurred—primarily during the Waning Moon of March—the gift of foresight was also said to have been bestowed upon the child.

Armand thought back to the strange occurrences that happened around the boy. He couldn't classify these as being directly related to foresight, but he couldn't rule it out either. Jimmy was certainly an enigma.

Another interesting myth about Pisces people was that of being aligned with water spirits. The Norse and Celtic assigned great significance to this idea, as they believed these people carried unpredictable fates, ending in either great victory or great calamity.

This made Armand think about the boy's fascination with the stone maiden in the garden, and the pool of water that surrounded her. If Jimmy wasn't in the house, there was a good chance that he'd be near the stone maiden. Numerous times, Armand had watched through the kitchen window at apparent conversations the boy had had with the statue.

He sometimes felt bad for Jimmy, considering he had no friends. And with Del being busy starting her own life, he often feared Jimmy was being neglected. But the boy had different needs than the others, some of which Armand struggled to understand. But he was often put at ease when seeing Jimmy return from the stone maiden with a look of serenity upon his face. He could only compare it to how some people described their feelings after a church service. Jimmy seemed to find solace from the silent gaze of the maiden, reflected in the still waters. And Armand thought there was a universal thread that connected all the strange things about Jimmy, and that the thread ran straight through the middle of the stone maiden in the garden.

Other superstitions pricked Armand's mind, many of which he had trouble letting go. But perhaps the one that was the most intriguing, was the idea that people born near the Spring Equinox—March 20th and 21st, a time historically seen as a portal between worlds, where veil-thinning, rebirth, and balance occurred—possessed an intuitive ability to navigate between worlds—both the seen and unseen.

And it was this line of questioning that he had explored the most. He pressed play on the tape recorder and listened to the recording again.

Admittedly, it had been a rather haphazard start. When the hypnosis session had begun, and Armand had told the boy that his question, Sparkle, needed to go look for its answer, he was unsure whether the suggestion would take. It had been years since Armand had practiced hypnosis on anyone, but it had been a significant part of his study as a young man. In fact, a hypnosis session from long ago had been the catalyst which converted Armand from a skeptic of the supernatural, to a fervent believer. But that incident had nearly been the early end to his career, one which he'd avoided reliving. One day, when his nerve was up, or with the help of Del or Mama D, he'd explore that unfortunate event again.

But for that reason, and the fact that Jimmy's mental faculties were different from most hypnosis patients, he'd decided to take a different approach. The idea of Sparkle, a friendly entity which had lost its answer seemed absurd to him in the beginning. But after much consideration, the idea seemed more plausible. After all, Jimmy was enamored with shiny and beautiful things. The boy was protective of those around him, especially butterflies—although black crickets were squished mercilessly without regard. And, Armand thought, Sparkle could be the medium for asking any number of questions, because he would implant the idea that it was very forgetful and frequently lost track of its answers. In this manner, Armand could ask a question, and if the answer was not apparent to Jimmy, perhaps his subconscious would work on it, and over time produce an answer.

Questions about Jimmy's parents, or his pre-orphanage life went nowhere. But Armand was OK with that, as he was trying to set the stage for Sparkle to do its work.

"Now, Master Jimmy," he'd said, "this question is very important to Sparkle. Maybe you can help it find this answer. Can you try to do that?"

Jimmy nodded. His eyes hadn't opened once.

"Very good. Remember the time when Del came back to us, after her long adventure, and when Mama Dedé got better?"

He nodded again.

"And we were in the library, and you wrote some strange words on a piece of paper. Sparkle was wondering why you wrote them. Can you help Sparkle find the answer?"

Blank at first, Jimmy sat passively, then a look of confusion formed on his face.

"No," he said.

"No? You don't—I mean, Sparkle can't find the answer?"

"Yes," Jimmy said.

"Yes, it *can't* find the answer, or it *can*?"

Jimmy's face wrinkled at this, and Armand became concerned that the confusion would break the trance. Perplexed, Armand thought for a moment, then tried a different line of questioning. Perhaps the Sparkle approach was too abstract after all.

"Can Sparkle remember the words you wrote that night?"

"Yes."

"Can you tell me what they were?"

A brief flicker of concern passed over Jimmy's sleeping face, then, like an actor waiting for his cue, he spoke. "Cha'thul ungh ah mwu'lla nigh—"

"Ahh, no, no! Stop! Stop!" Armand said, frantically waving his hands.

Jimmy stopped suddenly but remained asleep.

With his hands clenched in front of his mouth, Armand held his breath, listening intently for any supernatural repercussions he may have just caused. Mama D's words of warning about not reading things he didn't understand, echoed in his mind.

When he was relatively sure that he hadn't just called forth a demon—or even worse, the wrath of Mama D—his hands slid from his mouth to cover his eyes, then to his forehead. He patted his head gently as he waited for his heart to stop pounding.

His voice was quiet and apologetic when he spoke again. "Master Jimmy, forgive me, but perhaps it is best to leave those words unspoken."

After all, even though they had all *seen* the strange words on the paper that night, no one had read them aloud, because no one knew what they meant.

Then a thought occurred to him. Del had been the one to find the sheets of paper on the library floor after they'd fallen off his worktable. Had she read them? If so, even silently, if she'd read them completely, would that trigger the magic in them?

He had a strange recollection that she had stared at the paper for several seconds—long enough to read the words—then flinched with a twinge of pain in her forehead. Was he remembering that correctly? He couldn't be sure. So, he couldn't say that *no one* had ever read the strange words, but whatever they were, and whatever harm they may cause, surely had already occurred by now.

He squeezed his head at the absurdity of the situation. The words could simply be gibberish, after all. The confused scribblings of a boy trying to learn his letters.

But if he truly believed that, that it was nothing more than coincidence and circumstance that swirled around Jimmy, then he wouldn't be sitting at this table right now.

There had to be another way.

He raised his head from his hands and looked at the boy.

"Master Jimmy, what is Sparkle doing now?"

"Waiting."

"For me to ask another question?"

"Yes."

"So, Sparkle is not afraid?"

"No."

"What is Sparkle doing while it is waiting?"

"Looking."

Armand flinched at this unexpected answer.

"What is it looking at?"

"Me."

A strong wind blew outside, and the old house groaned, causing Armand to jump. His nerves were running high as his eyes flicked around the room, looking for spooks. He rubbed the goose bumps down on his arms and dismissed the sound as odd timing. He needed to be calm as he was getting to a delicate subject.

After a deep breath he continued. "That night in the library, there was another letter written in crayon. Do you remember that one?"

"Yes."

Armand remembered it as well, cryptic and oddly written. A warning from Mama Dedé echoed in his mind, not to go reading things he didn't understand. But he felt reasonably confident they could speak the words aloud.

"What did it say?"

Jimmy thought for a moment, then said, "Hello. Is someone there?"

"Very good," Armand said, "that's correct." Although he distinctly remembered that the letter had quite an unfortunate capitalization problem, reading more like a bizarre warning.

HELLo IS some one tHERE

"Do you remember why you wrote it?"

"No."

"You don't?"

"No."

"If we give Sparkle time, do you think it can find the answer to why you wrote it?"

"No."

"Really?" Armand was perplexed. "Why is that?"

"Jimmy didn't write it," Jimmy said.

Armand lurched back in his chair, causing the legs to scrape loudly against the floor. The sudden screech broke the trance and Jimmy opened his eyes.

He stared blankly at Armand.

Armand stared back, cautiously, a whirlwind of warning bells going off in his head. Silently, he prayed that he had not just done irreparable harm to the boy's mind. Uncontrolled exits from hypnosis could leave unresolved impressions on the mind. They'd have to have another session soon, to ensure this hadn't happened.

But an even bigger issue weighed on Armand. He hadn't realized until just now that the voice responding to his questions spoke without Jimmy's characteristic speech impediment. In fact, based on the third-person reference, it appeared to not have been Jimmy's voice at all.

CHAPTER 22

(That is the nature of your deal with Legba. Your binding transformation will continue. What you will become... I cannot say.)

The old fortune teller's words echoed through the Gris-gris man's mind, as he flickered in and out of existence. Without constant feeding from the wraiths, his subsistence was a poor one. Also, the thing in the third boat was waning rapidly. Sullen and miserable sounds were all it could make, vibrating on a low frequency that unnerved the soul.

When the wraiths arrived to feed him and his family, he'd been deeply grieved to find only two had returned: Umbra, his first disciple, loving and devoted, and Sussurus, also devoted but cautious and untrusting of others. Often, she had warned him of some of the bolder disciples. Now the two of them hovered above the Gris-gris man, the wispy, tattered form of their heads bowed in shame at the betrayal of their brother, Praeco.

After The Gris-gris man had fed, shedding some of his life-energy to Mr. Sandgrove, he questioned the two remaining wraiths.

What of Praeco?

He did not speak the question but merely thought it, wanting to save as much energy as possible. In a mothering gesture, during his feeding, he'd sent some of his Aether to the other disciples who were still struggling to form.

Umbra and Sussurus quivered in their shadow-form, telling of Praeco's betrayal. The language was that of shadows and mystery which few could understand, but they whispered it nonetheless, for it told of weakness.

The Gris-gris man understood the implication and lauded them for their discretion, especially with the realization that the Shadowfire had been discovered. He had not foreseen that possibility and wondered now if he'd been shortsighted.

He had discovered the Shadowfire by accident in his former life, and since then, had taken great pains to understand it, use it—and most importantly, keep it hidden. The intentionally violent ripping of the soul—or gluttonous feeding as had been the case here—was what triggered it. Somehow, the friction of such a violent act was more than the soul—or more likely, whatever it was made of—could handle. And when it finally ignited, it consumed everything in its vicinity. Even the physical body. Just being able to call it forth on demand, much less control it, would give one great power. And the Gris-gris man had no intention of sharing that.

The unformed shadows skittered nervously in the corners waiting for their master to address them.

What of us? They asked.

When will we form?

Will we fo—

Some of their questions would never form.

Patience my dears, the Gris-gris thought. *All will be well soon. Soon, we shall walk amongst the living, and breath the air of our youth. Soon, we will return to our beloved bayou, and from there, we will rise up and our destinies will be realized.*

A shudder of murmurs vibrated through the structure. Most were approvals, the last fleeting hopes of the disciples who still believed in their master. Some were grumblings, disciples whose beliefs had begun to wane.

Quiet, my dears, the Gris-gris man coaxed. He knew that his hold over the crew was tenuous, and his time was growing short. *The hunger will end soon enough. We are nearly at the end of our journey. And when the hunger ends, and we are restored, we will feed and live like kings.*

Something low and black rumbled in response to his pleadings. It began as a feeling in the center of his mind, but he quickly felt it materialize into actual vibrations. The beast raised its shaggy head when the rumbling started and growled weakly in response. The thing in the third boat was moving.

The Gris-gris man reached out in the dark and patted the beast's head with a ghostly hand. *Quiet, Mr. Sandgrove.* This thought, sent the same way he'd spoken to the wraiths and the other disciples, was heard only by the beast. They had a special bond, for they were of one another. *Yes, the Knot is stirring, but it is still asleep. It will not escape. And although Praeco has betrayed us, I believe in Umbra and Susurrus. They will hold true.*

A vibration came off Mr. Sandgrove as if a whimper of fear had started in its body, but having no voice to form it, had to worm its way to the surface to be heard. A secret message had been passed from beast to master.

I understand, but it will not come to that. We will absorb the others before I let that happen.

He patted the air where the beast's head lay, flickering in and out of existence.

Rest now. We still have time.

And somewhere in the dark, the Gris-gris man and the beast, closed their eyes, trusting that they would open them again soon.

CHAPTER 23

Later that day, Del realized she was far from home. She'd spent hours wandering the streets of the Crescent City, trying to get lost, and now stood in a part of town she didn't recognize.

Her escape from the throng of people that morning had been a chaotic one. After seeing Detective Valcour staring back at her with his crossed arms and indifferent gaze, she'd practically fled, but something had stayed her will. She didn't care for the detective, but felt he cared for her even less. He had grilled her hard over the deaths of Tasha and Billy Bash, and seemed not to believe parts of her story. But in the end, what could he do?

At the alley, she remembered standing up with a cloud of voices swirling around her. Whether the voices were from the crowd of people, the detective, or both, she couldn't be sure. She even imagined ghostly whispers of the dead woman pleading with her. But in the end, she'd mumbled some weak apology and practically dragged her bike through the crowd of people to escape. At one point, arms had reached for her, presumably to help, or to test her strength, but they quickly withdrew. Del felt this.

No one touched her, but she felt them pull back—mentally, instinctively withdrawing. Somehow, the people, feeling sorry for the strange girl convulsing on the sidewalk, had reached out to sooth her, but felt a type of danger that resided in her. Del felt this as well. A type of energy had radiated out of her, immediately after the surprise rain shower had drenched everyone, and had continued to radiate for several minutes after. She knew the people around her could feel that energy, and not understanding what it was, pulled back their reaching hands. People who had one moment been concerned for the strange girl, suddenly feared her for a reason they didn't understand. But the fear was primal within them. Like an animal who instinctively avoids a fire, the people withdrew from her, shunned her, and turned their eyes away.

Del felt the revulsion in the people, as easily as she'd felt the burning of the wraiths. It surrounded her like a plague, first subtle and foreign, then close and intimate, like her own personal stink. She imagined it—the revulsion—as something that seeped from her pores like an odor. Half a block away from the scene, she couldn't stand it any longer—she could still feel the sideways glances at her back—so she mounted her bike and began peddling.

She rode, helter-skelter through the streets, not thinking where she was riding. She just rode. Careening through intersections without looking, the oncoming drivers seemed to have sensed a disturbance in the air, a flash of intuition that an accident was about to occur, and they slowed instinctively, just as she flew through the intersection.

She couldn't say how long she rode like that, only that she finally stopped when her legs could no longer push the pedals. She was dripping with sweat and exhausted.

This part of town was unfamiliar to her. Whether it was a good or bad part, she couldn't tell, but she had to stop and rest. Besides, she doubted anyone would bother her with the way her body radiated out the dark energy.

Finding an old park, abandoned and overgrown, she wheeled her bike into the cool shadows of a large magnolia tree and collapsed onto a bench.

*

The air under the magnolia tree hung heavy, thick with the scent of damp earth and rotting petals. The shade from the overgrown trees cast her and the bench into a serene, mottled twilight. She heard very little noise here. In her frantic ride, she'd seemed to outrun the sounds of the city. A quick flash of the park layout told her she was utterly alone.

Del slumped back on the bench. Her chest had been heaving for hours, but now the adrenaline rush was over, and she was crashing. Sweat plastered her shirt to her skin; her arms and legs felt like rubber. The bike lay sideways on the ground, its front wheel lazing to a stop.

Fragments of her frantic ride flickered through her mind, tangled with memories she couldn't yet sort. Her life had been quiet for the last few months. She was close to starting the job she wanted. Then this had to happen.

Her life outside the orphanage had always been stop and start. Every time things seemed to go right, something crawled from the swamp—or found her in the dark—and all hell broke loose. Her own mind had even begun to betray her. But this time it felt worse. Whatever was happening to her now, with the new visions and strange sightings, this felt different.

Ever since returning to Armand's after the Billy Bash incident, she'd avoided talking much about her gift. Granted, they all spoke about it that night after Frank and Armand prepared the big home coming dinner. But she *had* to talk about it then. They all did. There was so much to clear up. So many pieces of the puzzle that needed to be put into place, there was no way to avoid the topic. But after that night, no one had spoken much about the supernatural things that had happened. It was like a big family secret that everyone knew but just pretended wasn't there.

Perhaps everyone hoped their fears were unfounded, and that silence would make them fade like old bruises.

But Del now feared this had been a mistake. They suspected that the Gris-gris man had been behind their bad fortunes. That he had somehow orchestrated Mama Dedé's failed health. And somehow, he had taken on the guise of a spirit known as Victor Vermis and spoken to Armand and Jimmy through the Ouija board. But to what end? To return? If so, was he already here? Or were these supernatural killings something completely different? Perhaps they were just another layer of New Orleans that had decided to finally show itself.

The thoughts were heavy on her mind.

The wheel of her bike had settled to rest several minutes ago.

Following its lead, she lay over on the bench, with her knees pulled up and her arm bent beneath her head. The sweet, cool air lay heavily on her eyes.

I'll just rest my eyes for a minute.

She was asleep almost before the thought crossed her mind.

*

With exhausted body and mind, Del slept on the park bench beneath the Magnolia tree. Long periods passed where her mind was simply blank, doing whatever necessary repair work it needed to do. The wraith-hallucination and Well of Life incident had taken a toll on her. More than she knew.

But her body knew.

And something in her mind knew as well. Her mind wanted her body to be as strong as possible, for, although it could travel on its own—through the power of the trance—it could not exist on its own, so had to take care of its vessel.

After the major repair work was completed, her mind began to drift, and a dream surfaced.

She was standing in a dark place of trees and overgrown shrubs. A random park that her dreaming mind had produced. A night fog had rolled in, obscuring the perimeter. A fat moon hung in the sky lighting the area with a ghostly glow. Shadows twisted between the trees as the fog crept in, curling like fingers over the grass. Then she saw her—Arlo—emerge from the gloom, silent as a prayer. She moved as if her billowing robes floated on a breeze. She moved like she owned the night.

Just then, Del felt a tingle in her right hand. She looked down at her palm and gasped in surprise. Her palm was covered in glowing, arcane symbols. The etchings of their old pact.

"You look like hell, girl," Arlo said. Her ancient voice scraped like gravel. She stood a few feet away, arms crossed, head tilted as if inspecting Del for the first time.

"Where have you been?" Del said. She remembered seeing fleeting visions of Arlo after her incident with Billy Bash, a mix of visages floating outside her old apartment window, and possibly while in the hospital. How real they were, she didn't know. They could have been dreams, just like this one.

But the old woman had been mysteriously absent for months. A low kind of angry frustration had built up in Del during that time. She didn't know if she'd been tricked, abandoned, or forgotten. But none of those options felt good.

"Been aroun.'"

In her dream, Del crossed her own arms in response. A strange power buoying her confidence.

"Oh? I thought maybe you would have wanted to know how I was." Her foot began to tap out her agitation.

"How you was?" Arlo eyed her sideways. "Bah! I knew how you was. You needed time to heal. You needed time to find yer path."

"Ha!" Del interrupted. "Find my path? A lot of good that did."

Arlo's hooded head tilted back slightly, as if not understanding the girl's frustration. Then it came forward again. "Yer on it, ain'tcha?"

"I'm not on anything," said Del.

Arlo shook her head. "Remember me sayin' 'You cain't halfway folla' a path; you won't get anywhere. And you cain't folla' no path at all, 'cause you'll end up where you doan wanna be.'"

"But I haven't found anything," Del blurted. "Nothing but paranoid dreams, weird trances with double vision, and, and…" Her frustration bound her to a stop in the form of a tight line across her face. "…and what about this?"

Del thrust her open hand toward the old woman.

"Why is this back?"

Arlo's eyes darted over Del's palm.

"Back? It was never gone," she said, looking straight into Del's eyes. "Dat's part of our pact, you remember?"

Del crossed her arms, tucking the hand away, out of sight. "I remember you were going to help me."

"Mmm." Arlo nodded. "I did. You on yer path now, but doan even know it. Open yer eyes and see it!"

"What? So, is this my path?" Suddenly they were standing on the sidewalk where they had first met. Across from them sat a dark alley where Del's *commotion* had taken place just a few months back. It seemed perfectly normal to be here, and Del continued without pause. "Wandering around, seeing spirit monsters, watching people die. Is that the path you set me on?"

Arlo's eyes narrowed. "Spirit monsters?"

"What have you done to me?" Her words came out jagged, half-accusation, half-plea.

Arlo's lips twitched, not quite a smile. "I helped you find yer path, Delphine Larouche." She floated nearer. Now they were in the cemetery where Arlo had taught Del about the spirit cord. "It's right in front of you."

Del flinched as a quick burst of heat flashed through her body. The burning image of Maggie DuBois jumped to her mind, and she watched as imaginary embers of the woman floated off her body, then winked out of existence.

"In front of me? There's nothing but death in front of me. Is that my path? What, am I supposed to burn up like them? Am I supposed to feel every bad thing that happens in this city?" Her voice rose, cracking. "Those marks you gave me—they're alive. I've felt them growing."

Arlo didn't move. Her eyes, deep pools of knowledge, watched Del. At that moment, Del thought back to the night she'd made the pact with Arlo, and not for the last time, thought she had made a mistake.

"They're growin' cause you're growin'. Those lines and symbols are the knowledge I gave you. You've added to that knowledge. You already had da sight. Now you ken see what others cain't—auras, spirits, the cords! Pert near the whole damn tapestry. Ain't that what you wanted? To see? To know?"

"Not like this." Del opened her right hand again, the symbols glowing faintly on her skin pulsed like a heartbeat. And Arlo could see that they *had* grown. What had started as just a few small symbols in the palm of Del's hand, had grown over the last few months. Tendrils now extended up each finger and had begun to snake out onto the inside of her wrist.

"I saw a woman die today," Del said. "She burned from the inside out. The things tore her apart and she burst into flames. Then I thought I was burning. I could feel what she felt. And then *I* was screaming. *I* was the one dying. Everyone looked at me like I was crazy."

"Show me," Arlo said.

And in her dream, it was easy to share the wraith experience. It began with the air in her lungs—after all, she had smelled the woman burning—which simply swelled up in her head and leaked out of her eyes in a type of dreamsmoke. The smoke became the wraiths, and a small image of Maggie DuBois, highlighted by an invisible spotlight, faded into view in the center of the smoke cloud. And there was Maggie, writhing and screaming as the things tore her apart, starring in her own movie trailer, on a miniature stage that had floated out of Del's mind. Her fifteen seconds of fame, literally going up in smoke before their dreaming eyes.

The writhing woman disappeared with a flash, and the wraith image was gone.

"Wraiths," Arlo murmured. Her gaze sharpened as her head

nodded. "You saw a wraith's work, today. They're hungry, them things. Dat's bad business."

"What are they?"

Now it was Arlo's turn to be perplexed. A gnarled hand came and rubbed her chin. After several seconds she spoke.

"It's been a long time since we've dealt with da likes of dem." Her eyes flashed to Del. "A long time. Wraiths ain't like spirits or ghosts."

"Aren't they all spirits?" Del interrupted. "How many layers are there to this damned tapestry?"

"Heh… how many layers? Why, if I knew dat, I don't spect I'd be here banterin' with you! I'd be on to my business and done." A sharp wave of her hand emphasized the point. "As far as what dey are, a spirit is just da essence of da soul. Da energy. Sometimes you ken see it floatin' around. But it doesn't have a direction or a purpose you know. It's just… left over. People think they see a ghost, but it could just be da left-over spirit-energy that collects together. Mayhap it wasn't even from da same person, just somethin' pulls it together like a cloud. It's dark and lonely on da other side, yeah."

Del remembered the time that Arlo had pulled back the veil and let her peer into the tapestry of the dead. Dark and lonely weren't the words she would use. Desolate and despairing seemed more appropriate.

"Spirits don't have a memory, but ghosts do. Enough of da spirit survived and it kept its memory. It can form a shape and often likes to show people who it was. Ghosts remember places, which is why dey haunt. But dey cain't always remember people."

"So, what about wraiths?" Del asked.

"Mmm… yeah, dat's bad business," Arlo said again. "Wraiths have been worked on, spirits dat have been cursed and manipulated, to a purpose. Old magic, black magic, is needed fer dat. A wraith has a will of its own to some degree. But it's tied to da one who created it, ya see. Why would someone create such a thing, just to let it loose? It works at da direction of a master, da one who gave it its power."

"So they were created to kill people?" Del asked. "That's it, just to kill?"

"Bah! Don't be stupid, girl! I said dey have a purpose. Whoever created them, gave 'em a purpose."

"So, what's the purpose?"

"To feed," Arlo said flatly. "It's da Aether they're after."

"Aether?"

Arlo nodded. "Aether. Da spirit-energy of one can bring life to another. Da strong feed off da weak."

At that moment, a Saturday morning cartoon flashed in Del's mind. Jimmy loved Saturday mornings, never failing to get up early and plant himself in front of the TV in the den downstairs. Del—if she was awake—would pour herself a cup of coffee, then join Jimmy as he ate bowl after bowl of cereal and watched the progression of cartoons that filled the morning airwaves.

The cartoon that had just flashed through her mind was of a small fish, which was suddenly swallowed up by a larger one. Then, as the camera zoomed out, a larger fish ate that one, then yet a larger one ate the last.

How many things were in the tapestry, she wondered, waiting to eat a weaker thing? And where was she in that hierarchy? In many ways she felt like a small fish which had just left the safety of its shallow pool, and through some cosmic hiccup, had been thrown into the ocean. Her problem was that she didn't know how big this ocean was, or how many creatures where in it.

Del shook her head. "But why now? What does it all mean?"

"Bah! Open yer eyes, girl. What'choo think it means? It means you finally seeing how this city works." And here Arlo spread her hands wide. "How the world works. Someone got eaten. Dat means someone is feedin'. Someone died, so someone ken live. It's as simple as dat."

Del stood in silence. She'd known this, in a way. Smart enough not to need it spelled out. But at times, she wished she couldn't see it all. It made her head hurt. Not just seeing unbelievable things only to learn that they're real, but then to have to contrast this idea of *real* with what could be completely made up in her brain. The tapestry was everchanging, and Del was lost somewhere in its weave. If only she could control one small part of it. If only she could weave the strands of the tapestry just enough to see through the confusion.

Arlo's eyes snapped up to Del. "You ken control it."

Del started at the comment. "I didn't say anything. How did you—Are you reading my mind?"

Arlo chuckled. "Heh, readin' it? I'm in it, ain't I? Besides," and her hands dismissively smoothed her long sleeves, "it ain't dat hard to read anyway."

Del caught the teasing tone.

"OK then, now what?" Del asked.

As if on cue, Arlo produced an amulet from within the folds of her robes. A small black stone, bound up in silver thread, hung from a thin cord. She held the amulet out to Del.

"Weave," Arlo said.

Del's hand instinctively reached for the amulet. Before she could ask what it was, its weight was in her palm. The arcane lines of knowledge—of the pact—that had pulsed dimly in her palm, flashed with a sudden brilliance. Whatever magic the amulet held, had just been shared with Del.

Del watched in amazement as the arcane symbols that lived within her palm grew with the new knowledge the amulet presented. Filigreed lines of insight wound around her fingers. Tendrils of understanding stretched up her arm. And somewhere in the back of her mind, something was pleased. The pieces of the cosmic puzzle that wove the everchanging tapestry of dead, were coming together, for she'd just been given another piece.

"Now you have to do something fer me," Arlo said quietly, her voice a distant whisper. "As written in our pact. As witnessed by the night. I have a task."

"Wha?" Del tried to ask, but her mind was fading rapidly.

"Free my sister."

Del's dreaming mind was retreating. Arlo was fading. Like the wraiths, the dream had fed on Del long enough, suckling her thoughts, and it was satiated. At least for now. Her mind was sinking into the void. Floating away. Almost gone.

"Sisss-terr?" Del mumbled.

"Free Dred."

"Dred?"

"Free Dred and you'll find yer path," said Arlo. "Free Dred… and weave."

Del fought the heavy darkness that was swallowing her. Her watery eyes burned to shut, but she forced them open one last time. She had one final question for the old woman.

"How… how did you… find me? In my dream."

"Find you?" Arlo said, curiously. "I didn't. You called me."

Then, like in a dream, Arlo was gone.

CHAPTER 24

"Have you seen Del today?" Armand asked Mama Dedé from the doorway to the den.

After a light dinner with Mama D and Jimmy, Armand had tried to focus in his library, but his thoughts refused to settle.

He'd roamed the big house for a while but needed to speak with someone.

He'd found her sitting in the downstairs den, which had been no surprise. She'd been spending a lot of time here lately. He assumed he knew why, but had yet to inquire on the subject.

"I was gonna' ask you the same thing, Frenchy." She set her cup of tea on the ornate table next to the couch.

"May I?" Armand motioned to a chair.

"Come on." She motioned for him to get on with it. "Not like I'm gonna charge you rent."

He smiled as he crossed the room. Day by day, he could see the old Mama D coming back, at least in spirit, but something was still off.

Armand settled into an armchair across from her, part of the cozy seating circle they now shared. Setting his brandy on the other end table, he gripped the wooden arms of the chair and looked around the room as if he were appraising it for the first time.

"I quite like this room," he said. "It's a wonder I haven't spent more time in it."

"Don't let me run you out," she said. "I can plop down anywhere."

"Oh, no, no!" Armand said. "That is not what I meant. In fact, I believe it suits you quite well. Besides," and he motioned to the ceiling, "I am perfectly happy… you know."

"Mmm hmm," she said. "Is that why you're wearin' a groove in the floorboards?"

Innocently, Armand pointed at himself as if to confirm she had the right person.

She waved her hand at him and a tangle of bracelets rattled. "Hell, Frenchy, you're walking right over my head most nights." She pointed to the same ceiling, indicating that part of the library sat right over the den. "You think I don't hear you shufflin' around up there? I don't need to trance for that."

Armand flushed. He'd planned to avoid that topic. He looked down at his hands in his lap.

"And on top of all that, Del's out all kinda hours, Frank ain't been around for a coon's age. And… and…"

Armand held his breath.

"And I'm sitting around here like an old cushion collectin' dust! Give me that brandy!"

Armand started as if he'd just been caught not paying attention in class. He looked up and saw Mama Dedé staring at him, a ringed finger pointing at his glass.

"Oh!" he said. "But of course." And grabbed up his glass, handing it to the woman.

She downed the liquid in one large gulp. A visible shiver moved through her.

"One moment, madame," Armand said with a gleam in his eye. And before the heat of the liquor had left her mouth, he was out the den door and heading up the library stairs.

She set down the glass and quickly wiped away the tears of frustration that had sprung into her eyes. Her growing frustrations had weighed heavily on her for months now, and she felt bad that her concerns had just been unleashed on Armand.

"Here we are," Armand said, returning from the library. His voice chirped with an almost musical quality. He held a full decanter of brandy and another crystal glass. "I believe this is long overdue." With that, he refilled her glass, poured his own, and put the bottle on the table. Then he sat on the other end of the couch from her.

He raised his glass. "Here's to getting our house back in order."

Mama D chuckled. She was pretty sure that Armand had no idea how out-of-sorts the house was now—at least her mental house—but she couldn't deny his optimism.

"Frenchy," she said, grinning, "you have no idea what's really going on."

Armand considered this a moment, thinking about the hypnosis session with Jimmy and all the other theories that swam in his head. He was pretty sure that Mama D didn't know the extent of his concerns, and he would keep those to himself for now. Why burden her with his wild theories, he thought. However, they were long overdue for a chat. So, as if accepting her challenge, he smiled broadly, clinked her glass, and said, "Do tell."

*

They chatted by candlelight late into the evening. Armand, so happy for the adult conversation, even if it was only half the normal audience, tried to mimic the ambiance of the library fireplace by lighting whatever candles he could find. By the time he'd finished, the room looked as if they planned to raise a spirit through the floor.

They talked about trivial things first, expertly skirting the real topics of concern that plagued them both. Mama D was pleased with her weight loss but hated the extra skin. Armand complained of a hip that was acting up. She mentioned that Jimmy probably needed to go to a dentist since his brushing habits weren't exactly the best. Armand hoped that Del's job was going to work out this time.

And in this way, they passed the time, each privately wondering if the other suspected their deception. But it was for their own good, they both thought. No need to burden them unnecessarily.

The old grandfather clock had just chimed. It was midnight now and Del had yet to return. Both noticed but said nothing.

"When's the last time you talked to Frank?" Mama D asked.

Armand had just refilled his glass and raised it to his absent friend. His cheeks had been rosy for an hour now. "I spoke with him briefly this morning. Or… perhaps yesterday. He said he was going out, so we didn't talk long." He took a sip in Frank's honor.

"How'd he sound?"

"Sound?" Armand shrugged slowly, the brandy softening his movements. "Eh, like Frank, I suppose. Why?"

Her mouth tightened into a scowl of exasperation. "Men. You don't know nothin'. Tomorrow you drive over and find out what he's doin'. You don't think it's funny he ain't been here in a spell?"

Armand watched the brandy swirl around the inside of his glass.

His thoughts went back to the spinning watch and the hypnosis session with Jimmy. He was anxious to get back to his research, and a second session with the boy. The abrupt end to the first weighed heavily on him. It had only been a day since it had occurred, and Armand had secretly watched the boy for any negative signs but had seen none. Perhaps they were in the clear.

"Well?" Mama D said.

"What?" Armand looked up from his glass. His fogged mind tried to replay the last thing she'd said. "Oh… yes, Frank can be funny, I suppose." He wiggled his fingers as Frank often did when whistling his *Twilight Zone* sound and smiled. He raised his glass again.

"Frenchy! You didn't hear a damn word I said. You need to take your nose out that glass."

Armand looked at the glass and squinted. Small specks of light sparkled off the edges of the cut crystal, pulling his gaze forward. Behind that, inside the dark liquid, several random, unformed thoughts swirled.

Around and around, the dark liquid and the plaguing thoughts played a game of follow the leader. They chased after the other, leading, following, fleeing. Their axis, that central point of connectivity at the bottom of the glass *(pit of his stomach)* where all the concerns were born, was hidden from him. No matter how fast he swirled the liquid in the glass, he couldn't see the bottom.

But something was there driving the whole thing.

The warm light of the candles cascaded like diamond rain from the cut edges of the glass.

Bright flashes hiding dark thoughts danced before him, and like a fox chasing a rabbit, his fogged mind blindly followed.

Sparkling, sparkling thoughts where great mysteries were hidden.

Sparkle.

Jimmy.

The strange voice.

(A man's voice.)

He squeezed his eyes shut, trying to focus, then opened them wide. He suddenly thought of the tainted brandy that had nearly done them in last summer. His hand pulled the glass away as the swirling liquid began to settle.

Those random thoughts, the seemingly unrelated ideas that had driven his pacing feet night after night, were suddenly combined in the amber liquid. They melted together, like a phantasm, into a single idea.

"…tricky old bastard," he mumbled, staring at the glass.

"What?" Mama D said. She'd been watching him, staring into his glass, but was taken aback by this statement. "Tricky ol'— why'd you say that?"

Armand continued staring at the glass, which now rested on his knee. "You know we never talked about it," he said. His words were slushy, but coherent.

"Oh, lawd," Mama D muttered. She could see that he'd suddenly slipped into the next level of inebriation. Like most people, Armand had several stages of intoxication. She'd witnessed them many times with Frank. He'd just hit his deeply contemplative stage. "Frenchy, you might want to—"

"No," Armand said, waving her off. "We said." An unsteady finger went up to emphases the point, then began to wag with the syllables of his words. "Remember? We said. One day. One day we'd have to talk about it."

Her voice was low. "Frenchy, I don't know if tonight is the—"

He shook his head, stopping her. "But we never did." He squinted at her and began nodding, as if to say, *See, I told you so. I knew we'd be bad. Let's confess. We should have talked about this before now.*

"Frenchy, don't—"

"What if he's back?" He whispered conspiratorially. "The tricky ol'—"

His waging finger went to his lips to emphasize the secret nature of the idea. He whispered past his finger with exaggerated lips. "—tricky ol' bastard."

Mama D instinctively tranced around the room, as if the mere mention of this idea would call something from the shadows. The trance was acceptable, but still not as sharp as it should be.

Armand continued. "The strange words on the paper," he pointed again for emphasis, "we never spoke about the strange words."

Mama Dedé knew quite well what Armand was referring to. The night they had celebrated Del's return had been a heart-felt reunion. Many missing pieces about the events of the previous months had been put into place. However, a new puzzle had emerged. The strange notes that Del had found. They attributed them to Jimmy, due to the childlike lettering and use of crayons. But they had an unsettling look about them. Then there had been the odd giggle that had come from Jimmy. No one knew what to make of it. Furtive glances confirmed that it was not a topic to be discussed in front of the boy, but an implication was made that they'd discuss it later.

They never did.

Each person grappled with their own issues after that reunion, and it was simply too easy to avoid the topic altogether. But here it was, surfaced again through a sparkling glass of brandy.

"You about done?" Mama D tilted her head towards Armand as her eyebrows curved up.

Armand squinched his face and raised his hands in question. This time some of the brandy did escape onto the back of his hand. "What?" he said. "I'm simply—"

"You're simply drunk is what you are," she said. "And that ain't no time to have a real discussion about… you know what."

Armand thought about the hypnosis session. Was Sparkle still working on the boy's subconscious? Did the voice inflections—or the lack of the impediment—mean anything? Had he misunderstood Jimmy's answer? He wasn't sure. He hadn't been sure right after the session, and his addled brain certainly wasn't sure now. He debated telling Mama Dedé about the session, then thought better of it. Another hypnosis session was in order first.

"—help Del if he is, and I can't tell what's goin'—."

Armand blinked and looked around the room, realizing he'd just missed part of the conversation.

"Have you read the paper lately?" he interrupted. Sitting the glass down, he reached for his cold pipe.

"What? The paper?" Mama D looked around the den as if one were lying nearby. "Well, I—"

"Spontaneous. Human. Combustion," Armand said. Two fingers in a V-shape went up. "Two cases. The second one just last night." He pointed in a random direction. Then he pulled his pocket watch from his vest and squinted at it. "Or… this morning rather."

Mama Dedé said nothing, only looked at him, listening.

"It's only a theory of course," he said. His mind seemed to have cleared considerably in the last few seconds, now that it had something to latch onto. "And, it's quite rare. I haven't heard of another case for many years."

"In the paper?" she asked.

Armand nodded. "The only reason I know of the second—because it only happened early this morning—is because of the late edition of the paper, you know, the afternoon version."

She nodded.

He recounted the deaths of Buddy Tibbets and Maggy DuBois, as the newspaper articles had reported them.

Incredulous, Mama D crossed her arms and said, "Two people go up in flames, and you're blaming the boogeyman?"

He raised his hands in defense. "Of course, the paper can't definitively state they are spontaneous combustion. It is an unproven theory, you understand. But the evidence is compelling."

"What evidence?"

A grimace slid onto Armand's face. "It's the way they burn. In many cases, only the appendages remain. The fire seems to start in the torso and burns from the inside out."

"There were witnesses?"

Armand shrugged, he knew it was a wild theory, but he also knew something that Mama D didn't, and that was Jimmy's strange response. "The newspapers, you know how they are, they never tell the full details."

Mama D's mouth twisted sideways. The skepticism was clear.

"Frenchy, I think you're lookin' for a spook story."

"There's a way we could find out for sure," he said.

"How?"

"Ask someone in the newspaper business." He twisted his mustache.

"And who do you know in the—?"

He raised his hands in defense, as if to say, 'I know a secret'.

"Oh, no you don't," Mama D said. "That girl don't need to be lookin' into—"

She stopped as the grandfather clock struck one a.m.

"Damn!" she said. "Where is that girl?"

CHAPTER 25

(Wake up.)

Del bolted awake at the sound of the strange voice. It was both inside and outside of her head at the same time. In one lurching move, she rolled upright on the bench, legs curled in front of her, ready to strike. Her hands were pulled up in front of her face positioned for both defense and attack.

Étienne stepped back, surprised at the response. But more surprising was the faint flash of light he'd seen spread out around Del. It had been brief, only a fraction of a second that most people would not have seen, *could* not have seen. But most people did not have his eyes. To his eyes, the moment the words left his mind, the faintest glow had started somewhere within the sleeping girl. A protective spell, perhaps, that he'd never witnessed before. A heartbeat later, when his words seemed to register, the faint light exploded around her in silence. Then he watched as her body coiled into itself. She was sitting up before her eyes had opened. But when they did, they were awake and deadly.

And somewhere within those split-second motions, he even imagined that the flash had illuminated something down the insides of her arms. But he couldn't be sure.

"Don't be scared," he said. "It's me, Étienne."

He squatted down to show he was no threat and rested on his haunches. Elbows on knees, he steepled his fingers in front of his mouth and leaned forward. He held her in an intense, curious gaze.

Del blinked awake and relaxed slightly. Resting her feet on the bench she wrapped her arms around her knees. She wasn't cold but now felt the effects of her long nap. The hugging embrace was more for balance than anything.

"What are you doing?" she asked, sleepily.

His gaze never left her. "I was going to ask you the same thing."

Del looked around, saw her bike laying on the ground, then remembered where she was. But it was darker than it should have been.

"I dozed off," Del said. "I had…" Something inside her resisted against dredging up the wraith story. Whether it was concern for sharing the story, or a simple weariness, she couldn't tell. But she trusted her instinct. "I just went for a ride and ended up here." Looking around, she added, "Wherever here is."

"You should be careful," Étienne said. "It's not safe to sleep where there are—"

He tilted his head back, considering his words.

"Where there are what?"

"So many prying eyes," he said.

Del flashed the park. They were the only ones here.

"There's no one else here," she said.

Her confidence in the statement surprised him. And a flash of that surprise escaped his face before he could conceal it. How odd it was that she did not seem afraid of him, he thought.

Del arched an eyebrow. "So, I guess that makes *you* Mr. Prying Eyes."

His steepled hands went to his knees. "My dear, Del," then he locked his long fingers together, hanging between his knees, and leaned forward. "I don't pry." The slightest smile curled one side of his mouth. "But I do observe."

Now it was Del's turn to steeple her fingers. "So, why have you been observing me? Just out for a stroll before dinner at—" She glanced at her watch, then held her wrist out in surprise.

"At three a.m.?" he said, then shrugged. "Not unheard of. But—"

"Oh, my God," Del said. "It's 3 a.m.? Mama D's going to be worried sick."

Étienne continued. "—alas, not tonight. Instead, I was checking up on something."

"I gotta go," Del said, then tapped her watch with her finger. "Is it really this late?"

Étienne stood up and extended his hand to Del. "Late? Early? Who's to say. It really depends on one's perspective."

Del stood up without his help. He politely withdrew his hand with a nearly imperceptible nod.

"However," he continued, "my perspective on the risk still stands. You really should be careful. I've had several reports of—." He paused.

Del had picked up her bike and just thrown a leg over the seat when he stopped. "Reports?" she asked. "Reports about what?"

Étienne extended his hand towards the park opening and began to walk. "Please," he said. "Allow me to escort you for—"

"I can find my way home, thank—"

His hand came up swiftly, cutting her off. "I'll escort you," he stated. It wasn't a question.

The moment his hand had moved she instinctively flashed but found no threat. However, in that microsecond of movement, she did see the doppelganger view of his hand. Quickly replaying the scene, with his body standing in one place, one moment his hand was at his side, then a fraction later it was swiping the air to cut her off. Somehow it had jumped forward faster than her eyes could see it. She thought back to the day at Café DuMonde and her forgotten bike; one moment it was missing, the next moment it was there, leaning against a pole. She'd caught a doppelganger view of him then, only didn't know who he was. How fast had he come and gone through her field of view to cause the strange vision? Or was it that her vision was simply shorting out due to overload?

This thought flashed through her mind then was gone. *I'll escort you,* still echoing in her head.

"Have it your way," she said. Then began walking her bike forward as she straddled the seat.

"So," she said, "do you patrol all the parks, or just the ones with napping girls?"

With hands sunk into the pockets of his suit *(tuxedo?)* pants, and with white dress shirt open to the night breeze, Étienne looked perfectly comfortable, as if he'd just stepped out of a late-night reception for a bit of fresh air. His matching coat would be draped across the back of a chair, somewhere, with an untied bowtie *(definitely tuxedo)* hanging from an inside pocket.

He smiled crookedly. Del caught a glimpse of the smile, and for a moment thought it was because of the elegant party image she'd just conjured of him. It was as if he'd just read her mind.

"You mean, do I seek the damsel in distress?" He spread his hands to the night. "There are few things left for me to seek that I have not already found. But I have learned over the years that a damsel in distress?" He tilted his head in consideration. "Is rarely in distress."

Intrigued, Del looked at him. "Oh, really? If not in distress, then what?"

Étienne looked up, seemingly to study the stars. "I don't know. Lying in wait?"

"Lying in wait?" Del chuckled, not sure if he was serious. "Wow, a real renaissance man you are."

Still walking, Étienne feigned indignation, then bowed his head towards her. "Correction, madame. Not *a* renaissance man, but *the* renaissance man."

"Oh, I see," Del said. She thought she heard a jest in his tone but wasn't sure. Flashing the area again, she reassured herself that she wasn't being led into a trap. Only the two of them were present on this part of the street.

"How do you do that?" Étienne asked.

"Do what?"

"That thing you just did with your mind. I felt it."

Del stopped and stared at him. "How do you know I—"

"I felt it," he said, pausing for emphasis. "I'm not sure *what* I felt. It's hard to describe. But I felt it, nonetheless. It was not completely unpleasant."

Del studied his face closely. She had interacted with other people who had the sight. Certainly, with Mama Dedé, but also with a few others that she had been introduced to. It was well known that you could see when someone had been trancing into a vision that you were looking at, but she'd never heard of someone being able to feel it. The cord business was a different matter. Billy Bash had certainly felt that. But a trance was just looking at an afterimage. The person wasn't even there any longer.

To prove this to herself, she flashed again, tracing their journey back to the park.

They both flinched and blurted out.

"Please don't do that," Étienne said.

"What are you?" Del asked.

But their words fell over each other, tangled and urgent. The night had suddenly become very small around them as they stared at one another, two enigmas drifting dangerously close to each other's orbit.

A shudder ran through Étienne.

Del's heartrate ticked up, not understanding what she had just seen in her trance. But also imagining that she had seen a snarl flash behind his eyes, only to disappear just as quickly.

Each one waited for the other to speak.

Étienne finally broke the silence. "Please, you must understand, whatever you're doing, with your mind, I can feel it. I know it's not aggression, but my… my instincts can't always tell."

"I don't know what you're saying," Del said. "Your instincts? Like, they're not under your control?"

"I've had to work very hard, over the years, to learn to control them." He wanted to get off the topic, but then added, "It's a work in progress."

Del nodded and began to walk her bike forward again.

"But enough about that," Étienne said. "What did you see when you… looked into me?"

"I'm not sure," Del said. "I guess I'm still trying to figure out my own instincts. Mama D—she's... well, she's sort of like my mentor and, like an aunt I guess—but she just calls it the sight, or trancing." And Del described the general process and what it looked like. "But with you, there are... well, missing scenes, I guess is the best way to describe it. I can't see the full trail. It's like you're there in a few scenes, but not all of them. I know that doesn't make any sense, but that's what I saw."

"Or didn't see," he said.

Del nodded, then remembered the day at the café. "It was the same thing the day you returned my bike. You know, to the café? When I noticed it there, I tried to follow the scene back to see where it had come from, but there were all these missing frames in the vision. I couldn't make sense of it."

"I see," he said.

"What did it feel like?" she asked. "The trance, I mean. I've never heard of someone being able to feel it."

With hands in his pants pockets, and a contemplative look on his face, he considered the question. "Like fingers, I suppose."

"Fingers?"

He turned and looked at her. "Yes, fingers, in my mind. Down my spine. It's rather alarming if you're not expecting it. It's as if you can sense the predator behind you but can't see it."

It was Del's turn to contemplate this new bit of information. "Did you feel it the day you returned my bike? You know, afterward, when I would have been trancing?"

He shook his head. "Not that I recall. Perhaps it's the proximity that makes it possible to feel. Which brings me to why I came looking for you in the first place."

"You came looking for me?" Del said.

"Yes. I had reports of a… disturbance, let's say."

"A disturbance?"

"For lack of a better word," he said. "I'm sure you know, there are many layers to this city, any city really, but this one especially."

Del thought about all the strange things she'd seen over the last year and a half. Then she thought about the wraiths. "Yeah, I've realized that."

"And you know that there are… forces, at play as well?"

"Yes," she said. "Well, some of them, I guess." She didn't know Étienne very well and was unsure how much to tell him. Perhaps she knew more than he did.

"That's why you need to be careful," he said. "That's why I insisted on escorting you tonight. You were drawing too much attention to yourself."

They stopped and Del realized that they were in front of the Monteleone hotel.

"You're talking about my dream?" Del said.

Étienne nodded. "Yes, partially. I'm unclear on the implications, but I can feel the tension building."

"Tension?"

"Yes. It's in the underbelly of the city. There are forces at play that we haven't felt for a long time."

Del's eyes narrowed. "How long?"

The sly smile returned to his face. "Let's save that for another time. Would you like a further escort?"

"No, I'm fine from here," she said, knowing that she was fine from the beginning. "But thank you."

He nodded. A mix of compassion and concern ran through his eyes.

"Please be careful," he said. "You've come into focus for some. I need to check on something, but we'll talk soon."

Del held his gaze for another moment, then started peddling down the street, her head even more jumbled than when she'd rode away from the wraith vision in the alley yesterday morning. Too many things at once. Too many strange faces emerging from the dark. It felt like before—that slow build before the storm. The time the Gris-gris man first showed up, even the time Mama D and Armand fell sick, too many things were happening at once, and no one paid much attention until it was almost too late.

And it was happening again. Only this time, she wouldn't be caught off guard. This time she would be prepared. She decided then and there to find out where the wraiths had come from and why they were here. Only, for the life of her, she couldn't figure out what Étienne was about.

Halfway down the block, she flashed behind her and saw that he was still watching her from the steps of the hotel.

She let the trance fade just as he brushed a phantom touch from his arm.

CHAPTER 26

It was late morning, and Del sat at the kitchen table sipping coffee. A damp towel was wrapped around her head from her shower. Having slept late, and missing breakfast, she now scrounged whatever leftovers she could find. Half of a bacon and biscuit sandwich sat on her plate with a glob of grape jelly smeared on top. She was scanning the newspaper.

"Woo-wee!" Mama D said, as she entered. She'd just started a load of laundry. "Those clothes were rank. What'd you do, sleep in 'em for a week?"

She went to the coffee pot and while pouring a cup, tranced to see what Del was reading. To her surprise, the trance came through clearly and she smiled to herself.

She felt good until she saw the article.

Del was reading about the strange burning deaths that Armand had mentioned last night.

When Del didn't respond, Mama D turned towards her, leaning against the counter, and said, "Well?"

Del looked up, bleary-eyed. "Wha? Oh, I'm sorry. I guess I'm not awake yet. I was just..." She looked back at the paper as her voice trailed off, her fingers tracing over the newspaper article.

"Mmm-hmm," said Mama D. "I'd be tired too, if I came in after all kinda hours."

"I'm sorry," Del said absently. "I didn't mean to worry anyone. I was..." And her mind drifted from the story on the page to the reason she'd left the house so early yesterday morning. "...just following up on some work stuff and..." Scanning the black and white columns of the newspaper, reading about the strange deaths, had triggered the visions all over again. Like an evil movie projector stuck on PLAY, she replayed parts of the alley scene in her head, then the bike ride, the park, over and over. Each repeating scene showed a new detail, a new bit of horror, and she couldn't look away. Whether it was a trance or not, it no longer mattered. Images were images. Until they burned you to cinders.

A small sound slipped from Mama Dedé's mouth, but Del didn't hear.

"...and I guess I lost track of time," Del said to the paper.

Wraiths swirled in Del's vision, and like a drunk spotting a fresh bottle, something primal in her stirred. Dark dreams swirled up around her, probing at some grotesque pleasure center deep in her brain.

(Drink. Drink deep. The juice is at the bottom.)

The cup in Mama D's hand tilted as her fingers went slack. A splash of coffee spilled over the side before she could tighten her grip. Watching the girl, who seemed to be half in a daydream remembering something, Mama D saw what Del was remembering. Whether the girl was trying to share her trance or not, Mama D couldn't tell. In fact, she couldn't tell if *she* was trancing at that moment. But she was seeing. Everything that played through Del's mind, through her memories, played through Mama Dedé's. And it was all consuming. It was like nothing she'd ever felt before.

The wraiths in Del's vision morphed, twisting from one horrid shape to another. Sometimes they had faces, sometimes not. Sometimes there was a whole body, other times a twisted mass of people writhed in the air.

There were too many legs, too many body parts. What had gone into making these abominations Del could not tell, nor could she look away.

"Oh…" Another sound slipped from the woman's throat. Through some magnetic power of Del, Mama D was pulled fully into the girl's trance. This wasn't their first shared trance, like when they'd seen each other's essence in the shared memory.

This was larger and more terrifying.

"There's something I…" Del said, absently.

Del's mind devoured the wraith scenes, and Mama D was forced to feed with her. The woman saw the people fall under the weight of the assault. She felt their fear as the black shapes tore at them. She felt goosebumps run over her skin just a second after they did Del's neck and arms. Her own throat swallowed in response to Del remembering the overwhelming desire to drink from Billy's cord.

"…need to ask you about," Del finished.

Sparks.

Mama D saw the sparks as the souls were torn apart, violated, devoured.

"Del," she whispered. "Stop."

The bodies burned chaotic, hectic, racing towards their fiery end. Mama D held up one ringed hand and squinted her eyes against the bright sparks shooting from the burning bodies. They looked like human sparklers, she thought morbidly.

"Del!" the woman yelled as her coffee cup shattered on the floor.

Del's attention snapped to her mentor. She saw many things at once. A wet stain of coffee creeping down her blouse. The doppelganger vision of the coffee cup, breaking against the floor, then unbreaking, as her mind replayed it. The ringed hand moving up to shield her eyes before it came back down. The look of terror that had steadily grown on her mentor's face.

And Armand.

Her doppelganger vision showed a long ghostly trail of Armand-images as he had walked towards the kitchen to greet them, stopping just outside the kitchen door when they'd begun to speak. He'd witnessed the entire thing.

*

An hour later, after Armand had made a full second breakfast for his favorite ladies, Del had finished her story. She'd told them about her first session after meeting with Mr. Bobby and how she'd peered into the death of Buddy Tibbets. They understood why her mind had the need to look for safety concerns after the Billy Bash incident but were concerned about it wandering off on its own dreaming-trance sessions.

"Fascinating," Armand said, slowly pacing the kitchen. "It's like sleepwalking, only—" His hands absently patted his vest for his pipe which was sitting securely in the ashtray on the kitchen table where he'd left it only moments ago. He'd suddenly realized that one didn't actually *walk* during a trance, so he needed a different analogy. "No, more like Lucid dreaming I suppose. It's really quite fascinating."

The women looked at each other with hidden grins. *Here we go, again,* was the message.

Talking to no one in particular, Armand's mind tumbled down the rabbit hole of curious ideas. "Lucid dreaming is where one realizes they are dreaming but doesn't wake up. And by not waking, they can control the dream. Fly around. Visit… the moon I suppose. But..." Not finding his pipe, his hands had wandered to random objects in the kitchen, searching for hidden clues. "…but, no, you're already in a trance-like state, so you didn't awake." He corrected his thought process. "Of course!" His finger shot up. "Trauma-induced, random, lucid, sleep-trancing!" Armand stored this new term, with the touch of his finger, onto a used notepad that hung next to the telephone on the wall. He tapped it twice for safe keeping, as he had every intention of researching the idea.

Mama Dedé cleared her throat. "Alright, Frenchy, save some for Sherlock."

"Wha?" Armand turned and saw two patiently waiting faces. "Oh, my apologies," he said, returning to the table. "I just get so… you know."

"We know," the women said in unison. Their faces told him they wouldn't want it any other way.

Del had lost the shower garb at some point during breakfast and now sat in her standard T-shirt and jeans. With her head titled, resting in one hand, she fidgeted with a bandeau trying to get it to contain her hair

"But we think we got bigger problems than just your wandering mind," Mama Dedé said to Del.

Del's eyes turned towards her mentor. After the Billy Bash incident, they'd all told each other that to get through these supernatural issues as safely as possible, they needed to be honest with each other. Del had done that, to a degree, but so many things had happened lately, she didn't know how much to include them in. She wasn't sure if what she'd experienced over the last few days was all connected to a new threat, or simply the way her life would always be. It was exhausting to think she'd need to explain every little nuance of a shadow her mind focused on, just to stay true to the promise of sharing.

But Del thought she knew what Mama D was getting at. There were some large concerns that had been consuming her thoughts of late, as well. Not to mention the strange request from Arlo and warning from Étienne. But when she'd told them that one of the wraiths had seen her, had actually looked at her during her episode outside the alley, they nodded as if their late-night, brandy-fueled hunch had been prophetic. There was simply too much evidence to ignore.

"Bigger problems like—?" Del asked Mama D.

Mama D sipped the last of her cold coffee and set the cup down. It clinked in the saucer, where a light circle of coffee marked its resting place.

"We need to look," the woman said. Her head nodded slightly. A clock on an open shelf ticked off the seconds, patiently waiting for the next and the next, until the words would be spoken. "But I can't do it on my own." The words were delivered quietly and with humility.

For months they had been bitter words, slowly forming in the pit of the old woman's stomach. Bile and acid had formed them, sour breath and heartache had raised them to the back of her throat. But, it had been her pride that had chewed them back, kept them in place, kept them hidden in the event that one more practice session, one more pot of tea, one more prayer would restore her power. But she felt their time was running short. There were multiple facets to her concern, but overall, she felt their time was running short.

Over the many months they'd lived in Armand's house, despite the spirit attacks and misadventures, a loving family had formed. But in the eyes of the law, in the courts of formality and procedure, there was no family. There were simply four people living in a house, two older, two younger, and that was it. If something happened to one or the other of them, would the rest survive? Could they survive?

It was these thoughts, among many, that had consumed Mama Dedé during her recovery. And it was the concern she felt for Del which had finally taken the bitter words from the back of her throat and shaped them into the words she had just spoken.

Mama Dedé shook her head slowly. "I can't do it on my own. The vision is slow to return. Mayhap it won't ever. Not like it used to be, anyway." She was holding Del's hand now across the table. "But this mornin', whenever you were… daydreaming, or whatever it was. I could see then."

Del's head snapped up. She knew something had happened to cause Mama D to drop the coffee cup. And they'd started to explore it when Armand had first walked in, but the conversation had quickly turned to Del. She was watching her mentor intently.

A pinched grin creased Mama Dedé's face, and she nodded. "I could see through your trance, Del. And not just, you know, from the side. I was in it. You pulled me into it, somehow."

It was Del's turn to shake her head. "I don't… I don't know how that…"

"I didn't think so," Mama D said, releasing her hand. "But ya did. And before that," she nodded her head towards the coffee pot, "when

I first walked in, I could see what you were readin'. My own trance was crystal clear, like before." Here she looked wistfully at some point in the air. "But it wasn't me, not completely. I know that now. It was you. Somehow… I… I used a bit that you didn't need. Some bit that you sort of… shed off like that damn hair all over the place."

A short laugh caught in the woman's throat, causing tears to spring to her eyes. They were quickly wiped away but not hidden. Everyone knew anyway.

Del started to reach for her mentor, but the woman drew herself up.

"But I still have a thing or two to teach you," she said, rubbing her eyes and cheeks. "And you too." She pointed at Armand for good measure. "I just…" She looked back at Del. "…need a little jumpstart."

Del smiled, wiping tears from her own eyes. She was silently nodding. If in any way she could help restore her mentor's ability, even if it only ended up being a loan, she would do it. This was her family after all.

"Arghh," Armand said wiping his eyes, "blasted smoke went right in my eye." He peered suspiciously at the pipe he'd just lit.

Del put her hands over her mouth, covering a smile, and simultaneously wiping the last tears away.

Looking back at her mentor, Del spoke through her hands. "The tricky 'ol bastard?" Saying the name too loudly seemed a sure way to curse the decision before they could get started.

Mama Dedé nodded, then looked at Armand. Just as quietly she said, "The tricky 'ol bastard?" The unspoken question to him was if he was ready to go down this road again. Ready to help protect them once more as they actively sought an evil they didn't really understand.

"We'll need Frank," he said. "I'd feel much better if he's here. I'll call him. Then…" He looked slowly around the kitchen, as if he may never see it again. "Yes, then… the tricky old bastard."

The three sat nodding solemnly.

Jimmy, sitting upstairs in the library, engrossed in another *black queen endgame*, absently nodded in unison.

CHAPTER 27

The Gris-gris opened his eyes to nothing.

(Void.)

This thought, as random and fleeting as it was, stirred an unease in him which he did not understand. The word was not familiar to him, but nonetheless, caused his core to tremble. Had he been more formed, he may have actually trembled, but floating in the darkness of the unformed, he was weightless.

Had they made it through? Had they moved into the *Misi sipokni* and traveled outside of their time? Had they been called forward to another place by a spell he'd cast into the great beyond?

He floated in this dark space for an unmeasurable amount of time. He nearly closed invisible eyelids over his unseeing eyes when he felt a faint presence near him. It was that of Mr. Sandgrove. The feeling was very weak, but it was there, and because of its proximity he suddenly remembered where he was.

But why couldn't he see?

Where were his eyes?

Something that should have been his hand reached out and felt nothing. Nothing was there to touch, because his hand wasn't there. Only the memory of it.

He raised what should have been his head—at least the idea of it—and the thought-motion sent him floating away like a spider-silk shadow.

He struggled for existence, struggled to maintain control.

Something had happened. Something was resisting his effort to reform. He was expending too much energy. It was as if his energy was being consumed by...

(A Void)

...some unseen force. It was as if whatever time he'd arrived in did not want him here. And the thought terrified him.

Feeling their master's torment, Umbra and Susurrus were suddenly by his side, feeding to him what they could of their own essences, but they were barely there themselves.

What has become of us? The Gris-gris man thought to the two remaining wraiths. *Have we failed?*

An image of Praeco flashed in his mind and he remembered the betrayal. Then it all came back to him. They *had* made it through the mist. All of them, even the Knot.

They had begun to feed, they had begun to reform, but it was too slow. There was too little Aether to sustain them all, even to get them to a point of equilibrium. And that's what they needed more than anything right now. The Gris-gris man needed to stabilize. The feedings from the two remaining wraiths had grown thin and watery. After Praeco's betrayal, they had fled back to the hiding place and in their predictably protective manner, hovered close to their master, fearing an even greater betrayal by their brother. Their hunting trips had become infrequent and ineffective ventures, consisting mostly of animals found near the riverbank. But animal Aether wasn't the same. In fact, one couldn't really categorize it as Aether at all, but it was something. It was something more than air, yet almost as thin as the mist. And in his rapidly deteriorating state, his two closest disciples had nearly starved the lot of them into oblivion.

But he was awake now, or at least, he was thinking. And that gave him a final chance to save himself, and possibly some of his family.

He remembered—the Knot had begun to stir. The thing in the third boat was trying to wake up. All he had to do was feed from that, begin consuming the Knot, which was why it was created in the first place, and he would be renewed. In fact, he would be renewed to such a state that he may become like a God. Yes, he'd become like a God and then he would deal with Legba and any other entity that thought to oppose him.

But the thought was folly. His addled mind was at least able to understand that. He didn't have the strength to feed from the Knot. In fact, if he mistakenly came too close to the third boat—or let his thoughts wander too closely—the Knot was liable to feed on him. It was awaking after all. He remembered hearing the rumblings of the giant, multi-chambered stomach, groaning with hunger-pain as it struggled to wake up. It wanted to awaken so it could feed. It had other plans for its future.

So, with the risk too great to approach the third boat, with his essence draining faster than anticipated, and with the two remaining wraiths skittering around him like nervous birds, there was only one other thing for him to do.

(Remember the words.)

*

(Remember the words, John. That's the only way.)

In his floating degraded mind, he remembered this thought. How long it had taken him to pull the memory forth he could not tell, for he was no longer anchored to a specific time. His presence was so thin now, so tenuous, he felt he was stretched across all times and places, leaving him no place at all.

But he was here.

He thought, therefore he was.

And if he was, he had a memory.

And if he could remember, he could pull the words forth.

It was a spell that had been tied to a ritual, the darkest of covenants.

He remembered setting the hook during a long night in the swamp. When the twelfth disciple had been gathered, all had performed a ritual of sacrificial communion. Performed by all for the benefit of their savior. It was a blood-binding summons.

"Come now, my bones, my blood, my breath—
Come forth from shadowed, darkest death.
I summon thee, who bound thy soul—
To feed the flame that keeps us whole."

And when the disciples had performed the ritual in the swamp around the roaring fire, they had each, of their own accord, spilled their blood, first into the fire, then into John's open mouth as he knelt to accept their offering, then a final drop back into the fire. This ritual was the only time John Montanet, Dr. John, or the Gris-gris man had ever knelt before the disciples, but it was this act that bound them to the words. And John knew that once the words were spoken, they were upon the wind and would live forever.

And in this most dire moment, the fading essence of what had become the final abomination, the Gris-gris man, remembered the words and prepared to say them.

But he had one bit of charity left to give.

Umbra, Susurrus, he thought weakly, *hunt and feed me.*

The two nervous wraiths vibrated in their diminishing states. If they left now their master may die, dissolve completely, and if that happened, who would hold the magic together? How would they survive without their master?

Hunt and feed me, was his final command to them, a faintest thought. And in a desperate, hectic state, the two remaining wraiths flew off to hunt for their final time.

*

An indeterminate amount of time passed, the Gris-gris man had no means of measuring it now, but he dared not wait any longer. He only hoped they'd gotten far enough away to not sense his next thought.

The shadows in the void moved uncomfortably, they felt a shift in their world. The shadows—what remained of the disciples—moved in the darkness toward the essence of their master. He was somewhere close but was nearly nonexistent.

Then a thought came into their shadow minds.

"Come now, my bones, my blood, my breath—
Come forth from shadowed, darkest death.
I summon thee, who bound thy soul—
To feed the flame that keeps me whole."

Just one little word. That's all that was needed. Such a simple ploy, changing 'us' to 'me' and the meaning was altogether different.

The words had been spoken and were upon the wind. All who

heard them, and who were bound by them, had to obey.

And the sacrificial communion began again for the last time.

The first of the disciples, in their tattered-shadow state, to come forward, did so with little hesitation. The spell had been set into their very being. Wriggle and pull as they might, they could not throw the hook. When the disciple came forward, there was no slicing of the wrist to spill the blood, for there was no hand nor blood. There was only the will to be devoured, the desire to be consumed, to take what little Aether was left that kept them tethered to existence and give it away.

And with a mental ripping of the soul from imagined fingers, the first disciple tore themselves open and felt their Aether float free. Their existence quickly faded but not before sensing a great sucking force, like depleted bellows that suddenly found air. And with a tiny spark, the Gris-gris man absorbed the first disciple.

Then panic set in.

Like sheep smelling the first drop of blood in a cold morning slaughter, the disciples began bleating and shuffling. They felt the pull of the spoken spell, had just begun to understand what it meant, but could not escape.

The next disciple moved forward in space and time as it ripped open from the inside out. This one had been a bit stronger than the first, and thought it remembered pain, if not felt it. But an instant later, its Aether floated out into the void and was absorbed by the Gris-gris man. Only then did the ember begin to glow.

Like the last ember of a long dying fire which is touched by an errant breeze, the ember glowed to life one final time. Usually this was the final act of the ember as all fuel around it had been burnt to ash. But there were seven more disciples to go. And when the remaining disciples saw the glowing ember, a strange thing occurred. A mad terror washed over them. A final terror to carry them to the Desert of Dust on the screams of insane finality. They began ripping themselves apart, some from madness, some from confusion, others from ecstasy. The mad-terror glowing ember was the first they'd seen in a void-night, and it was a beacon. It was a beacon of their master's voice and salvation and beyond the mist and into the promised land and the Aether was their gift unto the ember, a way to get back to the light, back to their savior. And the Gris-gris man drank of their sacrifice, gorged himself of their desire and his ember became a flame, and the flame roared as it sparked with energy and the disciple-ghosts flung themselves onto the fire, ripping and tearing themselves, for the final sacrifice.

During the communion, as the Gris-gris man's mind was restored of all the worldly knowledge he'd gained through the years, a faint warning was lost in the maelstrom. It could have been something a demon had snickered at him, or it even could have come from Legba himself. It was a warning to not consume all the power you could. That if you only ate of abominations, it only fed the abomination within you. But, not heeding the warning, he ate of the abominations, for that was his nature.

And when the carnage was done, when the sacrificial communion was over, the Gris-gris man emerged from the void-shadows that had nearly been his death shroud and opened his eyes. His vision was clear. His mind was whole. And since arriving in this place and time, he no longer felt the faint sucking of a memory; a memory of a swirling black void that was somewhere in his past. Perhaps it had been something he'd encountered while in the mist. Perhaps it was an effect of traveling through it.

He looked down as the beast, also fully formed, bumped its ragged head against his hand. Because they were of the same essence, the beast had enjoyed the communion as if the disciples had crawled into his own gaping jaws.

"Mr. Sandgrove," the Gris-gris man said. "You look well."

Mr. Sandgrove, the beast, emitted a low guttural growl. Yes, it was well again.

"Yet," the Gris-gris man stroked the beast's neck, "you are still incomplete." Toth was still missing. "We'll have to see about that."

Just then, the two wraiths emerged through the wall of the boat. They glowed feebly with the thin Aether they had collected. Confusion rippled across their surfaces as they detected the carnage that lay at the feet of their master. Shadow-stains on the floor were all that was left of their siblings.

"Fear not," the Gris-gris man said. "All is well now."

The shadow-forms of Umbra and Susurrus swirled at the feet of their master, awaiting their fate.

"My faithful disciples," he continued, "rise up, and you will be rewarded."

He raised his hand slightly, extending his fingers as if to absently brush the top of tall grass. The motion called the wraiths, and they moved to his hand. Faint blue arcs of energy swirled up from behind his fingernails and crackled across the tips of his fingers. There, they fed from the fingers of their master; it was their time to suckle.

Having fed from the other disciples—a last resort, but one he had considered in the other time—he had fully restored himself. Blue Aether, like tendrils of lightning, arced out and around what would be the wraith's heads, and they began to form into dark, dense shadows.

A memory of a painting came into his mind. Many memories had flooded back over the last several minutes, but this was a picture of a famous painting he'd seen in a book. It adorned the ceiling of some old chapel in Europe. It was a picture of God creating Adam with the touch of his finger from an outstretched arm. He looked down and smiled at the things he had created. He had become god-like himself.

Before the wraiths could reclaim their original forms—they'd had legs and arms once—he withdrew his fingers, leaving them mewling for more.

"Not yet," he said. "You are perfect in my eyes, exactly how I want you."

And with this, the two remaining wraiths rose up to his full height, supported on their own dark wind.

He smiled and nodded. "Very good. Now, I believe it is time to leave this boat.

"I believe it is time… to find Delphine."

CHAPTER 28

Madame Broussard stood up from her chair. She was nearly ready but needed to check on something first.

The Toth-skeleton stood up also, as if to follow her. With a quick mental correction, she instructed it to stay.

As the hollow eyes of the skull, and the tiny red bead eyes of the doll looked at her, she couldn't help thinking that it looked like something one would see propped outside the freak tent of a carnival. The bones that had been damaged in previous wanderings had been lashed together with sinew. Remnants of the skin which had been so violently sucked away by the winds of Scarmish's feeding still clung, like ancient, cracking papier-mâché, to the bones and skull. And then of course, there was Toth, riding high on its hatpin. She still couldn't recall how the thing had come to be on her table of curiosities—something that would have been traded away like so many *(children)* others—but for a fortunate turn of events; she'd discovered it had life. Or a semblance of it anyway. A masterful job had been performed on this thing, but what had it been before it became Toth?

Had it been a person? A dwarf? A baby?

Had it come from *that* time? Is it possible it came from *him*?

She nodded absently and the Toth-skeleton agreed.

(Yes.)

Strange bedfellows indeed. Could this be one of John's creations?

She knelt to stare at it. When she did, the slightest movement of its stubby arms pushed against the empty eye-socket skull, and the skeleton leaned in. A flicker of light flashed across the red bead eyes of Toth in recognition of its new master.

Yes, it had had a different master in another lifetime, although it had not the capacity for long memory, so those details were lost to it. But desiring life, as Toth did, along with a means of transportation—which it now had—it had only one other desire: to use those gifts to serve.

What a strange turn of events, she thought. Toth had been in her possession for over a year now, and yet, it was as if she were seeing it for the first time, again.

What had consumed her time so, over the last year, the last ten years, that she now looked upon this curiosity as if it were new?

How long have I been here?

She absently fingered the black pearls around her neck.

When was the last time I removed these pearls?

(You know.)

Yes. She knew. She also knew the last time she'd put them back on, just after she'd had the fresco created.

The fresco was funny, it gave her vision yet kept her blind. It provided a window, yet hid the walls. And like moldering paper, all things changed when kept hidden behind walls.

Hidden behind walls…

An image of a wooden crate flashed in her mind, and she flinched.

Toth, feeling her surprise, flinched as well, and then, like a protective dog, turned the skull to look around the room for the invisible intruder. But the only intruder here were old thoughts creeping from the shadows of her mind, thoughts of an earlier version of herself. That, and a young girl.

The image of the crate grew, overtaking the walls of the room and filling her mind, consuming her and any thoughts she had of Time.

For time was different in the crate. It played by its own rules, rules that had no meaning and no end. There in the darkness of the crate, with no way to escape, time pressed down on you, on your mind, like a cosmic weight. It squeezed your mind until it caved in upon itself, until you were less than a speck of light, until you were no one and nowhere. And only then did Time remake you.

I was remade in that crate, she thought.

Such a strange story that was, the crate, a memory that had been buried for a hundred lifetimes.

The girl in the crate, what had her name been?

(Which girl?)

Which girl? There had only been one gir—

But that wasn't correct. At some point in that long journey, there *had* been another girl in the crate. But not in the beginning.

In the beginning, the *very* beginning, there had only been one girl. A young, beautiful girl who loved flowers, was loved by many, and who had fallen victim to a terrible curse.

The rose!

(Yes. The rose.)

It pricked me. I bent to smell it and... and it... reached out, and pricked my finger.

(A cursed rose.)

Yes, she remembered now. The rose bush, which had been sent as a peace offering after a terrible tragedy had occurred. But it was no peace offering at all. It had been a Trojan horse.

She had been that girl.

She had been the one to go into the crate, who was *put* in the crate.

And before she went in, she'd had a different name. Her name had been Ana Dalca.

Ana Dalca had gone into the crate and endured a long journey. Her time in the crate, and the cursed blood running through her veins, had changed her. When she'd finally escaped, she was changed. She was no longer Ana Dalca, so needed a new name. And someone had given her one: Broussard.

*

The daydream of walls and crates had led her—not unlike a shadow-road—to the attic door. And like the memory of the crate, she hadn't visited this place in a long time.

Unlocking the door with a hidden key, it groaned as she pushed it open. Waving away dust and cobwebs, she ascended the half flight of stairs to the low-ceilinged third-floor attic. Somewhere behind her, the Toth-skeleton slowly clacked its way up the steps.

A strange little wobble ran through her legs as she walked deeper into the room. It had been so long since she'd been up here, she'd forgotten to expect it. But the instinct of balance—and hers was very good—quickly overcame the imagined tilt of the room. It was as if one were standing on a moored boat being jostled by gently lapping waves. Once the body acclimates to it, the subconscious takes over and you no longer think about keeping your balance. It wasn't exactly like that in the attic, but close enough for comparison, she thought. Just the slightest tilt of reality seemed to twist this room a degree or two off level. And depending on the mood of its occupant, one could never tell when, where, or how the sensation would present itself.

But the room's occupant is what kept her safe. So, the disorientation was a minor nuisance.

The attic was like many other attics in the Crescent City, stuffed to bursting with old furniture, boxes *(crates)* trunks, and all manner of family memorabilia. But unlike other houses, none of the heirlooms were hers.

Oh, they were in her attic because she had put them here, but they were not from any family member of hers. Not real family anyway.

Her hand found the back of a chair, and without looking at it, she recognized it by the feel. The dark mahogany top rail ornately carved with leaves, flowerets and grape clusters. Her hand slid down, fingers brushing over crushed gold velvet material. A blood stain was on the left side of the back cushion. Her fingers found its outline.

Further into the room, beneath a writing desk, carefully covered with a sheet, was a crib. Again, she didn't need to see it to know it was there. And unlike many objects in this room, buried under decades of dust, the crib was one of the few objects she had taken the time to cover. Surely, the small satin white mattress and cover had yellowed by now, but this object above all—save one, perhaps—deserved to be handled with care. That would not be a memory she'd revisit anytime soon.

She made her way around the room, in a haphazard sort of path, the Toth-skeleton bumping through the maze as best it could. Toth, seeing where its master was from its elevated position, but not the path forward, had driven the Alvie-bones of its new body forward into several dead-ends. With frustrating little grunts—always some form of, "Ngyihng…" the doll pushed and pulled at the skull, turning it this way and that.

In the center of the attic, she finally came to her destination. The gravity warp of the room was different here. Today it felt as if the object she sought had gained tremendous weight and the floor of the room bowed beneath it. Yet, it was a rather small thing.

A wooden box of approximately two-foot square sat in the center of a small table. Unlocking it with another hidden key, its front doors swung open, and its top, cleverly hinged from within, folded back to expose the contents within. Inside was a smaller wooden container shaped like a helmet. Flat on the bottom and round on the top, the container was less ornate than the outer box and strapped with thin metal bands. It was split down the middle whereby undoing a silver clasp, the two halves would swing open on a hinge in the back. It was shaped like a head.

Sliding it forward onto the table, she thought she felt it stir but quickly dismissed the idea. Where would it go if it had the means to move?

Nowhere was the answer. After all, it had been in this position for so very long.

An even smaller key would unlock the silver clasp that held the two halves together, but that was not needed now. Her goal was to simply look at the thing again, knowing that this was the cause of her pending struggle.

And remembering it for its salvation.

To the left and right of the center line were two thin strips of metal, about an inch wide, that were held in place by small metal guides running up and down the container (mask). They were designed to slide up the mask, uncovering a hole hidden behind them. They could just as easily be slid back down, covering the holes back up. Little trap doors they were, hiding a whole other world.

Slowly, she slid up the band on the left side, then the right. Two dark eye holes which had been carved into the mask, were now visible.

Madame Broussard waited, wondering if the thing in the box was still viable. She heard Toth scuffling behind her, trying to get a better look.

"Ngyihng…" Toth whispered, as it spied the wooden mask.

And at the sound of Toth's voice, eyelids sprung open behind the eye holes. The eyes were as white as the day they'd gone in there.

CHAPTER 29

Del puttered around the house most of the day, waiting for Armand and Mama D to return. Armand had driven over to Frank's house, after he didn't answer his telephone, and Mama D ran her own errands.

She did some light chores, mostly in her room, and went through the motions of trying to clean the downstairs, which didn't need it. Mama D, needing something to keep busy with, had the downstairs rooms under control. Most of the rooms didn't get used much anyway, so there wasn't much to do. Straightening the library was mostly left to Armand—certainly his research table—but a stray glass could be plucked from the fireplace table with little risk.

The only real tug-of-war area was the kitchen, which contained an invisible line that held back the forces of bachelorhood from encroaching upon the organization of Mama Dedé. It was a battle of wills, and Del thought that Mama D would ultimately win it, but Armand was a formidable disorganizer.

More than once had the older woman found a ladle, whisk, or

some other needed implement, hiding in a most obscure place. And when asked about its placement, Armand, looking thoughtful, but perplexed would say, "Has it not always been kept there?"

In response, Mama D would either roll her eyes, sigh, plant her hands on her hips, or a combination of all three, then go back to her cooking, muttering prayers under her breath.

Exiting her room, she saw Jimmy sitting at the chess table, staring intently at the pieces. She knew he'd spent a lot of time there lately but admittedly had not asked him about the game. She felt bad that he didn't have any friends to play with and on more than one occasion had told herself to do something about it.

Walking up behind him and lightly touching his shoulder she said, "Hey, watcha—?"

"AHH!" Jimmy yelled, starting in surprise.

Del jumped in response, withdrawing her hand.

Looking up, Jimmy saw who it was, and his eyes went wide with fright.

He spun around and threw his arms over the chessboard and pieces.

"Don't 'ook. Don't 'ook!" he said.

"Jimmy, I—" Del stammered. "I just wanted to—"

"You mess it up! You mess it up!" he continued. Then his hands were moving, swiping at the pieces, sending them flying in all directions. "You can't see. You can't see!"

Del stared, open mouthed, and stepped back.

Frantically, as if trying to wipe away the evidence of a crime, Jimmy flung his hands out in one last arc, jumped up from his chair and ran down the stairs.

"You mess it up. You mess it uuuppp," trailed after him.

Del stood silently, looking around the library for a long moment, trying to understand what had just happened.

She sat down in the chair Jimmy had just occupied, and let her eyes scan over the scattered pieces. Although she didn't know how to play the game, she knew what the pieces looked like, and wondered at the strange objects Jimmy had added to his version. There were regular chess pieces, mostly consisting of pawns, there were small stones, a butter knife, a small bird feather, and three empty cicada carcasses. Some were on the floor, and one was all the way under Armand's workbench. The remaining pieces lay—as if defeated by the great storm of Jimmy—on their sides; all except one.

Despite the tumult, the black queen had miraculously survived—knocked out of the square of play, but still on the table—standing alone.

Del slipped into a trance and began inspecting the moments that preceded the outburst.

*

After some time, Del still hadn't determined what may have caused the uncharacteristic outburst from Jimmy. He was normally quite calm, except for the times he had a bad dream. But even then, he didn't respond with anger or frustration.

Having tranced on Jimmy's exit from the library, she saw that he was sitting on the edge of the pool that surrounded the stone maiden. When she realized that he was 'talking' to her, or his imaginary friends in the water, she looked away. She'd done something to upset him and even though he couldn't see that she was watching him, she felt it to be an invasion of his privacy.

However, she did not feel the same about looking into his past. She couldn't change the things she saw in his past, only learn from them, so somehow, it didn't seem as bad.

Del floated through scene after scene of Jimmy's daily routines. It was amusing to play the reel of his life backwards on high speed. It reminded her of some old black and white movies where the characters moved faster than normal people, scurrying around like ants. She scanned Jimmy's movie reel, backwards then forwards—always skipping over the bathroom scenes—and watched him move through the house in a funny, accelerated, clipped motion. There was a definite pattern to where he went each day, and she imagined she could see his path worn into the floorboards of the house.

Then, as Jimmy's movie reel went to autoplay, she began to think about Étienne. What was he about, anyway?

He was handsome for one thing. But oddly proper—if that was the right word—in a way she wasn't used to. In her short life, Armand was the most sophisticated person she'd ever met, but over time she'd learned that his sophistication had a degree of eccentricity to it. She'd become used to the random object-touching he did when searching for an answer but had begun to learn that it may be some form of disorder. Étienne on the other hand seemed to be sophisticated in a different way.

Maybe he's from another country, she thought. And that excited her for a reason she couldn't explain.

She'd never really been attracted to older men before. The only ones she knew where Frank, Armand, and now Mr. Bobby. And they were like Friendly Uncle, Eccentric Uncle, and friend of the Friendly Uncle, if she had to rank them. She also knew Jonesy, the old bartender from the Jazz Note, but he was more like an ex-work mentor, sort of.

She'd thought for a while that she should stop by and see how

Jonesy was doing but never got around to it. She didn't think much about her old job anymore—which wasn't surprising considering both Sasha and Billy Bash were associated with that bar.

Ugh, that reminded her of Detective Marcel Valcour. How could she forget him? He didn't fall under the friendly-anything bucket. And he certainly wasn't a mentor. He was like a school principal she supposed, although she had no real reference for one.

Her only reference for a disciplinarian was Sister Eulalie. And he certainly wasn't like her. Nobody could be that bad. But she knew that Marcel would never be a friend to her either, and if she never saw him again, it would be fine with her. But something in her stomach told her that wouldn't happen either—*not* seeing him. She was sure their paths would cross again.

So, Étienne was the only unrelated man in her life. And although she hadn't snooped on him yet—just taking a harmless peek at what he might be doing—she couldn't say she hadn't thought about it. In fact, she'd been thinking about it a lot.

Her mind went back to the movie reel of Jimmy, and she rewound, then let them play forward. She'd completely missed them, as her mind flashed between competing thoughts, but she really didn't expect to find much anyway.

She was surprised at how much time Jimmy had been spending at the chess board—even Armand had become interested—but what was the harm in that?

Images flashed back and forth:

Armand watched Jimmy from behind his worktable—

—Flash—

Étienne, Armand, then back to Jimmy—

—Flash—

Back and forth, Jimmy, Étienne, then Armand.

Armand, Jimmy—

—Flash—

Jimmy—

What was that flash?

Del focused, and like a pendulum settling at the bottom of its swing, the movie reel of Jimmy came to rest on a set of scenes that she had glossed over. It was a nighttime scene. She'd just watched herself and Mama D go off to bed. Jimmy was playing. Armand was watching.

She moved the scenes forward and Armand was speaking with Jimmy, sitting at the table.

—Flash—

She saw his pocket watch dangling from his hand.

What's he—?

It began to spin.

Tiny flashes bounced from the gold watch, painting Jimmy's face with a kaleidoscope of yellow light.

Del watched in fascination as the hypnotism session unfolded. She'd never witnessed one before. And had no idea that Armand knew how to do that.

What's he looking for?

The whole concept of Sparkle as a question and its lost answer was bizarre to her. Perhaps this was just another of Armand's strange pursuits, she thought, and almost left the scene. But then her whole attention snapped to a bizarre statement.

"Because Jimmy didn't write it," Jimmy had said.

Del gasped, freezing the movie reel in place. She sat staring at the still image of Jimmy, mouth partially open, which had just spoken in a different voice.

See didn't need to replay the scene. She didn't need to double check that she'd heard him correctly. The words were so surprising, the voice was so alarming, that she knew it was correct and that she'd never forget it.

She didn't know what to do with the information, so only sat there staring as if hypnotized herself. What was it that lurked in Jimmy's mind?

And through her staring eyes, something else made notice of the strange boy. It hadn't noticed him before, but only recently had it begun to peer outside of Del's mind. Before now it had only been a splinter, a black thought deep in her subconscious. But like all things that desire life, it had wormed its way up from some blackness, toward light. From where it came, it didn't know, nor did it care. It only cared about gaining life, gaining control over itself, gaining power that it had recently glimpsed and felt. And although it knew not how the boy could be used, it felt—because Del felt—that he was special.

And with that knowledge, the Dark Dreamer fell back into the shadows of Del's mind, taking Jimmy's image with it into the dark.

CHAPTER 30

Mr. Bobby, resting comfortably against a stack of bed pillows, grabbed his pack of cigarettes from the nightstand, and launched one at his face. As if on an invisible string tied to his upper lip, the cigarette flew towards his mouth where he caught it between dry lips.

"How do you do that?" said Odetta, lying next to him. Slender brown fingers came up and made a scissoring motion, as an ample breast slid out from under the thin top sheet of the bed. "Gimmee," she said.

He lit it and placed it in the waiting fingers, then launched another into his mouth. "We all have our talents, honey," he said.

Odetta inhaled, tilted her head back onto the flat pillow, and sent a heavy cloud of smoke shooting upward.

"Yeah," she said. "And what are mine?" With her free hand she reached beneath the cover, searching for him.

"Yours are exhausting," he said, pushing her hand away. "Sorry darlin', no more left. I'm dry as a desert." He grabbed the half empty bottle of beer from the nightstand and took a swig, as if to emphasize the point.

"Well, that won't help it," she said, sitting up.

"Doesn't hurt either," he muttered. "All it wants to do is take a nice long nap, then get some grub."

Odetta dropped the half-smoked cigarette into the watery remains of her vodka and soda, which sat on the nightstand next to her, and stood up. "Well, you do that," she said, stretching her arms over her head. "Mama's got to get back downstairs."

"It don't sound too busy. Those girls can't handle a few old drunks?"

"The drunks I'm not worried about," she said. "The cash register I am. Besides, it should be picking up in a bit." She glanced at her watch. "Come down later, I'll fix you a sandwich."

He crushed out his own cigarette, watching her get dressed. "I think I'm gonna take a walk. I have an article due tomorrow and need to get it written."

"Cuttin' it kinda close, aren't you?"

"Nah, a good reporter always has a couple of stories in the bag, just in case."

"What about your new girl, how's she doing?"

"New gir—? Oh, Del you mean." He put his hand behind his head. "OK, I guess. Favor for a friend, really. She's…" He looked at the ceiling to consider. "Hell, I can't really say. Eager enough, I guess. But it's a hard road to get started down. Hard to find your path, ya know? I mean, who in the hell can guess what'll make people pick up a newspaper anymore? That is, besides the same old yellow journalism we've been plagued with for the last fifty years."

Odetta's brow wrinkled in question at the term.

"You know, blood-and-guts-economy-gone-to-hell stories. Big

flashy headlines. Death. Despair. That damned Hearst and his New York Journal." He shook his head. "Mark my words, this Gulf of Tonkin resolution is a bad deal for us. Just wait until the draft numbers go up, you'll see."

Odetta reapplied her lipstick in the mirror on the dresser. "Nobody even knows where Vietnam is anyway." It came out as '*Vee-it-naam*'.

"They will soon enough," Bobby said, shooting another cigarette into his mouth.

Odetta turned and looked at him, with her hands on her hips. "Now don't go gettin' your drawers in a knot."

Bobby sucked the cigarette to an angry red glow.

Odetta rolled her eyes. "Well, I see it's too late for that." She walked over and gave him a quick kiss. "Go walk it off and don't come back 'til you're in a better mood. I don't want you gloomin' up my place."

She winked at him and turned towards the door. "Besides, if you come back in a better mood, I might have dessert for you later." She flipped her hip as she walked through the door, closing it behind her.

*

A cold September rain had begun to fall on the Crescent City. To the residents of New Orleans, the rain wasn't the surprise—it was nearly October and hurricane season after all. The surprise was the sudden drop in temperature. Normally the rain came up on warm winds from the Gulf, buffeting the trees and shop canopies. But this rain was different. It was as if December had suddenly descended on the city, chilling the souls in preparation for a freeze. The people were sluggish in the rain, shuffling along the sidewalks with slumped shoulders and bowed heads. Mouths were silent.

Thoughts were somber. And in this preternatural gloom, a dark shadow moved unseen through the streets.

The shadow, the thing known as Praeco, having gorged itself on the Aether of Maggie DuBois, had broken free of its master's hold. That *untethering* had happened by accident, as the hold had been tenuous at best; they all had been starving. And had the other two wraiths consumed the Aether and absorbed it, instead of saving it for their master and siblings, the untethering may have happened to them as well.

But after feeding on Maggie, and feeling its power restored, the wraith felt the call of the dark city—the pulsing underbelly—and was pulled into it. Being sucked into one of the many shadow-roads that crisscrossed the city, it floated like a leaf on a black river, to no particular end.

It did this with almost no knowledge of itself; it simply was and was not.

It was a thing of substance, but without direction. It was an entity of power with no tie to land nor even an anchor to steady it at sea; for that matter it wasn't even a vessel. And all it had to do, like the pollen of a mighty live oak, was float around until it landed on fertile ground.

And there, it could take hold and grow.

*

Étienne, having been warned of the wandering wraiths, and the sleeping girl, just the day before, had barely risen from his own sleep when this new menace had come to his attention.

His people had alerted him to the untethered wraith, something they had not dealt with before. And its whereabouts were unknown.

*

Mr. Bobby wandered the rain-soaked streets with his jacket collar pulled up around his neck. He held a soggy newspaper over his head as he plodded forward. Wavery neon lights announced the end of one establishment and the beginning of another. He was surprised to learn that even in their water-color distortion, he recognized some of the signs.

The warmth of Odetta's bed had been cooled by the rain, and his mood had grown steadily darker. Things were going wrong in the world and he suddenly felt that his little light-hearted column was a waste of time. Maybe he *should* be writing something different. Maybe he *was* doing his readers a disservice by ignoring the larger problems. It had been years since the imposter syndrome of writing had afflicted him—that internal nagging voice of self-doubt—but it was never completely gone. And the bitch of it was you never knew when it would turn up again. Like it had tonight.

So, with these troubling thoughts, he walked until he realized the neon reflections on the sidewalk had changed. He had passed out of the bar district which had pacified his mind, and into a commercial area. He knew where he was immediately. The lights of the Touro Infirmary now lit the wet streets and sidewalks.

As the page three story of Maggie DuBois slowly dissolved and ran down his forehead, he stopped and looked down the alley. It was fog-choked and dark, a black abyss next to the glaring lights of the hospital. It was an alley that one would typically not walk down, especially since the streetlights did not penetrate its darkness. But he knew he would walk down it, anyway. Why else had he come?

He couldn't recall the woman's name from the hospital, but he remembered the story. She'd been the second strange burning death, and it had happened in this alley.

His feet turned, pivoting on the balls like a marching soldier. He squinted into the gloom.

There was something down there, he thought. He just saw it flutter in the rain.

Police tape?

With a tentative step, he walked into the alley.

*

The dark shadow that was Praeco, having been tossed about on the currents of the shadow-roads, felt familiarity looming. There were many forces in this city which pulled at it, coaxing it through one hidden crossroads only to pull it suddenly another direction. Like an iron filing, Praeco floated, aligning with the psychic winds of the city, and awaited its destination. A constant low thrumming, like a cosmic wave, vibrated it along its path, turning it this way and that. There was a power source—many of them—nearby, but it was already tuned to a certain vibration. There was a signal that was tuning it in, and it felt itself pulled along ever closer to the source.

It knew instinctively that it had been on this shadow-path before. How it had ended up back at a familiar point, it never considered. It was just *here*, which was different from where it had been, but similar.

The similarity may have been like that of an old memory, if it could catch the concept, but it did not. It only felt a *speeding up* of its journey and knew that it now had a destination. A destination that would become an unfortunate anchor.

As the tunnel of the shadow-road grew larger, a type of scene began to form. It was a watery scene, shrouded in fog.

It was a familiar place.

It was an alley.

It was *the* alley.

And in the alley, it had come face to face with a force beyond anything it had ever felt. A girl. It had looked into the young face with the dark eyes, and the power beyond knowing, and had peered into the eyes and glimpsed its future. And that's where the shadow-road was taking it. Back to the alley and the girl.

*

But whether it was the shadow-road, the alley, or the combination, a trick would be played on Praeco, for the girl was not in the alley.

But someone else was.

And like two automobiles destined for a head-on collision, Praeco and Mr. Bobby moved toward each other, with no power to move out of the path.

Mr. Bobby was squinting through the rain, looking for something that was waving in the fog.

Praeco was speeding up, moving forward, being propelled out of the tunnel by an unknown force.

The gust of wind—centuries in the making—arrived. It was the wind that slid through ancient trees, that had skimmed over oceans and above mountains. It was the wind that had fled before a thousand thousand moons. And it was the wind which was at the right place at the right time, just when the shadow-roads shifted to move an untethered wraith to fertile ground. It was the wind that pushed the wraith out of the tunnel, right into the startled face of Bobby Dupre.

*

Bobby gasped as the wind buffeted him. He stiffened as he felt the cold fog surround him, then began to seep into him.

Not seep… crawl.

No, not seep. It was crawling. Somehow the fog was *crawling* into him.

Deep.

His mouth went slack as his eyes glazed over.

Deeper.

His arm dropped, letting the sodden newspaper fall to the sidewalk.

As Praeco latched onto Bobby's soul, a most unfortunate thing happened. It did not feed.

Still satiated from the feeding of Maggie, Praeco did not have the animalistic instinct to gorge. It knew the Aether was there. It could feel its nourishing warmth. And that warmth, as if cast forth from an ancient fire to also arrive at this very time and place, brought with it something unexpected.

The warm feeling of memories began to flood into Praeco. Whether from Bobby's mind or a much older source, it did not know, but memories flooded it.

And with those memories, a sense of self—no bigger than a grain of sand in an oyster, but there nonetheless—began to form.

And at that moment, Bobby Dupre tried to scream—but the memory of how had vanished.

CHAPTER 31

Jimmy finished his macabre game of chess and grumbled in anger.

"Grrrr, 'tupid rasa frasa..." His voice trailed off with a Saturday morning cartoon curse word.

He stood up, pushing the chair back, and left the pieces lay where they had died. All except the black queen of course, who stood triumphantly in the middle of the board.

He slipped downstairs and through the kitchen where he grabbed three cookies from the cookie jar before heading outside. One cookie was for his friends in the water to share—if they were out today—and the other two were for him, which went into his shirt pocket.

He nibbled at the ends of the windmill cookie, which he always ate first, and walked onto the back porch. There he paused, surveying the garden, with a new, keen interest. Something about the garden looked different to him today.

A passerby on the street glancing casually through the gate may have thought he was the young lord of the manor, the way he cocked his hands onto his hips. "It's a fine day to be lord of the manor," said his stance. So, he chomped the top half of the windmill off and headed to the fountain.

Walking through dappled sunlight, he looked for butterflies but saw none. Birds chirped from flowering vines that had scaled the stone wall that surrounded the courtyard. He waved. A dog barked somewhere down the block.

Reaching the short wall that surrounded the stone maiden, he leaned and slowly looked over the edge into the dark, still water. It was like a mirror of the sky, with the stone maiden standing guard as tall as the clouds. He didn't see anything in the water, but couldn't see the bottom either, so took the last bite of his cookie and looked up at the stone face.

Despite having had an accident when he first came to live here, and almost drowning in this pool, he felt safe sitting here, *if* the maiden gave him the sign that all was safe. Whatever bad thing that had pulled him into the water back then, wouldn't come around when she was here. And even though her stone body was always here, sometimes her voice wasn't, because it went away whenever she did, which was only natural, so he always had to check before sitting down.

Jimmy wasn't sure where she went during those times. He'd tried to ask before, but she didn't want to say. For some reason he thought she went into the water where his friends lived but couldn't be sure.

The maiden, haven taken an appropriate amount of time, nodded to Jimmy that it was safe to sit down. It was only a slight nod that he would catch from the corner of his eye when he started to look away, but it was there. She had to be careful so that no one else would see her talking to him. This was another reason her voice always came from the water.

Today, he had an important question to ask her, but somewhere between the cookie jar and here, he'd forgotten it. It had probably been about Del, which meant it was very important. But, it could have been about Mama Dedé or Armand, which was also important, just not as much as if it were about Del.

He didn't have any questions about Frank.

Sitting down on the stone ledge, he saw a slight ripple run across the surface of the water. The maiden had said it was good to see him.

"It good to see you too—"

(Shhhh...) said the water.

"Oh," Jimmy said, remembering her warning from long ago. *Sorry,* he thought, the words silent in his head.

(You have been away a long time.)

Jimmy thought about this. He couldn't remember the last time he'd spoken with the maiden, and because of that, he agreed, it must have been a long time.

Yeah, I kinda busy, I guess.

The water rippled.

(Much has changed since we last spoke.)

He thought about this and wondered what it could mean. Del had come back, so that was a change. But that had happened a while back, so maybe it didn't count. Mama D was better, he didn't have to bring her cookies anymore, but that felt like the Del thing, so he ignored it and said nothing.

(Have you found a way through?)

No. The thought, like a tattletale, escaped his mind before he knew it was there.

(You must find a way. She grows stronger every day.)

Jimmy squirmed. He didn't like it when the maiden talked about this. But, she'd saved him before and talked to him almost every time he came out here, so he trusted her. They were friends after all. In fact, he was beginning to feel like the stone maiden was almost as good of a friend as Del was, now that she was busy being a grownup. *Almost* as good.

Sometimes I fohgot, Jimmy admitted. *'tupid head.*

The stone maiden knew this about Jimmy. The many errands she had sent him on, testing his reliability, had told her much about the boy. But there was power there, she knew that also. She felt it—but so did many things, she feared. How long did they have before others felt it? How long before she was simply too strong for them all? These things were beyond the ability of the stone maiden to answer. But she'd been given a task, a responsibility, and if she could not perform it, everything that came before her would be for naught, for nothing would matter after. But still, the question of how to harness the boy's power, help him to understand the threat, had eluded her.

Until a few nights ago.

The stone maiden's voice rippled over the water, but it was false. There were no words for Jimmy to hear.

There was only the rippling.

And through some strange cosmic alignment, a high gentle breeze, perhaps a remnant of the one that had shuttled the wraith from the shadow road, brushed against a dangling leaf and moved it, allowing a single ray of sunlight to filter through the tree to cascade off the water in a thousand thousand sparkling shards.

Sparkle found Jimmy's eyes.

And because Armand had told him to always protect Sparkle, he snatched his eyes closed to keep it safe.

And there, already behind his eyes, burrowing deep into the boy's mind, was a question looking for its answer; *What is the way through?*

A cool feeling of calm settled over the boy as the question settled, already in the back of his mind. There, it spread out through the gray folds, exploring, seeking, for the answer was here somewhere. Somewhere in the vast folds of Jimmy's mind, a single clear answer was waiting to be found. But he'd hidden it from himself long ago, not realizing it, for it was a terrible thing to ponder. But at some time, somewhere in his dreams, he had.

His head tilted forward, and he opened his eyes. Sparkle needed to show him something.

The stone maiden felt the answer emerging from Jimmy's mind, and despaired.

(It cannot be this.)

But some things are exactly what they seem.

The boy watched, open-eyed, as the answer played out in the water. The sparkling diamonds of light that had triggered his hypnosis had disappeared. What remained was the answer to the question.

Just then a bird flew overhead, casting its shadow into the water. The shadow-image of the bird printed itself on the surface, then began to sink. As it did, the stone maiden whispered her despair, and the surface rippled again, changing the image of the bird.

It had become a falcon.

One corner of Jimmy's mouth twitched, battling between grimace and smile.

He recognized the bird. Somewhere in his past he had dreamt it, conjured it out of thin air perhaps, but he knew this creature.

He watched it as it soared through the night air of the pool becoming larger. The larger it grew the more details he could see: the ragged feathers, the midnight blue talons, the remnants of a thousand,

thousand faces, the dying ones, trailing behind the bird on their journey to oblivion.

Another ripple and the scene changed again. Now Jimmy was on the bird. He was riding the falcon, guiding its flight by its neck feathers. An acrid smell of burnt wood and flesh wafting from its body.

The corner of Jimmy's mouth twitched, grimace overcame smile, smile overcame grimace.

High in the air the bird screeched. The falcon of death had caught a scent. Laser beam eyesight shot from the bird's head, scanning the land far below. It was looking for Del.

And as the answer to the question played out in the shadows of the pool, Sparkle left the boy, and the hypnosis ended. But the image of the answer remained. It was left behind, tucked away securely in his mind, where it would leave its imprint for another time.

Jimmy blinked and looked around; unsure how much time had passed. He had a bad taste in his mouth, something like burnt ash.

As he walked across the courtyard, the stone maiden gazed into her own pool of water, looking for another answer.

She found none.

Jimmy, trying to remember what he'd come to ask, walked in a daze, his mouth twitching.

Grimace over smile. Smile over grimace.

CHAPTER 32

The Gris-gris man, having yet to choose his final form, moved along the country road like a shadow which had torn loose from the tree which had made it. His partial man-shape was recognizable around the head and shoulders. But below that, long wisps, like stickly fingers of tree branches, hung down where his arms would be, and floated over the dirt road. And since he didn't care for the real shape of his lower body, it hadn't materialized at all, giving him the appearance of being propelled along silently on grotesquely long arms that ended in spider-fingers.

After leaving the boat in the hidden cove near River Ridge, he'd wandered northeast towards Lake Pontchartrain. He felt a twinge of remorse at the loss of the grand old plantation houses, where he'd traded his services for live specimens. The old or infirmed slaves had diminishing value to their owners, but for John they had provided an answer to a critical problem, that of scarce resources. Besides, the soul didn't really age, as far as he knew, so for his purposes they weren't infirmed at all. And this fortunate partnership had provided him something that he hadn't realized he'd needed, until it had almost been too late. His own escape.

He thought back to the time of his feud with one of his disciples, Marie Laveau. She had been a quick study, a natural practitioner, as well as a part time lover. That was, until they'd had a falling out and she'd cursed his mule which had killed his favorite dog. From there, the feud escalated until her son was dead and his daughter had been cursed with such a terrible fate that she'd gone mad and disappeared into the swamps. He knew at that point that the feud would only end when one, or both, were dead. But by that time, his own transformation was underway, and the seer had told him to go into the mist, to find the one called Del who could cure him. Knowing that Marie had raised a possie of men to catch him—trap him like an animal—so she could unbind him, he'd devised a plan. He needed a decoy. Only with a decoy, someone who Marie would think was him, even after she killed him, could he slip into the mist and wait for the time of Del to come. He knew he'd be vulnerable while asleep and that if he suddenly disappeared that she, or one of her own disciples, would hunt him through time. So, a decoy was the only way.

The man John had chosen had come from one of these very plantations, although he couldn't recognize where it had been. But he remembered the man. He had the same ebony skin as John, and the same country marks on his face. He should have, for he was from the same Senegalese tribe as John—a half-brother that John had loathed as a child. So, when the time came, and the half-brother had proven to be a trouble-making voice amongst the other slaves, the plantation owner was more than happy to trade him away. Traded for a single spell—that amounted to nothing more than a hypnotic suggestion—

which caused his wife to suddenly desire a more carnal means of showing her affection.

It was this man, a half-brother who shared the face of their father, who John cursed one night, binding him to John's very essence. This had to be done to infuse him with the abomination that was growing in his own body. He knew that once Marie put him down, she'd look for signs of the curse that ran through him, gator skin or teeth, leg bones that bent backwards, anything animalistic.

He'd tried passing these traits onto others with no success. His thought then was to dilute his curse by binding others to him, but it never took the curse away. And in all other cases, the process had killed the newly bound. But when he realized that someone with the same blood as him may be able to survive—after all, he had—he knew what must be done.

And shortly after the supposed great capture and unbinding of Dr. John had occurred, he and his disciples had slipped into the mist and were forgotten.

*

But that time, like his fond memories, had moved on and he let them both slip from his mind. Now that he was whole and thinking clearly, his mind was filled with the excitement of exploring this new life.

This year nineteen-hundred and sixty-four—based on the parts he had seen—was a marvel. The river boats and carriages moved under their own power. Towns and roads sprawled everywhere. And the things in the sky, well, he didn't know what to make of those. But exploring these wonders to understand their magic would have to wait. He had more pressing decisions before him now.

The sacrificial communion had been a last resort, but not wholly unplanned. After all, he had bound them for that purpose, among others. It was the timing of the act for which he hadn't planned. He thought he'd have more time.

But in the end, all was as it should be, he thought. After all, why shouldn't he receive his disciple's Aether? They were there to worship him. What better way to show their devotion than that? He in turn fed those who needed it and were worthy.

At this thought, he looked at the beast—which had fully assumed its original form—plodding along ahead of him. Its wide shoulders and powerful strides were juxtaposed by its slightly drooping head, whole, yet not whole.

Although it was a moonless night, he cast his own living shadows along the path. The two remaining wraiths slunk along the dirt road in front of, on the side of, and behind, the Gris-gris man, in the ultimate position of fealty, as shadows of Him.

The countryside changed as he traveled away from the town of River Ridge. The backwater town gave way to isolated farms, and those decayed to abandoned fields which were being reclaimed by forest and marshland. It was possible that the road he was on would wander off into the marsh and simply disappear. If that were to happen, he'd have to travel closer to the outskirts of New Orleans, but something told him that that was not the right move, not yet.

In his original time, before going into the mist, there had been many other things within the city. Old things, which had come over on the European ships. And he suspected—no, he felt—that they were still there. But they were not slaves. No, not slaves at all, but they *were* refugees in a way. The creatures which had fled the old country—persecuted as he had been—had brought old powers with them which others had wanted to stamp out, but which had allowed them to survive. And like all things, when creatures of power accumulated in a close area, rivalries formed, territories were marked, and they made things harder for themselves, instead of easier.

This was one of the reasons he had stayed near the swamps and rarely ventured into the city. And this was the reason he was now looking for a suitable residence. He had to stake a foothold so he could learn the ways of this time. Only then could he begin his search for Del.

And as if the mere thought of her name carried a strange magic with it, he rounded a bend in the road and found his salvation.

Ahead of him, set far off the road, hidden by fog, something lurked. He felt its presence before he saw it. But it was there. The weight of it was upon the wind and the wind carried its meaning.

And again, as if responding to his desire to see it, a faint light suddenly sprung up and could be seen flickering from one window. His shadow-mouth smiled sardonically as he recognized its form.

It was a small country church.

*

Isaiah Thomas sat within the small room at the back of the church which served as a combined office and storage closet. A makeshift workbench comprised of two sawhorses and three flat boards stood in one corner, a fold-out cot sat in the other. Everything he owned, everything that defined the life of Isaiah, was in this one tiny room.

One side of the workbench was reserved for his personal belongings, which consisted of a bruised suitcase and a worn army-green duffle bag that had been his father's. The other side of the bench held a smattering of tools, a few paint cans, and an oil lamp. In the middle, as if demarcating the two lives of Isaiah, was some canned food, a box of crackers, and a tattered box of used bibles which had been donated from his old pastor in his hometown of Quincy, Alabama. His smock, jacket, and priest's collar were hung neatly on a metal hangar that hung from a nail in the wall.

Isaiah was in his mid-thirties and was considered a handsome man. His dark wavy hair tended to the unruly side if he didn't keep it cut. In what he considered his wild days, he'd sported a beard and moustache of the same black color but tried to keep clean shaven now that he was a man of the cloth. But that was difficult when his five-o'clock shadow tended to show up around two in the afternoon. His blue eyes could be disarming when angry, but when behind the pulpit, they could convince even the most stalwart sinner that his words were true.

He'd just sat down for a light dinner after a long day of work on the little church where he'd planned to continue his father's legacy. It had been a long road for him, physically and spiritually, to finally realize his calling. And despite the lamentations of his father, Isaiah's path hadn't been that difficult because he had never been really bad, it had been because he'd been really good at not being good. And that was the truth of the matter.

The single candle which stood guard in the front room window flickered a warning to him—something was coming—but he was tired and didn't notice. A long night's sleep was the only thing on his mind.

That, and contemplating one of his favorite passages. He flipped his bible open to Isaiah 47:10-11 and began to read. *"For thou hast trusted in thy wickedness: thou hast said, None seeth me. Thy wisdom and thy knowledge, it hath perverted thee; and thou hast said in thine heart, I am, and none else beside me…"*

*

The shape of the Gris-gris man materialized before the front door of the church, and something like a hand formed from the shadow-mist which was his essence. The hand paused, hovering above the knob as if its owner were afflicted with indecision. But it was more a sense of poetic irony than anything else.

Should he open the door, stride in, and announce himself?

"I'm home," he might say gleefully.

Or would it be more polite to knock, and wait to be invited in?

The implications of the existence of this place were maddeningly seductive.

The beast, sniffing the ground around the steps leading up to the door snorted as if to say, "Foolish pretense. Get on with it."

The Gris-gris man, looking back at the waiting beast, caused a shadowed look to pass over his face. "But it's our new home," the look said, "and we would be polite."

So, he knocked.

*

"Therefore, shall evil come upon thee; thou shalt not know from whence it riseth: and mischief shall fall upon thee; thou shalt not be able to put it off: and desolation shall come upon thee suddenly, which thou shalt not know."

Isaiah jumped at the harsh rap upon the door.

It was louder than a polite knock. A polite knock he may not have even been heard back here, especially considering he'd been reading aloud.

But it wasn't a knock of desperation either. Someone in trouble—assuming they hadn't just burst in, the door was unlocked after all—would still be banging. Or would have at least delivered four rapid knocks to indicate the urgency. Three knocks would have indicated a possible neighbor, but the closest was nearly a mile away. And he doubted they'd be out here at…

He looked at his pocket watch.

Midnight?

Exactly midnight?

Isaiah rose, dusted breadcrumbs from his pants, and turned towards the door of the office.

If there were kids around here that had already taken an interest in what he was doing these late nights, then maybe his new church would be a welcome distraction to youngsters playing pranks at midnight.

What kind of parents didn't know that their kids were out at—?

KNOCK.

KNOCK.

He froze.

Two knocks, just like before. Not one, giving the perpetrator time to run away. Not three polite or four frantic. But two. Measured and decisive.

Isiah wiped the palms of his hands on his workpants, not realizing that they had suddenly turned clammy.

*

When he opened the door Isaiah was greeted by a face surrounded by smoke. For a brief second, Isaiah feared the man was fleeing a fire which was just outside his church door. He started to go outside to see but quickly stopped as a strange smile broke over the man's face.

"Good evening," the Gris-gris man said.

Isaiah stepped back, his mouth partly open, as he stared at the strange visitor. All at once, his mind was overwhelmed with input from his eyes. For a brief second he considered he might have fallen asleep and was dreaming.

A man waited in the doorway, surrounded by living smoke. It moved like… like it had a purpose. It swelled up behind the man's head, almost seemed to be *part* of his head, and began to take on the shape of a cowl.

No, not just a cowl, something else.

Yes, at the first instance Isaiah had thought of a man wearing a hooded jacket, or more like the cowl of a robe that a monk would wear. But a second later, after it had begun to grow, had become larger, he changed his mind. As it morphed his mind changed its opinion, always trying to move away from its gut feel, but was drawn back to the same conclusion, nonetheless. He knew what the thing looked like now. It looked like the swelling head of a cobra.

Isaiah's eyes flicked back to the face of the smiling man, then a movement behind the man caught his attention, and his eyes flicked there. And they widened.

Behind the stranger, standing on the overgrown path that led up to the church, stood an animal. It was a wolf, or… a rabid dog… or….

Isaish shook his head to clear his mind. *It can't be*, he thought. *It's not real. That can't be…*

His eyes went back to the smiling man as his hand went to his chest, searching for the cross necklace which hung there. The smoke-cowl-cobra-hood had grown larger in the time it took for his hand to move, blocking out the image of the beast. It seemed to want his attention on the smiling man.

Before he realized it, Isaiah had staggered back several feet, but only because his brain had realized at the last second that he was about to fall over. There was too many stimuli all at once, and his brain almost forgot he was standing. When he righted himself, he saw the entirety of the smiling man, and that's when he saw that the man had no legs.

Oh, God, he muttered. *He has no legs…*

The smoke man with the cobra hood slid quietly through the door of the church. The wraiths, which had formed the cowl as a protective measure, suddenly sprung out from his head, filling the space within the church with an inky blackness. But their task was not to feed. The Gris-gris man was perfectly capable of feeding himself now. Their job was only to restrain. After all, the Gris-gris man had yet to choose his form.

He's walking on ghost fingers, Isaiah thought maddeningly. *He has no legs and he's—*

"Thank you," the Gris-gris man said, as he began to assume the body of the preacher.

CHAPTER 33

Bobby Dupre sat at his kitchen table, staring at the glass thing. How long he'd been there, or how he'd arrived, no longer registered in his black-hole mind. He only knew that he was here and not inside the glass container with the white grains.

The thing had a companion which held black grains, but he couldn't remember the names of either one. Although they sat next to one another, he avoided looking at the black one the best he could. In a black hole, your eyes sought light.

He wanted to pick the thing up, but his arms wouldn't move. He thought that if he could just touch it, he could name what it was. He felt it was important, or that he liked it, but didn't know why.

Nnnnnnn… A feeble type of vibration, with his tongue pressed against the roof of his mouth, was all he could manage.

Another wave of disorientation washed over him and he realized that his ears no longer worked. He couldn't even hear the vibration he'd just made. He had been sightless in the black hole for a long time, but his vision had finally made it to the other side of the hole. He could see the glass thing after all. But sound didn't work here. Maybe the sound waves had disappeared, or he'd simply gone deaf. Or maybe the glass thing on the table was turned off.

Yes, that's it, his mind told him. One or all of those things could be the answer—or none of them.

His thudding heart agreed and disagreed, pounding out its opinion in his chest. Each time it did, tiny lightning bolts of pain shot through the cavity of his chest and up his windpipe.

Thump thump. *(You're deaf.)*

Thump thump. Thump thump.

Thump thump. *(You're dead.)*

Thump thump. Thump thump.

(You're dead. You're dead.)

Thump thump. Thump thump.

The knot of terror in his stomach formed into a scream. It swelled until it filled the space and began to push up his windpipe. It wanted to go somewhere. It needed to escape, but he'd forgotten how to let it out. Sharp pains radiated out from his chest.

Now it was in his lungs, swelling like a water balloon. His lungs struggled to expand. They couldn't get the air they needed because the scream couldn't get out. His lips, now purplish-white, pursed out like a drowning fish.

Then the scream was inside his mouth, swelling into the air passages, filling his nose, blocking all airways into his body. Surely, he would suffocate any minute, he thought. He'd choke on the terror rising in his body because he'd forgotten how to scream, and he'd die with it pushing his tongue down his own throat.

"...ehhhhhhhh..." A weak puff of air was squeezed over his vocal cords, mocking his desire to scream.

The scream swelled further. The only place it had to go now was to squeeze up the narrow space behind his eyes. He felt it moving there, pressing against the backs of his eyeballs. His vision blurred under the pressure, blood seeping into the whites of his eyes. The pressure was immense. His eyes bulged, threatening to pop free of his eye sockets. His head was swelling. The weight of the scream took on mass. It was now a skull busting thing, and he felt the sagittal suture at the top of his head begin to pull apart. He felt the bones separate; the nerve ends tear. He heard his skin begin to rip.

He was coming apart from the inside out.

*

The thing known as Praeco, now firmly attached to the essence of Bobby Dupre, sat in a room as the man's eyes roamed over strange objects. It was a small room where one would feed. The barely sentient part of Praeco had a vague recollection of similar rooms. It was a memory from another time. But despite its age, it was so deeply engrained, it could never be forgotten.

The experiences of its existence were nothing more than a series of disconnected images. They mostly consisted of dark places, fire, and mist. These images flashed randomly through the empty space of the wraith's mind. If the images would align, or settle somehow, into an order of occurrence, perhaps Praeco could understand their meaning. But the wraith had not been created for deep thought. It had been created for a different purpose, which it had performed. That was, until it had become untethered, then, it simply existed in this imperfect state, struggling to progress.

It didn't help that the body it had inhabited was revolting against it, either. The vessel it had inhabited was squirmy and uncooperative.

Praeco, having no plan when it attached itself to this person, had planned to simply feed from it until it was used up, then move on. Yet, there was a connection here that it felt it could use. A connection back to something that could change its situation.

So, mostly because it did not have to share its Aether, it had no desire to feed yet. But neither would it leave.

*

Bobby, suffocating on his own scream, slowly going mad as the pressure of his own terror split his head apart, prayed for salvation.

If only someone could release him from this living hell, end his terror and pain, he'd pay them anything. And although he wasn't a religious man, if Satan himself walked into the room and offered him reprieve from his torment for the price of eternal servitude, Bobby Dupre thought that he'd seriously consider the offer.

As the image of the glass thing continued to blur, Bobby Dupre knew he was slipping back towards the black hole of unconsciousness. He struggled against it, fighting to stay awake, but knew that darkness was only moments away.

In a final attempt at salvation, a whisper of a prayer formed in his mind. It was a tiny thing, barely able to survive on its own. But it's all he had. And with every bit of energy he could muster, he sent the prayer, wrapped in a thin bubble of thought to the top of his mind. There, all he had to do was push it through the top of his splitting skull, in hopes that it would float away on the wind and be caught up by some benevolent being floating by.

"Pheh…" A feeble cry of frustration escaped his lips as a few meager tears spilled out of his eyes. He truly was losing his mind, he suddenly realized. The hallucination of the prayer and the benevolent being was a trick of his mind. The final effort of a dying organ as it slipped towards madness.

But when the scream expanded again, a white-hot fracture broke across the top of his head.

"Errrrrrr..." he moaned.

He felt his skull split as tiny cracking sounds like breaking ice filled his ears, and the prayer bubble had just enough room to slip up through the crack in his skull, just before his mind sealed the breach.

And suddenly, as if the first part of his prayer had just been answered, Mr. Bobby's tears of pain and terror became something like joy. His final wish had escaped his mind right before it was plunged back into darkness.

CHAPTER 34

Sitting on her bed, Del tapped a pencil rapidly against the yellow legal pad that sat on her lap. She was supposed to meet Mr. Bobby tomorrow and needed an article outline to discuss with him.

She had nothing.

With all the crazy things that had happened lately, her mind was scattered. She didn't know what to focus on, or even how to decide.

The first page of the yellow pad had more doodles than words.

Maybe I should become an artist. I could draw illustrations for Mr. Bobby's articles and—

(Doodles aren't drawings.)

They could be! They just need some detail.

(They're doodles, that's all. They're practically Jimmy doodles.)

No, they're not! This one could be—

"Stop!" she said suddenly, throwing her pencil down. "Just stop." She exhaled. Sometimes her wandering mind, and its competing opinion, needed a firm hand.

She rubbed her eyes and looked at her watch. It was 10:19 and she had nothing. It was going to be a long night.

Staring at the page, Del began to see patterns in the scribbles that she hadn't drawn. They weren't moving—although she wouldn't have been surprised if they had started to right then—but she began to see something she hadn't seen before. Her brain had just detected it and was trying to understand what it was. It was like those hidden picture posters, where it looked like a bunch of noise, but if you stared at it long enough another picture came out. She felt that was happening now.

Then she thought of the Mad magazines that Jimmy had started reading. It was a satirical magazine that had just been published this year and was a hit with teenagers. It was like a news magazine for young adults, but in comic book style. Jimmy couldn't read much of the text, but loved the cartoons, especially the Spy vs Spy episodes. In the back of the magazines there was usually a crazy drawing with all kinds of characters doing wild stuff. If you folded the pages just right, where the middle third of the image became hidden, you'd see a completely different drawing.

Del tore the doodle page from the pad, looked at it as she tilted it this way and that, then began to fold it. When she did, the doodles began to line up and form other pictures. The partial drawings that she'd been scribbling matched other pieces in random ways. The more she twisted and folded the paper, the more intricate images came forth. Then her heart leapt into her throat.

Her right palm had just started tingling. And glowing.

As if triggered by the process of folding the paper and trying to get the doodles to line up, the rune lines that lived deep within her palm, the evidence of her secret pact with Arlo, had begun to resurface.

Startled, she shook her hand and rubbed her palm on her leg, but to no avail. She knew they couldn't be rubbed away, but she still wasn't used to having the tattoo scrolls pop out of their own accord. She stopped and looked at them. The runes, a type of scroll work of sorcery, she thought, were now fully visible. And they'd grown since she'd last inspected them in her dream in the park. From the tips of her fingers, across her entire palm, and stretching down the inside of her wrist, an intricate design of curves, symbols and strange marks, could be seen.

She clenched her fist tight, which dulled the tingling a bit, then reopened it. When she did, soft waves of light pulsed beneath the runes, backlighting the lines and symbols, causing them to glow faintly. She watched as the light ran up and down her palm. A heartbeat of hidden knowledge waiting to be used.

(Or looking for a way out,) the cynical part of her mind said.

I can control it.

(You don't even know what it is.)

A long moment passed as Del watched the power pulsing in the palm of her hand, and at some point, she thought,

but it's mine.

As if to gently grab the light and hold it for inspection, she partially closed her fingers. She could have been holding an invisible ball. This action caused the crease lines of her palm to deepen.

She knew what the major lines of palm reading were: the head and heart lines mostly ran horizontally across the palm, while the life and fate lines ran up from the wrist and around the fat part under the thumb. Each person's lines were different, and although she didn't really know how to read them, she thought it was curious that the four major lines on her right palm overlapped so much that they were basically two. Her head and heart lines were right on top of each other, forming a deep crease across her palm. And her fate and lifelines carved a deep crease in a half arc around her thumb joint until they met the other line where her thumb and pointer finger came together.

As she watched the interaction of pulsing light and runes, with the deepening creases on her palm, she saw the truth that was hidden there. New images, new runes, were formed when she bent her fingers, or rolled her thumb in or out, causing the creases to deepen, thin out, or touch in places.

Del was fascinated by the effect. She watched as the pulsing light changed its pattern according to how she held her hand. Sometimes the light pulsed up and down her palm—but always following the lines of the scrollwork—as if scanning it. Other times—and this was primarily when she cupped her hand around the invisible ball—the light would swirl around her palm as if being drawn to an imaginary hole in its center.

"Or mix together," she said absently.

Yes, that was a more likely explanation. Whatever the power, or knowledge, was that lived in Del's hand, it appeared to be searching for new connections.

Del put her hand through a series of movements: almost closing her fingers completely, pinching the two inside fingers into a claw with the thumb, while the outside fingers stayed extended, touching her third finger and thumb together while extending the first two fingers, etc. Each new configuration caused a different connection to form on her palm. If Mama Dedé had walked in right then she would have thought Del was casting the evil eye at herself.

That thought brought Del out of her daydream, but straight to another—and into a sharper realization. Some of the scrollwork on her palm looked exactly like that from the amulet Arlo had given her.

Her eyes flashed to the dresser drawer where the amulet was hidden. She suddenly felt an overwhelming desire to take it out and look at it.

*

Sitting on the floor with her back against the bed, Del scribbled furiously on the yellow legal pad. Her hand was beginning to cramp, she'd been writing steadily for the last thirty minutes, but she was so excited to finally have an idea and to be writing something, she didn't really notice.

After the light show on the palm of her hand had reminded her of the hidden amulet, she'd taken it from the drawer and studied it. The black stone wrapped in its fine silver thread was heavier than it should be, she thought. It was a small thing, after all. But it was surprisingly dense, and it felt good in her hand.

She thought about the article she needed to write; she'd been stressing over it all week. She wondered where the words would come from, and if she would find them at all. All she wanted to do at that moment was to think of something to write about.

Cradling the stone in her palm, she wasn't surprised to see the rune lines light up in greeting. The silver threads sparked, forming a new connection. And with that, she slipped into a trance.

*

Del's vision hovered in her room for only a moment, then moved outside it to the library. It was looking for Armand.

A strange light had suddenly ticked on in her head; she had a need—the words for her article. And she had power, and that power knew where to find the words. So, it went and got them.

It was a strange sensation being in Armand's head—or anyone's for that matter—but not watching a scene. Granted, most trancing sessions didn't involve her being *in* someone's head. She was typically outside of it. But this time was different. She felt as though she was floating around in his thoughts, picking through them, looking for the words to form her article. And if anyone had the words, it would be Armand.

*

Sitting at his workbench, pouring over copies of family trees that had been recorded in the fronts of old bibles, Armand paused briefly in his work. Something pulled at his mind—which itself wasn't a surprise—but what he didn't realize at the time—and never would—was that he'd have no recollection of this pause.

There would be no memory of the next five minutes of his life, no fleeting image of a dream, not even an unsettling feeling of Déjà vu. It was, and would remain to be, a hole in time. And it would never ever be recovered.

It was as if those five minutes had just been stolen by a thief in the night.

*

Del finished the last sentence, then with a flourish wrote *The End*, and signed her name.

She wasn't sure if The End was appropriate for newspaper articles but figured Mr. Bobby would tell her. Then she underlined her name with a curly cue, held the pad out at arm's length, and marveled at her first article.

New Orleans: A Tapestry

By Delphine Larouche

People don't try to be invisible. It just happens when the world forgets to look at them.

Your mind seeks out the connection points of your life: the bus stop, the light that just turned green, the eyes of a stranger that didn't meet yours, and you rate your day on how well these points align with your expectations.

But what did you really see?

Did you see the invisible people?

Yes, that's right, the invisible people. Your eyes collect their images. They see them in passing—the man who mumbles at the bus stop, wearing three jackets even in July, the woman who sweeps the sidewalk every morning though no one knows where she lives, the boy who tap dances in Jackson Square with bottle caps stuck to his bare feet, but doesn't have a tip cup. But do we see them? Or have we made them invisible?

Where did these people come from?

Who wove them into our tapestry?

"The Weaver," I say.

"The Weaver?" you ask. "Who is this Weaver?"

The Weaver is all of us. I am the weaver. You are the weaver. Time, weather, the sun, and the moon are weavers. And we live within the weave we make, yet we see so little of it, it's a wonder we comprehend anything at all.

Like the mosquito, we wave these people away.

What a waste!

Unfortunate Noise.

Necessary Background.

Bad Mojo.

They become something to smile at or look past, depending on our moods. They become conversation fodder when our own lives don't meet expectation. They are the requisite clowns in our mad little circus.

But through their eyes, what are they?

They are the anonymous helping hand from the crowd. They are the silent prayer for the stranger, the shoulder for the lonely, the spilled tear for the dying.

They are the invisible, and they are the yarn with which our tapestry is woven.

I think about this a lot.

These are the people we pass. Not because we mean to ignore them, but because we don't always know how to see them. They don't ask for much—just a second glance. A little attention. A name in print that isn't followed by a crime or obituary?

So, I will be writing theirs now. Their names. Their stories. Because they are part of this city's story. The quieter part. The part that smells of jasmine, old wood and sometimes smoke.

And if you see them—if you really see them—you might realize something unexpected:

They've been seeing you all along.

Del, vaguely aware of her visit to the mind of Armand, smiled, beaming at the paper she held in her hands. She knew it wasn't perfect and hoped that it wasn't too *out there* to be considered for publication. She didn't know where the concept of the weaver had come from, but it felt right for some reason. On top of that, she was excited about the idea of writing stories about other people, in a way other orphans, who had lost contact with their families, or in some cases, society all together. Wasn't she the perfect person to do that? She thought so.

A feeling of hope hit her so thoroughly it was like a revelation. She was going to be a newspaper reporter after all!

And she couldn't wait to show her article to Mr. Bobby.

CHAPTER 35

After checking on the head in the attic, Madame Broussard returned to the main floor and her fresco. The Toth-skeleton, like an unruly child denied its plaything, was ambling around the room looking for a way back up to see the thing in the wooden mask. Why the sound of Toth's voice had caused the head to come awake, she could only guess at, but feared it was not for a good reason.

Why she'd gone up there in the first place, she couldn't say. The fact that the building remained hidden was proof enough that the thing in the mask was still viable. After all, that was the source of what kept her and the building hidden. But she knew that cracks had begun to form in the whole process. After all, over the years hadn't the locals, the few sensitive ones that could still sense the other side, begun to whisper about an invisible building? Hadn't rumors reached her ears about a nefarious tradesman that dealt in all manner of trade, whether bone, flesh or spirit?

Of course they had.

And although some of that had been planned marketing—she had to survive after all—she'd been so very careful to stay hidden. But nothing remained forever, and over time, the head's ability to keep them hidden had begun to fail. And when she'd heard the rumors of the invisible building—the mere idea that something like that could exist—she knew that her end would eventually come.

She supposed that her trip to the attic was for no other reason than to ensure herself that a mouse hadn't chewed the nose off the thing. Or that a rat hadn't eaten half the head, which was causing its power to fade.

Though she hadn't removed the wooden mask from the head inside—and wasn't sure she could—she'd had the sense that it was still effective. But for how long? After all, how had Arlo found her? And this thought took her back to the black ring of spirits that surrounded her, the spirit hunter seeing her, the wraiths, and the whole feeling that her time was rapidly drawing to an end.

And in an ironic sort of revelation she realized that that end would play out, to some degree, on the fresco in front of her.

*

Thinking over her plans, mapping out her best escape route, she peered closely at the fresco. Toth, with its skeleton bones clacking softly behind her, came to the wall as well, mimicking its mother. Toth's eyes gleamed red as its little arms directed the skull eyes to scan the arial view of the Crescent City.

So many spirits, she thought.

So many lost opportunities.

But she was tired of this prison. Once, she'd thought the journey in the crate was the most horrible thing that anyone could endure. But she'd been wrong. The walls had closed in over the years, the many long decades of her banishment, to the point where they were as close as the walls of that crate, from so long ago. But at least then she'd had someone to speak to. Here, she had no one.

"Ngyihng..." Toth alerted, as it focused on a spot.

The Alvie-skull, driven by the demands of Toth, banged into a spot on the fresco, backed away, then, in a mockery of frustration banged forward again.

"Ngyihng!" Toth cursed.

Madame Broussard looked down in time to see Toth's stubby little arms jerk in frustration. This caused the skull to tip backwards again, then forward, crashing into the fresco with even greater force.

"Ngyihng! Ngyihng!" Toth reprimanded.

The unseeing eyes of the Alvie-skull stared dumbly forward, waiting for its master to plow its head into the wall again. It was a sad looking thing, doomed to live out its life at the insane demands of its tiny demon master.

Madame Broussard steadied it with her hand, as she looked at Toth. Its red-beaded stare never left the fresco.

She gently raised one arm of the skeleton, helping it to extend a boney finger. Toth's stubby arm raised to mimic the motion. Whether or not Toth would ever be able to control the bone arms, while moving its head for direction, and general motion forward, she did not know. It was a clever little thing, but that was a lot to ask of something that was basically a cursed bit of... whatever Toth was. She'd yet to identify what the lumpy brown skin was, or how the initial magic had been born into it, but that wasn't important now.

Supporting its bone finger with her own, she raised it up, then down, then to each side, showing—*hoping* to show—the whole of the

Toth-skeleton that its arms and fingers could be used as well.

After a general lesson on the four cardinal positions, she touched the fresco with her own finger, causing the sketched images there to grow larger. It was a way to see more clarity within the fresco, but the effect was localized. A strange expansion affect, like someone blowing a bubble from behind the fresco, caused the image there to expand, in a distorted way. If the detail was already there and she used a magnifying glass, she supposed it would have a similar effect, but it didn't work that way.

"...ohhh..." escaped the red bead mouth.

She was so surprised at this, she jerked her finger back as if she had received a jolt. The boney hand and arm, having lost its support, swung down to the side, and rocked to a stop.

"...ngyihng?" Toth said mournfully and motioned as if to drive the skull into the fresco again. It wanted to see the spot.

Lifting its hand again, she supported its finger and touched the spot on the fresco. The ballooning picture gave her a few distorted details as they both slid their fingers, one atop the other, around in a slowly widening circle. Something of importance was here somewhere.

They both saw it at the same time, although neither would realize they'd seen something slightly different from the other.

Madame Broussard saw what could only be the wraiths. But there were only two of them, she thought. She couldn't be sure, as they were all huddled in a tight mass, but the density of the object made her think there were only two. This meant that one was unaccounted for.

Staring, she also detected another presence. It was not a wraith, but something more. And she couldn't say that she was seeing it, at least all of it, but she knew more was there. It was like when she'd detected Scarmish on the fresco, in whatever form he'd returned in, but different. This was larger and more powerful, but nearly impossible to see. And the only way she knew of a spirit being able to hide from her view was if it had inhabited, or possessed, a living being. And that was the worst thing she could imagine. For once a spirit or wraith found a living vessel to attach itself to, it could move, day or night, through the city undetected. And it would be impossible to find and defeat.

Toth on the other hand stared at the same spot on the fresco but saw something else. Its bead eyes were not those of the enigma which had given it a second life, and which now guided its bone finger. Its mind did not hold the centuries of knowledge that had kept its new mistress alive. And it had no concept for how it had become separated from the thing on the fresco, but with every ounce of its borrowed life, it knew that it had been something different before. Toth understood that it had had a different life-source in a past time. And if that were true, it'd had a different master as well.

And from what little it could piece together—from a glimpse deep within the fresco, its master had been blue mist.

And was at this very moment, calling it back home.

*

Madame Broussard pulled back from the fresco and left the Toth-skeleton to stare in wonder. Suddenly everything made sense.

Why it had taken her so long to understand, and why it had happened now, was something else she couldn't explain. These lapses in judgement, in seeing, would have bothered her to no end in her youth, her she no longer had time to worry about such things.

Granted, Arlo had found her somehow. It made sense because she had something of the witch's. Something that was very dear to her and had caused the witch to search for her throughout the centuries. She had the head of her youngest sister, Dred, trapped in an enchanted mask in her attic.

And before the time of the witch sisters, before the time of Arlo, Barlo, and Dred, when the creatures of the Crescent City—creatures very much like herself—roamed freely and ruled the night, there had been others. There had been the onslaught of the abominations, a veritable invasion of wretched creatures formed by the unholy binding of animal spirit to human, human spirit to animal, or worst of all, a combination of all. These abominations had come out of the swamps, first by ones and twos, then as a great hoard, as if an entire town of women had given birth to the same adulterated seed. And eventually it was discovered that this sire had been one John Montanet, who had taken the title of Dr. John the Conjurer, and who had famously been put down by Marie Laveau herself. Or so went the story.

And of course, there had been Étienne. Amongst all the chaos of that time, amongst all the debauchery of the creatures, there had been one who rose above it all and brought the creatures under control. But not by himself. No, as powerful as he was, he could not reign in the likes of the creatures by himself. Deals had been made. Alliances had been formed. And in the end, some trusts had been broken. During the dark days of New Orleans, it had been the only way. Had it not been done, the city would have first devoured itself, then been consumed by the swamp and the still older things that lived there.

But now there were the wraiths. And the last time the city had seen such things, had been the time she had just recalled. And if they were back, it only made sense that John's magic was back. Either it had been rediscovered, or... if this were even possible... John had somehow survived.

And in the middle of this storm, this perfect storm, hidden away for most of her life in an orphanage, was perhaps the center of the whole thing. The spirit hunter had been born into a time that would see some of the greatest foes ever matched in the new world, many born of the old world, brought back together in a final epic battle. And she would come into her power at the very start of it.

Her hand went instinctively to the black pearls around her neck. Touching them brought a thought into her mind. First, it was of feeling, a feeling of presence. Second, it was of voice, a pleading yet defiant one. Lastly, it was of innocence, tarnished, yet unbroken. She was remembering innocence in the face of evil. She was remembering the face of Zoe, the other girl in the crate from so long ago. A girl who had been surrounded by evil, but who had persevered, somehow. A girl that was not unlike someone she had watched on this very fresco.

At that moment, Madame Broussard knew what she needed to do. She had no time to consider an escape plan. She had to send a message.

She looked at the Toth-skeleton, her only means left of communicating with the outside world. Bending her head to it, first Toth, then the skull, looked up. She put her mouth very close to Toth and whispered. Its red bead eyes pulsed once as if growing with surprise. Then she whispered to the skull, a separate, but related message. The Alvie-skull only stared dully forward.

Standing back, she pointed to the opposite corner of the room where a dark shadow had just begun to bleed out of the wall. It was as if the corner of the room had suddenly given away to a black oozing cancer that had finally burst through a thin crack in the wall.

Toth steered the head to look at the spreading shadow and the clacking leg bones began to move. With each step the Toth-skeleton slid forward a tiny bit, covering more ground than its short legs should naturally allow. It was being pulled to the opening of the shadow road by whatever ancient force had created it. There, it would move along the network of invisible paths that ran through the city and hopefully end up at its intended destination.

Madame Broussard had used Toth to send a warning to Del.

CHAPTER 36

The morning was cold and overcast, unusually cold.

October Country had already settled into the northern states and was making its slow descent towards the Crescent City, but it was never this cold in September. It should be in the low seventies, Del thought, rising quickly into the eighties by the afternoon. But this morning, standing outside the office of the Times-Picayune, she felt that it was barely sixty degrees.

Del rubbed her arms for warmth, wishing she had brought her jean jacket. She'd been so excited to speak with Mr. Bobby today and show him her article, she'd rushed out of the house without even thinking about the weather. And it wasn't until standing on the sidewalk for fifteen minutes after her body cooled down from the bike ride, that she'd noticed how chilly it was.

She had been showered and ready by seven a.m. but knew that Mr. Bobby was a late sleeper, so she'd spent some more time rereading her article. She'd almost shown it to Armand for feedback but then felt a strange fear that he may be able to recognize his own thoughts written on the paper. She didn't know if that was possible, but she'd never had a trancing session like that before, one where she felt like she was rummaging around in someone's head. So, with the tiniest bit of guilt on her conscious, she'd tranced on everyone's whereabouts that morning and conveniently left out the back door while Armand and Mama D where in other parts of the house.

Now it was almost nine-thirty in the morning and there was still no sign of Mr. Bobby.

She'd thought about going inside the office to ask about him, but still didn't feel like she belonged there. In her mind, she imagined there was some type of ritual, or rite of passage, that a reporter had to go through before they'd be invited into—much less accepted within—a newspaper office. So, she'd stood outside as the cold crept into her body.

A man came out of the front door that she thought she recognized. He had the characteristic *harried and hurrying* look of a reporter. Besides, the press pass sticking out of his hatband was like a beacon, yelling, "Out of my way! My finger's on the pulse of the city and I have a story to write!"

What she wouldn't do for a press pass like that one. Although, she wasn't sure how good she'd look in a hat, so didn't know where she'd put it. She absently felt the bandeau wrapped tightly around her hair, and wondered if she could carry it there, but quickly dismissed the idea as silly. Besides, she had to find Mr. Bobby.

"Excuse me," she said after the man had already passed her. He was weaving his way through a crowd of people and getting further ahead with every harried step he took.

She tried following but only managed to do the awkward *side-step-excuse-me-gotta-get-around* dance with the people in front of her.

And trying to push her bike through the crowd wasn't helping either.

"Excuse me!" she said rather loudly in a woman's face, meaning it for the man who was almost out of sight.

"Well, excuse me!" the woman said, and pushed past Del.

Del watched the woman go by, and it was only for a second, but when she turned back around, she panicked. She'd lost sight of the man.

"Stop!" her unspoken voice bellowed in the man's head, despite not being able to see him. Up ahead, the man stopped so abruptly that another man walking behind him, plowed right into his back. "Hey, watch it," the guy said and moved around.

The man with the press pass in his hatband looked around as if he'd heard his own name called. Del, flashing quickly at the minds of the remaining people coming at her, saw her opening and in three quick steps maneuvered her way to the reporter, who was just beginning to think the sound *had* been all in his head. Which it had been.

Not seeing anyone he recognized, he started to turn away.

Chiding herself for her stupidity—she could have just spoken into his head in the beginning—she sent a more pleasing greeting to him.

"Excuse me," his mind heard. He shook his head, poking a finger in his ear. "My name is Del," Del said aloud, as she pushed her bike up beside him. "Can I ask you a question?"

The man, now looking at Del, removed his finger from his ear as she spoke as if to test whether the sound was inside or outside of his head.

"Say again?" he said, tapping his ear.

His accent was strange and reminded Del of her favorite T.V. show *The Naked City*. It was a gritty police procedural set in New York. "*There are eight million stories in the Naked City. This has been one of them,"* was its tagline. She imagined what it would be like to be a big-time reporter in that city.

Del smiled. "I didn't mean to yell back there. I just couldn't get your attention."

The man looked back at where the girl had motioned with her head and seemed to give up on understanding the strange hearing issue he'd just experienced.

"Oh, ok," he said. "Can I help you?"

"I'm Del. Uh, Delphine Larouche." An awkward pause hung in the air. "You may have heard of me. I'm Mr. Bobby's uh, appren… uh, under…" She'd almost said 'apprentice' then almost changed it to 'understudy,' but wasn't sure if either of these words were correct. The man's eyes narrowed in confusion as she fumbled for the right word. "What I meant to say," Del began.

And at that moment the man thought of the word she was searching for: *mentee.*

Del's face brightened. "Yes, that's it! Mentee. He's helping me—"

As quickly as Del's face had lit up when she'd plucked the word from the man's mind, his mouth dropped open in shocked surprise. She realized what she'd done just a moment too late.

His eyes narrowed again, then slid back and forth in their sockets, looking past her and for the person who was surely trying to prank him.

"I'm sorry," Del said. "Sometimes… well, sometimes I just…" She pointed at her own head as a sheepish grin crept onto her face. "… kind of, hear the words, you know… as they're being spoken."

The man's eyebrows went up as his head tilted down. With a quick flick of his hand, the front brim of his hat shot up, revealing a forehead creased with worry—or suspicion—lines. He stared at her like this for a moment, then cleared his throat.

"Yeah, OK," he said quietly, "let's just pretend like I heard something out loud. I'll sleep better that way." Then he grabbed his hat and scratched his head with it. "Jeez, this city..." he mumbled.

Straightening up, he left his hat cocked so that the brim pointed to the sky on a sharp forty-five-degree angle. His hands went into his pants pockets as an inquisitive look settled onto his face. "Now, *how* is it that I can help you?"

*

Del was disappointed.

After making a fool out of herself in front of one of Mr. Bobby's colleagues— *"You've probably heard of me. I'm the non-apprentice that has never written anything."*—then reading the man's mind and spitting his own thoughts right back at him, he hadn't been able to help her at all.

The man—his name was Dick Wynthrop, from New Jersey—had only been in New Orleans a couple of months. Yes, he knew Bobby Dupre. No, he didn't know where he was. He didn't remember seeing Bobby over the last several days, but that didn't mean a lot. And unfortunately, he couldn't even guess as to the reason for his tardiness. Although—and he had added this part as a kind of afterthought—now that he thought of it, Del's name had sounded familiar to him, and it was his mistake not to have recognized it.

Without trying, Del knew that was a bunch of hooey. And she wasn't guessing either, she knew. Whether it'd been a trance, a flash, or an outright theft of his thoughts, she saw the little white lie in his mind, would swear that she had even seen it forming somehow before he spoke it, but couldn't explain how it had happened.

But she appreciated the fact that he had told it—the little white lie—to minimize the embarrassment that probably had shown on her face during her awkward opening.

And with a polite goodbye, he had left her standing in the street.

CHAPTER 37

Forty-five minutes later Del was riding north on Montegut Street—one she had never heard of before—and wondering if she wasn't in the wrong place. After finishing her talk with Mr. Wynthrop, she'd realize it was closing in on ten a.m. and began to wonder what she'd do with her day.

(Find him!)

She'd jumped at the sternness of the command, causing several people to eye her oddly as they moved around her.

In response, Del just shook her head as the two halves of her mind battled. She wasn't really surprised at the harshness of her self-reprimand. That part of her mind—the occult part? —was often dismayed and frustrated when Del didn't rely automatically on her ability. Perhaps that was because the other half of her mind seemed to actively try and forget—or at least to not remember—that she could simply trance on Mr. Bobby and find him.

Yet, the occult part wouldn't always just come forward with the idea. It was as if it sat around waiting for her to slip up, so it could scream at her, "Just use it! Just use the gift! What are you waiting for? You could be the best reporter in the city if you'd just look at what people are thinking. What's wrong with you?"

Her battling mind frustrated her to no end. And she didn't even begin to try and figure out how her gift worked. But she was beginning to understand that there was an odd sense of fairness somewhere in her core. It was as if the one part of her mind thought, "Well, if you're *really* good at this or that, you don't *need* to trance. That'd be like cheating. No one else can do it, so why should you?" Which was why it always tried to forget.

These thoughts, amongst many others, were what kept her up at night, and were what was responsible for the shadows that crept ever darker beneath her eyes.

But, as the voices in her mind subsided, the concern for Mr. Bobby grew. And if anyone could find him quickly, it was her.

So, that's what she had done. No sooner had the thought crossed her mind that he might have had an accident, or even worse, a medical issue, her mind was flooded with images.

Her vision did not go back to their last meeting. If it had, and if she'd followed it forward, she would have understood, she would have *seen* the thing that awaited her. But she had not done that.

Instead, she had pictured him coming and going into the Times-Picayune office, where his path was as well-worn as the spirit-paths she'd seen in Jackson Square.

It was like that in front of the newspaper office. Del saw the path that Mr. Bobby walked nearly every day. It was like looking at a map of a river and its tributaries, the widest part of the river was his main route, the smaller tributaries were his many detours. Granted, this map had many right angles on it as he moved from block to block, but it served her purpose.

Once she had the aerial view anchored in her mind, and thought she knew which path to take, transposing the image to something she could follow on the ground was the last trick she had to master. Again, this was something new to her and brought back a sudden feeling of vertigo as her vision-mind adjusted to the sensation, but she managed it well enough.

It didn't have the same doppelganger effect as before; she wasn't watching someone walk towards her. It was more like moving along in someone's old dust cloud, as they slowly decayed. She wrinkled her nose in disgust when the thought came to her.

Faint and shadowing outlines of Mr. Bobby, from the many times he'd walked this path, were imprinted in the air in front of her. Most of the outlines were so old they no longer resembled him, and had begun to drift away as a vague distortion of his original shape, but somehow she knew they were his. If she were to draw a picture of the experience, there would be a million Mr. Bobby images stretching out before her in a long, loose tunnel of dust. The more recent imprints still looked like him, although even those were faint, nearly invisible, shadows. The older imprints had begun to… fall apart, in a way. It was like looking at a picture of a dust cloud in space—the one that looked like a horse head came to mind—where you knew something had exploded but it would take another billion years or so for it to stretch out of shape.

A strange thought struck her at that moment. She imagined the cosmic dust of Mr. Bobby's path as a visual representation of the long-lasting impact each one of us has on the people around us. If his mere presence on a sidewalk lasted this long, how long did his deeds last?

And for that matter, how long of an impact did someone's words have?

A sudden pang of guilt dropped into her stomach. She thought she may need to take an inventory of her own impact before all of this was over. But she wasn't sure if she was ready to see all the devastation left in her wake.

Merging deftly into traffic, she rode north through the streets from the central business district, where the Times office stood on St. Charles Avenue. From there she'd skirted the Quarter by taking side streets and the occasional alley. Once past the tourist area, she turned East and wound her way through the old Faubourg Marigny neighborhood. Although, somewhere along Dauphine Street she saw something so strange that she nearly wrecked her bike right in the middle of the street.

She'd been clipping along at a good pace. Over the last year and a half, she'd become quite adept at navigating the traffic on her bike—and no longer felt the backpack slung over her shoulders—so much so, that half the time her eyes wandered off to take in the wrought iron balconies covered with flowers, rather than the boring task of watching the cars. But this time, as she let her gaze wander—it was mostly her eyes, but some of her mind as well—she thought she saw the edge of a building that one moment was there, then the next moment was gone. It was like the building had started to materialize in the air, or more like, was pressing against the fabric of the air leaving its outline, then with a puff of wind the fabric of air moved off the building and its outline had disappeared.

When this happened, she was looking straight over the roofline of another building where she thought the clouds were about to break apart. That's when it happened. The top corner of a building—

although she felt it wasn't built very straight, the geometry was all wrong—briefly came into view, then disappeared. She'd been so startled by this, she did a double-take, veered into the lane of a taxicab trying to pass her, overcorrected away from its front fender, hit a loose piece of asphalt that was trying to form a pothole, and almost spilled herself into the busy street. Fortunately, something pulled her attention back to the road at the last minute, allowing her to stay on the seat and keep her out from under the milk truck behind her. A quick flash showed her the scared and angry driver of the truck behind her as he clenched his fist and sent a series of curse words at her through his windshield.

Ten minutes later she was away from the busier roads. She was headed north on Montegut Street, then turned right onto a no name street and skidded her bike to a stop. She didn't know what street this was, the sign had either been stolen or knocked down, but she didn't like the area. She was just north of an area known as Bywater which still bordered the river on one of its many bends.

The area she was at now sat unceremoniously about a third of the way between Bywater to the south, and Lake Pontchartrain to the North. It had a large trainyard running north and south along which Montegut ran on its east side until it was abruptly stopped by some industrial land works related to the trainyard. It was this portion of Montegut that she had followed before coming to this little gem of a dead-end street.

She was surprised, and a little disappointed, that Mr. Bobby lived in such an area. Her idea of a famous newspaper writer had placed him in a much different area. Certainly not a mansion like Armand's, but at least a nice house with a yard for barbequing. Or a cool apartment uptown where he could easily attend late night soirees with important people, discussing important topics.

But this place wasn't any of that. And yet, she knew this was the right area. She could feel it in the pit of her stomach.

She began to walk her bike forward as she took in the desolate view. The no name road ran east for about a block and a half before it made a sharp left, sending it north, where it would also dead-end at the same piece of unpassable ground that had stopped Montegut.

As soon as the road swung left, she knew that Mr. Bobby's house was up on the right. His imprints were exploding out of it, spilling out past the barren front yard, and drifting aimlessly out into the street. There the dust of Mr. Bobby's existence hung in the air like a specter, refusing to float away.

Del paused her forward movement, but her mind was in overdrive. Looking, flashing and trancing simultaneously, she searched to discover what was wrong with this place. It was as if the entire street was dead — nothing moved. And there was no sound.

Well, a little, she thought, but it was muted and seemed far away. Much further than it should be considering she was only ten minutes from a major highway. Why was that?

Up ahead, the floating imprints of Mr. Bobby looked to be frozen in place. But as she moved closer, she realized they were simply moving very slowly, again, like the exploding cloud of space dust a billion miles away.

And like in space, there was nothing here to move the air. As far as she could tell, the trainyard was dead. If not dead, certainly out of use. And there was little to no traffic here considering the roads had been cut off.

One way in, and one way out.

Looking around again, each small house seemed to peer at her with their unblinking black windows. They seemed to watch her move deeper into this isolated place. This place where nothing moved, and time had slowed to a crawl of the ages.

And then she realized that she no longer felt that the little neighborhood was dead or abandoned, but only laying in wait for someone to stumble into its dead-end world.

She inched her bike forward, but even though she was still three houses away, the place felt downright bad to her.

The knot in her stomach had turned to acid. For at that moment, she fully expected to find Mr. Bobby dead in his living room, covered with flies. Or worse.

*

Despite the cold, a slick of sweat covered Del's skin from her bike ride. But despite the bike ride, Del felt the wave of cold that emanated from the house. It shimmered before her like a curtain.

Standing on the sidewalk at the edge of the drive, she felt that she stood at the edge between two worlds. The world she was in, the one where she'd ridden her bike following the cosmic dust of Mr. Bobby, was still humid and temperate, despite the weather change. The other world, the one that surrounded the house in a type of invisible bubble, was silent and cold. A cold which she not only felt as it wafted towards her, but curiously, one that she could see. As her exhausted body puffed out the last of its used-up air, she watched her breath—invisible as it exited her mouth—become a specter of mist six inches in front of her face.

Tentatively extending her hand, she felt when it passed into the bubble of cold and watched in fascination, and more than a little concern, as the heat waves rose off her arm and turned to mist.

One way in, and one way out.

That vague thought was somewhere in the back of her mind when she stepped forward, leaving the sidewalk and her world, and entering the world of whatever was in the house.

CHAPTER 38

Sitting at his worktable, absently doodling on a sheet of paper, Armand tried to collect his thoughts. They were scattered today, more than usual, and he couldn't seem to get them in order.

He had quietly watched Jimmy over the last few days, looking for any signs of distress. The hypnosis session that had ended so abruptly, weighed on him, but he was reluctant to probe too soon. If it had left some type of lingering impression on the boy's mind, he thought it better to let it heal over first, much as one would allow a cut or scrape to heal. Too much probing in the beginning would only prevent it from scarring over and introduce infection.

Infection?

Armand wrote the word on the paper as if to inspect it further. That was a strange term to associate with someone's potential mental state. Why had it come to him?

Although he was not a licensed practitioner, he knew a fair amount about psychology and general *maladies of the mind*. They were tricky things to diagnose. And although he realized that Jimmy's limitations had been present at birth, he couldn't discount the feeling that some of his recent behavior hadn't been caused by the hypnosis session, or even worse, the Ouija board incident.

The image of the crazily spinning puck came to him, followed closely by the eerily printed crayon message, both a result of the Ouija board. Then there was Jimmy's strange third-person reference to himself, the weird chess game, and the growing infatuation with the stone maiden.

Had these all been triggered by the hypnosis session?

He didn't think so. Jimmy's fascination with the maiden had been established from the moment he'd come to live here. But after the episode with Clara…

Armand began sketching a rough draft of the stone maiden and the pool of water she stood over. His thoughts went back to the days after the Clara incident and the significant repair that had to be done to the gate and backdoor. And there was something about the maiden…

Hadn't he found strange scratches on the courtyard stones around that time?

And there had been something about fresh cracks in the maiden herself. He recalled mentioning this to Frank. Or, thinking that he'd meant to. But one thing was certain, try as he might, Armand could not escape the idea that many of these events had been triggered through some action that he himself had taken. Good intentions be damned—that was the core of it. And to that end, he suddenly thought that perhaps *he* was the infected one.

The idea bloomed in him like the totality of an eclipse, an idea so large and dreadful that it cast his entire world into shadow.

His mouth tightened into a grim line beneath his moustache. His head nodded imperceptibly at the realization. Victor Vermis, aka the

Tricky 'ol Bastard, aka the Gris-gris man who once was Dr. John and possibly had many other names, had exploited the weakest link in his line. And it wasn't a mentally handicapped boy or a practitioner who had lost her ability to see. It was Armand himself. Through sheer negligence, he had let this spirit captivate his imagination, which caused him to be careless. And in that manner, The Gris-gris man in whatever form he'd been in, had left an indelible mark on Armand and his family.

But now that he understood the level of deception that they were dealing with, he meant to do something about it. He would not be so easily fooled again.

*

Mama D puttered anxiously around the downstairs den. A nearly full pot of tea sat on an end table, and most of what she'd poured into her cup sat cold and undrunk. She was trying to catch the vision that had nearly come to her in its complete form.

Over the last few days her trancing vision had grown steadily stronger. She wasn't sure if it was the constant practice she'd gone through, which had been significant, or if it was the residual effect of being in Del's presence during one of her trances. But she wasn't complaining.

In many ways she felt like she'd been exercising for weeks on end trying to melt away twenty years of bad eating or turn back the clock to a younger version of herself. She was exhausted.

And this had nothing to do with physical exercise. It was a mental exhaustion that dripped down from her overworked brain and seeped into her shoulders and back, tightening them a little more, and a little more throughout the day until they were taught as a drum.

Most nights—excluding those when Armand tricked her into being his drinking buddy in place of Frank—she'd gone to bed early, falling asleep as soon as her head hit the pillow.

But tonight was different.

Thinking about nothing in particular, a vision had practically come knocking on her mental door. Perhaps it was because she hadn't been trying to force the issue. She'd simply been wandering around the house looking for something, and suddenly it was there.

Or, more accurately, the feeling that a vision was coming was there. She felt it like a pleasant memory she hadn't thought of in years. It was like a lost song title that suddenly revealed itself, like a…

Like a…

Like a ghost in the night.

*

One moment the Toth-skeleton had been stumbling along in the hidden room of Madame Broussard's building, and the next moment it had been sucked into the void that had opened in the corner of her main room.

The sensation—if the creature had the mental capacity to have one—was like the first time it—meaning the bones—had passed through the shadow roads: immediate and abrupt. One moment it was somewhere, then, after an arbitrary length of time, it was somewhere else. It didn't really care *when* it was, as creatures of its type had no notion of time. It simply knew that it existed in the here and now, and that place was somewhere other than where it had been.

So, when it arrived in its new location—drawn there by the power of the one it was sent to find—it stepped out of the shadows and into a room that vibrated with the very essence of power. It was a room that was saturated with the power of Del, her bedroom. Only *stepping out of the shadows* for something that had just arrived via the shadow roads didn't mean that it appeared through a door. The darkest shadow in Del's room, which happened to be near a point of intense saturation, was the one under her bed.

It recognized the feeling of the power immediately. It had felt it before.

At some point in the past, before the birth of the Toth-skeleton, the Alvie-bones had been sent on a similar mission, but somewhere along the way, it had been pulled askew by another force in the house.

Now, the bones of the Toth-skeleton vibrated with the memory of the power, practically clacking themselves apart, sending vibrations of energy up the long hat needle into the body of Toth.

"Ngyihng!" Toth said, as its eyes began to glow. "NGYIHNG!"

It tried to step forward, to move completely out of the shadow and closer to the saturation point but couldn't navigate the small space. It didn't have the muscle memory of crawling.

After several minutes of clacking and scraping about, the bones grew tired, which sent less energy to Toth. Its glowing red eyes dimmed, signaling its loss of power. Then, it stopped moving altogether, essentially asleep until another wave of energy would give it a semblance of consciousness and life.

So, there it lay, mostly obscured by shadows, beneath Del's bed.

*

(CLICKETY-CLACK the bones are back.)

"AHHH!"

Jimmy screamed from his seated position on the floor, sending comic books and marbles flying. He'd been sitting in front of his treasure drawer debating on reading an Archie comic book—which consisted mostly of him finding the scenes that Betty was in—or picking a special marble that he didn't mind sacrificing to the black queen in his next chess game. He'd yet to find a way through to the end of that never-ending game and thought that a cat's-eye marble would do the trick. He'd avoided this type of marble up until now because it reminded him of a monster he'd dreamt about some time ago, but he was running out of ideas on how to defeat the queen and the stone maiden was getting impatient, so he thought he'd try this.

But as soon as the sounds hit his ears—a sound like that of a Halloween windchime made of bones—his mind had been flooded with a skin-crawling feeling of invasion. He couldn't remember where he'd heard the sounds before, but he felt like his own bones had begun to vibrate and were trying to walk right out of his body.

Leaving the dresser drawer open and his treasures exposed, he ran and hid in the walk-in closet where Slinky and the other shadows lived. The closet could be scary, especially when the door opened on its own. But out of all the scary things in his room—the talking mirror, the cannibal shadows, even the train lampshade—the noise of the bones was worse than all of them.

And he knew without a doubt that they had just entered the house.

CHAPTER 39

Dropping her bike on the overgrown path that acted as a narrow driveway, Del didn't notice the absence of sound.

She no longer thought about sound, or the cold, or the staring eyes of the other houses. Those were things outside of her current world, and she was in a different world now. She didn't know it, but she had just walked into her own episode of the Twilight Zone: New Orleans style, and she was one of the lead characters.

The air around the house was thick and dense, concentrated somehow into an immovable cloud. As if knowing a secret of their own, her hands floated up, reaching out in front of her, just as her mind flashed towards the house. Then she wobbled, slightly. Something was wrong with her balance, and her hands moved to help keep her upright.

But something else was wrong as well. Whatever was affecting her balance, was also interfering with her vision; she couldn't see into the house.

She guessed it was the fog causing her vertigo, but didn't remember this happening before. A flush of worried heat ran up her neck as beads of sweat broke on her forehead.

She flashed again towards the interior of the house, but nothing happened; she couldn't see anything. Then, as if on an escalator that had suddenly begun to move, her hands shot out to her sides, working the air for balance again. Mist swirled about her in random not-random patterns—an intricate weave, not unlike that buried deep within her palm—which spelled out an ancient warning. But only the mist could read it.

She spread her feet, anchoring her stance and tranced again, then she tried with her eyes closed. Nothing. She couldn't see inside the house.

Her heart pounded out its warning. *This isn't right... Something's not right. Get out while you still can!*

She started to turn, but just as quickly as her hands had come up, a presence entered her mind.

(One way in, one way out.)

Del flinched at the invasion.

She was used to her mind arguing with itself. She was even used to having to tell the two sides to shut up and be quiet. But the two sides had always been different versions of the same whole, her pessimistic side warning her optimistic side, or the pragmatist berating the dreamer. But this had been different. The reprimand that her other side had just given her was more forceful than usual; it had a heavier hand. And in some strange way, it hadn't felt like hers.

One way in, one way out. What did that even mean?

She wasn't sure how long she had stood there steeling her nerves but felt it had been too long. When the thought of Mr. Bobby came back to her and the possibility—no, the certainty—that he was lying somewhere inside the house close to death, she pushed her fear away and took three more steps towards the side door.

The second time she paused was to look back outside the fog and down the street for any movement, in case she needed to call for help. What she saw sent another wave of vertigo-inducing-dread through her.

She saw nothing, nothing at all.

She could no longer see *outside* the fog bank. It was all encompassing and endless. She was blind to everything but this world of gray fog, and she panicked.

In her terror she turned and took several stumbling, low-reaching steps towards where her bike should have been.

It wasn't there.

She turned left thinking she'd missed it and clawed at the ground. Then she turned back to the right, swinging her arms around in a wild arc.

It wasn't there.

Grasping frantically through the fog, she fumbled in all directions, tripped, stumbled and righted herself. Her bike had to be here somewhere! It had to be!

It wasn't.

So, she ran.

Running was the only thing that made sense to her at that moment. The fog couldn't stay thick forever. And the dead-end she'd followed to get here wasn't that far away. Five steps. Ten steps at most. Hell, in twenty steps she'd be across the road and headed for the trainyard. She'd run until she tripped over the old steel rails that she knew to be lying out there.

But they never came.

*

She didn't know how far she had run or in which direction she'd gone, but she couldn't run any longer. It was hard to breath in the fog. It was like trying to breath through a wet towel, and she stopped.

When she did, wide-eyed and gasping, and bent to feel the pavement or trainyard rubble beneath her, she recoiled in terror. All she felt was the dead lawn and the overgrown driveway.

And at that moment her mind seized on a bizarre realization. Her bike was gone, just as the dead-end neighborhood was gone, just as the world as she knew it was gone.

She was in a Place of Gone.

And in that place her sense of self nearly left her. Her mind, reaching out in search of something to touch, something to latch onto, nearly failed. And it probably would have, leaving her to wander endlessly in the gray fog, had she not stood up, willing herself to move forward.

One way in, one way out.

Because when she did, her outstretched fingers brushed against something so familiar, yet so terrifying, her knees buckled and nearly sent her sprawling again.

Suddenly, and from a sense of direction so distorted she could have been standing upside down, she knew where she was. And the impossibility of it sent a plume of acid belching up her throat.

She was standing in front of, and touching, the side door.

In this Place of Gone, with her senses muted and her vision blinded, she hadn't needed to run anywhere.

The house had come to her.

*

Praeco felt a presence outside the house and awoke. Whether it awoke from a true sleep or an imagined one, it could not tell, as it had not the reference. But it had been disturbed from a pleasing vision of pictures.

Ever since it had attached itself to this vessel, and having no need to feed, it simply existed in a perpetual state of shared space.

If it had the sense of uncomfortably close quarters, it may have complained about its neighbor, but it did not. It only knew to exist, which it did. And in its existence, it saw pictures and scenes, and they had words and feelings and people, and its neighbor tried to hoard the things, tried to hide them, but Praeco liked them as well. So, it took the images for itself which left the neighbor mumbling and gibbering. And since it hadn't discovered how to make the noise stop, Praeco simply let it drone on.

It liked the images it had found. They reminded it of something it could not remember but was worth trying to, it felt. So, it took them, molesting them in its own voyeuristic way, and strung them together in random orders which caused blue babies to slide back up into their mothers and undie as the cord relaxed from around their necks. It caused exploded people to recombine and fly back up into the air, disappearing through unshattering windows. Heads and bodies switched places and became siblings that never existed. People died and undied, going in all directions at once. Words were spoken and sung in garbled ways, like too many voices screaming from the same mouth. Then something slick and wet was on it, then gone too soon, leaving a sense of crushing loneliness.

And Praeco may have lost itself in this menagerie of images, lost itself so completely that it would have forgotten to feed and eventually faded away in its sweet nightmare dream, had it not been for a most unfortunate thing.

Outside, Del stood up

(One way in, one way out.)

and began to move forward.

*

Once she had the door, Del walked into the house like it might have been her grandmother's. And as such, the house had been expecting her.

Not only was the door not locked, but it swung open with a heartfelt greeting of entry, then closed amicably enough. There were no screeching hinges, no thunderous slam behind her, nor was there the maniacal laugh from above and beyond.

There was simply the house, sitting in the Place of Gone, and as far as she could tell, it was empty.

In the kitchen she shivered and for the first time realized how cold it really was. It wasn't just cold, it was like an icebox.

During her frantic search outside for her bike, she'd forgotten the cold bubble that surrounded her. But now she felt its full force as her frozen breath puffed out in small wisps. It hurt to breath too deeply here and she found herself taking small shallow breaths.

She knew Mr. Bobby was in the front part of the house, not by trancing, but by feeling some primal vibration that rippled through the frozen air. It bent itself around the walls and down the short hallway that connected the front part of the house to the kitchen in the back. A small bathroom stubbed off the hallway towards the side of the house she came up on. A single bedroom sat in the back corner of the house opposite the kitchen. It was a simple four-room layout common to the area.

She could almost see the waves of his heartbeat disturb the frozen fabric of this place. But they were shallow, and… fading, she thought. He was alive, but whatever state of life he was in, she could not imagine. And she felt it was fleeting.

Her mind reached out to him but came back with only images of herself standing in the kitchen, half of the short hall that stood before her, and the bit of bedroom she could see through the open door. In short, her supernatural vision saw no more than her physical one. And this worried her. It was as if the walls and ceiling of the house were frozen so solidly that her mind could not penetrate them. Much less, her screams, she thought.

Three more steps and she was halfway up the hall, even with the bathroom. Here she could see into the open area that served as an eating nook.

There was no grand dining room here, just a plain living space for a normal person who had suddenly landed in the Place of Gone.

To the left of the eating area—as she looked towards the front—would be a small living room. That's from where the frozen waves of Mr. Bobby emanated. He seemed to be waiting for her.

*

Mr. Bobby, choking on the scream that would not come, felt his head split again. He recognized the hot line of pain that ran from the base of his neck, up the back of his skull, then over the top, before it split off in multiple directions. His skull was cracking like an egg.

He had the oddest thought at that moment. *This must be what a baby bird feels like, blind and deaf, but suddenly deciding it needed to leave its—*

Then a new level of terror blinded him.

Oh God. That's not right! That's not right! It's not the bird I feel like… it's the egg.

Oh God, I'm the egg!

And the tiny fragment of his mind that was left couldn't fathom what might crawl out of him when his skull finally cracked wide open, once and for all.

*

A wrenching shiver wracked Del's body as she neared the end of the hall. In just the last few steps the temperature had dropped severely. It had to be in the fifties, she thought, maybe lower.

She rubbed her bare arms briskly wishing she had anything to cover them with. Her thin T-shirt seemed to invite the cold into her core, and once it sunk in, it found its way up to her head, where a dull pain began to throb behind her left eye. She pushed the pain back with the palm of her left hand while wiping a frigid right hand across her runny nose. The cold always made her nose run.

But if she'd had the wherewithal to look, she would have realized that she'd just wiped away a smear of blood.

Her nose had begun to bleed.

*

Praeco felt the presence when it entered the house and hovered, hoardingly, around its Aether well. It had yet to feed from it, but the time was drawing near. It had to feed on the Aether before the body expired, or it would be no good. It would spoil then slip away on the wind. And this body, for some reason, was nearing its end.

It had exhausted the source of the pictures. Either there were no more, or the source had stopped working, dried up, no longer viable. But that no longer mattered, because something new was here.

The wraith, born from the power of one and the soul of another, had a fundamental understanding of ownership. Perhaps *understanding* wasn't the right word, considering what it experienced was more of a physical thing. A *tethering* may describe it better. That familial link from one being (a creator) to another (the created) could not be undone. Yet again, the word didn't quite fit the circumstance.

What Praeco experienced since it had been pulled from its menagerie dream, was so close to ownership it felt as if it were back with all its siblings.

It had siblings once, it felt. And like all siblings they had had chores. One of its chores had been to feed the others.

And, to feed its master.

The wraith known as Praeco, once named by its creator—by its old master—began to tremble like an abandoned dog. And like a dog which has been whipped so many times, the involuntary tremble could be triggered by nearly anything: the quick movement of a boot, the raising of a switch, or the simple presence of a stronger dog. The presence of a stronger dog meant that it would be made to give up its food. And although the other dog had not been the one to sire it, it would soon come to master it.

And Praeco remembered the terrible master it'd had before. And it planned to never bow to one again.

So, it hovered. And it waited.

*

Del stepped into the front room and turned to face the thing in the house. For all these long minutes—perhaps it'd even been hours, for time was different in this place—she'd dreamt up every imaginable scenario for how she might find Mr. Bobby. Dying of a heart attack was the most common image—he was an avid smoker after all—or immobilized by a terrible accident. The possibility that she'd find him dead by his own hand had even entered her mind until she'd felt his presence. But for all the things she could imagine, for all the things she had seen, she had no reference for what sat before her now.

She drew back in terror and screamed.

A three-headed monstrosity resembling some type of man sat on the living room couch. It was simultaneously vibrating, swelling, and shrinking all at once.

It had a singular body which was half dressed in Mr. Bobby's clothes. A button-up shirt, torn open to the waist, hung like a death shroud from its shoulders. One bare foot spasmed randomly against the floor, as its hands clawed at the remnants of its pants. Bloody finger marks streaked the upper thighs where the skin of the fingers had been worn away from spasmodic clutching. An overwhelming smell of shit and piss filled the air and Del thought she could hear the cushions squish as the body vibrated.

Backed all the way to the opposite wall, Del clawed tears from her eyes, fearful of losing sight of the monster for even a second. She felt as if the thing was waiting to pounce at her even then.

Bulging eyes looked at her as the mouth opened, stretching grotesquely out of shape, before falling back into place.

He was trying to scream and cry at the same time.

Suddenly, the mouth shot open further in an unbelievable grimace. A brief image of the ghost of Bob Marley came into her mind when it unwrapped the rag from around its ghostly head, letting its mouth fall open. But at least it could speak.

Mr. Bobby, or what was left of him, was trying to scream but nothing came out. He was choking on a scream that wouldn't come. Behind the tumult, she heard a muffled snap as a bone broke somewhere in his mouth.

And the whole time he did nothing but sit there and vibrate.

And in a way, the vibrating was the worst part.

She'd seen people with Parkinson's disease before who couldn't control their head or an arm. But she'd never seen a person's entire body shake. Not like this. It was as if he was tied to some medieval torture device that instead of pulling someone apart, was meant to shake them to pieces.

Focus! She scolded herself.

And in the face of it all, she did. Locking her jaw, she overpowered her terror, even as tears streamed down her cheeks.

Now do something!

And as commanded, her vision began to sharpen. It had taken time to understand what she was seeing, unraveling the scene layer by layer, but she finally understood. She saw what the three-headed monster was. And her knees buckled.

The three heads where an illusion which only her trancing mind could detect—but had also partially caused. Mr. Bobby's face was there, but not there. His head swelled almost to bursting, but at the same time caved in upon itself. And the entire time, a black ghost face flickered in and out of existence behind the swelling, pulsing face of the man.

The illusion had been enhanced by her doppelganger vision gone crazy. She saw Mr. Bobby's essence swell up then contract, in rapid succession. And when her brain tried to make sense of it, tried to rewatch it to understand it, it made the effect worse. But there was an incredible force working on him. Something pushed, then pulled on his very being, causing it to stretch outside of his physical body.

Oh, God. How—?

She thought she would vomit. The human body wasn't meant to do that.

The pressure from the infestation had a monstrous effect on his body. The skin, and even the skull, was pushed and pulled out of shape, first grossly expanded almost to the point of bursting, then cruelly compressed as if in an underwater pressure tank. That was the explanation for two of the heads. When the supernatural pressure from within expanded, it pushed his head out of proportion. But his skull could only expand so far, and at that point, whatever was inside of him broke the boundaries of his body—which her vision could see. This released the physical pressure which allowed his skull and body to deflate. Each time this happened, as his bones cracked apart from the outward and inward pressure, he expanded a bit further, only to deflate a bit more on the return. He was turning to rubber as his skeleton slowly broke apart one snapping, crumbling bone at a time.

The third head was formed by the thing itself. She now saw the black shadow in the shape of the man which hovered in the background.

The wraith!

(You should have known.)

But how?

(Use your gift!)

Yes, the wraith was what inhabited the shell of Mr. Bobby. It was causing the expansion and contraction of his body. And the entire time, it had been watching her, moving rapidly back and forth in the shadows as if to stay hidden, waiting to see what she would do.

But she had done nothing. Until now.

And just as she considered what she was going to do, the wraith-head began to swell. It went from cowering dog to bristling wolf in an instant. The shadowy man-shape with the skittish head solidified—no more vibration. Barbed tendrils of smoke which had been deeply embedded in the man pulled free, adding substance to the wraith—no more swelling for Mr. Bobby.

Then it morphed again. It swelled like the head of a cobra.

And it prepared to strike.

CHAPTER 40

Mr. Bobby, can you hear me?

Del's mind reached out in a sluggish representation of speech. Seeing the wraith swell, positioning itself for an attack, she needed to understand if the person that Mr. Bobby had been was still there. Was he dead and the wraith was simply inhabiting him? Or was he still alive somehow trapped, speechless, and broken beyond repair.

As if in response to this thought, and as the last of the wraith-tendrils slid from his body, Mr. Bobby deflated in a dying-balloon sort of way and slumped sideways on the couch. Del watched in incredulous stomach-churning horror as he shrunk to two-thirds of his normal size. He was a balloon man that had lost some of his air. He was a wax dummy that had been left too long in a warm room and was melting from the inside out.

He was a rubber man who had no bones.

But there was one thing that he still had, air in his lungs. And as he collapsed, preceded by a thin bubble of spit, a faint wheezing sound escaped his mouth, "...ehhhhhhh..." And with the sound, Del heard his new voice. A voice which came from vocal cords squashed and stretched out of proportion. She saw his thoughts which had been smashed in an expanding, cracking skull.

She saw everything now.

The frozen fog had prevented her from seeing inside the house. The squashed body and mangled mind had prevented her from hearing his voice and seeing his thoughts. But now she was here. She saw him and heard him. What he had become. What the shadow-leach had done to him. And she understood.

At that moment, the tiny prayer bubble that had escaped Mr. Bobby's mind, which had been suspended, floating slowly to nowhere, had finally reached someone who could hear it.

Del heard the final pleading prayer of Mr. Bobby before his mind had become a squeeze toy. "Kill me," he had prayed.

And just like that, as if also hearing the prayer and understanding the impact, the wraith began to feed.

*

Del saw the movement as it happened. A shadow-barb, thin as a needle, shot out from the body of the wraith, piercing the essence of Mr. Bobby. A tiny spark of light flickered on his body where the Aether began to leak out. The head of the barb, initially sharp, now changed into a living funnel—a proboscis made for sucking.

Then ten shadow-barbs pierced him.

Then a hundred.

Then a thousand, thousand needle-barbs punctured the fat, ripe Aether sack that hung suspended in the air, still attached to the dying body by a fraying silver cord. And once the skin of the fruit was split, the feeding began.

"NOOOO!" Del yelled. Rage overwhelmed her. Tears of anger burst from her eyes, blurring her vision again.

All of this happened in an instant. She saw everything as it happened, but her response was still too slow. The final molestation of Mr. Bobby had begun, and she wasn't fast enough.

"STOP IT!" she screamed.

She felt herself draw up. All at once she was pulling energy from somewhere. Her hypothermic body, cold to the point of pain, began to warm.

"GET AWAY FROM HIM!" she yelled. "GET AWAY!"

Tears of hatred and fear erupted out of her. She wept for what was happening to Mr. Bobby. She cried for not being able to stop his pain. But she also sobbed for the loathing she felt, for the deep well of hate she'd suddenly found. A white-hot column of poison gas, tapped from the very lakes of hell, had begun to move. The pressure was too much, and she felt the poison, the black streak that had been buried within her for so long, rise and fill her. And she cried for her own salvation.

Then she let the hate take her.

And suddenly, her mind was free. Caught up in the swirling maelstrom of her own power, it broke free of her body. Her vision changed as energy poured into her. The room became smaller as her vision grew. The wraith began to feed faster as the sweet taste of the Aether stirred its appetite. Her body began to warm as hell's fury rushed into the cracks of her psyche.

Her perspective shifted, first viewing the feeding scene in close detail, then floating back and up. She was seeing the room from an elevated point of view. Her mind expanded. She was floating. She was rising.

She was becoming…

Power.

Rage.

Retribution.

And so, she became.

With a loud crack of electricity, the swirling orb of Del snapped into existence. The heat of its arrival evaporated the frozen mist in a flash sending hot droplets shooting in all directions. The force of the arrival shook the walls of the tiny house, sending cracked plaster raining to the floor. Del's body was first thrown forward, then pulled back violently, yanked up into the swirling orb that was her mind; for it was a physical thing now.

*

The swirling mass of energy inhabiting the small room grew rapidly. Like the creation theory of the universe, where after it popped into existence, it began a rapid expansion, the swirling Orb of Del now went through its own inflation stage, pressing out against the walls.

The wraith, equally fast, and being fueled by the Aether, also grew in power and size. Like a mass of storm clouds that draw energy to itself by sheer mass, it had no choice but to grow. And soon, like many storms when the conditions are just right, it may become a twister, a black tornado, or even a hurricane, depending on conditions. But the storm of Praeco was different. Whatever it would become, it would not be random, for it had a sense of itself now. And hovering before it was another source of power, perhaps even greater than its old master.

It could feed forever on that source.

And if it could do that, it could be the master.

*

Del saw into the wraith and knew its mind. Its growth was startling, but there was something beyond that. It was beginning to think. She felt the thoughts emanating from the black space of its mind and sensed that it had just formed plans beyond that of feeding. She had to stop it before it could grow any stronger.

The wraith, swelling in height, pressing itself upwards to mimic the size of the spinning cloud before it, felt danger. But it also felt desire. Danger for the sense of destruction that radiated from the orb, but desire for the power within it. It could not reconcile these ideas beyond rudimentary needs but knew them to be true.

Looking deep within the wraith, Del hunted for a way to kill it. It was a black shadow nightmare that had been raised from the depths of hell and set loose on the world. And like a nightmare, there was no way to catch it. It had no life force that she could see, beyond that which it fed from. It was a thing made from nothing.

As the wraith grew, it peered into the spinning orb, saw through it, and there, it saw the source of its power. A body, like the one it was attached to, but different in many ways, hung suspended in the air like an imprint. Arms outstretched and motionless, legs rigid and still, gave the body a look of levitation. A levitating body caught up and held motionless in the center of a storm of energy. But what the wraith did not see, for it could not understand it, was the black streak that had suddenly appeared near the bottom of the orb. There, as faint as a shadow, was a black streak which, as if smeared by centrifugal force, began to snake its way up the outside of the orb. It was a thin but dangerous thing.

(Bite it,) the voices said, echoing off one another. Discordant things, the voices were familiar and not familiar at the same time. She knew them all yet did not recognize the whole. At least not yet.

(Bite it before it's too late. Bite it before it bites you.)

The voices, at least three of them, echoed in her mind, piercing deeply into it. The pain behind her left eye flared with great brilliance. The flow of warm blood from her nose began anew and slipped over her lips and down her teeth.

I can't! She yelled at the voices. *There's nothing to bite!*

Her anger grew beyond comprehension. Frustration overwhelmed her. The deflating body of Mr. Bobby pleaded to her. The gluttonous slurping from the wraith sickened her. The chastising voices mocked her.

(Bite it! Kill it before it's too late!)

"*Kill me,*" echoed the prayer bubble.

(Bite it!) screamed another voice.

(Kill it!) they urged.

"Kill him!" Del yelled in three distinct but merging voices.

And in that instance, she recognized them, the three voices. Somehow, they'd come together. Somehow, they had just merged. And they'd spoken for her.

The first voice was Arlo's, the person who had first taught her about the silver cord.

The second voice was the Dark Dreamer's, the black streak that lived in the shadows of Del's mind and which had, up until this moment, remained silent and hidden from her.

And the third voice was that of Del herself. The part of her mind that she argued with almost every night. The only *other* voice that she really interacted with, as if that would control the many voices in her head, or at least, keep them from coming forth.

All three voices had shaped Del in some way or another—even the silent one—leaving their imprint on the clay of her being while it was still wet. And through the heat and pressure of her anger, the outer shell of Del had just hardened a bit. And there, the impact of the voices would leave a lasting mark.

*

A blinding flash of light filled the house when Del bit. Once she'd screamed out the command to herself, willing it into reality, she had not hesitated. In a fraction of a second her focus had shifted from the wraith and how to potentially defeat it, to the obvious choice: Mr. Bobby's silver cord.

And in that split second, knowing that if there was still an ounce of life in him, and that she would be responsible for his death, she did not hesitate. The cord materialized—summoned by will alone. And when it did, she bit clean through it.

But the result was not what she had expected. It was nothing like when she'd bitten the cord of Billy Bash.

As the brilliant flash of light momentarily blinded even her trancing vision, a powerful gust burst from the cord, rocking her backwards. She inhaled in shocked surprise as the stinging cord juice—a taste she would never forget—blasted her mouth and nose, causing her to recoil in disgust and terror.

Despite the stinging sensation to her eyes, she forced them open the best she could—she still had the wraith to contend with and needed to use all the vision she had. Through blurred and watery eyes, she saw a brief glimpse of the spirit of Mr. Bobby floating away. His appearance wasn't fully back to the cigarette-flinging newspaper man she'd known so briefly, but neither was it the deflated rubber man with no bones. She saw on his face a combination of confusion at realizing he was dead, mixed with something like relief at being free of his torment.

Then a violent sneeze wracked her body. A fine spray of blue cord mist shot out of her nose and mouth, filling the room, and she began to cough. Now the cord mist was caught up in the swirling maelstrom of her anger with no way to avoid it.

Three more equally violent sneezes, interspersed with coughing fits, caused her to double over, even as the spinning Orb of Del kept her aloft.

She sneezed and coughed out the life force of one, which she knew could be deadly to another. Or perhaps even worse than deadly.

"Whatever you do, don't swalla'!" came the remembered voice of Mama Dedé. *"Don't swalla' the juice!"*

But there was no time to worry whether she had swallowed any or not, for a faint but unnerving realization was quickly dawning on her. Upon the severing of Mr. Bobby's cord, which hadn't frayed a strand at a time like Billy's had, a strange backwards flow of pressure occurred when it exploded.

Touching the cord, which connected one's spirit and life force with their physical body, meant that Del and the wraith had also been connected in a strange umbilic way, the moment she bit. The wraith had been feeding from the Aether, which was Mr. Bobby's life force, which flowed along his silver cord, which Del had just severed. And when the cord exploded, sending pressurized air gushing into her face, a part of the Aether, and anything else attached to it, had been sucked along the cord and exploded out as well. And as she had gasped in surprise, she'd also inhaled, or been infected by, a part of the wraith.

Regardless of the sequence of events, the impact it had on the wraith was immediate and dramatic.

The instant the cord had been severed, a high-pitched, warbling shriek filled the room. It drew back from the sucking pressure as if to escape, then began to blindly lash out at her. Whether caused by pain or frustration at losing the Aether, she couldn't tell. All she knew was that for a brief moment she thought she had overpowered the wraith by severing its link to the Aether.

Then her face was stinging from a thousand invisible needle-barbs.

*

The power of the wraith hit her like a tidal wave, rocking her backwards. Had she not been suspended within the spinning orb, she would have been slammed into a wall or thrown completely through it. But in this swirling cloud of madness, the physical manifestation of the orb had acted like a net, and she'd suddenly become the center of a madly spinning gimbal.

In her mind she spun out of control with a wet needle blanket wrapped tightly around her; the wraith was trying to smother her.

Her body screamed out as the shadow-barbs first stuck, then began to burrow into her. Unlike anchoring barbs like those on annoying burrs that stuck to your pants, these were feeding barbs—a supernatural tick—where once its head was buried within your skin, it began to suck the life force out of you to feed its own grotesque and bloated body. Only it wasn't interested in blood. This thing was searching for her soul.

Her mind scrambled for purchase as she fought to restore her vision. The spinning disorientation was not unlike the time the Gris-gris man had trapped her in her own trance, nearly destroying her.

Blurred images flashed through her mind like a projector stuck on fast-forward.

The burrowing needle-barbs sent arrows of pain shooting into her body as they burrowed for her core, but they also had a strange anchoring effect which first slowed—then stopped—her body from its spinning gimbal state.

She was suddenly fixed in mid-air, frozen in a rictus of terror with outstretched arms, and a face contorted with pain.

Her instinct was to flee to her Well of Life, to escape this physical place and heal herself.

(No! Don't take it there!)

The warning came from somewhere in the dark.

(Not your well! Not there!)

But the pain was unbearable.

Red-hot needle-barbs.

Invasion to her very core.

Exquisite pain that set her mind on fire.

And in that pain, she had a premonition of green flames.

*

Del screamed as the green flames flickered in her mind. Like the time at the murder house, where she saw dwindling possibilities for the man and woman's futures, she saw her own possibilities quickly disappear to that of greasy green ash.

She saw a premonition of her own death.

In a blind panic there was only one thing left to do. Her trancing mind, protected for a few more brief seconds behind the spinning Orb of Del, mentally pulled herself into a tighter ball. It had one last chance.

Like a figure skater going into a spin, she gained momentum. And as her mind spun faster, she remembered the morning Mama Dedé had dropped the coffee cup, after getting caught up in the wake of one of Del's own trances.

Del's lips curled slowly back, first resembling a strange smile, then becoming a snarl.

Instead of pushing the wraith away, trying to dislodge its thousand needle-barbs that were inching their way ever deeper, she could only try to absorb it, to pull it into her trance in hopes of disrupting it the way she'd disrupted Mama Dedé's thoughts. She'd either disrupt it as her own life force ran out, hoping to not be its next meal, or kill it by burning it up in her own atmosphere.

She mentally clamped her arms around the wraith, pulling it and the barbs closer to her. For a brief second the wraith leaned in thinking it had the advantage, and when it did Del thought she'd made a grievous error. Then a strange thing occurred.

As the Orb of Del spun faster, it gained mass, and as it gained mass, its gravitational pull increased.

She felt the wraith hesitate, momentarily unsure what was happening. Then it was struggling to free itself from her. It began shedding layers of itself, first the smothering black wetness on her face, then the layers wrapped around her body. It shed these layers in a desperate attempt to escape, but it could not. The needle-barbs were deep and held tight.

In a last desperate attempt for freedom, it began eating itself, devouring its own shadowy substance to escape the death spiral it had fallen into.

Around and around they spun, two cosmic entities, black holes, caught in one another's wakes. And as they spun, like all cosmic entities, one began to eat the other.

The shining Orb of Del with its silver sheen and small black streak began to change. Imperceptibly at first, then with greater clarity, the black streak of Del began to grow. Whatever force that was shedding from the wraith, whatever substance that was being peeled off, did not fly away into oblivion. It was being absorbed into that mysterious black streak of Del. And as it grew, the Dark Dreamer laughed just as the multi-voice of Del laughed just as Del laughed, and the voices were one in their celebration.

The wraith began to shake, first subtly as if in confused denial, then with greater violence. Faint tearing sounds, not of Del's flesh, but of the needle-barbs being ripped from the wraith, were cast into the wind and lost to the violent storm of Del. The wraith shrieked another insectile scream as its needle-barbs splintered away, then—as if to mock Mr. Bobby in its final act—it rapidly deflated, first into a comical version of its own rubber man, then dissolved into a greasy stain that disappeared into the spinning silver orb before blinking out of existence.

The wraith was no more.

The shaking house settled. The spinning orb receded. And Del collapsed to the floor as she felt her own consciousness begin to slip away. The feeling was becoming all too common. But in her final moments of consciousness, she had the strange sensation that the deflated head of Mr. Bobby slipped forward in a final bow of appreciation.

CHAPTER 41

The Gris-gris man opened his eyes and sat in stunned silence.

In the small church that stood alone somewhere deep in a forgotten farmland, he had just completed inhabiting his new body when a strange vision overtook him.

The two remaining wraiths felt his mental return and warbled excitedly to come greet him in his new form, but a mental signal held them at bay.

The vision was too strange. He didn't understand it yet and couldn't risk them seeing something that he could not explain. Besides, he still needed them to patrol their new domicile. He wasn't as concerned with nosy neighbors as he was with other creatures of the night. He'd been away a long time and wondered what may still live hidden in the swamps.

During the process of inhabitation, he'd been too far away, mentally, to have detected the vision, so he felt himself fortunate that he saw it all. He didn't need the priest's body for feeding, considering he was now in a state of equilibrium, but he did need one to fit into this world of nineteen-hundred and sixty-four. Some of that could be accomplished by simply changing his clothes, but he didn't have the mind of someone from this time and needed one to share. Then there were his troublesome legs to contend with, and those he couldn't hide very well. So, in choosing the new body, he had also chosen a new pair of legs. And fine legs they were.

The vision had come to him as if Praeco had reached out to find him. He knew it was the errant wraith, because the only entities he had direct contact with were here in the church. Or, in the case of Mr. Sandgrove, in the woods nearby. But their mental connection was so strong that he could look out of the beast's eyes just as he looked out of his own.

But with Praeco, a wraith of meager experience and less intelligence, he had lost the connection easily in his previously weakened state and had yet to be able to reconnect it. But something had changed in the wraith during his absence. The Gris-gris man felt that very clearly. It had grown in strength but had locked itself away from communication somehow. It was as if it had slipped into its own void and disappeared.

That bit was unclear to him as an entire part of the vision was shrouded in fog. But the part that concerned him, the part that his mind now grappled with, trying to understand, was the spinning orb that he'd just seen.

Praeco had encountered another entity during a territorially fight over food, the best he could gather. An Aether store of great value, apparently, for two entities such as these to engage in mortal combat. And in the vision, he felt that Praeco had the upper hand. He felt the power growing in his creation as it fed from its store, but the thing it battled was powerful. It had done something to the Aether store, destroying it as opposed to even sharing it, causing a fantastic explosion.

Then it had done the unbelievable. It had latched onto the wraith, physically restraining it. Although this part of the vision was obscured by a terrible static, he sensed a great struggle had unfolded. Then, as if these many surprises weren't enough, the orb actually tried to absorb the wraith.

And as Praeco lost equilibrium, it began to dissolve in a way, degenerating into a small pool of black tar. Yes, the main body of the wraith had been destroyed, the Gris-gris man was sure of that. And whatever energy it had stored, was lost. But he knew it wasn't entirely gone. A part of it remained. It was now in its elemental form, a liquid representation of wraith-carbon perhaps, but it was still there. He could feel it.

And with this thought safely tucked away, the Gris-gris man turned his attention to the final piece of the puzzle, a strange image that hung before him in the night air.

Praeco, even its final and violent dissolution, had still managed to serve its master. The wraith had captured an image that the Gris-gris man now pondered.

It was an image of a girl, suspended in mid-air, encircled in power. And reflected on the surface of the orb.

CHAPTER 42

Del's eyes shot open, wondering how long she'd been out, or if she'd lost consciousness at all. Getting used to the feeling of passing out after something like this, her mind had learned to pull her back quickly, if possible.

Laying in the dining area opposite the living room, she sat up and felt a wave of dizziness well up around her. She closed her eyes and waited for it to recede.

Upon opening them again, she saw the deflated and dead body of Mr. Bobby through the open door to the living room. It had finally slumped over as if to sleep.

Broken remnants of furniture, plaster and dust were scattered throughout the place.

She stood up, struggled for balance, then fell against the wall. Sliding down to a crawling position, she watched as a stream of blood fell from her face and pooled on the floor beneath her.

"...uhhnngggg," she moaned. Her bloody nose had swelled, giving even her moans a nasally stuffed-up sound. The copper-blood taste in the back of her throat caused her to wretch and spit a bloody glob of mucus onto the floor. A shiver wracked her body, causing her arms to buckle. She vaguely felt splinters sticking into the palms of her hands.

Then darkness began to invade her senses.

Stay awake! She demanded. *You can't pass out here.*

No, it would be a difficult story to explain if she was found here.

Crawling on all fours, she moved into the living room and towards the front door. Bright flashes of light exploded in her eyes with each slow, agonizing movement.

She wished there was something she could do for Mr. Bobby, cover him with a sheet or something, but now she felt like she was going to vomit, and had an urgent need to get away from this place.

She flashed outside the house and was dismayed to see cars moving along the short street. Long shadows spilled across the pavement—late afternoon. People would be coming home from work soon.

Pulling herself up the inside of the front door, she looked back once more at Mr. Bobby and whispered a silent apology. She was so deeply sorry for what she'd done but had seen no other option. And with that thought, she weakly turned the knob, yanked the door open, and stumbled down the front steps.

The air felt good on her face. The normal smells of the city were a welcome replacement for the burnt smell of death that now saturated the house. The throbbing behind her left eye had receded some, but the physical toll on her body was just setting in. She felt as if she'd been badly beaten and needed to get home quickly. She recognized the feeling of her body wanting to shut down to repair itself, and wasn't sure how long she could stay awake before the next wave of unconsciousness crashed over her.

Starting down the sidewalk, she almost left her bike lying in the overgrown driveway, then remembered it. She turned back and grabbed it. It was unbelievable to her that only a few hours earlier this had been a frozen fog bank but then laughed.

Why should that be so unbelievable?

(If you'd stop being surprised by the unexpected, maybe you'd have an easier time with this.)

The words, just common noise in her already noisy head, were spoken in a slightly different voice. She remembered that some type of convergence had happened with the voices in her head; or maybe it had been more of an introduction. Regardless, they weren't helping her right now.

Please be quiet. Just for a bit.

Mounting her bike, she began peddling slowly down the street. Her balance was so poor, she nearly fell over twice in the first ten feet or so. Her pounding head revolted against the forward movement.

A few people were out and about. Keeping her head low, she flashed each one of them as she went by. Most ignored her, which was good, but some seemed to take a keen interest in her. She instinctively turned her head away from those who did and soon was out of the little dead-end neighborhood and onto busier streets where she hoped to be more inconspicuous.

But she was anything but inconspicuous.

For the normal people, the ones who only saw what was on the surface, a girl of Del's beauty who was covered in sweat and plaster dust may have just been an oddity. But one with a bloody nose and rapidly swelling face, left a lasting impression. Not to mention, the torn T-shirt and wild hair—which really needed a restraint—made her quite memorable.

For the other people, the sensitive ones that heard the words upon the wind and the whispering dead, they may have noticed something else. And there were a few of those along Del's journey home, as well.

Those people may not have noticed the dust, the sweat, or even the furtive glances when the girl turned her head. They may have noticed a strange shadow. Not quite her own.

A shadow, that despite the time of day or angle of light, always seemed to be beneath and slightly behind the girl.

A shadow, that on the occasion she had to stop at a street crossing waiting for cars to pass, puddled beneath her like a small pool of black tar.

A shadow that had eyes of green flame.

A TASTE OF THE FUTURE

I very much hope you enjoyed ***Shadowfire***.

If you did and would like more in the same vein, here's a sneak peak at the fifth book in the *Spirit Hunter* series…

CHAPTER 1

Somewhere in a bayou, Louisiana 1964

The two boys jostled one another and their night shadows tangled together. Dark silhouettes stretched out across the road, casting them as a strange beast with too many arms and legs for the single body. But they always walked like this, nearly hip to hip, unless they were running.

"Race you to the signpost," said Robby Carter. The eyes of his black face studied his friend, watchful for movement.

"Telephone pole beyond that," said Harold Wickham. His white face nodded to a point further down the blacktop road, although his eyes never left his friend's face.

"Go!" they cried together.

Then their shadows made an even more impressive monster, flying across the pavement with pumping madness. Painted bird skulls hanging around their necks on old shoelace cords, flew backwards as if trying to take flight one last time.

The closeness of the boys was due in part to their upbringing, both lacking fathers and having part-time mothers. They'd learned early in life that there were few people they could depend on. And having grown up next to each other, in houses with walls so thin they could hear each other's nightmares, it was only a matter of time before they became inseparable like brothers. For here, poverty colored each one the same.

But on this dark night, with its hide-and-seek moon, the boys felt closer than ever. They were going to the hanging tree.

"Do ya think we'll really send a man to the moon?" said Robby. He chucked a rock into the darkness, then jiggled his flashlight again. "Dang, batt'ries," he mumbled. The bulb glowed with a dim white ember, the light struggling to fall to the ground.

"Got to," said Harold. He picked up his own rock and chucked it further. "'Fore da commies take it over."

The blacktop road—if they were to turn around—would take them back home, to one of the many unincorporated communities in St. Charles Parish. There, most areas were unincorporated and without names, because most of the land—both North and South of the river—was swamp. The people there lived a different type of existence, rural and disconnected, despite the fact they were within fifteen miles of the Quarter.

But tonight, the two eleven-year-old boys were determined *not* to turn around until they found the hanging tree. After all, they had their talismans.

"Commies?" said Robby. "What they want it for?" He threw another rock; this time it thudded against something in the dark.

Harold chuffed. "Man, they already sent a guy up to space." He shook his own flashlight, hit the rim, and the light brightened a bit.

"I heard his real mission was to look for some place they could set up their nukes."

"Nukes?"

"Yeah, that way, one night, when there's no moonlight…"

His voice drifted to a whisper as he clicked off the flashlight. A cricket chirped somewhere in the darkness to fill the silence.

"KABLAM!" Harold flipped on the light, right in Robby's face. "They blast us to smithereens 'cause we can't see 'em comin."

Robby jumped from the noise and light, then shoved Harold's shoulder. "Nuh uh!" He took a moment to collect himself, and to think of a way to pay back the scare. Silently, he jiggled his flashlight again, hoping for a beam, but it was now dead.

"Yeah, well how they s'posed to get all that stuff up there, anyway?"

"I dunno." Harold shrugged. He clicked off his light and shoved it into the back pocket of his jeans. "More rockets, I guess." He squinted skyward as if searching for one.

"Hey, lookit," said Robby. "Last pole."

He pointed to a lone telephone pole that marked their turnoff. The dark outline of a rusty transformer hung askew high overhead, the skull of a long dead giant, and looked forlornly down at the boys.

Beyond the pole, an overgrown path slithered away into the bayou. The hanging tree was somewhere out there.

The boys stopped at the entrance to the path and glanced back at the way they'd come. The road disappeared into the darkness. Neither would suggest they go back without first reaching the tree, so they turned towards their destination.

"How far ya think?" Robby asked. He squinted into the night as if searching for the tree.

"Mmm, a mile?" Harold said. Although, he really wasn't sure. The location of the hanging tree was a closely guarded secret.

Still scanning the darkness, Robby whispered, "Man, I hope we don't see no rougarou toni—"

"SHHH!" Harold whispered harshly. "Man, don't call 'em."

"I wasn't. Just sayin.'"

Of all the swamp creatures, both natural and unnatural, the boys feared the rougarou, or swamp werewolf, the most. Getting eaten by a gator was definitely a bad way to go. And they knew not to follow any floating lights out into the swamps. But if a rougarou got you—and didn't eat you outright—then you'd be infected by its curse and become one yourself. Then you'd spend the rest of your life in the swamps eating wild pigs and killing people.

Moments ticked by and neither one spoke. They weighed the seriousness of mentioning the things name outloud.

Then, without speaking, the boys turned toward each other, for they knew the other's mind. They had stalled long enough. So, they simply stepped onto the path, simultaneously touching the bird heads hanging around their necks. "By cross and bone, leave us alone," they whispered.

One never knew when errant spirits where about.

*

Thirty minutes later, Robby reached out and touched Harold's arm. "What time is it?" he whispered.

They had fallen into a rhythmic cadence during their walk. First, as the path had closed in, and with the cutgrass nipping at their arms, they'd moved to single file with Harold in the lead. Having the best eyesight, he could follow the path by moonlight, saving their last flashlight for later. Then, as if subconsciously trying to minimize the noise they made, their footsteps fell into sync. Soon, they began to hear the chirps, hoots, and howls of the nocturnal creatures, as they passed through the night, silent as shadows.

Harold stopped, clicked on his flashlight and squinted at the old wristwatch that hung loosely on his arm. His mom had told him it was an heirloom of his father's and that he should treat it with respect. But he doubted the story. There were an unusual number of watches that showed up in their house from time to time.

"'Bout twelve-thirty. Why?"

The boys, who still stood outside the door of adulthood, but close enough to peer into it, were on a mission. Venturing into the bayou at night and placing your talisman on the hanging tree was a rite of passage.

"Jus' wonderin," Robby muttered, as he scanned around behind them. "Turn it off 'fore it runs out."

Harold turned off the light with a click of finality, and the darkness swallowed them. After his eyes adjusted to the blackness, he said, "Come on. I bet it's not too far." And they resumed walking.

That summer they'd decided it was time for them to take the journey but had postponed it for a variety of reasons. If asked, they could not explain what the reasons were but would have adamantly agreed they *were* necessary.

By the time school had started, and the tall tales of summer began to circulate, the boys knew their time had come. They couldn't go past Christmas without having made the journey; that was practically the next grade. And the only thing worse than being poor—which a lot of them were—was being poor *and* being a chickenshit. They might as well be from Mississippi.

So, the boys found their bird heads—crows for both—and cleaned them to a brilliant white. Unique designs were painted on the skulls.

Robby glued two feathers to the sides of his in honor of the Greek guy with flying sandals whose name he couldn't remember. Harold, having painted his mostly black, reminding him of the Black Plague masks they'd learned about, glued the butt of a cigarette into his beak. He thought this morbidly ironic.

Now, traveling over the spongy ground of the overgrown path, the bird heads took on new meaning. Originally made as offerings to help them pass out of childhood, then as protectors when they entered the path, they now signified the end of the night's journey. The sooner they could place these in the hanging tree, the sooner this adventure would be over. The journey had already been longer than either of them expected.

*

Somewhere above the boys, as night things often do, a shadow moved silently through the air. It had not been cast by branch or cloud, and in fact, moved against the wind, and with a singular purpose. It had come to inspect the boys.

Whether it was the boy's dark thoughts, the strange talismans they wore, or a combination, something had called out to the shadow, alerting it to their presence. So, it came to see.

Slipping far ahead of them, the shadow floated to a high branch where it began to take shape. First, a single black eye formed, watchful and unblinking. Next, the outline of a sleek feathered head materialized around the eye. It watched the boys moving toward it. The old path would take them very near its branch. Finally, a beak, body and legs emerged from the mist, and a Raven sat where the shadow had just been. It cocked its head and watched the boys with one glossy eye.

*

"Lookit!" Robby whispered. "Is that it?"

Harold stopped and hunkered, as if their sudden arrival may cause the mystical tree to disappear. Robby squatted beside him.

"I think so," Harold said quietly. "An old weeper just north of the path? It's gotta be it."

The boys knew their trees and could name many by their silhouettes. They also knew that Live Oak branches didn't start reaching for the ground until they were close to forty years old. Even then, they rarely touched it. But to be considered a *weeper*, a granddaddy tree with gnarled branches that reached the ground some twenty feet from its base, it had to be pushing eighty to a hundred years old. And the giant silhouette that stood before them told them it was at least that old.

"Is it talkin'?" asked Robby.

Harold held up one finger and turned an ear towards the tree. "I don't hear nothin'. Let's get a little closer."

The legend that the old weeper would talk to someone before they hung their talisman upon its branches was hotly debated amongst the schoolboys. Some claimed the tree's voice was from the spirits of dead boys who had died of fright beneath its great canopy, for each boy had to enter the canopy alone to hang their offering. Others claimed it was the mystical voices of the bird heads, somehow turned to something other than tweets and chirps. Regardless, one wasn't supposed to enter the canopy until it heard the voice inviting them in.

They crept closer but stopped about forty feet from the edge of the canopy.

"Shine the light," Robby said.

Harold took the flashlight from his back pocket and slowly pointed it at the giant tree. He jiggled the light for good luck, then clicked it on.

The boys gasped.

Highlighted in the harsh circle of light was the outer canopy of a giant Live Oak. The grandaddy weeper of weepers. Its ancient branches, thicker than many other trees' trunks, arched out from a hidden center like gigantic arthritic spider legs. Spanish moss hung from the branches in long clumps as if a thousand grandpa beards had been hung there in some other strange ritual.

"What's that?" Robby asked, pointing.

"What?"

"Those… white things."

Then Howard saw what his friend had called out. Beyond the foliage, past the Spanish moss, hung hundreds of small reflective items.

"They're skulls," Harold whispered.

Hundreds of tiny bird skulls—maybe more—hung inside the canopy of the great hanging tree. Bits of their white skulls were visible from the glare of the flashlight.

It might be five hundred years old, Harold suddenly thought.

The boys stared, stunned by the enormity of the sight in front of them. Harold slowly panned the circle of light over the tree, left, right, up, then down. Everywhere they looked, every place the light touched, the same white brilliance was reflected back at them. Bird skulls were hanging from every branch of the tree. Even at the very top.

But in their mute surprise, as they grappled for words, they both felt the wrongness of the thing that stood before them. They didn't know what it was, but there was something wrong with the whole thing.

Then, as if to give the boys a hint, a soft night breeze brushed the tall grass in front of them. The sudden movement highlighted the problem.

"It ain't movin'," whispered Robby. "Them things ain't moved at all."

And Harold knew his friend was right. Wherever he shined the light, not a leaf moved, not a strand of moss waved, and not one of the tiny bird skulls twisted on its string.

The boys eyed each other when the realization hit them.

"Do you hear anything?" Robby asked. "Do you hear the voi—"

The Raven, which had been watching the boys from one of the very branches they had scanned, cocked its shiny head. It had seen the boys. It had learned them very well. It had decided.

So, it pecked three times on the branch.

Peck.

Peck. Peck.

And the hanging skulls began to move.

A NOTE FROM THE AUTHOR

Thank you for reading *Shadowfire*. I know it took a while for this book to come out, there are a couple of other series competing for my time, but I was excited to get back to it. I know there's still a lot of story to tell and I hope this didn't feel like too much of a cliffhanger, but I felt it ended at the most logical spot. As you know, there are a lot of plot lines working, but rest assured, I see their most likely futures. Sort of like Del does when trancing, I suppose.

One of the most interesting things to me was the backstory of John Montanet and how he hid in the timeless mists of the great river. I realize this creates a conundrum with his emergence in the first book, but I suspect there's an explanation for it. Besides, the Gris-gris man appears to be wondering about this already. He seems to be very aware of Toth's absence. Did you catch it?

And what about the thing that's trying to awake in the third boat? That my friends, is a true monstrosity. I'm not sure when it will be exposed, but I know its backstory. In fact, there were several backstories pulled from this book. Nearly two chapters about Frank, and a few chapters about the boat's previous owner. These weren't excluded because they were bad, per se, they just slowed the main story down too much.

Let's see, what else is waiting to be explained? The thing in the attic? That must come out in the next book. It's pivotal. Jimmy's dilemma? This will certainly be exposed, but not for a while yet. The previous relationships between some of the characters? Yes, those also, will be explained. However, a quick note here for the followers who saw the post with the story title hints. Because we learn in this book that some of the characters knew each other before Del was ever on the scene, the working title of this book was Strange Bedfellows. In fact, Madame Broussard thinks this very thing as she wonders what to do. But in the end, the title *Shadowfire* was just too good to pass up. And this also, like many things, has future ramifications.

Well, I could go on, but now I want to go back to writing. I think I'll go to either book #5, or perhaps, a precursor story to this whole thing. For a while now, I've been wondering about the fire that killed Del's parents…

As always, thanks again for reading, and please think about leaving a review. Each and every one counts.

ACKNOWLEDGEMENTS

Thanks again to my wonderful wife Mary for the long hours reading and discussing this story. You're a tough critic, but I wouldn't want it any other way.

MORE BOOKS BY D.S. QUINTON

The Spirit Hunter Series (A Supernatural Thriller)

Book 1: A Grimoire Dark

Book 2: Scars of Redemption

Book 3: A Tapestry of Dead

Book 4: Shadowfire

Way of the Vampire (A Supernatural Thriller) – Related to The Spirit Hunter Series

Prequel: The Cursing of Ana Dalca

Book 1: Final Voyage of the Carmilla

Evolution Series (A Technothriller)

Prequel: The Phoenix Stone

Book 1: Devel Django

Milo Savage and the Gargoyle Hunters Series (Middle-grade Fantasy)

Book 1: The Secret of the Moonstone

Book 2: The Curse of the Chimera

Splinters – A short story collection for fans of the Twilight Zone and Night Gallery.

ABOUT THE AUTHOR

D.S. Quinton was born in the Midwest USA and attended the schools of daydreaming, foosball, and mixology. His is an avid student of the unknown and grew up on Greek mythology, the Twilight Zone and Night Gallery.

He is the author of the Spirit Hunter supernatural thriller series and the Circus Sideshow supernatural oddity series, along with a few other interesting tales.

Although his guitar slide is rusty, the piano keys are warm, and despite the lure of many untraveled paths, his feet are generally moving forward.

You can find him at *dsquinton.com*, some social media platforms, or on his deck solving the world's problems with his wife and a good bottle of wine.

www.ingramcontent.com/pod-product-compliance
Lightning Source LLC
Chambersburg PA
CBHW020927310726
48980CB00010B/824/J

* 9 7 9 8 9 9 3 5 8 5 1 0 9 *